NATALKA BABINA

D1073340

DOWN AMONG
THE FISHES

Glagoslav Publications

NATALKA BABINA

DOWN AMONG THE FISHES

This book has been selected to receive financial assistance
from English PEN's "PEN Translates!" programme,
supported by Arts Council England. English PEN exists
to promote literature and our understanding of it, to uphold
writers' freedoms around the world, to campaign against the
persecution and imprisonment of writers for stating their
views, and to promote the friendly co-operation of writers
and the free exchange of ideas.

www.englishpen.org

DOWN AMONG THE FISHES

by Natalka Babina
Translated from the Belarusian by Jim Dingley
Edited by Camilla Stein

© 2013, Natalka Babina

Cover art by Edward Gałustow

© 2013, Glagoslav Publications, United Kingdom

Glagoslav Publications Ltd
88-90 Hatton Garden
EC1N 8PN London
United Kingdom

www.glagoslav.com

ISBN: 978-1-78267-076-6

A catalogue record for this book is available
from the British Library.

CONTENTS

Down Among the Fishes *(A note on transliteration)*. 7
Dramatis personae 9

The business with the Devil. 13
A sack came rolling... 15
Holes in time 18
Velkom to Dobratyche. 25
Velkom to our polyphonic world. 27
Henik the Uruguayan — his love and luck 31
The night after the rain came 39
The Black Bog 46
A death intended for someone else 54
He used vulgar words being besotted with power. 63
I encounter Mr Ivan Kukal for the first time 75
It's nothing!. 89
I know full well how things are 97
Onwards and upwards lead us to bliss! 104
Time to call a spade a spade 112
I feel old 116
The diesel train south from Brest to Vladava 121
My sister and two stations 124
Aksana's not at home 129
What did you ask me that for? 130
Another soul, another language. 132
A charming neighbour 135
The red jacket. 144
It smells of people. 148
Full circle 160
Maria Vaytsyashonak gives me a good telling off 163
You aren't going to win the elections 166
Greetings from Taras Slyozka. 170
To the frontier and beyond 176

Not every boomerang chooses freedom. 186
On stakeout. 190
Sasha and Dzima do their job 193
From America with sorrow .198
It's better to bow down and worship your own arse. 203
I don't even have a catapult 205
Death hangs over Dobratyche 212
Everyone can have their say. 215
A blood-soaked rag comes to my rescue again 222
Cancer 230
Trap for a middle-aged woman
    who kicks hornets' nests. 239
Down among the fishes. .251
Yet another decree 256
Mad Meg on the march. .264
What kind of medicinal herbs do we have
    in Dobratyche? 270
The dog it was that died .279
Despair is the damp of hell... 281
... as joy is the serenity of Heaven 283
I didn't get his autograph .289
Makrynya's fifth child. 299
Wives on the catwalk aboard the "Royal Barge" 313
By the light of the moon .319
Sotheby's acquires a new client 329
A world created anew. I learn who the apparition
    in the white shroud really is. 336
E Day. 347
1465 words. 350

DOWN AMONG THE FISHES

A note on transliteration

Personal names are transliterated from the Belarusian forms, unless they are obviously the kind of officials who would never speak Belarusian, or are clearly Ukrainian, e.g.

Belarusian: Babylyova, Henik
Russian: Graychik, Kuleshov
Ukrainian: Ponomariv

Placenames and names of rivers are transliterated from the Belarusian forms, e.g. Chachersk, Lahoysk, Buh, Prypyats. This includes names of places that are now in Poland; in such cases the Polish forms are given in a footnote. Ukrainian placenames are given in the appropriate contemporary form: Lviv.

A whole chapter is devoted to the names of the villages which are at the heart of this story. The real complication is the name of the city that lies closest to them. Its Russian and official Belarusian name is 'Brest'. The author also refers to the city by one of its truly Belarusian forms: Berastse (with stress on the first syllable). It also appears in the form 'Bereste' as it would be written in a document dating from the seventeenth century. On one occasion the author refers to the city as 'Brest-Litovsk' (literally 'Lithuanian Brest'). This brings me to a little bit of history, as Brest has never had anything to do with the country we now know as Lithuania:

What's in a name?

A great deal, as it turns out. Part of this story is played out in what is sometimes called the Polish-Lithuanian Common-wealth, a federal state comprising the Kingdom of Poland and the Grand Duchy of Lithuania. Do not be misled by the name: the Grand Duchy was a predominantly Slavonic state in which the ancestors of the citizens of the modern Republic of Lithuania were a tiny minority. — *Jim Dingley*

Although inspired in part by facts of real life, the following story and characters in it are fictional and do not depict any actual person or event.

DRAMATIS PERSONAE

AKSANA. Old schoolfriend of Ala and Ulia. Now the head teacher at a local school. Married to Syarhey (called Syarozhyk as a schoolboy). Has three children and two grandchildren.

ALA [ANATOLEUNA] BABYLYOVA. The narrator. On official occasions, when Russian is being spoken, the surname will be spelled 'Bobylyova'. There are also occasions when she is addressed solely by her patronymic 'Anatoleuna' — most notably by the governor of the remand prison in Brest. Twin sister of Ulia [Anatoleuna] Barysevich. Daughter of Eva and Anatol [Tolik] Hadun. Granddaughter of Makrynya Hadun. One daughter — deceased.

ANATOL. First name of the governor of the remand prison in Brest.

ANATOL HADUN. Husband of Eva, father of the twins Ala and Ulia. Also called Tolik.

ANATOL HADUN. Leader of the treasure hunters. Married to Handzia. See Tolik.

ANDREY [ILICH] RUDKOVSKY. Local police officer.

ANTANINA DLUSKAYA. Singer of a kind. Girl friend, then new wife of Ala's husband, Anton.

ANTON BABYLYOV. Ala's husband.

DZIMA. See Sasha.

EVA HADUN. Daughter of Makrynya, wife of Anatol Hadun, mother of the twins Ala and Ulia.

FYODAR KOPATS. See Khvedzka.

GOSHA. Drug dealer in Mensk.

9

GRAYCHIK, E.A. Judge.

GREY TOPER. Nickname given by the villagers to one of the townies in the dachas.

HANDZIA. Wife of Anatol (Tolik) Hadun.

HARABETS. Leading opposition candidate in the upcoming presidential election. Ulia is his campaign manager in Brest province.

HENIK HADUN 'THE URUGUAYAN'. Husband of Auntie Katsya.

HORST DAVID. American journalist in Mensk.

IVAN [DMITREVICH] KUKAL. Brest-based 'businessman' (racketeer).

KAZIK. Son of Ulia Barysevich.

KHVEDZKA. Employed by Lena Zarnitskaya. In a more formal situation he is referred to as Fyodar Kopats.

KULESHOV, A. T. Public Prosecutor in Brest.

KULYA (THE WORD MEANS 'BULLET'). Nickname for Kuleyeu, a 'businessman' and rival of Kukal.

LENA ZARNITSKAYA. The local vet. Runs a private practice. Old schoolfriend of Ala and Ulia.

LINA. Daughter of Ulia Barysevich.

LYALKA SENIOR (UNABLE TO WALK) AND HER DAUGHTER LYALKA JUNIOR (MENTALLY RETARDED). Villagers from Dobratyche.

LYAVI. Gypsy racing driver.

LYONIKHA. The village gossip. This familiar village way of referring to her tells us that she is the wife of Lyonya (who in more formal circumstances would be called Leanid). Only local people would call her this. Outsiders, e.g. the police officer, would call her 'Auntie Masha' or 'Auntie Manya'.

MAKRYNYA [LUKASHAUNA] HADUN. Grandmother of Ala and Ulia.

MARIA VAYTSYASHONAK. Ala's rescuer.

MIKHAS YARASH. Pen name of the local poet. Grandson of Yarashykha. Also referred to very familiarly in the text as 'Yarashyshyn Mishyk' — Yarashykha's grandson Mikey.

NGWAASI. Leader of a group of refugees trying to cross the frontier to get into Poland and head further westwards.

POCHTIVY. Spetsnaz officer.

PONOMARIV. Head of the Historical Documents Department of the Lviv Archives.

PYATRO KLIMUK. Belarusian astronaut.

SANALEYEU. Electronics expert, sent from the Harabets campaign HQ in Brest to debug the house in Dobratyche.

SASHA AND DZIMA. Former KBB (state security) officers, sent by the Harabets campaign to protect Ulia.

SHUSHKO. Spetsnaz officer.

STEPAN FYODOROVICH. KBB (state security) officer.

SYARHEY. Husband of Aksana. Called Syarozhyk as a schoolboy.

TARAS SLYOZKA. Ukrainian. From Lviv.

TARASENKA. President of Belarus.

TOLIK. First mentioned by the narrator as Tolik-the-alcoholic, then as 'My Tolik'. Works for Agrovitalika Plus. Married to Handzia. Leader of the treasure hunters. Also referred to in a formal situation as Anatol Hadun.

ULIA [ANATOLEUNA] BARYSEVICH. Twin sister of Ala [Anatoleuna] Babylyova. Daughter of Eva and Anatol [Tolik] Hadun. Granddaughter of Makrynya Hadun. Her husband is Yurka, an architect. Two children — Kazik, Lina.

VALERYK. Son of Henik the Uruguayan. Home on a visit from the United States, where he now lives.

VALIK. Works for Agrovitalika plus. One of the treasure hunters. Married to Volya.

VITAL CHAROTA. An incomer to the area. Director of the private agricultural company called 'Agrovitalika Plus'. His son is a drug addict.

VERA MIKALAYEUNA. See Yarashykha.

VOLYA. Valik's wife.

YARASHYKHA. Village way of referring to the wife of a man called Yarash (a familiar form of Yaraslau). Grandmother of the poet who calls himself Mikhas Yarash. (By outsiders she is referred to formally as Vera Mikalaeuna).

YURKA. Husband of Ulia Barysevich.

ZOSKA. Granddaughter of Henik the Uruguayan.

THE BUSINESS
WITH THE DEVIL

There was a time when the Devil used to torment me terribly. He would track me down almost every day. I did have a few ways of driving him off, but he's a really persistent object (there's no way you can refer to the Devil as a person). Time and time again he would come and jump out at me whenever and wherever I least expected it. Bald, disgusting. Yuck... I was permanently stressed out. After all it was my immortal soul at stake, nothing more or less. Just imagine the horror of it — expecting to see a vision of hell under a saucepan lid, behind a mirror or beneath the surface of your bathwater. Anyone who's ever had any dealings with the Devil will know what I'm talking about. Fear completely sapped all my strength. Yet all the same, and to my own astonishment, I managed to sort him out once and for all. I found a way of doing it. I can recommend it to anyone. Or, to be more precise, to any woman. As I recall, it happened one evening, after a heavy, sultry day. I dragged myself home from the city all sweaty and totally knackered. I pulled off my dress. My tights were stuck firmly to the soles of my feet, and I literally had to rip them off. The smell of exhaustion mixed with — yes, I couldn't ignore it — an overweight woman's body odour. Pulling off the blood-soaked bit of old bed sheet that I had been using in place of a sanitary towel, I headed for the bathroom to get under the shower. And here, in the dark corridor, the devil suddenly jumped out at me from round a corner. He had been relying on the element of surprise, but it was the very unexpectedness of it that led to his undoing. The shock of it caused me to lash out at him with the bloody rag (and at that time the blood was simply pouring out of me), hitting him across his bald pate so hard that dark red stains spattered all over the white wallpaper. I hit him again and again, and again. The first blow had been a kind of reflex action, but by now I was thumping him faster and faster, driven by all the loathing that had piled up inside me: 'Fuck off and die, you bastard, you piece of filth'. And he did. He squealed and disappeared. And never came back.

To this day I still don't know — does menstrual blood have the power to ward off devils, or was he ashamed that a mere mortal had frightened him?

Either way I don't really care, so long as he doesn't come around me any more. And doesn't stop me digging holes in time. For my part I never bought hygienic pads after that. It was, after all, a matter of considerable importance to me. A sanitary towel would not have been of as much help to me in driving the devil away as a blood-drenched torn piece of old sheet had been.

So physiology does bring some benefits after all, even to people like me.

And the smell of blood is something I can still sense in the air from time to time — even if I don't know where it's coming from.

A SACK CAME ROLLING...

In spite of everything that had happened here, I did actually come back. But not for long. I'm going to leave soon and never return.

It's beautiful here. Really lovely. Misty steel-grey sheets of fine rain divide the air over my head and all around me into tiers — close up they're greenish-grey, further away they look greyish green. The rain runs down my face and the oilskins I'm wearing. In a way they are just like each other. Oilskins lose their shine when they're old, and an old face no longer lets the soul shine through. I'm standing right on the frontier. Or, to be exact, where the frontier used to be. On my right, on the other bank of the Buh*, I can hear people shouting in Polish — in spite of the rain someone is swimming in the river. To my left there are people speaking Russian; these are the townies who have dachas**, at least those whose crummy shacks haven't yet been bought up by Tolik the alcoholic. They're always on guard, keeping watch over their fruit and vegetable patches, even in a downpour.

So here I am, standing on a narrow strip of water meadow right by the old frontier in my oilskins and wellies, one scar on my stomach, another — just for the sake of variety — on my back; the bones in my fingers have healed but the calluses haven't worn away yet. The rain is just teeming down, making the grass

---

* *River Buh:* better known in its Polish form 'Bug'. The river is sometimes called the 'Western Bug'.

** *Dacha:* a cottage in the countryside with a bit of land, owned or rented by someone who lives in a town, somewhere where they can grow their own fruit and vegetables. The 'cottage' can vary from a large purpose-built mansion to something that is little more than a shed.

bend under the weight of water. A little lizard swims calmly past my foot in a stream the rain has made; it's bright green with a yellow pattern on its back. This is a top-grade lizard. When I was a child, we got really excited whenever we caught one like this — much better than the common-or-garden plain grey ones. I'm amazed at just how much the feet of the lizard– when it spreads them out — are like the tiny hands of a young child. Meadow. Water. Ripples on the surface of the enormous puddles of rain water. Calm lizard with a child's hands. Poland on one side, Russia on the other. And from this narrow strip of land between them I hear a whisper, although I have no idea where it's coming from precisely:

> *A sack comes rolling down the hill,*
> *In it is food, take what you will,*
> *There's rye and wheat,*
> *And soft white rolls to eat...*

I get a sense of being rebuked by these words, or mocked, or even of being thanked in a patronizing kind of way... This is the earth talking to me, the thick black waterlogged mud of the river, in a voice you can't hear, you can't pinpoint where it comes from, it's indistinct, but you feel its power. And the earth speaks Ukrainian.

A sack did come rolling down the hill, straight into my arms.

The price of the sack was a human life.

You hold out your arms to catch the sack, but what you catch is Death.

And then here you stand, under the pouring rain, and the water runs down your faded face, your khaki-coloured oilskins and your green wellies.

Right now I'm going to wipe the water off my face, take a last look at the tiers the rain has made in the air, and then go

---

* A counting rhyme for children. Various things can be put in the bag.

home, sit down in the one cosy corner that's left where I can write, and put everything down on paper, just as it happened. And when that's done, I'm going to leave this place and never come back.

And there's something else: not everything in this story is fictitious, and any resemblance to real persons, living or dead, or real events is by no means always purely coincidental. If this means that so-called official personages will come and pay me a visit, then I'll simply deny everything. For the benefit of these plainclothes art experts, I can add that the events of the story take place in 2012.

HOLES IN TIME

What I like most of all is digging holes in time. When I'm digging them I now and again hear the earth whispering to me. But not very often.

Stradche, Lyubche and Dobratyche

Everything in my life went arse up right from the very start — literally. Against the advice of her mother — so, my grandmother — my mother went off to have me in the out-patient clinic of the hospital that had just been opened in the neighbouring village. Granny Makrynya — that's what they called my mother's mother — didn't see any need for it and so tried to dissuade her in her usual manner: with a big stick in her hands. She did not, however, dare to hit her pregnant daughter. So off my mother went to the clinic. After all, she was a teacher, young, educated, with a firm belief in the necessity of progress, drug and hygiene. The paramedic who was assigned to deliver her baby was also a believer. Maybe his faith wasn't strong enough, or he just didn't have enough experience, or he put his faith in vodka as well as progress, but as soon as the baby was born — my sister Ulia (or, as they say around here, Vlyana) — and without waiting for anything else to happen, he started to stitch up my mother's lacerated vagina, concentrating on trying to make the stitches even.

"No, no, no, we have to stitch it up," this in response to my mother's agonised protests, "otherwise we'll have your uterus dangling between your knees. Not a pretty sight!"

And so on he stitched. My mother, of course, was screaming — not surprisingly, if your skin and muscles are being sewn up without anaesthetic in an open wound, and if, to top it all, the needle being used is a really thick one …

She was in such agony that any other feeling was completely blotted out; it came therefore as a complete surprise, to both her and the paramedic, when I suddenly broke through the fresh stitches and burst out into the world.

"What the fuck!? There's something else coming out!"– according to my mother, these were the exact words used by this latter-day Asclepius as he stood there rooted to the spot, flabbergasted, with a surgical needle in his hand.

In the teacher training college that my mother had gone to in order to get an education, they had no courses on how to give birth, and so she, barely conscious and in terrible pain, was unable to dispel his astonishment. In any case she didn't have any idea of what was happening either. She had exhausted all her strength during the birth, and when the pain had let up a bit, she had tried to get her breath back at least. So the paramedic simply stared goggle-eyed at what the medics call the birth canal — and which in normal language we try to avoid giving a name to. The entrance to the canal was framed by pubic hairs that weren't exactly what you would call nicely shaved, full of pain and shimmering blood, and gaping wider and wider like a pulsating star.

Fortunately for me, it was right at this moment that the nurse came back into the ward. Thanks to her, I didn't end up being dropped on the floor: she grabbed me from the arms of the gob-smacked labourer in the vineyard of public health care and managed to prevent him from starting to stitch my mother up again until the placenta had come out. Only an hour later everyone in Dobratyche already knew that *Makrynya's girl Eva* had given birth to twin girls. That's us, me and my sister.

After the nurse had washed and swaddled me and Ulia, they all — that is, the nurse, my mother and the paramedic (who still had an utterly gormless expression on his face) — noticed how alike we were. Peas in a pod. Mum always used to say that we stopped crying once we had been born, and just lay there looking at the world with identical dark eyes. The paramedic said we were OK, but neither my mother nor the nurse took any notice of him. I now think that we weren't crying because we had no idea what the sequel was going to be. We didn't know that people are not born for their own benefit. At best they are born so that someone else benefits from it.

Although my sister and I looked alike it was easy to tell us apart once we had begun to walk — I walked with a limp. Mum was in despair when she saw this and rushed me off to a woman doctor in Brest. She said that the limp was the result of an injury sustained during birth, because the baby came out feet first, and it should soon pass. It still hasn't passed, although you don't really notice it now.

It was late spring when we were born, a spring of a self-confident kind that you don't get any more in our parts. There were occasional gusts of cold wind; on the sandy hills the pussy willows drooped even more with catkins in full bloom, the railway embankment was speckled white with the flowering spurge that had come with the gravel strewn under the tracks. Tiny white five-petalled flowers of chickweed trembled on beds of brown moss in forest clearings. Yellow marsh marigolds flourished on the silt left behind when the river changed its course. These are the earth's soft colours. There were hardly any people around. That was the spring when they replaced the wooden posts on the frontier with concrete ones that lasted for about thirty years. They were constantly replacing the barbed wire.

My mum Eva and my dad — whose name, by the way, wasn't Adam, but Anatol (or Tolik, as my mum called him) — won't appear in this story, so I had better say a few words about them now, just out of filial respect. Both of them died when Ulia and I were nine. I don't even remember what they looked like (I've got a bad memory for faces), especially when I try to imagine them close up; I don't think I can recall what they were actually like as people. But I can remember that the focal point of my mum's life — second only to her fear of hunger, something that everyone in our parts had a phobia about — was her fear of anything associated with machinery. She was afraid of cars, of roads, of electricity, of domestic appliances and even of the drugs that brought progress and hygiene, things that it was her job — as a teacher at a primary school — to promote. I vaguely remember how, whenever dad was held up at work or anywhere else for more than ten minutes, her face would change (although I still cannot remember anything about her facial features) and she would start howling and weeping, and so gradually reduce my sister and me to a state of tearful hysteria. Tolik, our daddy, was the one we have to thank for the fact that we can both speak Russian without an accent. Right from the time we were born he deliberately spoke only Russian to us, so that we would learn it. He had had to learn the language on his own, because his parents, of course, didn't know a word. He made his way in the world so well that the factory where he worked gave him a flat in Brest, and a year later he reached the top of the queue to get a car. There weren't any car dealerships back then, where you could just walk in and buy a car. You had to join the queue and, when your turn came, off you had to go to Tolyatti, the town where the Volga Car Plant was, to collect it — just over 2,000 kilometres away from where we were.

Mum, despite her fear of cars, wanted a Zhiguli* so much that she scrimped and saved every copeck; she made dresses and coats for herself and the two of us, stitched on extra strips of cloth to the sleeves and hems as we grew, and fed us just enough to make sure we didn't die of hunger. The sea-blue Zhiguli that they had bought at the factory and in which they were driving back, overturned and ended up on its roof in a ditch near Pinsk when their journey was almost over. They were already in their coffins when they were brought back home.

---

* Soviet-manufactured car of the 1970s, sold in the UK under the Lada label.

It's been a long time since I last looked at the photographs of mum Eva and dad Tolik that granny had kept. There weren't many, all rust-coloured as a result of the poor quality fixer used in developing them. Finger-smudged memories of a few seconds of lives long gone.

Dad's surname was Hadun, just like mum's, so she didn't even need to change her passport when they got married. People often used to tell me how like dad's mother Ulia I was. Nobody ever said anything like that to my sister Ulia, who was after all given the same name. My memories of granny Ulia are even murkier than what I can recall of my parents — just a general sense of boundless kindness and vulnerability in her eyes and wrinkles. According to granny Makrynya, granny Ulia was the type of woman who allowed herself to be used as a doormat. When she was young and the children were still small, she was regularly beaten by her husband. And he was a whole head shorter than she was.

Later on I saw both the paramedic and the nurse a few times. I saw her in the church in Stradche, a skinny woman with a weather-beaten face, definitely one of us, huge hands work-worn and callused, still wearing what had been fashionable in the first half of the twentieth century — blouse, jumper, skirt and headscarf. The paramedic had a round, well-fed face covered with a web of fine red veins, his fingers were chubby and squeaky clean. His clothes were drab and cheap, bought in the Brest shop called simply "Clothing". As an educated man and therefore a member of the intellectual elite — the local elite, of course — he was always getting himself elected on to the local council. Neither of them is with us now. Nor is the rural hospital in Duryche where Ulia and I first came into the world. Duryche has been renamed; presumably the association with fools (*dury*) was too strong. Now we call it Znamenka; I suppose this was to make us think of the banner (*znamia*) of communism leading us forwards. So the hospital is in Znamenka. This, we must assume, has made it a better place.

We were driven from the hospital in Duryche to our home village of Dobratyche along a road that twists its way through fields right next to the frontier, past tumbledown little farmsteads basking in the warm sun, to one side adder-infested oak woods and a marsh. Then comes the Hill; from here you can see the houses of Dobratyche next to the cemetery. Then there's another marsh — white cotton-like seed heads of bulrushes, reeds swaying over the mucky brown water, yellow irises. There's a place right by the barbed wire of the frontier, where — if you stand on tip-toe — you can just about make out a few apple trees and lilac bushes some distance away. You can see it all much more clearly in springtime. It was here, right by the lilac, where the village of Dobratyche once stood. Before 1939. Before the Soviets came*. Before the arrival of progress and hygiene.

*Stradche, Dobratyche, Duryche** — this was how the locals still said the names of the villages in our area when I was young, with a very soft-sounding 'ch'. The names hadn't changed in the slightest since the register of 1566 was produced. I came across this document when I was a student doing field work in the archives of the town of Lutsk in Ukraine and read it, trembling with excitement. Who had these villages once belonged to? Was there someone called Strada, and had he been a martyr (*stradnyk*) to some kind of cause? Was Dobratyche founded by a kind (*dobry*) fellow? And had Duryche been rudely named because

---

* 1939 was the year of the Nazi-Soviet pact. The westernmost frontier of the Soviet Union was fixed along the river Buh,, and remained there after the end of the World War II.

** A modern map of the Brest region of Belarus will show the road leading southwards towards the Ukrainian frontier. Driving along it, you would first arrive in Pryluki after leaving Brest, followed by Zakazanka and Stradche (although the map, if it is in Belarusian, will tell you that you are in Stradzech; if it is Russian, you will be in Stradichi). Then you will come to Znamenka, once Durychy. The one village you will not find on this road is Dobratyche, the village in which the narrator of this book lives. It exists, but on the Polish side of the river, where it is spelt Dobratycze. The author has exercised her right to place the village wherever she wants.

the people living there were regarded as fools (*dury*)? There was another village listed in the register — Lyubche — that, by that time I came along, no one living locally had ever heard of, or even knew where this settlement of forty homesteads had once stood. It had simply disappeared. It was no more, this little place that may have belonged to a woman called Lyubou (*love*). All the other villages were still there. It was in Duryche that we were born, me and my sister, and in Dobratyche we lived.

For centuries my ancestors had toiled away here — in Stradche, Lyubche and Dobratyche — living out their lives day after day with no sense of order or purpose. Beings with no faces, freezing cold, bodies covered with sores and pus. Living in holes. With no idea who they were. Fortunately, there are none of them left. Progress, hygiene and the Soviets have won. Basking in the warm sun and fanned by the occasional breeze, the ghosts of ancient farmsteads and the people who once inhabited them, the ghosts of the adder-infested oak woodlands live on.

The very first — wow! — Belarusian astronaut Pyatro Klimuk was born not far from us, in the village of Kamarouka. The composer Ihar Karnyalyuk comes from Hershony. Andrei Dynko, editor of *Nasha Niva* ('Our Pasture'), was born in Zakazanka. And, as my readers in Belarus probably already know, the poet Mikhas Yarash lives in our very own Dobratyche.

If I hadn't invited our famous poet Mikhas Yarash over to our house for a visit, there wouldn't have been two murders.

The Baptists wouldn't have built a chapel for themselves.

And that airship — the very latest model, by the way, all shiny, fast and completely see-through — would never have started flying tourists on excursions over Dobratyche, Stradche and Zakazanka.

A great deal would never have happened if I had taken my laptop out of the house into the yard. But it's old and won't work properly unless it's plugged into the mains; it keeps shutting down or playing up in all sorts of odd ways. So I invited Mikhas to come over to the house, and soon after that the phone rang.

VELKOM TO DOBRATYCHE

Come on over and visit us in Dobratyche; we'll be really glad to see you! This is the place where the whole story — *as dangerous as literature itself,* it's hard to believe that I was the one it happened to — actually took place. This is the village eulogised — well, that's perhaps a bit of an exaggeration — by our local poet Mikhas Yarash, a guy so talented that even in Belarus one person in every twenty has heard of him, let alone in Europe. And that's in spite of the fact that he writes in Belarusian. OK, he writes in Ukrainian as well.

Our village is situated in a glorious forest of fir trees — they call them *baryaki* round here (a word you won't hear anywhere else). These trees really do remind you of people. We've got real sand dunes as well, although there's no sea round here, invisible or otherwise. On the other hand there are several springs; in one of them the water is salty. These days we're allowed to go right up to the river Buh — it doesn't take more than fifteen minutes to reach it — but back then you couldn't get anywhere near it. The frontier was shut fast, there was barbed wire, the ploughed-up strip of no-man's land — don't even think of trying to get across it — and an alarm system. Yes, indeed, we had a real problem with water in Dobratyche at the time. That explains why the little bay by the sluice gates on the drainage canal was so popular; people even came down from Brest to enjoy a day by the water.

There was also a problem with the "primeval lack of human-kind, the boundless solitude" in Dobratyche that Mikhas writes about. That goes some way to explain why, when I was a child, meeting another human being among the ancient firs and aspens was a real event. More often than not all you met were ferrets, pine martens and striped wild piglets. Then came the cancerous growth of whole estates of dachas and a station on the railway line. Almost all the animals disappeared. In their stead came the townies.

Maybe Mikhas meant that you couldn't call them people.

He was wrong there. These folk are the cream of our society. The best of the best. The gardening clubs, that sprang up around Dobratyche, had names like *War Veteran, Defender of the Fatherland* and *Rainbow*. They were slightly dotty, these rulers of our world, but they were also dangerous, and my grandmother always put on a special respectful vo ice when she was talking to them. Granny was ninety seven. The last of the Mohicans among the original inhabitants of our village. Whenever a retired major or lieutenant-colonel — always in well-worn blue trousers that sagged at the bottom and the knees — came near our fence, she would always offer them a drink of water and bring out a metal cup that was covered in chicken shit.

Granny was one of the poor in spirit. One of those to whom the Kingdom of Heaven belongs. If she had succumbed to the temptation to commit suicide some twenty years earlier, as she really wanted to, then she most likely would never enter that particular kingdom. As things are, there's no problem. She will.

In the era of dachas, fences around the village houses began to make their appearance. There had been no use for them before. You simply put a twig through the latch as a sign that you weren't at home, and that you would rather no one entered while you were out. Now there are high fences everywhere, and anything that weighs less than a ton is securely locked away... Previously it was only the gypsies that people were wary of; now they're afraid of each other.

But I should get back to that evening in June when a young fellow with a gun opened our gate and came into the yard.

VELKOM TO OUR POLYPHONIC WORLD

It's people like my granny who support the world on their shoulders. She's sitting opposite me right now, at a table that's gone black with age. From time to time dry pine needles drop from the tall tree next to us on to the table, and in to the pan with fried potatoes and our mugs of kvass*. People round here call these needles *shypata*, presumably after the sound they make when the wind blows through them. We're having our supper in the open air, just like we've done many times over the past fifty years. There were times when other people joined us — mum, dad, Ulia, her children, my daughter... But now Ulia is in Norway, where she is lecturing to the scholarly descendants of the Vikings about the journeyings of their restless ancestors. Her children, Lina and Kazik, are in Mensk. So here we are, just the two of us.

The seven o'clock train has just chugged off to town, taking the townies from the dachas with it. Dobratyche is at peace again; the wind has dropped and the voices have fallen silent. There are just the villagers left, five homesteads in all; they too are eating their supper under the ancient oaks or settling their domestic animals down for the night.

So, imagine our surprise when at this quiet hour a young man with a holster on his hip came casually walking down our village street — if, that is, a deeply-rutted sand track with patches of wild oats growing here and there is worthy of the name 'street' — and, looking round in a perfectly relaxed way,

---

* A very slightly alcoholic drink made from fermented black bread.

NATALKA BABINA

stopped by our gate, opened it and came into the yard where we were sitting.

What did he want from us? Where had he come from?

Young, dark-haired, open honest face. And with a gun. You could see at once that he wasn't some kind of robber, but then what do I know about people? So who was he?

Everything soon became clear.

"Good evening, I'm your local police officer. Rudkovsky's the name. Call me Andrei. Can I come in?" This in Russian.

Granny looked at him with interest.

"What do you want, sonny?"she asked in reply. In Ukrainian.

"Can I ask you to draw me some water? It's still terribly hot."

Granny nodded in my direction, so I handed a clean mug to the lad. He 'drew' — his word, after all — a bucketful of water from the well, enjoyed his drink and then rinsed out the mug.

"The body of a man was found on the road not far from here. Do you know anything about it?" he asked, looking at me.

"We didn't hear anything," replied granny. "What sort of man was it?"

Through the thick lenses of her spectacles granny gave him the kind of look that demanded a reply. The lad heaved an almost imperceptible sigh and began his story.

Stop, hang on a minute. What language should I use to tell you what happened here? This is in fact not a simple question. The people of Dobratyche speak Ukrainian, but there aren't many of them. The director of the firm called 'Agrovitalika Plus', Vital Charota, speaks Belarusian. He was evacuated here after the Chernobyl disaster of 1986, from somewhere near Chachersk. Now and again my readers in Belarus will occasionally mumble a few words in Belarusian, but on the whole Russian dominates here. Charota, or the local police officer, the local newspaper or the doctor, or the Baptist pastor will sometimes lace their speech with a juicy Ukrainian phrase or two — something that the young local Orthodox priest and his good lady wife would never do.

As I've already said, the earth speaks Ukrainian, but only very, very rarely.

The wind whistles in its own way, beyond any human language.

So, *velkom* to our polyphonic world.

This is what the young police officer told us:

Our local Dobratyche news agency, our newsmaker or, in other words, our local gossip, is known hereabouts as Lyonikha, which is our village way of saying that she is Lyonya's *missus*. So her husband's name is Lyonya, or, to be formal, Leanid. The police officer, who doesn't come from our village, politely calls her Auntie Masha, which means that her official first name is Maria. Anyway, Lyonikha was the primary source of information on this occasion as well. Yesterday she was taking milk to sell to the townies in the dachas, when all of a sudden she spotted someone lying on a slope by the road. It turned out to be one of the townies — Grey Toper we used to call him, because of his grey hair and his fondness for the hard stuff. He was lying in a position that was unnatural, even for him. On closer inspection, Lyonikha saw that he was dead, so she went back home and called the police. They soon arrived on the scene and ascertained that aforementioned Grey Toper had been despatched by three drinking companions to the shop in Pryluki to replenish their depleted supplies of alcohol. It looked like he had been knocked down by a car. All this had been put on record yesterday; today's visit by the police had however been occasioned by the fact that Grey Toper's widow had reported her husband's bicycle missing. According to her, it was on this bicycle that he had set off on the final journey of his life and, when the police turned up, there was no sign of it near the body.

"No, we don't know anything about it. Lyonikha didn't come and see us yesterday," this was me confirming, in Russian of course, our complete lack of information.

"OK, thanks for the water. Really tasty. I'll get off then, maybe Auntie Masha's already got back."

So off the young fellow went, obviously in no great hurry. There's a copse of aspen trees between us and Lyonikha's house, but even so we soon heard a great racket coming from that direction. Lyonikha's gone as deaf as a post in her old age, so the police officer really had to strain his voice to get his message across.

"Was there anyone around when you found the body? Did you see anything else?" we could hear the officer yelling.

"Believe me, I didn't see anyone. There wasn't anyone around at all. No, I didn't see a bicycle." Lyonikha's loud replies came drifting towards us.

Strictly speaking this episode with the police officer was not directly linked to what happened afterwards. It wasn't the actual pebble that started the avalanche. That particular pebble shifted in another place and at another time. But it was the first abnormal, unexpected event in a whole string of such events that came tumbling down on me so insistently that I was soon suffocating beneath a whole avalanche of them.

HENIK THE URUGUAYAN — HIS LOVE AND LUCK

It's possible that the first pebble was dislodged by Henik Hadun the Uruguayan. That same slim, handsome Henik Hadun the Uruguayan who's fond of cheap booze and chasing skirts, whose wife Katsya often moans about him to the other women of the village when they're out working in the fields. Carpenter, beekeeper and all-round general handyman, in old trousers and usually with no shoes or socks on, he's so closely tied to the earth that he may well have been the one who set the avalanche rolling... If I'm right, then it all started the following morning.

The grass in the yard had turned yellow with the heat, the sun was blazing down on us more and more fiercely. Even the fir trees sound different in the completely dry air than they do normally. These tall, majestic trees managed to look as though the all-consuming, scorching heat was of no concern to them whatsoever, but of course they do have roots which reach down almost as far as the Earth's core. The ground beneath our feet is one mighty network of roots. A living world beneath the surface. The invisible part of God's great miracle.

Granny flung her stick at one of the chickens. Her stick is an inseparable part of her. It's both a symbol and a tool of her authority. She uses it to hit the chickens, wallop the cat or poke the cow. That's her all over. True, she never actually hits them. The chicken flapped its wings a bit, just to show how frightened it was, and jumped away from the porch where it had been headed.

"I'll give you what for!", shouts granny as she always does when she tries to hit the animals. I never did understand what it was that she would give them.

I hand granny her stick. She's washing herself at the battered old washbasin that stands in the yard. She's placed her glasses on the shelf and rested her stick against the fir tree. I look at her — she's all skin and bone, almost blind, and I'm sure she's grown shorter. The hard skin of her hands is cracked and encrusted with earth that will never wash out. Her face — once so powerful, gaunt and sharp — has gone dry. Her grandchildren call her a witch whenever they come down to see us in Dobratyche. Her hands tremble as she pours water on her eyes. The hands are filthy, she'll never get them clean.

Looking at her jogs my memory: I am lying in bed with really bad stomach ache and throwing up all the time. Some infection that children catch from dirty hands, the soil that gets ingrained in tiny cracks in the skin. Granny is cussing and swearing all the time while waiting for my parents to arrive from town. My being ill is stopping her from going out to the fields. Everyone gets the rough edge of her tongue: her thoughtless, worthless daughter who swanned off to town, leaving her behind with these 'bleedin' kids', me and Ulia together, because they prevent her, Makrynya, from going out to the fields. "You wipe their bottoms, and they won't so much as give you a drink of water in your old age." The only thing she does for me, is to shove a bowl under my face when I'm being sick and then, cursing again, she takes it away. As soon as my parents turn up, she leaves us and runs off to the fields. She has no time for tablets or doctors. Still, for all that her hands were filthy, she did bring me up. Whereas I, with clean hands, was unable to do the same for my daughter.

"Gran, where's the basket for the windfall apples?" I ask.

I know perfectly well where the basket is. When I'm ninety seven, my granddaughter is not going to ask me where something is, just to hear the sound of my voice. And every day, when she's cooking something, she will never ask me to taste it to see if there's enough salt in it. Simply because I will never have a granddaughter.

Granny, with a triumphant face that clearly says "What would you do without me?!" brings out the basket.

"Should I go down to the apple trees?" I ask, and again I know what the answer is going to be.

"No, no need for that, I'll do it myself. You'd do better to go to the woods and see what mushrooms you can find, and make soup for supper."

Granny is always looking for something to do, like collecting apples or weeding the rows of vegetables and flowers. Then I have to go and replant the growing onions, carrots and asters that she has torn out by the roots because she can't see what she's doing.

"O'er there, on the hill, the reapers are reaping?" A line from a Ukrainian song suddenly came drifting over the fence. For some reason there was a question mark distinctly audible at the end.

It was Henik the Uruguayan. His legs had given way, he grabbed hold of the fence, swayed a couple of times, and then, with a downward gesture of the hand that eloquently said "sod it", he succumbed to the inevitable and collapsed on the ground at full stretch, after deftly placing his cap under his head.

"My wife, my dear heart, we don't get along?" He continued to address questions to the sky until granny and I got to him.

He has a fine, silky smooth voice. His face is lean, his arms tanned by the sun and hard work.

"Henik, get up!" Granny gave him a poke with her stick. "The sun's still up, and you've already had a skinful."

"When the Sun goes down, love goes out the door," Henik parried in response.

The nickname *Uruguayan* was passed down to Henik from his grandfather, who at the dawn of modern times had gone off to seek his fortune in Uruguay. So all his heirs were now called Uruguayans. When I was a child, I believed that this was their actual surname. Only later did I discover that their real surname was Hadun, the same as everyone else in Dobratyche.

Yes, that's right. We all come from the same stock, with the same surname. We're like each other: heavily built, with faces that look as though they've been rough-hewn out of wood with an axe, flat noses broad at the bridge, high, prominent foreheads, strong jawlines and uneven teeth. But no one can say that the people of Dobratyche are ugly; there's an urge to live within us that gives us something more than mere saccharine beauty.

However, at this particular moment Henik Hadun's urge to live had drained right out of him into the ground under the influence of alcohol. All he could do was declaim verses.

"*Oh, 'twere better had I ne'er known love,*" he uttered, turned on one side and closed his eyes.

Granny and I exchanged glances.

"We'll have to let Katsya know," I said. "She can come and collect him."

"She'll never be able to lug him home. He's far too heavy. Get the sheepskin coat and put it under him so he doesn't lie right on the ground." This is granny giving instructions.

As it turned out, I didn't need to fetch the sheepskin coat. Remember our poet Mikhas Yarash? He's better known around here as Mishyk Yarashyshyn. Think of him as Yarash's missus's grandson Mikey. Well, he appeared all of a sudden with a rake slung over one shoulder and wearing a t-shirt proclaiming "Irmoshyna can't count".[*] He was on his way back home from haymaking, and decided to call in on us.

"I'll take him," he said, quickly sizing up the situation. "I'll leave the rake here. I was going to come round to see you anyway," and now he was talking just to me. "I wanted to ask you how you can get Ukrainian spell check in Word."

Mishyk lives quite close to us. It won't be long, I reckon, before busloads of tourists come to visit the house where the

---

[*] This is presumably a dig at Lidiya Ermoshina, the chair of the Central Electoral Commission in Belarus. Accusations of vote rigging are always being levelled at her.

Famous Poet lives. For the moment, though, not a day passes without some bearded intellectual type calling on him. Mikhas' granny, Yarashykha herself, is a practical woman who gets them involved in all sorts of urgent domestic work such as haymaking. Today, however, Mishyk was going back home after haymaking on his own.

"It's easy," I said. "Drop in when you come back for your rake, and I'll show you."

Mishyk grabbed Henik unceremonially under the armpits and brought him to his feet, brushed him down and said:

"Off we go, old man. Katsya's waiting for you. She'll pour you a glass of something good, I'm sure."

Henik lifted an ironic eyebrow but allowed himself to be led home.

Mishyk was laughing when he got back. "I don't know about a glass of something good. What he did get from Katsya was a good walloping. Henik had been up at the place that belongs to those venereologists, reroofing their root cellar. They were the ones who got him drunk. Katsya's locked him in the house and gone off to have it out with them. So what about the spell checker?"

We went through into my room where the big table that served as my desk was. On it, next to the computer, stood a great pile of files and papers. I really had intended to do some work on them, but as things turned out, all my hopes were in vain. I didn't have time to wipe my nose, let alone do anything constructive on the computer.

I switched my notebook on and showed Mishyk what he needed to do to load the spell checker.

The phone rang. I ran to the kitchen. It was Ulia calling from Norway, so we didn't talk for long.

"How are things with you?" she asked. "Why don't you pay your mobile phone bill? There's no point in having one if it's always blocked. How's granny?"

"Everything's OK. Don't worry, just get your Vikings sorted out!"

"I'll be arriving in three days' time. I've bought the ticket already. You don't need to meet me. What can I bring back from here?"

"Rain. It's like the Sahara here!"

While waiting for me to finish on the phone, Mishyk was fiddling around with the different options on Word.

"Ulia's coming, is she?" he asked.

Ulia is an archaeologist. She's giving a paper at some conference or other in Norway. As far as I remember, the title of her paper is "Archaeological evidence for the presence of Vikings on the territory of the Principality of Polatsak* in the 10th century". But maybe that's not it. I may have got it completely wrong. I'm not all that strong when it comes to dealing with scholarly topics, even though I am a historian by training.

"Yes, in three days' time."

It was right at that moment that I got to witness an act of poetic creation. Poets forget completely about everything around them and go off into their own world. All of a sudden Mishyk seemed to be staring at something a long way away. He asked again about the spell checker, something that I had already explained to him only a few moments earlier. I quite enjoyed the spectacle of another poem taking shape in his head. Could he perhaps have a soft spot for Ulia? Was it the news of her imminent arrival that had had this effect on him? I patiently explained everything to him again.

Granny clattered into the house, bringing with her the windfall apples from our orchard. The noise aroused Mikhas from his reverie; he stood up and went home. Then he had to come back a bit later for his rake.

The sun continued to sear us with its ferocious heat. It became impossible to walk barefoot on the sand. The leaves on the lilac bushes had shrivelled up. You could at least cool off a

---

* *Polatsak:* the oldest city in Belarus, and in early medieval times the centre of a large principality that is regarded as the first Belarusian state.

little inside the house. While I was cleaning the mushrooms, I thought lazily — in that heat there was no other way to do anything — about Ulia's arrival, about how happy she would be to see granny still strong and active. About how happy she would be to see me. I knew she would have to do no more than quickly cast an inquisitive glance in my direction to see, instantly, right through me. She is the only person who knows exactly what things are like between me and Anton. She is better than I am. She is my mirror image, except the image I see is better and purer, and doesn't walk with a limp. When she was giving birth to her children, I felt the pain. When I was in prison, she lost weight. Our lives are like two streams; the waters run side-by-side but they never mingle.

I was still a student when I married Anton (Good Lord, where did my life go!?). He did well for himself in the business world, and we bought ourselves a flat in Mensk. Then, of course, I became trapped in the vicious circle of running between the kitchen and the dining room and back again, until I was given the diagnosis: You will never be able to have children. That was seventeen years ago.

"Your stories are full of extremes," Dynko said to me not long ago. "A Frenchman comes to study the habits of townspeople who rent houses in the country for the summer. He gets himself murdered and his body is dumped on the municipal tip! Not very likely, is it?" What about the tasty aroma of food, cooking in the kitchen, the cool fragrance of clean linen in the cupboard, the gentle homely feel of a lamp-lit room in the evening, the waxy shine on the leaves of a ficus plant? How likely is it that all of that can in an instant be robbed of any meaning by a guilty verdict consisting of eight words: "You will never be able to have children". Barren fig tree, seed cast on stony ground. And then there was Anton's face — utterly lost, not knowing where to go or what to do.

And then there was the miracle. The birth of my daughter.
And then there was Death.

The doctor who first diagnosed my little daughter with cancer worked in Hospital no. 2. I simply don't recall how I ever got out of there. Somewhere on Starazhouskaya Street I stopped being able to breathe. I collapsed against the rough wall of some old building. Everything went dark and I began to vomit, curled up on a manhole by a food store. I was lying on the snow, but the snow wasn't cold. I came round when a little dog started barking right above me. A woman shook me by the shoulder:

"What's wrong? Can you get up?"

It was Maria Vaytsyashonak with her little dog Murza. Two years later she would rescue me again. When I was high on drugs and oblivious to the world. She helped me get into the psychiatric hospital in Navinki and undergo treatment for my addiction.

When Anton and I got married, both of us experienced — as far as we possibly could — that thing called love. We were open to each other — as far as we possibly could be. We were drawn to each other. But then the stage of infatuation passed, and we entered into a stage of close friendship, so close that it seemed unbreakable. But break it did. It's difficult to put up with a wife who happens to be a drug addict, even if you really want to. And he didn't.

A drug addict for a wife. No children. No desire to go on living. No light in the eyes. No life in the hair. That's why I wasn't surprised when a woman phoned me out of the blue and — obviously relishing the moment — said, "In the circles they move in it's considered bad form not to have a mistress. It's simply a must-have in business. You must be either blind or completely out of your mind." So there it is, then. No mind and no sight. Just soft in mind (no will to do anything) and body (rolls of cellulite on my hips). What was there to be surprised about?

THE NIGHT AFTER THE RAIN CAME

At last the long-awaited rain came. Once rain has fallen, it's absolutely essential to earth up the potatoes before the heat has had a chance to dry out the soil again. This is serious work, much more serious than it might seem to an ordinary internet user or, say, some kind of high-flying manager. Granny wanted to rush out and do the job on the same day, and I had difficulty in holding her back. The previous winter she had had a cataract removed and the doctor warned her not to do anything that involved heavy labour. There was, of course, no way in which she would willingly refrain from doing anything that needed doing, and it was virtually impossible for anyone else to stop her. She's become so used to doing everything herself, there's no job that she thinks is too hard for her. As a result, she occasionally suffers from a discharge of the eye that was operated on. The only way for me to stop her was to do it all myself, before she had had a chance to realise what had happened. We had been talking for a long time about the need to earth up the potatoes, all we were waiting for was the rain. I simply hadn't managed to get around to the potatoes today. I had been busy all day — of course under granny's close supervision — with weeding and replanting the beetroot, another urgent job that needs to be done after rain. That's why I knew that first thing tomorrow, while I was still cooking breakfast, granny would be raring to get out to the spuds, hoe in hand. Then she would have trouble with her eye again. There was only one thing for it — I would have to go out myself tonight to do the job.

It was eleven o'clock in the evening when I smothered

NATALKA BABINA

myself in a good litre of liquid to keep the mosquitoes off and crept quietly out of the house, so as not to wake up granny.

The villagers of Dobratyche have their allotments right on the frontier, at a spot where the soil is rich with the silt left behind whenever the river floods, as it has done for centuries. To get there you have to go through the forest for a little way. There's nothing finer that a moonlit night in our village. The full moon bathes the world in a fantastic silvery light that contrasts sharply with the dense shadows. The sand dunes remind you of some exotic scene in Algeria with those crystals they call desert roses, and the grass lower down the slopes looks like pictures out of a book of fairy tales. Nights like this are not only valuable for their own sake. They give some meaning to an otherwise empty existence.

I had already hidden the hoe in one of the rows on the allotment. It would take me about four or five hours to finish the job, I reckoned, and there would be enough moonlight for me to do it properly in that time. I retrieved the hoe and got down to work. Down on the river the frogs were giving a concert. I tried to work smoothly, without haste, so as not to tire myself out too quickly. Fitness classes and the swimming pool aren't enough to prepare you for working out in the fields. I had never known the kind of hardships that the old women of Dobratyche had had to endure in their lifetime in order to survive, I lacked their stamina and skill. At the age of ninety, granny could dig potatoes faster than I could at forty. It was with enlightening thoughts like these that I worked my way up and down a few furrows and stopped for a rest.

I heard a gentle tinkling noise coming from the path at one end of the allotments. Someone was riding a bike. The bell jingled every time the wheels went over a rut. I instinctively crouched down behind a blackcurrant bush. Meeting anyone face-to-face was not part of my plans. Especially as I could clearly make out by the moonlight who it was on the bike — the imperturbable Lyonikha, the village gossip. Where on Earth could she be going at this time of night? She was riding along quite slowly, obviously afraid of falling off on to the path at night. As always she was muttering something to herself, but I couldn't hear what. At last the jingling died away. Just as well I had hidden myself in time, otherwise by morning the whole village — and all the dachas as well — would have learned that Makrynya's girl Ala goes out at night, hexing other peoples' crops, and Lyonikha, no doubt, would have been prepared to swear that she had seen a long spindle-like tail sticking out of my backside. I know her only too well.

I had scarcely had time to get my breath back when someone else appeared — this time on the other side of the allotment where the road is, walking quickly in the opposite direction. This was our famous poet Mikhas Yarash, striding out purposefully, but looking around now and again as if he was nervous of something. In the moonlight his face looked unusually pale. He didn't see me either. At least, I don't think he did. I waited for a few more minutes, then stood up from behind my bush, breathed deeply and picked up the hoe again.

Good Lord! I never knew that there was so much going on in our village at night! Never. Miracles will never cease. Where was Lyonikha off to in the middle of the night, and what for? Surely not a love tryst? You might think that her time for love had long since passed. Come to think of it, though, it's quite possible that she'll marry again — it will be her fourth time if she does — but it isn't really likely that she'd go riding round the village on her bike at night for the sake of a hug and a kiss. So where was she going? And what about Mikhas? Has he got a girl up there in one of the dachas? After all, that was the direction he was going in. Curiosity was biting harder than the mosquitoes. The perfumery departments of the big stores haven't yet begun to sell a scent that will ward off curiosity. As the saying goes, "there is no cure for curiosity". If we weren't curious, we'd be dead. And I still retain a sense of curiosity, even at the great age of fifty and even though it may well kill the cat.

I laboured on for several more hours. The froggy concert on the river had gone quiet, and the calm peace of the night was from time to time broken only by an occasional strange hooting noise, monotonous, infinitely sad, breaking off in a kind of howling. I recognised this sound from when I was a child. When we were young, we used to think that it had something to do with the mysterious alarm system on the frontier.

The full moon was gradually descending from its zenith, and I had almost completed my earthing up. There were just a few short rows left. Some distance away I could already hear the jingling of Lyonikha's bell as she rode back; I was keeping my ears open. Once again I hid behind a bush, and this time I kept my eyes on her all the time while she rode past our allotment. I noticed that she had a large suitcase tied to her bike... At that very moment I was gripped by a sudden sense of dread; right opposite me, on the neutral strip just over the frontier beyond the barbed wire, standing in a thicket of bushes and small trees was... something... someone...no, more likely to be something — a tall figure, taller than any human, in a white shapeless garment like a shroud, with a black blob where the face should be. This something was staring in our direction. Lyonikha obviously hadn't noticed anything and just kept on riding. The phantom in white stepped noiselessly back and dissolved in the mist that was rising off the river.

I stood rooted to the spot, and felt the kind of horror rise in me that a fifty-year-old woman ought not to feel, but which nevertheless was tugging at my guts and wrenching them open. Who or what was it that I had seen? Nothing sprang to mind apart from the one word "Death". This is exactly how death looks according to Dobratyche tradition. It's how we imagined death when we were children, and it's how I still think of death even now: a massive woman in white with a fearful, cruel visage. True, she is supposed to be holding a scythe, but maybe I hadn't seen the scythe in the darkness! My legs started running of their own accord. I've got to get away from here as fast as possible. It was absolutely forbidden for anyone to be on no man's land at night. And in any case this thing didn't look human! Maybe it was from the other world, and it had come either for me or for Lyonikha. That means it'll come again. People say that Death always shows itself first and then comes back later to collect you.

I hurried back to the house, wanting nothing more than to hide away in the comforting warmth of home. I pulled up with a start when I reached our fence. In the grey light of dawn that was just beginning to show — the time when people, who are obsessed with gathering wild mushrooms, leave their houses, torch in hand — I could see that there was someone in our yard looking in through the window. It was a lad with short hair, dressed in a dark jacket. After the shock I had experienced in the allotment, I felt no fear — there was no doubt that this was no ghost, but a human, and smaller than me to boot. Not hesitating, I flung open the gate. He turned round when he heard the noise. There was a scared look on his face — I could see it. He set off to make his escape, with me in hot pursuit.

There are three gates in our fence: one leads to the allotment, another opens on to the path to the railway station and the third is the one we go through when we set off for the forest to collect mushrooms. The lad had fled through the mushrooming gate. He left it open and disappeared behind some trees. I closed the gate and drew the bolt across (although what good would that have done, I now ask myself), ran up on to the verandah, and locked the door on the latch. I went right round the house to make sure that everything was as it should be, returned to the kitchen, checked the latch again and then my gaze fell on the coffee maker. Good idea, I needed to have a think.

Coffee's OK, but I felt as though I could do with a drop of something a bit stronger. To put it more exactly, I now had occasion to feel that way. The thought of having a drop of something strong had been flitting around in my head for some time. I had managed to hold off, and then stopped bothering about it altogether. Granny kept a strict tally of the stocks of alcohol in the house: it was all intended 'for export' — as payment for the use of the collective farm horse, and for guests. However, I had brought down a few bottles of duty-free whisky to entertain guests who would otherwise not be happy with the poor-quality vodka called "Blue-eyed Belarus" that the mobile shop sells. With only a moment's hesitation, I poured myself a generous measure into a tumbler, flopped down on the bench and took a quick swig in the hope of subduing the qualms of conscience I felt. Because I knew — in the depths of my conscience, and on the surface as well — that I ought not to be drinking.

By the time the glass was empty I was already taking a much more optimistic view of the world. I looked smugly out on the world from my haze of alcohol-induced well-being, like a goose sitting alone in a large puddle.

If you think about it, did anything really special happen during the night I spent on the allotment after the rain. No, of course it didn't! So what if Lyonikha and Mikhas choose to go wandering around at night. What of it? I know them both so well I couldn't possibly suspect them of being up to something bad. Well, OK, it's perfectly possible Lyonikha was out and about with intentions that weren't what you might call 'wholly pure' (like casting a spell on Makar's wife's allotment to ensure her potato crop failed, or some sly milking of the cows of the collective farm herd that's out grazing near the isolated farmstead some way from the village, and Mikhas — well, he's a gifted poet and therefore capable of falling in love instantaneously and passionately, and therefore really was on his way to call on a young lady in one of the dachas. It's all their own business. It's got nothing to do with me.

And as for that ghost I saw on the other side of the frontier, it was just a figment of my imagination. After all, I'm living in the 21st century, aren't I, and I've been to university, haven't I? There's no such thing as ghosts. It wasn't there. Something I dreamed up after a sleepless night and working so hard. And the lad at the window? One of the people from the dachas. Old Grey Toper's son and heir, another one fond of his drink and ready to pinch anything that isn't fixed to the ground to get the money to quench his thirst. Doesn't mean a thing. There are loads of people around like that. Bloody mosquitoes, the lot of them.

The door banged. In came granny, leaning on her stick and straightening her glasses. She expressed surprise that I was already up. With a big effort, and trying to focus properly, I asked her what I should make for breakfast. "Beetroot soup and potatoes," came the answer, and off she went to open the chicken coop.

Thus it was that everything returned to normal. The chickens started clucking loudly to greet their new-found freedom. The first ray of the sun pierced the window. The morning had begun.

But what a tongue lashing I got from granny when she found out that I had earthed up the potatoes during the night! How she savaged me for traipsing around in the forest at night! It quite reminded me of the good old days.

THE BLACK BOG

All this summer I've been like a hamster in a wheel. Whenever the wheel stands still I fill my pouches with food, look around my world with interest and even do some tidying up. But as soon as someone turns the wheel, off I run. I can't stop. It drives me mad. I'm exhausted. But I can't jump off — my brain isn't developed well enough to let me do that.

I moped around the house with no idea of what to do. Well, no, that's not quite right. I knew exactly what had to be done. The house needed a good clean before Ulia got here. The only thing though, I had absolutely no desire to pick up the cleaning cloth. Instead of poking around with the vacuum cleaner in all the dusty corners of the house, I plumped down on the sofa and started fiddling with the TV remote.

The TV sprang to life. A female commentator was haranguing us, in Russian. "*These self-proclaimed lovers of the people, these utterly bankrupt failed politicians and their friends, the wheeler-dealers of the business world — for whom bankruptcy is only a matter of time and the patience of the forces of law and order — have spotted in the recently announced pre-term elections an ideal opportunity for them to indulge the petty ambitions they cherish so much.*"

An idle thought occurred to me: "Where does Belarus Television manage to find such people?" It is theoretically possible to understand the selection criteria. But all the same... It takes a special kind of talent scout to unearth a woman like this one. First of all, there are the 'chops' — the only word you can use to refer to a face that's as wide as the shoulders beneath it. Then there are the eyes, like tiny little boreholes set deep in the midst of layers of fat. There's even fat on her forehead. Her tits look as though they are about to burst out of the shiny green garment she's wearing. She looks like a toad spawning. With her looks, the high point of her career ought to be to yell "I'm in here!" when she sits on the loo.

The big biddy on the telly continued to vent her righteous indignation: "*Today we have yet another candidate for election to presidential office. On this occasion someone by the name of Anton Bobylyov, director of a private firm calling itself "Gamma", has put himself forward.*"

This brought me up with a start. The picture on the screen changed: there was my husband, sitting in his office. He was obviously saying something, but all you could hear was the toad continuing its harangue:

"*The Belarusian people know only too well what pains they had to bear as a result of the gamma radiation from Chernobyl, all the sorrow and tears, mothers' sleepless nights, the sufferings of our children. Gamma is for our people a sign of grief. It is symptomatic — is it not? — that a man who heads a firm with such a dreadful name should seek to use the democratic freedoms offered by our republic — and there are many who maintain that these freedoms are excessive — in the pursuit of his own manifestly dubious aims, at the expense of the liberal nature of our laws. There is no doubt that the people of our republic can be relied on to distinguish between what is real and what is false. They will be able to work out for themselves exactly what each of the candidates stands for, and which of them is genuinely capable of protecting our country from disasters and dangers of all kinds.*"

She went rambling on, but I wasn't listening any more.

My head had started to ache. He's gone mad! I rushed to the telephone, but both his landline and his mobile were engaged. Gone completely mad! With unseeing eyes I stared at the TV screen. There were some bulldozers being driven across it.

He'd gone off his head, that much was obvious. There was no other way of explaining what he had done. He'll attract the attention of the Ministry of the Interior, and quite possibly the attention of a much more deadly organisation as well. He'll have his dirty linen dragged out for all to see, and then they'll dig around in his family's past to lay their hands on whatever dirt they can find. And then they'll start to focus on me and the horror that I thought I had buried at last.

I was in an anxious, agitated state the whole evening. Anton's telephones were increasingly irritated by the need to demonstrate just how engaged they were all the time, and I was afraid to switch on the television. I was also afraid that someone might try to phone me out here in Dobratyche, but so far there had been no calls. The old telephone on the shelf in the kitchen of this old house remained silent. The next morning, as I was cooking breakfast, I found myself listening expectantly for it to ring at any moment.

All of a sudden — as if in answer to my anxious expectations — I heard a child's desperate scream from the forest. It was the kind of scream you can't ignore. I literally flew out of the house like a whirlwind, snatched up the hoe that was standing by the porch and raced for the gate. Out of the corner of my eye I saw granny coming out of the chicken coop; she hurried after me, supporting herself on her trusty stick.

What had happened? Was there a rabid dog on the loose? Some drunk making a nuisance of himself?

A few seconds later, once I was through the gate, I saw the children, two girls and a boy.

Tears were streaming down their deathly pale, scared faces. The older one, in her early teens by the looks of her, was bent double and holding on to her calf.

"It's a snake! A snake bit me!"

"I'm frightened," and the younger of the two girls began to sob and wail.

"It'll bite us. I know it will," the boy kept repeating in horror.

There was an adder on the ground. It made no attempt to get away. It was fat with a small head, lying still on pine needles next to a clump of bracken. Aiming for the neck, I hit it with the edge of the hoe. I almost screamed myself when the headless body began to squirm and spew out blood on to the sand.

When a snake's blood is allowed to drip on to a loaf of bread, they say that the bread groans. Sand doesn't. Sand doesn't make a sound, whatever you pour on it. I'm not afraid of creepy-crawlies of any size, but this time I had rainbow-coloured circles dancing in front of my eyes.

"Lean on me," I said to the girl who had been bitten. "Stop crying, children! There aren't any more snakes. Stop crying, I said!"

The children could not stop crying. By now granny was almost running; I thought that at any moment she was bound to fall and most likely fracture her hip. But she didn't fall. She reached us, looked quickly round — her eyes were still surprisingly sharp despite her thick lenses — grabbed the hoe out of my hands, swung it round and drove it into the ground right by my foot. There was another snake, smaller than the first, wriggling and writhing on the moss. Another little head rolled away from its body.

I have no idea what kind of holes these snakes had been seeking for themselves here. Maybe it was some kind of get-together or symposium, or perhaps they were having a pre-election meeting. I simply don't know. We had never had snakes in Dobratyche before.

Granny took control. "Call an ambulance! Quick! It's the Uruguayan's grandchildren."

I stifled my feelings of nausea by an effort of will and ran off home. Already by the gate, I turned round; the girl who had been bitten was hobbling towards the fence, leaning with one hand on the hoe and with the other on granny's stick. Granny herself was leading the other tearful children by the hand.

Blindly stabbing at the dial, I dialled Lena Zarnitskaya's number. (She's our local vet.)

"Lena, I've got a girl here who's been bitten in the leg by an adder. What should I do?"

"Don't panic. Get the leg comfortable. Don't put any bandages on it. Give her some strong tea, coffee would be even better. Are you in Dobratyche?"

"Yes."

"I'll be with you in five minutes. I'm in Stradche at the moment."

I put the kettle on the gas and rushed out to meet Zosia. Now I recognised her, it really was the Uruguayan's granddaughter.

Her leg was swelling up right before my eyes. A bluish black colouring was spreading beneath her tender skin. She could hardly walk.

"Hang on, sweetheart. Auntie Lena will be here in a minute, I'll give you some coffee, it'll make you feel better."

With a trembling hand Zosia wiped the sweat from her forehead and tried to lie across my arms. I grabbed hold of her tiny body under the arms and carried her to the hammock on the verandah. Zosia fainted and flopped backwards. She was making a funny gurgling noise in her throat, as if she wanted to say something. Stupefied, I looked at her, not knowing what to do.

"Her head, turn her head!" Granny suddenly appeared behind me and herself turned the girl on her side. Zosia vomited.

The kettle began to whistle. I made some coffee quickly but did not have time to give it to the girl — I heard Lena slam the door of her Mercedes, and there was my dear old friend running towards us in her customary bright scarlet suit, opening her trusty old case and breaking off the head of an ampoule with some clear liquid inside, ready to give Zosia an injection.

"Right, then, off we go to hospital," Lena was now organising things. "Don't worry, no one's died yet from an adder bite, but we've got to move now. There's no point in her suffering here, she needs to be put on a drip with the antidote."

We carried Zosia into the vehicle and placed her carefully on one of the seats with its back right down — Lena has an MPV — I sat the two younger children down in the car and jumped in myself.

"Be careful,"said granny who had come out as far as the fence. "God be with you!"

We dropped the young ones off at the Uruguayan's house and quickly explained to Katsya what had happened.

"What did you have to kill the snakes for?" Zarnitskaya voiced her dissatisfaction in no uncertain terms after I had told her in detail about the morning's events. "You don't know anything, do you?"

"What was I supposed to do!?" I was indignant at her reaction. "Give them a bowl of milk to drink?"

"What you should have done is catch them and take them deep into the forest! Or out to the Black Bog," Lena snapped as she overtook a battered old Ford on a corner. "It's like we're back in the Dark Ages. As soon as something happens, the first thing is to kill the snakes!" She was so cross that she put her foot right down and the speedometer began to creep up to 140 (an aside in brackets: there are advantages to having the cobblestones laid by the Polish authorities in the 1930s covered with modern tarmac). "Every instance of death from a snake bite in Europe is caused by giving the wrong kind of first aid. Some help that is! People tie a bandage on the leg and the net result is poisoning caused by tissue decay. They put the patient on his back and he then chokes on his own vomit (a chill came over me as I recalled granny's words "The head, turn the head"). None of you have any idea of the simplest things. But when it comes to chopping heads off with a hoe — you can do that all right, can't you?"

The wheel stopped and the hamster realised that it was coming into Brest in a filthy skirt and a worn tee shirt with tiny holes all over it. Lena was driving while lecturing me on the basic principles of first aid, holding the steering wheel with one hand and dialling the emergency admissions desk at the local hospital with the other. She's a well-known figure there — after all, doctors also keep domestic animals.

As I said before, Lena is a vet. Her mother fought tooth and nail against the idea of her going to veterinary college;

when we were young, the best an "animal doctor" could hope for was a job on a collective farm, and that wasn't something that Lena's mother wanted for her daughter. She wanted her to become a teacher, a job that would guarantee good pay and a certain status in society. Lena's mother could not possibly have foreseen how things would turn out; she simply wanted what was best for her daughter. Lena could not have foreseen either, but she insisted on getting her own way. For as long as I have known her, Lena has this boundless love for all living things. So she became a vet and not a teacher. This meant that she cut herself off from her family; her mother could not forgive her disobedience, something that amounted to an act of rebellion. Now Lena runs her own veterinary clinic, has two daughters by different husbands, and a grandson. Her scarlet jacket has become a familiar sight in Brest and the surrounding area; just before she came to help us get young Zosia into hospital, she was over at Stradche, delivering the puppies of a St Bernard bitch — the beloved (and expensive — it cost 1500 euros) pet of the Baptist pastor and his family. Her hands are striking, wide and strong with long, flexible fingers. Add to that her phenomenal intuition and her ability to go for days without sleep, and it comes as no surprise that she is now a wealthy woman. Her third husband is fifteen years younger than she is; she agreed to marry him after he had told her that for her sake he would willingly become a gerontophile, or even indulge in a bit of necrophilia.

Ulia and I first met Lena Zarnitskaya when we were on compulsory potato-harvesting duty. At the time she was a pupil in year six of School no. 13 in Brest, and she was the first to talk to us village yokels collecting the spuds on the row next to hers. Another thing about her then was that she didn't make fun of the way we spoke — unlike everyone else, including the teachers. Later on, when we had become firm friends, Ulia and I gave her nicknames that we based on her surname Zarnitskaya — *Zara-nad-Buham* (*Zara* means "dawn", so *Dawn over the River Buh*) and *Zarnitsa* ("summer night lightning"), and on the way she signed her name — *Zara* followed by a squiggle.

Zosia was put into a little room of her own in intensive care. She was beginning to feel better — the antivenom was obviously having an effect. The doctor assured me that there was absolutely no danger. Lena needed to get back to Stradche right away, so we left, after arranging for Lena to visit Zosia in the evening, and for me to drop by tomorrow.

Lena stopped in Dobratyche to let me off and opened the bonnet of her car to check the knocking sound that had been coming from the engine. She asked me to fetch her something to drink. That's how I was the first to see granny: she was sitting on the bench by the table on the verandah. Her head was thrown back and her headscarf had slipped down a bit. Her mouth gaped open. Her glasses were sitting askew on her thin, yellow face.

She was dead.

A DEATH INTENDED
FOR SOMEONE ELSE

All the funeral arrangements, and the funeral itself, went past me in a kind of fog. Ulia managed to arrive in time. Not many people came, but they had come from all over. The paths they took to reach granny were all overgrown with grass, hellebores and puffballs, but come they did. Beneath the storm clouds, gathering over the river, from Stradche, Duryche and Zakazanka they came, all of them younger than our granny. The villagers of Dobratyche were all there, except for old Lyalka, but it's been ages since she was able to walk. Afanasy Petrovich came — a pal of granny's, one of the townies up at the dachas. Today he hadn't tucked his axe behind his belt as he usually did, but his once blue trousers were the same, only freshly washed. He was the only one who cried when they carried the open coffin out of the house into the yard. Oh yes, there was a heron as well. At that very moment, with its neck bent in a hook shape, it flew over the yard and cried "Ay". I saw everything like through a dark veil — the people, the coffin, the heron that was brighter than the stormclouds creeping after it... Ulia, the Uruguayan, Lyonikha, the poet's granny Yarashykha, Aksana...

Aksana was the last to arrive, on her bicycle. She was out of breath. I didn't recognise her at first; she hadn't put on any weight, something that she might have been expected to do, but in the time that we hadn't seen each other — at least ten years — she had changed completely. She looked as though she had been drowned. We had been in the same class at the school in Stradche, and she was now the headteacher there. She nodded in our direction and placed her bike on the grass, went up to the coffin and kissed granny on the forehead. She straightened up, thought for a moment and then gently stroked granny's light-brown hand.

Although tradition has it that I ought not to have done so, I had helped Yarashykha and Katsya the Uruguayan's wife wash granny's body. They wouldn't have managed it on their own. All the same we could not get her hands and feet completely clean. It was quite impossible to wash away the earth that had collected under her finger nails and in the tiny cracks and broken capillaries of her skin. The earth was so ingrained that we couldn't shift it with soap or even pumice stone. It was then that the thought occurred to me: granny will soon be completely at one with the soil beneath our feet here in Dobratyche, but she had in fact always been at one with it, at least partially. At least her hands and feet.

Holding the edge of the coffin, Aksana began her funeral oration. Even her voice changed. Gone were the high and low tones; the voice was now steady, almost too steady. She spoke in our dialect. People raised their heads in astonishment; they hadn't expected that of the headteacher of a school.

Here we are gathered together once again. Once again we are burying a friend. Now you, our friend Makrynya, have left us. You worked hard all your life, never knowing what it is to have a holiday or even a day off. But now you will rest. May the earth be for you a soft downy bed. God will receive your soul and seat you next to him. And we will be left without you. The paths you trod in your lifetime will become overgrown with weeds. No more will we hear you speak, nor will you give us advice on how we should live our lives...

A single fair curl peeked out from beneath Aksana's black headscarf, just like it used to when we were children. Tiny drops of sweat appeared on her face and chest, although it was rapidly getting colder out in the open air.

We are here to bury you today, and we are sad, deeply sad at heart. We were long ago left as orphans, and now we feel ourselves orphaned twice over; today we bury you, but when our time comes, who will be there to bury us? Will there be anyone still left? But... When our time comes, we will be judged according to our works. Rest in peace, dear Makrynya, you lived your life righteously and with dignity. We shall not forget you.

Aksana bowed down and stepped away.

A cold wind blew up and the storm clouds drifted past us; once again there would be no rain. Gusts of wind wafted the scent of sweet scabious across the yard; the aspen trees were giving off an odour that reminded me of granny. The coffin was taken to the cemetery on a horse-drawn cart. The people who had come from other villages followed it in procession. No one from Dobratyche went to the cemetery, except the Uruguayan. They were all too old. Aksana didn't go either. She put her arms round Ulia and then hugged me, and explained to us that she had to get back to her school urgently — a delivery of new blackboards and desks was expected. She promised to drop in to see us in a day or so.

It's not difficult to talk about the actual burial. About the burial service held under the tall fir trees, about the sand which was drying out before our eyes and would now and again trickle down into the freshly dug grave, about the moment when the lid of the coffin was closed and the coffin then lowered into the grave, and the moment when hand-embroidered towels were thrown in the shape of a cross on top of the coffin... Standing next to me was a living reflection of myself — my sister, goosebumps on her arms, her face pale. Granny had many times instructed us that we were on no account to weep at her funeral. Weeping for such an old specimen as her, she said, would be against Dobratyche tradition. Ulia didn't cry, and neither did I, but not so much because I was following granny's strict instructions as because my mind was clouded by a problem that I had not yet had time to talk to Ulia about... Talking about the funeral is not difficult; actually standing in the cemetery was.

There was so much to do over the last few days, and Ulia had not even managed to unpack her things. Her suitcase was still standing in the hallway of the house where she had left it upon arrival from the station. We had had no time to talk, and what I had to tell her wasn't something we could talk about in a hurry. We followed the old custom and sat by granny's body at night while it was still in the house, but we took turns, so we couldn't talk then. And in the daytime the old ladies came to follow the tradition of watching over the body. They had to come in the daytime because they were no longer of an age to go wandering around in the forest at night. And we had all sorts of things to do during the day — buy the coffin, dig the grave, arrange with the priest about the burial service, clean and gut thirty two herrings and as many carp, fry a pile of meat cutlets that were soft enough for the old teeth of Dobratyche, Stradche and Zakazanka to chew, buy in quantities of vodka and fizzy flavoured water — and a hundred and one other things to do besides. It was just as well that Zarnitskaya was able to give us a hand, driving to and fro between Dobratyche and Brest in her "little Merc", as she put it. When she came yesterday, she chose her moment and whispered in my ear, "Have you told her?" "No," I replied, also in a whisper, "Not yet".

Neither Anton nor Yurka came for the funeral. Yurka is Ulia's husband. At that moment he was in Krakow, making the last-minute preparations for a conference of architects of which he was the organiser in charge. We decided that he should stay where he was and finish things off; if he didn't, the whole conference might turn into a disaster. But I had reckoned on Anton coming. I never did manage to get through to him on the phone, so I had to send him a telegram. Later that night he phoned himself. In a distant-sounding voice he expressed his sympathy and offered to send an assistant of his with money and a car. This upset me and I rejected the offer out of hand. I was about to bang the receiver down when I suddenly remembered the toad on the television, the toad that was in the hole (Ouch! What a terrible pun!) that serves as my memory, so that I had completely forgotten about her and everything connected with her.

"Anton dear (an endearing way of addressing my husband that I haven't used for years), what have you got yourself involved in now? What do you need it for? I'm really afraid for you..."

"Don't worry," and Anton's voice softened, it somehow grew closer to me. He obviously hadn't expected that "dear", a memory of our times together when we were young that had somehow floated to the surface. It was unexpected for me as well. "Everything's going to turn out fine. You know me, I always play for certainties when I hold the trumps." How out of place that word "play" sounded! It's been a long time since the two of us played. In fact, I've completely forgotten what it is to play — everything in our life together was much too serious. But I didn't have the chance to say all this — the Uruguayan came into the kitchen where I was talking, closely followed by a worried-looking Ulia. My presence was urgently required for the discussion of yet another domestic matter, so I hastily said good-bye to Anton and put the phone down.

Ulia and I didn't feel like clearing up when the funeral repast was over.

"Let's go upstairs," Ulia suggested after all the mourners had left the large table that was actually three smaller ones placed together. "We can have a lie-down. My feet are killing me."

Once in her room, Ulia sank down on to her sofa and covered her eyes with her hand. This was one of granny's gestures that we had adopted.

"I think we did everything that she told us to do," Ulia said without uncovering her eyes. "Just as she wanted. The only thing is I didn't like the priest very much. He was in too much of a hurry, if you ask me."

"Ulia, there's something important that I have to tell you."

Ulia opened her eyes wide.

"Granny didn't die a natural death. She died because someone mixed a heart drug — Cardiostim Forte — in with the coffee in the tin. I had made some coffee for Zosia after the snake bit her, but I didn't have time to give it to her because Zarnitskaya arrived to take us to the hospital. It looks as though granny acted as she usually did (*don't let anything go to waste*), put some milk in the coffee and started to drink it... With that heart drug in it."

"How do you know? Why didn't you tell me before?" Ulia's voice sounded hollow.

"There was a coffee mug on the table in front of her when I got back from the hospital. She had drunk half of it. I know about the drug because Zarnitskaya has an extraordinary sense of smell. When she heard my scream and came running towards the verandah, she rushed straight over to granny and almost immediately announced that she was dead. You know, once again I've seen just how capable she is in any situation, and how helpless and useless I am. She got me to help her carry granny into the house and then she called the ambulance, and asked for a resuscitation team just in case. She tried giving granny artificial respiration before the ambulance arrived. Later, after the paramedics had confirmed that granny was dead and left, we went back out on to the verandah. I just sat there like a stone, unable to say a word, and Zarnitskaya started dialling Khvedzka's mobile.. All of a sudden I saw her sniff the air, just like a hunting dog does when it's caught the scent of something. Then she went over to the table, picked up the mug of coffee, sniffed it and tasted it with the tip of her tongue... Then she looked at me in a very odd way and said: 'You know, Ala, something's been put in this coffee. Let me have the packet!' She took the packet with her to have it analysed. When she returned that evening she told me that she had found Cardiostim Forte in both the coffee mug and the packet. A really big dose. Big enough to cause a heart attack."

"But didn't the paramedics on the ambulance notice anything suspicious?"

"Of course not. Granny was ninety seven. There's nothing to be suspicious of, what else can be the cause of death, apart from old age? They wrote out the certificate and that's all. On the certificate the cause of death is given as "heart attack". It didn't enter anyone's head that it may actually have been brought on by some external agent. If it hadn't been for Zarnitskaya, no one would ever have found out."

We looked at one another. Two sisters, impossibly alike. Just that one is a little deformed in body and very much deformed in soul. I could read her thoughts just as if they were mine. Ulia had had more than her fair share of problems with me; I certainly wasn't an easy sister to get along with. When I recall everything that she had to do for me...! More than once she had to come and track me down in those awful old apartment blocks on Rosa Luxembourg Street in Mensk; when she did find me, I would always be out to the world. She had to pay doctors to cure me of alcohol addiction. At one time we didn't speak for a whole year. She's had to pay bribes to get me out of trouble. And there was that time I was suspected of involvement in a murder.

Now it's all starting up again.

And what's worse is that we're in a mess we don't understand. Who put Cardiostim in the coffee, and why. Why and who?

"Right," and Ulia paused for a second. "OK, what have you got yourself into this time?"

I shook my head.

"No, it's got absolutely nothing to do with me. I can't even imagine..."

"But I can," my sister cut in angrily and began pacing round the tiny room. "I can! You're up to your old tricks again, aren't you?" She sat down and wiped her forehead. "How much longer do you think this can go on for, Ala? We had an agreement, didn't we? You're soon going to be fifty."

I kept quiet, trying to hold back the tears that unexpectedly began to flow — just as they always did.

Ulia took hold of herself.

"I'm sorry, Ala," she sat down and hugged my shoulders.

I wiped my eyes.

"It's you who should forgive me."

"Where is your Cardiostim?" Ulia asked.

"Where it should be".

I have problems with my heart and I have to take this drug regularly, but no more than half a tablet a day. I had checked my stock of tablets; no one had touched them.

"So, OK then. What do we have so far? A powerful heart drug deliberately mixed in with the coffee. We can assume that the intention was to poison someone. As far as I know, a large dose of this stuff will be enough to kill a healthy man, let alone someone who's not well, like you for example..."

"Or you," I retorted.

Ulia thought for a second and nodded.

"Yes, or me. It would be enough to exceed the dose just by a little bit to cause a dangerous heart attack... If Zosia had drunk any, it would probably not have affected her. She's young and, thank God, there's nothing wrong with her heart... Granny's heart was worn out, but then again, she never drank coffee. At least I can't remember her ever drinking it. You were absolutely right when you said it was pure chance she drank some of that mug of coffee. That means... well, that means we can say with certainty that the Cardiostim Forte was not intended for her... For you, perhaps?"

"I don't know. But I have seen Death. Just over the frontier, at night."

"Ala, dear, I noticed an already open bottle of whisky behind the fridge on the verandah. I wouldn't be surprised if you saw little imps in the gaps between the cupboards."

I had been caught red-handed, so said nothing. It suddenly became very quiet in the house.

Then Ulia spoke. "Granny didn't die her own death. She died someone else's. Either yours or mine. That's all we can say at the moment."

"No, I really did see Death," I started to explain to Ulia what I had seen that night on the allotment, but then I faltered. It suddenly struck me what Ulia had just said. *Your* death? Someone might have tried to poison *you*?

Did an unknown criminal want Ulia dead? I simply said that

out of irritation. I was annoyed by Ulia's assumption that I was the guilty one here. And she takes it all so seriously?

Right at that moment, when I was still stunned by what Ulia had said, when the sun was already low in the sky, and its rays were drawing out the reddish hues in every colour, when the light outside shimmered magically, turning the trunks of the pine trees into pure copper, there came the familiar sound of a "Belarus" tractor briskly chugging its way towards our gate. It was followed by a little mare, looking a bit miserable but even so managing to pull its cart at quite a fast pace.

It was Tolik and Valik coming to see us. For all that Ulia and I are twin sisters and have many memories in common, our memories of this pair are completely separate. My part of these memories is linked with *my* Tolik: green moss, mist, the sand sticking to our damp, cold skin, the skinny body in which you can count the ribs...

HE USED VULGAR WORDS
BEING BESOTTED WITH POWER

My Tolik.

We never did get married. When we left school, Ulia and I went off to university and Tolik was called up for his military service. By the second year of my course I no longer thought of Tolik as my intended. Anton appeared in my third year. I can't say that I've never thought about what my life would have been like if I hadn't turned down the invitation to go to the dance over at the village club in Pryluki. But turn it down I did, so that's all there is to it.

Tolik now works as a tractor driver. More than that — he *is* a tractor driver. That's what he does. He's forgotten about everything else. And he's a terrible *alconaut* — he literally swims in the stuff. I heard that last summer he packed his son off to study at the Economics University in Mensk — what's more, the lad is studying in the section where they charge full fees. Tolik's face has been tanned by the sun to a deep reddish-brown, with wrinkles so sharply defined and deep that there seems to be no bottom to them. He's still a big man, but life seems to have worn him down a bit and his shoulders are starting to droop. His wife Handzia works hard to make sure he looks after the greenhouses and pigsties, and an orchard of espaliated apple trees.

Time has been a little kinder to Valik. He's a team foreman; he used to work on the collective farm called "The Path of Ilich"*,

---

* *Ilich:* this is the patronymic of Vladimir Lenin. Addressing someone just by their patronymic is somehow 'matey' or 'familiar'. The idea, presumably, is that any path taken by our good mate Ilich must good for us too.

and now he works for the private company called "Agrovitalika Plus". I can still see in him the boy with the full fresh face and grin that we went to school with. The main difference is that back then he was one of the real trouble-makers, always up to mischief or spoiling for a fight. Now he seems to have acquired some *gravitas*; "pensive" and "serious" are the best words to describe him. He travels around the district by horse and cart, lounging in a mound of hay and lording it over everyone, exactly as his grandfather did before him. He doesn't like driving the Land Rover-type vehicle that goes with the job. Indeed he hardly ever uses it. "I'm not in a hurry to get anywhere", he maintains.

However strange it might seem, I was really pleased to see them. Although we had had a funeral earlier on, I was delighted when Tolik switched off the engine and slammed the door of his tractor, and when Valik, once off his cart, tied the reins firmly to the gate post.

While Ulia and I were coming downstairs, the Sun had gone down across the river. The red reflections had all disappeared; the night, still dressed in blue, was gathering its courage and coming closer.

"Couldn't get away earlier," shouted Tolik from the gate. "Charota said to me 'I can't let you go. I should have gone myself to bid farewell to the old lady, but the weather won't wait. She knew what working on the land was like, she'll forgive us. Once we've got the hay in, we'll go to the grave together.'"

"He was right, there was that storm cloud on the other side of the river," added Valik as he came in through the gate. "But then a cold wind got up and we didn't get the rain we need so badly. Even more so now — we got the last of the hay in today. Please don't be cross with us for not coming to the funeral today. We just couldn't make it."

"There's no need to apologise," said Ulia, with a dismissive gesture of the hand, "It's great that you've dropped in to see us now. Let's go into the house. Go and wash your hands while we get the table ready..."

Ulia and I cleared away the dirty plates, glasses and forks, and put out clean ones. Tolik and Valik removed a couple of tables that we didn't need, and then we sat down.

Earlier today there had been no time for Ulia and me to sit down during the repast. We were busy bringing food and taking things away, making sure that there was enough to eat and drink for the people who had come to say their final farewell to granny. This was our duty at funerals; granny had a long time ago explained in great detail what we had to do. But now it was evening, the official part of the funeral was over and we could do things differently. So we put all the leftovers that were on several different plates on to one plate.

Tolik opened a bottle and hovered over my glass with it, giving Ulia a look that clearly asked "Should I or shouldn't I?" She gave him a nod, and he poured me a shot. I don't take any notice of these little details any more. *What can you do with her? She's an alcoholic, can't control herself.*

It's quiet outside, and getting darker. Inside there's just one bare bulb burning. Every year on Easter Sunday we used to have a grand spread in this very room. Granny would never sit at the head of the table; she always sat to one side, close to one of the children. But she was always the first to propose a toast. She usually spoke in verse, simple thoughts with verb rhymes. Now there's only the silence; nobody says a word. We sit there, holding our glasses up in front of us.

"So, right then, what was it I was going to say?" Tolik got to his feet, something I hadn't expected of him. "Perhaps I shouldn't be the first one to speak, but here goes... This is what I want to say: the first person I remember in my life is granny Makrynya. Well, you know the story: when I was four, I was playing down by the oval lake, breaking the ice, and then I fell in, and she dragged me out. She saved my life. I can still remember what it was like. I was trying to hang on to the lumps of ice, but they kept slipping out of my fingers. One minute all I could see was the black water in front of me, and the next white snow and blue sky. All of a sudden a powerful hand grabs me by the collar, and there I am, lying on the snow, I can't get my breath and there's steam coming out of my mouth... She sweeps me up in her arms and carries me home at a run... "

Valik suddenly burst out laughing, only to realise almost immediately just how out of place his laughter was:

"You were four when she lifted you bodily. Now listen to what she did to me just a month ago, and I'm fifty four..."

"What's that then?"

"I was coming back through Dobratyche from somewhere or other, when I see granny Makrynya carrying a large sack, she's walking along, leaning on her stick. I get down from the cart and say 'Here, let me help you.' She peers at me through her specs, recognises me and says, 'Oh, it's young Valik! Thanks very much, but I can lift you up any day, not just this sack!' 'Bet you can't!' 'I'll show you!' So over I go to her laughing, she dumps her sack on the ground, puts her arms around me and lifts me up. OK, I bounced off her at once, but she did get me off the ground... So, let's remember her." And we drank to her memory.

We put our glasses down and Tolik went on, "Do you remember the day she sent that fat guy packing?"

"No one in Dobratyche got up earlier than she did."

"My dad used to say that she was the only woman here who could drive the combine harvester."

"Remember how she had that fight with the guy from the agricultural advisory service?"

"What about when she strung up that rabid cat?"

"And how she used to drown kittens, chase dogs away, and beat the kids that got in among her fruit trees..."

"If you understand granny, you understand the whole world," said Ulia.

"What an odd thing to say," observed Valik.

"The words aren't mine," replied Ulia.

"People are saying your husband's put himself up for election," this is Tolik talking to me. "Taking a bit of a risk, isn't he? So I suppose you're going to go off to Mensk now to help him, aren't you?"

Go off to Mensk? The thought hadn't entered my head. Anton hasn't asked me to come, and I don't want to invite myself. Everything connected with granny is here — her house, her garden, her plot of land and her animals, if you like... I can't just leave them. I know too that I have to get to the bottom of the mystery of granny's death. And that's something I can do only here in Dobratyche, where it all happened.

I looked at my sister and I could see in her eyes that she understood me.

After the second toast my sister briefly told the two men how granny had died because someone — we don't know who or why — had laced her coffee with Cardiostim Forte.

"We can't say for certain who the intended victim was," my sister said. "That kind of dose would kill Ala or me, or indeed anyone with a weak heart. But it was granny they poisoned."

Tolik was already on a vodka rush after the second glass and didn't take it very seriously:

"Oho! We've got ourselves a detective story! 'Murder in Dobratyche', a mystery in two parts."

His feeble attempt at a joke fell flat on its face.

"You've got to tell the police," said Valik.

Ulia and I exchanged glances. Tell the police? What can the police do? Even if they do begin an investigation, they'll do a little bit of work to show they're earning their wages and then close the case down for lack of evidence. Who's ever been helped by the police? Or are the police only of use to people in those detective serials they're always showing on the Russian TV channels?

"No, let's not trouble the police," Ulia shook her head, "they've got enough on their plates as it is".

"Right. We don't need the police. We'll work it all out ourselves!" This was Tolik, fired up with the enthusiasm typical of an alcoholic. Valik countered him with the sober judgement of a foreman responsible for a team of workers:

"How?"

"We've got to think." "We've got to think of anyone who would benefit from having someone bumped off!"

"Bumped off? Who? Granny?"

"Yes, her, and you, and you," Tolia pointed towards me and Ulia with his chin. By this time Ulia had left the table and was sitting on the sofa. We're going to have to make a list of all those who might want you out of the way."

"Maybe it's already..." Valik began to say something but then stopped. "What sort of coffee was it?"

"Nothing special", I replied. 'Jacobs Kronung'. I buy it a lot. The packet was already open, I'd used it several times."

"When did you use it last?"

"That's exactly what I can't remember! I've tried and tried, but I simply can't! What with everything else that's happened, it's gone right out of my mind. After all, I drink coffee a lot. Perhaps it was that morning, or the evening before? I do recall that Mishyk the poet dropped by that week, and I made him a cup of coffee, but of course I've made myself coffee since then..."

"We have to find a motive," Tolik continued to pursue his own line of inquiry.

"Sure, and then it turns out that our murderer is the kind that doesn't have a motive," Valik retorted.

"But we've got to start somewhere!"

"Whatever, but it would still be worth calling in the police. And, by the way, please throw out all your open packets of food, get new ones. You should do that anyway." Another sober observation from Valik.

"Listen, everyone," Ulia interrupted him from the sofa, and her voice was completely different. "Ala, do you have any idea of what you've got here?"

While we had been talking, Ulia had — just for the sake of something to do — picked out one of the folders that were in a pile on the little table by the sofa and had begun to leaf idly through the papers in it. Holding the open folder on her lap she was looking at me with a strange expression on her face.

"So do you know what's in these folders?"

"The answer's probably 'no, I don't'. They're documents I took out of the archive. I was planning to do some work on them."

"Have you even had a look at them?"

"There hasn't been any time. So, what then?"

"Just listen." Slowly — so that we could follow what she was saying more easily — she began to read from a document of the seventeenth century. The quaint, old-fashioned words sounded strange in the still of the evening.

Complaint of Khrystof Tryzna Esquire, son of Storyma Tryzna Esquire deceased, burgher of the city of Lvov, late Master of the Guild of Goldsmiths, against Bartosh Kostomlotski Esquire, for assault and battery, and for defamation. Sworn before us, burgomasters, councillors and magistrates in open court session in the Town Hall of the city of Bereste in the Grand Duchy of Lithuania, on the 28th day of the month of July in the year of our Lord 1650. Khrystof Tryzna Esquire aforementioned, burgher of His Most Excellent Majesty's City of Lvov, Master of the Guild of Goldsmiths, recounted in his own words the events that gave cause for his complaint laid against Bartosh Kostomlotski Esquire, gentleman of the Palatinate of Bereste, Master of the Village of Kostomloty and the lands adjacent thereto, that on the 26th day of the Month of July in this same year the aforesaid Khrystof Tryzna Esq., being an upright gentleman and of good repute, and protected by the Laws of our Commonwealth from all manner of insult and injury, was proceeding about his own affairs along the right bank of the river Buh, seeking a package concealed there by his father, Storyma Tryzna Esquire, when the said Bartosh Kostomlotsky Esquire together with his serving men fell upon Master Khrystof, grievously wounding him and those who were with him, threatening to kill them and shouting that he would not permit Master Khrystof to take possession of the treasure because, according to the law of the Commonwealth, the treasure

*belonged to him, Master Bartosh Kostomlotsky, as it was hidden
on his land. To which Master Khrystof replied that he was seeking
not treasure but a certain package of his late father, who two years
previously had been on his way back by river from Bereste to the city
of Lvov when he was attacked near the Kostomloty mill by godless
villainous ruffians who seized all the goods and slaughtered without
mercy. Without hope of rescue and before he expired of his grievous
wounds, Master Storyma Tryzna concealed the chest with all the
precious stones that he had with him in a certain place, and wrote
a note, which note his faithful servant brought to Lvov and passed
to Master Khrystof. Master Bartosh threatened him with a sword,
used vulgar words being besotted with power. His serving men were
armed with sticks and chains and forced Master Khrystof to hand
over the note, in which was set out the place where the chest of jewels
was to be found. Master Khrystof Tryzna, son of Storyma deceased,
swore on oath that he was his father's sole heir, and humbly begs their
worships the burgomasters, councillors and magistrates to compel
Master Kostomlotsky to return the note and to impose a fine upon
aforesaid Master Kostomlotsky, and because of the bodily injuries and
the besmirching of his reputation as a gentleman, wishing to have
the matter tried in court in accordance with the law, respectfully begs
that this his sworn statement be entered into the registers of the City
of Bereste. The which has been duly done."*

I held my breath and stole a glance at the two men. Valik
had a dreamy smile on his face; Tolik's eyes were gleaming
and his grin was nearly stretching from ear to ear. These last
fifty years disappeared without trace, so did the collective farm,
Agrovitalika Plus Ltd., all the poverty and stress, no more dachas
on the hills or the people living in them, no more green toads
on the TV. All that there was were the children of Dobratyche,
our lives were still ahead of us, and the ground beneath our feet
had become transparent like glass, and treasures — not only
the gems that had belonged to the jeweller of Lvov — revealed
themselves right in front of us... Ulia was looking at us with an
amused expression in her eyes, but I could tell that she too — a

historian and therefore well used to holding old documents in her hands — was impressed.

"Well, did you understand it all?" she asked.

"What's so difficult about it?" Tolik gave a deep sigh. "Some jeweller is sailing down the river and he's attacked by bandits..."

"Racketeers," Valik corrected him.

"OK, racketeers, just like the crooks we've got now, and before he dies he manages to hide the chest with the valuables, and pass a note to his son, a note that tells him where to look for the chest... So what happened next? Did that Kastamalotski guy ever hand over the note? What happened to the treasure?"

"It looks like that's all there is. The papers after it are about other things."

"To think that all that happened not far from here. I can't believe it."

"What did you think, that there weren't any people living round here at that time? That they didn't eat, or drink, or earn money?"

"It's really interesting, that job of yours, Ala. Not like driving a tractor to take manure out to the fields."

"What job of mine?! If Ulia hadn't started to look through the folders, I would probably have returned them all unread to the archive."

I have to admit that I had completely forgotten about those documents.

Before leaving Mensk to come down here, I had tried to find a job, if possible one that was somehow connected with what I had been trained for in university. Rather that than selling cooking oil in the central market. So I went to see some people that I knew. Volha Babkova thought for a moment, then said in that heavily veiled voice of hers — and I reckon her soul lives somewhere behind it: "Yes, you know, I believe that we do have some sort of little job that you could do in our archives — going through old documents, that sort of thing. It pays peanuts, of course, but on the other hand, you'll be able to work down in that village of yours — what's it called? Dobratyche or something? Yes, you could read the documents down there and transfer them to your computer."

I was overjoyed at the prospect of a job like that. It offered me an ideal opportunity to get back to working in an area that I had specialised in at university. (Although, when you look at it, I must have been stark, raving mad. There was I, looking for a job in my specialist area when other people of my age are already thinking about retirement. But I did have reasons of my own. I was looking for a job because I needed to feel independent. And I needed to feel independent because my husband Anton had got himself someone younger, and I had found out from a woman on the phone who did not give her name, and I had been betrayed by my husband because he couldn't put up with my general uselessness any more, and all he wanted for himself was a normal life...)

In the archive department they loaded me with a pile of xerox copies of old illegible documents. They had all been carefully bound into stiff folders. I went through all the copies quite thoroughly, and my initial enthusiasm began to wane. I couldn't make out what was on them at all! Lots of fancy curlicues and squiggles, and in two scripts — Latin and Cyrillic. Not surprising really, it's been a long time since I studied palaeography at university, and I hadn't had any practice. A whole mountain of things that needed doing landed on me here in Dobratyche, which explains why all that stuff was still lying untouched on the table.

Without expecting it, I suddenly came out with:

"Hey, what if that chest is still lying hidden somewhere around here? What if we were to start looking for it seriously. Ulia, how much do you think seventeenth-century jewellery would be worth nowadays?"

Ulia shrugged her shoulders.

"It all depends on where it was made and who made it. If

it's made of silver, for example, then maybe, oh I don't know, somewhere around several hundred dollars apiece... But if they're made of gold, and the workmanship is good, and especially if they're inlaid with diamonds, then they could be very valuable indeed. And if the pieces are of historical or artistic importance, there's absolutely no way of knowing how much they could be worth, it could run into millions... The jewellery must have been quite valuable and not some pieces of cheap stuff, considering that this man Tryzna was willing to risk his life in searching for it. I'm sure I've heard something about a jeweller called Tryzna, but I can't remember exactly where. I'm not an expert on the seventeenth century. Anyway", and here my sister, seeing how intently the two men and I were listening to her, obviously wanted to put an end to the discussion, "just get these ideas of going on a treasure hunt out of your heads. You shouldn't be taking it seriously."

"Why shouldn't we take it seriously?" I said. I could feel that I was ready to flare up at any moment. "Are you just saying that because I was the one to suggest it?"

"Several hundred dollars for each of us," Tolik repeated dreamily and scratched one of his bushy eyebrows. "Yes, Ala's right. Why shouldn't we take it seriously?"

"Come on, we've known each other for so long, there's no need to quarrel. There are treasure hoards like this one hidden in the ground all over the place. That's a fact. It's like Valik said, people lived here and they made money. Burying money in the ground was just as natural for past generations as opening a bank account is for us nowadays, and for every single individual alive today, there are many more who have already died. It follows therefore that there must be a lot of buried treasure around, but even so... Buried treasure is either found by pure chance, or after a lengthy period of gathering and analysing information. In this particular instance we obviously don't have enough information. Let's just go through what we know already. The jeweller hid his chest of jewellery somewhere on the Buh, maybe in the vicinity of Kastamaloty*, but this 'vicinity' could cover quite a large area and might well be on both sides of the river. Remember that we can't get down to the river bank on this side — the right bank is in no man's land — and the left bank is Polish territory. Kastamaloty itself is in Poland. It's all too vague. Then there's the fact that, as you already know, the jeweller's son went hunting for the treasure, and we must assume that this Kastamlotsky character did so as well, once he got his hands on that that scrap of paper. And there may well have been others after it as well. In any case, do we have time to go treasure hunting now? I for one certainly don't." Ulia stood up and returned to the table. "Let's have one more drink. After all, you're supposed to have three drinks at a funeral repast, and that's what we're at, aren't we?"

---

* In Polish: Kostomłoty

I ENCOUNTER MR IVAN KUKAL FOR THE FIRST TIME

More than anything the next morning I wanted to sleep for as long as I could, just stretch out and sleep. To give my frayed nerves a chance to calm down. To give my body some rest. But by dawn duty was already calling loudly outside in the yard. I had no choice but to haul myself out of bed with a groan. The stupid chickens flapped their way out of the coop; the geese honked furiously; the ducks quacked; the rabbits demonstrated their annoyance silently, just by twitching their noses. When at last and still half asleep I got the sty open, the pig let out such a high-pitched squeal that I was on the verge of killing it on the spot with my bare hands. Killing... the word brought me back to reality just as if I had been plugged into a socket. There had been a murder in the house. I had no idea who had done it, or why, but murder had been done.

Granny was dead.

"The whole ground's covered with apples," and Ulia suddenly appeared on the scene carrying two huge baskets of the sweet summer apples we grow round here, so pale they're almost white. She tipped them into a corner of the verandah. "Nobody's been out to collect them for four days now, it's like there's snow on the ground".

I made a start on chopping beetroot and mixing the grains. Then I put some small potatoes on the stove to boil.

"What did you get up so early for. Given half a chance, I wouldn't have got out of bed at all. But seeing you were up so early, you could at least have let the animals out."

"I didn't think I would enjoy myself so much picking up the apples. Do you want some coffee?"

"Go on. I'm not going back to bed anyway."

"Then we'll need to do something with the apples. We can't let them go to waste. Let me get on with making the breakfast, while you go and have a wash — you're a frightful sight. Then you can fetch that old bedcloth from the loft that granny used to dry the apples on," she shouted after me as I was already on my way to the washbasin.

The washbasin that granny had touched with her own hands. Her bench. The tree roots on the paths that she had worn bare. "All the paths I've trodden will soon become overgrown," she used to say, staring into the distance. Will no one ever understand what we trample all these paths for in our lifetime?

The aroma of the fresh coffee that Ulia had made was spreading through the house. She was using the new pack that she had brought from Berastse.

The smell in the loft, however, was musty and stale. Cobwebs and dust. In the corners lay the few odd bits and pieces that granny hadn't bothered to burn: a large loom, some old overcoats, a thin satchel of the kind children probably used to go to school with back in the 1920s... I picked through all this old stuff and couldn't help thinking of granny again. She was a remarkable woman, quite out of the ordinary and very talented. People like her easily make enemies... So what if she lived to be nearly one hundred and never set foot outside Dobratyche... Even here the blood runs hot in people's veins... No, it's more realistic to think that someone wanted her dead rather than imagine that the poison in the coffee was meant for me. Good God, who on Earth would want me dead so much? More precisely, whoever would think I am so unnecessary that they would go to such lengths to get me out of the way? It's a joke! Sure, I'm not very bright, but I'm completely harmless. Of that I'm certain. It's even more ridiculous to think that someone wanted my sister dead. She's the kind of person who just doesn't have any enemies. Everyone I know is very fond of her. She's a real mensch, someone with principles, someone whose shoulder you can always lean on. She's like a tuning fork, you can always hit the right note with her around. No, it's absolutely impossible to think that someone would want her out of the way.

A dusty wicker-covered glass bottle... In the days when we were children, finding a bottle like this — or even a humble sweet wrapper — was a real piece of good luck; we would take it off to the fields. Bottles like this were easy to carry — they had wicker handles as well. This one even had a stopper in it — a tightly-rolled piece of paper. I took it out. A yellowed page torn out of an exercise book unrolled under my fingers. In the semi-darkness I could just make out that there was a drawing on it. I went over to the little window. Was it one of my childish drawings? Or one of Ulia's? No, this was how grown-ups drew in the Middle Ages. The details were drawn well, but the lines were all slightly crooked; lots of detail, but the proportions were wrong. So, it was probably a grown-up who drew the picture, quite likely someone talented, but with no training, maybe someone who didn't hold a pencil in their hands very often. It was a picture of a stocky young man with a big nose, wearing a cap. The collar of his shirt, the buttons and even the steel tips on the heels of his shoes were all there in the drawing. His hands were large and strong. There was another, very similar drawing on the other side. I took a closer look; someone had written a name, *Stepan*, several times over, in handwriting that had now almost completely faded.

Beneath the drawing was a verse, oddly enough written with Ukrainian words, but in Polish letters:

> *Sonce nyzeńko*
> *Prychodź, serdeńko*
> *Tody pryjdesz*
> *Jak Lalku proženesz*

The Sun is sinking low into the west
Oh come, dear heart, the one I love the best
But do not come ere you can tell me true
That with that Lyalka you are wholly through

I guessed that it was our granny's handwriting. And that means that the young man in the drawing must be Stepan, or as we would now call him in Belarusian, Stsyapan. Lyonikha, that Dobratyche newsagency and archive rolled into one, had once told us a story of love and treachery in which the heroes were our still young and unmarried granny, Lyonikha herself in her younger years and this Stsyapan. According to Lyonikha, Stsyapan and our granny were in love with each other and wanted to get married, but then Lyalka came along and stole Stsyapan away — just to show she could do it; after all, that made him her umpteenth boyfriend. Lyalka soon got tired of him, so he tried to get back in with his Makrynya, but she was having none of it, and went and married our granddad Vasil. But she never, ever forgave Lyalka. For as long as I can remember our granny and granny Lyalka were at daggers drawn. Granny Lyalka is now completely bedridden — she was struck down with paralysis, but in contrast to our granny, she kept her good looks. She has gentle brown eyes and wrinkles that a writer like Gogol might call *harmonious*. Behind these good looks, however, hides a character every bit as strong as our *witch's*.

"So what are you going to say to her?" said Ulia, shrugging her shoulders, when I showed her the note I had found, and suggested that I should go and see granny Lyalka. "So what's all this then, granny Lyalka, did you poison granny Makrynya? You'll just be making a soap opera out of it, that's all, if you ask me..."

"I don't know about a soap opera, but it's just like Tolik said, we have to start somewhere. Maybe we'll find some kind of clue that we can follow up. Otherwise what are we going to do — just sit around here twiddling our thumbs? I want to know who killed granny and why. And besides, there may still be some of that poison around, or there may be something else nasty just waiting to happen."

"OK, alright, we'll go and see granny Lyalka, but let's get the apples sorted out first. Hang on a minute, though, she can't walk. No, she can't be involved, it's a load of nonsense."

Getting the apples "sorted out" took a long time. There seemed to be thousands of them and Ulia simply had to examine each one closely, didn't she? Then we had to feed the animals again, and tidy up in the pigsty a bit; the wretched beast had managed to dig holes everywhere. Evening was coming on when we finally got out of the house.

Lyalka's dilapidated abode was not all that far from our house, just on the other side of the hill. To get there you had to go past the manor house that some specialist in STDs had bought off the heirs of old Dzianis. It's been an absolute madhouse there for ages. He's had the house faced with bricks, he's had another storey built on top, and of course he's added the latest must-have, a sauna. There's a swimming pool in all its shimmering glory, right in the middle of what used to be the farmyard. There's even a fountain playing in it. There are kids running about all over the place, there's a smell of kebabs sizzling on the barbeque, the table looks as though it might break under the weight of the food piled on it, and over it all the breeze is flapping a brightly coloured gazebo. We walked along a fence made of chicken wire. Stout-loined buxom women were lying prone on sunloungers, working on their suntans, and men — types who know exactly what the purpose of the lives is — were drinking beer. On the brick wall there were hanging baskets with this season's latest gardening craze — purple surfinia.

Lyalka's house is right opposite. There's a dry snake-skin lying in the yard, and a blackened old wooden wheel all overgrown with weeds by the well. Granny Lyalka and her daughter — another Lyalka — were also having their meal outside, sitting on a bench. Between them was a saucer with chopped onion in a pool of oil and some bread. The food that we had hastily gathered together and brought with us served as the pretext for our visit — we know Granny Lyalka couldn't come to the funeral yesterday because of her legs so here we are with the *kutstsya** from the funeral repast and a few other bits and pieces — but it was obvious that our offerings had come just at the right moment.

Granny Lyalka gave us a warm welcome, but that's what she does to everyone who comes to see her. She bowed to us from her porch, thanked us for dropping by, sat us down beside her and began to interrogate us about what had been going on. I soon realised that it would be better for us to leave. Both of them — Lyalka senior and Lyalka junior — were obviously hungry. Hunger was a constant companion of theirs, as indeed it was of all true natives of Dobratyche. The local code, however, did not permit any open display of hunger. It wasn't the done thing to eat in the presence of outsiders.

Lyalka senior was able to control herself better, but Lyalka junior — poor simple-minded soul — could not take her eyes off the cutlets and brawn that we had brought. She's the same age as me and my sister, but is really retarded. All she does winter and summer is lurch from one fir tree to the next. She wears a headscarf, and poking out from below her skirt you can see a blood-stained nightie; her face is either thickly smeared with beetroot juice or smothered in awful-looking pink powder. She seems to be pondering deeply on something or other the whole time, but if you ask her anything, the only two sentences that she will come out with are "Last Sunday we were in church. And on the Sunday before that as well." She does understand some things and she helps her mother: she can dig and weed the allotment, and feed the chickens, but she has to be told what to do. She'd never even get water out of the well on her own.

---

* *Kutstsya:* a dish for a special occasion, a kind of porridge made from barley or other grain, mixed with egg, sugar, honey and raisins.

Apart from this pathetic creature, granny Lyalka has no other children still alive.

Ulia gave me a sly poke in the stomach with her elbow, and I was just about to stand up ready to go home, when all of a sudden the whole scene changed.

An expensive, black car — I think it must have been a Mercedes — drove up almost without a sound and stopped. The rear door opened and out on to the dusty, sun-parched grass of Lyalka's yard stepped shoes with a high-gloss shine followed by a dapper silk-trousered pair of legs. Then the whole man emerged.

If only I had known then what I was destined to suffer because of this man! I'm certain that when the two of us are dead, the good Lord is going to put us somewhere side-by-side.

A striking figure of a man; the facial features give the impression of someone who considers his actions carefully and then acts decisively. The head flows gracefully into the neck. He's a bit on the chubby side, but not excessively so. He obviously keeps his weight in check.

Here was the man who was to play probably the most important role in my life. His face was tanned and weather-beaten in such a way that the wind now seemed to fan him in a special way, not like other people.

"Good evening," he greeted us calmly.

"I wish you good health," Ulia replied, a little cautiously and in Belarusian.

"My name is Kukal, Ivan Dmitrievich Kukal," said the stranger, in Russian of course, swallowing some of the vowels and stretching others out a little. "You ladies, I presume, must be Ulia and Ala. I have some business I would like to discuss with you. I called in to see you just now, but you weren't at home," and he waved his arm vaguely in the direction of our house, "so it's lucky you're here". Then he turned to Lyalka senior. "Well, gran, have you had a think about my offer?"

"Goodness, sonny! I don't understand any of it! I'm old, I'm going to die here."

"Gran, I've already explained everything to you! Silly old bat, I keep trying to drive it into her head, but I'm not getting anywhere", these last words were addressed to us. "It's so difficult dealing with old people", he said — in Belarusian — and smiled in quite a kind way. "Now those people over there," and he nodded towards the occupants of the former manor house opposite who were all looking intently in our direction, "they're normal reasonable folk, we came to an agreement straight away."

The venereologist apparently took Kukal's gesture as a signal for him to approach, so he came scurrying over towards us.

"So here's the deal: I want to buy up all this ground," and he swept his arm over a wide area. "Including the hill, all the water sources and the oak woods. And your allotments as well. I'll pay a good price. OK, OK, I'll be over in a minute," this to the venereologist who obediently turned round and trotted back. "I'm going to build a sanatorium here. So, what's your price?"

"There's not going to be any talk of a price. Our house isn't for sale," my sister responded. There was a note of surprise in her voice.

"And you, dear, what do you have to say?" he asked me in a tone that was far too familiar for my liking.

"I'll thank you to be polite when you talk to me," I retorted.

"I'll pay a very good price. You can ask them over there," and again he pointed towards the house with the surfinia on the wall. "One hundred thousand. US dollars, of course. Well, do we have an agreement?"

Lyalka junior couldn't hold back any longer. She picked up a cutlet from the bowl and began to chew. She closed her eyes and her face took on the expression of a plant that was being watered in the middle of a baking hot day.

"Are you mad?" asked Ulia in the same familiar tone that Kukal had adopted and in Russian.

"I'm a businessman," Kukal persisted in speaking Belarusian, but still with that note of irritating familiarity. "I need this land. OK, I'll put another ten thousand on top. Just think of how much money that is", and he cast a quizzical glance at Ulia. "That's more than you'll ever earn in your lifetime. Think of all the things you could buy with it. It's real wealth, something you can leave for your kids."

Kukal was speaking calmly, even politely after a fashion, but Ulia was beginning to boil with rage.

"My children are no concern of yours. Like I said, the house isn't for sale."

"Listen, love. OK, the old girl here's lost her marbles, but you know what the score is, don't you? You're a modern woman. Don't be so stubborn. Go and buy yourself a much nicer place somewhere else."

"Why don't you go and buy a place somewhere else?"

He raised one eyebrow slightly. Two massive young bruisers got out of the car. Honest to God, it was like a scene out of a bad movie. Kukal was still just about managing to keep his voice steady. He wiped his forehead with the gesture of a man who's tired of it all.

"Just picture it to yourself. OK, you stay here. What pleasure are you going to get from sitting right by the fence of a sanatorium? There'll be people all over the place wanting to have a good time, loads of noise, shouting. Think about my offer. There'll be a whole range of buildings here. The main block's going to be over there, and there'll be a bar here. We'll fix the wellspring up good and proper, and build a sort of dome on top, clean it all up..."

The house that used to belong to Tolik's dad Yovik was just a bit further away by the hill. The old man had died ages ago and Tolik was now living with his in-laws in Stradche, but he still kept some land here to grow his fruit and veg. He must have heard the slamming of the car door, looked out of the barn where he had been doing something and came hurrying over to us just as he was, with a pitchfork in his hands.

"Right then, let's leave it like this," Kukal was now trying to bring the proceedings to some kind of conclusion. "I'll give you a day or two to think it over, but don't take too long, my time's precious. Don't forget, money will always get you what you want, but anything can happen to a house... Houses get old, they can get woodworm or dry rot, they catch fire, anything..."

He turned round, demonstrating to us that he was in no hurry, and, without bothering to go over to the venereologist or to turn round in our direction, got in the car. The Mercedes drove off.

"Has that fat bastard been round again about buying the house?" asked Tolik, who by now had reached Lyalka's house.

"Do you know him?"

"I've seen him around. I saw him go to your granny's and how she sent him packing — do you remember, I said something about it at the repast afterwards? — I saw him call in on granny Lyalka — Good health to you, gran! — and heard her make out that she was stupid..."

"So what sort of man is he?"

"He's a businessman. Bit of a wide boy, if you ask me, although "crook" might be a better word to describe him. Got his fingers in all sorts of pies in Berastsie, restaurants, allocation of pitches in the market, that sort of thing. There's a rumour, though, that he makes most of his money from drugs and prostitution. People know him only too well round here. Thinks he's the king. Something's got into him that he must buy this land."

"Has he been round to see you?"

"No, he doesn't need our plot of land. Where he wants to build is over there, further up the hill, near where the wellsprings are is. He says he wants to build a sanatorium, but the lads at work are sure he wants to build a brothel."

"A what?"

"A brothel. Whorehouse, if you like."

Words failed us. There was silence for a moment.

"But what about the police and the authorities"? I asked, and my voice sounded hesitant.

Tolik just shrugged his shoulders.

Lyalka junior took a piece of ham from the bowl.

"You know," said Ulia when we were on our way back home, "this Ivan had a motive for wanting to see granny dead. I can just imagine what his conversation with granny was like. He looks like the kind of man who doesn't let little things like doubt and conscience stand in his way."

"As I understand it, today we've given him a motive for wanting us out of the way as well. The feeling's mutual."

But was it mutual? I suspect I was trying to deceive myself by saying that.

Ivan's face has certain what I would call marks of mystery. Some faces are blank. Other faces look worn down by life. And then there are faces with these special marks of mystery. These are the most attractive faces. And Ivan has a face like that. The face, a person's bearing, eyes that have something to express — I have always formed an impression of people at first sight. Very few people have attracted me at first sight as much as Ivan did. Of course we aren't going to sell him the house, but why did Ulia have to be so rude to him him?

It's perfectly possible to fall in love with a man who has a face like that. More than that, it's possible to stay in love with him. Such were my thoughts as I, a faithful wife to my husband, walked in silence next to my sister along the valley. I don't believe a single word of Tolik's tittle-tattle. He's just jealous.

When we got back home Ulia's mobile — which she had left behind — was almost jumping around the kitchen in agitation, and Lena's minibus was driving up to the fence.

Ulia finished talking on the phone. She looked a bit upset.

"I've got to go to Mensk for the day tomorrow. They need me there urgently."

"Don't look so miserable about it. Go, if you've got to."

"I don't want to leave you all here."

"So what's new?" Lena had come to join us. "How are things going?"

"All quiet, or at least mostly." I shrugged my shoulders.

"We need to have a talk." Lena glanced at her watch. "I've got ten minutes. First off, Ala, have you seen any more UFOs recently? Like Death or some Woman in White?"

"You're free to think I'm out of my mind if you want to, but, please, don't say it out loud to my face! They weren't fantasies. I wasn't drunk at the time, although I did have a drink afterwards. I saw what I saw — a white phantom right on the frontier. And, Ulia, stop making a laughing stock out of me. It makes me look stupid."

"What are you getting so worked up about? All I did was pass on to Lena what you told me, and she then asked you that question... Who's making you look stupid? And anyway, we've had a visitor who's much worse than any woman in white," my sister had now turned to Lena. "He really put the wind up me."

"Who do you mean?" Lena raised her brows in surprise.

"I'll tell you." Ulia told her about the conversation we had had with Mr Ivan Kukal.

"So it's true then." Lena's face darkened. "I've heard stories about Kukal wanting to build a sanatorium somewhere. I've even seen the plans. And, come to think of it, I've even heard that it's going to be here in Dobratyche..."

"So you know him, do you? Do you look after his dogs?"

"He doesn't have any animals, but you can't live in Brest without knowing who Kukal is."

"Tell us."

"There's nothing much to tell. He's loaded. He's set up an annual prize they call 'Person of the Year in the City of Brest'. He's got a summer residence out in Vychulki. True, there are various rumours about him going around. I was once sitting with a group of people and heard that someone they called Kulya is supposed to have said when he was in the sauna that Kukal is the main man on the local crime scene, and what's more, he's not in any of the recognised criminal families. He operates entirely on his own.

"So who's this Kulia then?"

"Kuleyev's his surname, but the nickname Kulia (*bullet*) fits him exactly, given that it's something you fire out of a gun, and he's a thug, although admittedly he is a member of one of the criminal families. There he was, sitting in the sauna and expounding a whole theory about how there have always been people — going as far back as the courts of medieval kings — who have been close to centres of power and have helped the state regulate financial dealings between people. And that is what he, Kulya, does, and society needs what he does.

"So that means he's in on protection rackets, does it?"

"Spot on."

"Does he 'protect' you?"

"No, I'm too much of a mouthful for him, but that's not the point. Kulya said that Kukal was getting too big for his shiny shoes, he tears up agreements, doesn't keep his word, that he's used brutal beatings and even killings to get control of all the criminal activity in the area — the spivs on the frontier, the girls who work the main Mensk road, the drug dealers, and he's set up a whole network of gambling and drinking joints in the villages around the city. This is where he gets his money from, not from restaurants and the city market. Kulia is also supposed to have added, on the quiet, that it was Kukal who ordered the killing of Radyonau. You probably don't know about that. There was a particularly nasty murder in Brest last spring. The city police chief Radyonau was found murdered in the forest alongside his little son. Of course, the killers were never found, but afterwards the local papers stopped printing articles about customs men finding yet another drugs haul, and the police caught a gang making child pornography..."

We were stunned into silence. All we could hear was the rustling of the fir trees. What was there to say? What could you say? Evil was whirling all around us. It didn't matter whether Kukal was the evildoer-in-chief or not, there it was, evil was dancing, having a ball, creeping closer to the land that was ours. Land, not "ground", as Kukal dismissively called it. Left to myself, I would probably have accepted the situation, but there at my side was my sister, standing on the very threshold of the ballroom, barring the way to the advance of this mad, wild dance. I knew that she would never give way. I had no choice but to stand at her side.

"No, it wasn't Kukal who put the Cardiostim in the coffee," Lena shook her head when I suggested that version of events. "No, even if he probably is capable of doing such a thing. He's got a small army of bodyguards. He would have sent one of them in to do the job with a knife or a pistol. Clean and quick. No, you're dealing here with someone who knows you. Someone who knew something about your state of health..."

"But why? What the hell for?"

"That, girls, is a question you'll have to ask yourselves, not me."

"OK, then, but why has this bloody man Kukal got so interested in Dobratyche? Why did he get it into his head to build here of all places?" asked Ulia.

"How should I know? If you're filthy rich, you get all sorts of weird ideas. Maybe he just liked the look of the place. Right on the frontier, not far from the main road. Convenient for customers — long-distance lorry drivers, tourists. Or perhaps he's found something valuable, like oil, and wants to buy up the land before anyone else finds out. I don't know, something like that."

IT'S NOTHING!

Deep in thought I trudged wearily in the direction of the allotment, holding in my hands a hoe and pitchfork and in my head the firm intention to tidy up the row of strawberry plants, an act of homage to granny's memory – if it was up to me I'd let the bloody things burn to a crisp in this hellish heat, and the sooner, the better... This morning Ulia set off for Mensk. What with getting all her stuff together, and then feeding the blasted pig (what the hell do I need it for anyway? I know full well that I could never put a piece of juicy chop from those fat thighs in my mouth without seeing those bright little piggy eyes in front of me!)... I had managed to forget all the questions that had been troubling me over the past few days. But now, when I had a few moments to myself on my way to the allotment, they rose to the surface again like bubbles of marsh gas from the black bowels of the earth. In my mind I once again ran over everything that had happened and decided it was high time for me to get scared for my own welfare and to take measures to defend myself.

Suddenly a woman sprang out in front of me from behind a bush.

I had just enough time to get scared but not enough to take any measures.

"Aksana?! God, you gave me a fright!" and I wanted to heave a sigh of relief. The sigh stuck in my throat.

Her face was terrifying, like a mask of white death. At first I had been simply startled by her sudden appearance, but now, when I had had a chance to look at her more closely, I was seriously alarmed by the anger I could see burning in her eyes. The last time we had seen each other was at granny's funeral. We promised that we would get together some time soon and went our separate ways; all seemed to be well between us. Now it was like I had insulted her in some awful way, done her some kind of unforgiveable injury, betrayed her, killed her kid, she was in such a rage. Her thick lips were twisted with fury and her big eyes had narrowed to slits.

"You bitch, you cow!" she screamed and gave me a mighty kick in the stomach.

I fell flat on my face, dropping the agricultural gear I was carrying.

Aksana seized the hoe, lifted it up above her shoulder and brought it down right on me. Just at that moment I was trying to stand up and had no time to fend off the blow. The sharp blade cut into my back, just below the shoulder. This was granny's old hoe and she had kept it as sharp as any knife. A blacksmith had made it for her just after the war; it had a long light handle of alder wood that had gone shiny with age.

I fell down again with shock, pain and the unexpectedness of it all.

"Aksana, what are you doing!?"

"I'll kill you," and Aksana grabbed the pitchfork.

They say that in moments when your life is threatened you somehow find the strength to act swiftly and save yourself. Perhaps. But that doesn't apply to me. I'm not a strong-willed person, as I've had reason to find out all too often. And I was well aware of it now. Instead of crying out, running away or doing something — anything — I simply lay there, wide-eyed and uncomprehending, staring at Aksana and the pitchfork that she was holding up in readiness to plunge down into me. I couldn't move.

But I was not destined to die on the way to the allotment at the hands of an old school friend.

Suddenly her expression changed and grew softer. I realised that I wasn't going to die. She drove the pitchfork into the sand right next to my head with all her might, in a hoarse hate-filled voice uttered "Curse you, I hope you die", and disappeared back behind the bush as if nothing had ever happened.

I managed to work the hoe out of my back. The blood on the steel blade was like thick gouache.

I lost consciousness.

I remember only scraps of what happened next.

It's the grains of sand that I remember most. Tiny little boulders, white, golden and grey piled up right before my eyes. An anxious ant pensively curling its whiskers. A red stain on the sand near my shoulder.

Then there was Lyalka junior. Lips tightly pressed together, smothered in pink powder, her cheeks smeared with beetroot juice. She was sitting right next to me with her legs stretched out, sunburnt up to her knees and milky white further up, looking intently at me and using her finger to draw in the pool of blood.

"Lyalka, please, go and get help." It was difficult for me to get my mouth to open, but I managed. "Tell your mum".

"Last Sunday we went to church," Lyalka replied, "and the Sunday before that as well."

She was sitting next to me, pouring sand from one hand into the other. I noticed how delicate her hands are, even refined.

Then I remember Yarashykha's face hovering over me in a kind of blue haze — face deep brown from the sun, framed by a white headscarf, against the background of the sky way, way above us:

"It's OK, Ala love, it's nothing, just don't close your eyes." But I must have closed them.

The next I recall is the nurse from the ambulance nagging me in Russian:

"What on earth made you rip the hoe out of the wound? You shouldn't have touched anything," and she continued to grumble as she deftly bandaged up my back.

The first person to come and visit me in hospital was Lena Zarnitskaya; she literally flew into the ward.

"Now this is going too far," the first words she uttered as she burst through the door. "There I was, minding my own business, then suddenly the hospital phones and tells me you've been admitted with bad lacerations to the back!"

"I asked them to call you," I whispered.

The generous portions of drugs that she poured out for me made my tongue go numb, and I began to feel very sleepy.

"That neighbour of yours, the one who found you, Vera Mikalayeuna (the one we call 'Yarashykha'), said that she's going to feed your animals, so don't worry about them. But in God's name what happened to you? *Who* did this?"

I told Lena briefly how Aksana had attacked me – after all Lena knew her, they had met several times — stressing that I had no idea what could have caused her to do something so insane, and asked her to keep her lips sealed and say nothing about the incident for the time being.

"Insane, you call it!? She could have killed you," and Lena pulled her bright red jacket more tightly around her. She had obviously made a decision. "Right, this is what we're going to do!—You can do whatever you want, but tomorrow, when they let you out of here — and the doctor says that they probably will discharge you tomorrow, the main problem was shock caused by the pain, and that's been treated now — I'm going to ask Khvedzka to bring you four pit bull terriers! Don't say anything! He'll chain them up in the yard for you, and then I'll have at least some reassurance that no one is going to call on you without your consent. You can look after them for me until I get back — we're going off on a break tomorrow over to Poland, to Kastamaloty." She was then struck by another thought. "Do you know what? We can take Ulia's kids with us as well!"

Just after being brought out of one state of shock, I nearly fell into another.

"You're out of your mind. How many people are you going to take with you?!"

"What of it? Kazik and Lina aren't babes in arms any more, and my fillies are quite grown up. It'll be interesting for them.

We've been invited over by the local priest, he's set up a small open-air museum in Kastamaloty. We can make a tour of the surrounding area, there's a church that was built immediately after the Union*, and old houses with thatched roofs. My people from the clinic have already been over, it made a big impression on them. There's a lot to see. And then there's fishing on the Buh. It's like my husband's always saying — we live in Brest, they call it the city on the Buh, but we never actually get to see the river with our own eyes. So, there you are, give Ulia a call, tell her to run down to a solicitor's and fill in all the forms to get permission for the kids to go abroad. They'll be better off abroad. Ulia's got a lot to deal with at the moment, and you've got yourself involved with God only knows what. Let's keep the kids out of the country for a bit."

Ulia was due to bring her children, Lina and Kazik, down from Mensk to Dobratyche, which, with everything that had happened over the previous few days, wasn't the safest place for them to be. So Lena's offer was really quite attractive.

Lena is Lina's godmother and very fond of her. In fact Lena, despite her fiery scarlet jackets and her wealth, is fond of everything that moves, and — I may as well add — of everything that doesn't move as well. Her daughters — her "fillies", as she calls them — are just like their mother. I remembered that Ulia's two children already had passports for foreign travel, and that both she and her husband Yurka had already obtained the necessary permission for them to go abroad back at the beginning of summer. It would certainly be a good thing for them to get away, so I had a quick chat with Ulia over the phone. Lena rushed off to get things organised, promising to drop by again in two hours.

But what was all that business that Lena had mentioned

---

* *Union:* the union of the Catholic and Orthodox churches that resulted from the Synod of Brest in 1596.

about Ulia having a lot to deal with at the moment? I didn't have time to think for very long, because another visitor arrived.

He entered the ward without knocking, sat himself down uninvited right by the bed and looked at me intently. My drowsiness left me at once.

"Mrs Ala Bobylyova? We've already met. My name is Andrey Rudkovsky. If you remember, I'm the local police officer in Dobratyche."

It was the same young fellow that had come into our yard a few days ago to ask for a drink of water.

"Please tell me what happened to you."

A fresh, open, young face, a boy's face even, with fashionably cut dark hair. He opened his briefcase and sat expectantly, his eyes peering at me.

"What makes you think that something happened? Who called you?"

"The hospital did. They have to let the police know whenever a patient is brought in with serious injuries that could have been the result of an assault."

I like this young man. He has none of the falsehood and that 'don't-give-a-shit' attitude that stick out a mile from the usual upright representatives of the forces of law 'n' order. But how could I possibly tell him what had really happened? I lay in bed looking at him, but in my mind's eye I could see a completely different scene.

There we are, Aksana and I, nine-year-olds, alone at night in the cemetery. We're standing like a couple of wooden statues, waiting for phosphorus to rise up from a new grave. When we were kids we were all afraid of ghoulies, ghosties and will o' the wisps. We didn't doubt for a minute that there were such things. We had made a bet with the boys in our class that we weren't scared to spend a night in the cemetery watching for the phosphorus that we believed was going to appear from the grave three days after they had buried that bloke from the village.

And we really did see it! A white column rose up from the ground, hovered in the air and then began to move in our direction. Squealing wildly Aksana and I set off running as fast as we could. Our squeals were joined by screams from the boys who were hiding behind the fence. All of them started running away as well, all, that is, except one: Syarozhyk Basatski, — whey-faced, pockmarked and with hair flopping down over his forehead, who came running towards us, wanting to save us. Later we were all made to stand in line and given a dressing down for behaviour unfitting for members of the League of Little Communists. And much later, when we had already finished school, Aksana and Syarozhyk got married, and Syarozhyk became Syarhey...

...We're ten now, Aksana and I, on our way home from school. There's a snowstorm blowing. Instead of walking along the railway line, we decide to take a short cut through the forest and, of course, we get lost. It wasn't long before I wanted to give up. If it hadn't been for Aksana I would have frozen to death. She wouldn't let me stop or simply curl up in the snow and go to sleep. All night we stumbled round and round the village until we were found. Ever since then, whenever it's really cold, the pain in our fingers reminds us of what nearly happened.

Aksana and I are bent double, working in a field that stretches as far as the horizon. We're weeding beetroots and chatting. The Sun is burning our backs that are covered only by the straps of the swimming costumes we're wearing. Our future lies ahead of us, just like the field. The horizon is far away, there's no end to the rows we still have to weed, and no end to what we have to talk about. We're both fifteen.

Now the horizon is right on top of us. Aksana has three children and two grandchildren.

No, son, you're a nice lad, but I'm not going to tell you anything. How could you possibly understand, what kind of justice can you hope to achieve? I'll sort it all out myself.

"There's nothing to tell. Someone jumped out from behind an uprooted tree stump, kicked me and then hit me with something.

I lost consciousness and don't remember anything else. When I came to, I was already here in hospital."

"But the place where you were injured means that you must have seen who it was who attacked you."

I tried to shrug my shoulders, and my face grimaced with the pain.

"I didn't see anybody, I don't remember."

"You do realise, don't you, that if you didn't see anybody," and the young police officer looked straight into my eyes, "it's going to be very difficult for us to find whoever it was who attacked you? Indeed, we may never find them."

I didn't say a word.

"Right, then," and suddenly there was a note of irritation in the police officer's voice, "are you aware of the penalties for making false statements to the police?"

"I am, but I really don't have anything else to add to what I've already said."

The expression on the young officer's face changed suddenly; he looked at me as though he despised me. Without a word he clicked his briefcase shut.

"That's it. Get well," and off he went.

I KNOW FULL WELL
HOW THINGS ARE

The whole gang of them came to see me early on the following morning. Lena Zarnitskaya with her husband Aleh the gerontophile, their two grown-up daughters, one with a one-year old baby son, and Lina and Kazik with their little dogs Chappy and Doughnut. Their owners could not possibly have left them at home, and, thanks to Lena's amazing network of connections, they were allowed to come through to the trauma unit. The two dogs barked continually, and the humans were all talking at once. It was an impressive sight.

"We're not going to stay long," announced Lena as she marched through the door. "We're in a hurry to get to the frontier. I've made arrangements, so we have to be there before the border guards change shift, otherwise we'll have to wait three days in the queue. Ala, listen, I remembered right at the last minute that you need some clothes. You can't leave Byarestse in the rags you were wearing when they brought you in. Here's my suit. Khvedzka's going to come and collect you in an hour's time. He'll take you to Dobratyche and pick up the dogs at the same time. Right, that's it then, kids, off we go. This evening we'll go down to the river and give you some kind of signal, listen out for it. We've decided that we'll do that every evening, just to let you know we're OK so you don't need to worry. And, please God, so that we know there've been no more daft incidents happening to you. So saying Lena swept out of the ward with the tribe trailing behind her.

An hour later I went out through the hospital's main entrance and there was Khvedzka, lost in thought, sitting behind the wheel of his pickup truck and smoking. He didn't recognise me at first, but when I came up to him he gave a wolf-whistle:

"Wow! You don't look at all bad for a trauma patient. Quite the vamp, in fact! Red suits you."

So, now it can be said with absolute certainty: a blood-red jacket of the kind Lena always wears may not exactly have turned me into a vampire, but it did make a significant contribution to my subsequent adventures.

However, adventures left me in peace at least for the time being. It wasn't long before we were already in Dobratyche, and I found the house in perfect order.

The chickens hid under the lilac bush in terror when they saw the dogs that Khvedzka took out of the truck. There were four white thoroughbred pit-bull terriers, all of them with the sombre expression of desert ascetics who had had experience of the ways of the world, and knew exactly what to expect from it. They were Jean, Jida, Jim and Jack. Their jaws and little reddish eyes would be enough to scare anyone off. While Khvedzka unravelled the wire that would mark out the perimeter of the house, the dogs sat calmly by the porch, casting casual glances at their surroundings.

"Mistress is going to feed you in a minute," Khvedzka talked to them in the same tone that he used with me. "I told you, this is where you're going to live from now on. You're going to guard mistress here." Khvedzka hit a finger with the hammer and swore quietly. The dogs tactfully turned their heads away.

Khvedzka gave me some instructions while waving his injured finger. "Give them something to eat now. And don't be afraid of them. They won't bite you, and they won't go for anyone you invite into the house either. They're clever dogs, they are, sort of like psychologists. They can see right through people. After all, Zarnitskaya trained them."

I felt a bit nervous as I took four bowls of meat out of Khvedzka's hands and, with his encouragement, pushed them under the four pink, canine noses.

In the meantime Khvedzka had placed what looked like a portable kennel at each corner of the house.

"OK, that's everything, then. You're all set to go. Just keep calm with them. And don't ever lie to them. They really don't like it when people lie. They might chew something off of you if you do! If a problem comes up, ask them for their advice first. Otherwise give me a call. See you around!" Khviedzka's green pickup drove away and disappeared behind the fir trees.

"My greetings to you, hounds," I said as I sorted out the leads to take them to where they were to perform their duties. "I'll tell you as it is, no lies: I don't know who I'm afraid of most — the people you're supposed to protect me from, or you, my protectors. It was your colleagues' teeth that instilled a fear of dogs into me that will be with me for the rest of my life. But then, I suppose Dobratyche dogs weren't psychologists. But maybe they didn't like lies either. Perhaps they could already sense what a totally false individual I was going to become in later life — or better, how false all of us become eventually. And whenever Mukhtar struggled to break free of his chain, every living being in the neighbourhood that could find a place to hide, found one and hid. So tell me, hounds, how do you react to alcoholics? Because I'm going to tell you now, and I'm being absolutely honest with you, that I fancy a little drink. Do you have anything against the idea?"

Jean — I was just in the process of tying her up — lifted her heavy muzzle and gave a short bark.

The dogs watched intently, but silently, as I fed the furred and feathered gang that made up the bulk of the livestock in the yard, carried water and went down into the root cellar. However, it was the pig that aroused their special interest, and their chains began to rattle with agitation when I opened the sty. When I was done, I brought myself out a good plate of eggs with bits of fried pork fat and a tumblerful of whisky, and sat down to enjoy my lunch in the open air on the bench in the yard.

There are those who say that, if you want to overcome your addiction to alcohol, you must first admit to yourself that you're an alcoholic. I have no desire to do any such thing. How could I possibly have survived the past few days without alcohol? Here I was, having my lunch, taking the occasional sip of whisky, and feeling the tension inside me gradually ease off. Over my head the fir trees rustled. There was a breeze blowing, all kinds of different molecules stirred the needles in the canopy above the mighty sun-bronzed trunks, producing in the blistering heat the fresh chill of a shushing sound, an eternal sound, the arhythmic breathing of time itself. I was alone. The thought suddenly occurred to me that I had not been so entirely alone, so left to my own devices under the fir trees, for a long time. An awareness of being on my own, like the awareness of being young that I had once known, welled up from the dark depths within me and filled me entirely. It was like re-entering Paradise, but this time a murky paradise of eternal loneliness. It was me sitting there on this ancient, decaying, blackened bench — not just somebody's daughter or somebody's wife, not a burned-out mother, not just a customer in a shop or martyr for some cause, not a client, not a citizen, not even an absinthe drinker — it's me, head, shoulders, knees and toes, my heart beating, my blood flowing in my veins, somewhere inside there's my soul, and no doubt the process of decomposition is already under way... I don't want to think about anything, granny's death, Ivan Kukal, Aksana. Sweet Jesus, I've got to get them all out of my head, otherwise I'll go mad.

I walked slowly around the house, gave the dogs some scraps of pork fat and sat down again on the bench. Right at that moment, as if in continuation of a song that I had caught in the middle, there came the words from behind the trees:

> *How things are in autumn I do know full well...*
> *I waited. Came the sound or not, I cannot tell...*

Two powerful bass voices which, without a doubt, belonged to real people. The dogs half-raised their heads, the chickens ceased their restless movement.

I hadn't heard singing like that in the village for years. When I was a child, every evening when the sun was going down beyond the river, there would be people in each house, sitting on the porch and singing songs in a rich polyphonic harmony that has all been blown away God knows where by the winds of history. The last time I heard people singing live was when we were celebrating Yarashykha's birthday a couple of years ago. The Russian part of the family had left on the evening train for Brest. The sky was turning red in the west and dark blue in the east, and those who were left sang. Somehow they managed, just like they always did, to divide themselves into different voice groups. The first to begin the song were granny, Lyonikha and Yarashykha. Yarashykha looked down at the ground, and granny looked somewhere in the general direction of the clouds without actually seeing them; all she did was listen, and the words came back to her... That must have been the last time she ever sang. She was 95, and had lost almost all her faculties... I never sang, if you don't count singing lessons in school.

Now songs were once again to be heard coming from Yarashykha's house. I gulped down the last of the whisky and headed off towards the sound.

Two good-looking lads (muscular, shaved heads with topknots hanging down the back, broad thin faces, loose jeans, loose sleeveless T-shirts, chains hanging down to their bellies) were standing back to back in the middle of the yard and singing so lustily that the leaves of the vine above their heads were all atremble. The pots and jars that had been put out to dry upside down on the fence on which I was leaning, chimed in with harmonies of their own.

Yarashykha sidled over to me, so as not to get in the way of the camera that a third lad was using to film the singing.

"Good health to you, Ala! One of your chickens pegged out, did you see it?"

"Yes, I did. Many thanks for calling the ambulance, by the way. If it hadn't been for you, I would probably not have been here now. And for looking after the house.. I'll find a way to thank you properly..."

"Come into the yard, sit over there and listen to the boys singing! Find a way to thank me!? What else will you think of? Offer me a bribe as well?"

Yarashykha sidled off somewhere else. I liked the fact that she didn't start asking questions about what had happened.

The song ended and Mishyk came over to me.

"Hi! How are you feeling?"

I mumbled something in reply.

"These are friends of mine, a group that calls itself "Ї".* They're from Lutsk, over in Ukraine. They came for a festival of contemporary song in Brest.

"Your singing is simply great," I said to the lads. "You're bound to walk off with the first prize."

"Ala Babylyova," Mishyk introduced me.

"No, Mrs Ala, the festival's already over," said one of them in Ukrainian, stretching out his huge hand for me to shake. "We won a consolation prize. It was a Belarusian girl who took the first prize. By the way, the festival organiser, Anton Babylyov — is he your husband? It was his protégée who came first."

I looked at the Ukrainian and said nothing. Anton's started to act as agent for girl singers now, has he? That's a new departure for him. It didn't seem quite right to say that I had no idea what my very own dear husband was doing at present, so I just nodded wisely.

"We came to an arrangement with Mr Anton about some performances in Mensk. Your husband's a very nice man; it's good to do business with him. We've come to Mr Mikhal here

---

* *Ї:* this is a letter of the Ukrainian alphabet; it is pronounced 'yee'.

to get him to give us some texts for new songs. You can feel the spirit of this land in his poetry."

The young man picked up a piece of paper from the bench and began to sing the Ukrainian text in a deep, rich voice:

> *The wind whispers, but what? There's no telling.*
> *The rowan tree's still. The wind tickles its branches*
> *The yellow leaves fall, like parachutes sailing*
> *The grief of a bird can be heard in its twitter...*
>
> *My eyes are empty, devoid of all hope,*
> *My soul I smother with the boredom of silence,*
> *My thoughts are like straw, dry, ready for burning,*
> *For the wind, it does whistle and cut me to shreds.*

ONWARDS AND UPWARDS LEAD US TO BLISS!

It was obvious that Mishyk was simply dying to interrogate me about what had happened, but was too embarrassed to broach the topic in front of the Ukrainian lads. This gave me a chance to slip off home after a bit, and so avoid any unpleasant conversations.

So, Anton's been here and not dropped by. What am I supposed to make of that?

At seven o'clock I went down to the frontier. Spot on time, from behind the bushes and beyond the river came the sound of an accordion striking up, and an invisible choir began to sing:

> We're Belarusians, the children of freedom,
> Great Tarasenka forward leads us,
> Our country's pride and joy he is
> He onwards and upwards lead us to bliss!

I yelled "Bravo!" and banged a stick as hard as I could against a metal basin. Judging by the number of voices, Lena must have rallied all the Belarusians staying in the boarding house into coming down to the river's edge. And not only the Belarusians, because I thought I heard a slight Polish accent in the singing. They announced their presence by singing our national anthem. Of course, no one could remember the vacuous words, so they just made it up as they went along. A wave of applause from across the river greeted my banging and crashing on the basin. Contact had been made.

"Ala, what on Earth was all that?" Intrigued by the noise, Lyonikha came running down from her house to the frontier.

"Don't worry, It's a festival of contemporary song!"

The evening was soft and gentle, like a silk scarf. I could just picture Lena and the children returning home from the river bank, and the Polish supper awaiting them on the table — tripe soup, pâtés made from all kinds of poultry, leek salad, cakes, there'll be a candle on the table, maybe someone'll play the fiddle... Perhaps the priest, the one who set up the open-air museum, is actually one of us, a sort of Ukrainian — a descendant of those who survived in Kastamaloty after Operation Vistula*, and only now, sixty odd years later, have attained a real sense of who they are. If I'm right, then there'll be other things on the table as well — pickled cucumbers, kvass, smoked pork loin, potatoes with meat, and pancakes, and certainly there'll be someone playing the fiddle...

Harken to the fiddle playing,
Drawing out its flawless melody...

I've got whisky for supper. Along with the copper-coloured trunks of the fir trees and the slanting rays of the sun as it sets. The one thing I don't have is kvass. Now that granny's dead, there's no one here to make kvass any more, sour kvass from black bread and served up with spring onions. I don't doubt that kvass tastes better than any alcohol ever could, but I know that I won't have any luck in trying to make it myself. Of course I could put bits of black bread in the bottom of a three-litre jar and pour water over them, but I don't have the essential ingredients that granny had: the bitter sorrow of lonely winter

---

* *Operation Vistula*: the codename for the military action undertaken in 1947 by the Polish Communist government to forcibly move the Ukrainian minority in the south-east of the country to the territories — Silesia and part of East Prussia — that had been taken from Germany at the end of the Second World War.

nights when the wolves howl, the sugar sweetness of transparent autumn days, tiny particles of the scent of burning juniper, the vanilla essence of a melody half-remembered from long ago that came floating over the dark, mighty river... These are spices I don't have.

The eloquent stillness of the summer evening spread through the forest, and then kicked me so hard in the back that I shivered. I felt a sudden urge to go to granny. I locked the house and hurried, almost ran, towards the cemetery. It takes about twenty minutes to get there on foot if you go through the forest.

The cemetery is really quite a long way off and in the midst of the forest, so there was no one there at this time of the evening. No visitors at all. The only people there were those with permanent residence permits, fellow villagers of mine, peering out at me from photographs shaped like medallions and fixed to the gravestones — women in headscarves, puzzled-looking men without hats. Above it all the fir trees rustled. With no concern for what any of them thought I hurled myself on to the freshly-dug grave, spread out my arms as if to embrace it and howled. I sobbed like I had not permitted myself to sob at the funeral. I could feel the sand becoming wet beneath my face and shifting under my stomach. After a time I got the feeling that there were indeed some living humans watching me. Two young frontier guards were standing on the other side of the wire, looking at me intently. Our forest cemetery is hard by the frontier, and granny's grave is in the very first row. I was furious.

I gave full vent to the wrath burning in me: "What are you gawping at? Do you think I'm putting on a show just for you? One of those concerts 'For Belarus' that your boss loves so much? Get off out of it, go and do some guarding, otherwise we'll have spies running around all over the place!" Without a word in response the two boys, armed with automatic weapons and long knives, set off obediently to carry out their honourable duty and exercise their inalienable right.

I sat down, wiped away the tears and tidied up the sand on

the grave. I didn't feel any better, but a good cry can usually give you the strength to go on living.

Then I heard something that sounded suspiciously familiar — the tinkling of a bicycle bell. Could it be Lyonikha again? The tinkling stopped.

It was indeed her. I had no desire to meet anyone at all, and so scurried back on all fours to hide behind the wreaths. Lyonikha probably didn't want to meet anyone either. She left her bike by the gate. Looking around cautiously, she went right up to the frontier wire. Again she looked left and right, before bending forward much lower than usual, and slithered down to the burial vault.

Our cemetery has a little old chapel with a burial vault underneath. We don't know who built it and when. Maybe some landowner who lived round here had it built, but I don't really know. When we were children we explored the place thoroughly, in spite of our parents' strictest instructions not to go anywhere near it. All there was left in the little chapel was a faded picture of the Virgin Mary, and in the vault — half sunk in the ground — there was nothing at all except dust and cobwebs. One of the corners had broken away, and tree roots were sticking out of the earth floor, which — given their snake-like appearance — simply added to the air of mystery in the abandoned building.

Lyonikha's skinny figure flitted between the graves, and my eyes went wide in amazement when I saw my highly respected neighbour clamber — just like I had done forty years ago — through the tiny window of the vault! Her thin, brown arm lingered a little in the open window, then something clicked and all was quiet again.

I shut my mouth and, with a great effort of will, returned my jaw to its normal position. What was all this? Why had Lyonikha gone down into this nether region, and when it was nearly night as well? And why was she acting all stealthy so that no one would see her?

There was a stillness reigning over the cemetery at this hour when night was fast approaching, the kind of stillness — so it seemed to me — that is tense rather than calm. From behind the gravestones a dark blue haze began noiselessly to spread around. The gentle rustling sound made by the fir needles as they fell made me feel I could actually hear time flitting away... Somewhere the frontier alarm signal went off, a single note that could cut right through you. Then all of a sudden, just like that night on the allotment, I saw a huge white figure on the other side of no-man's-land. It was floating above the ground with a white shroud trailing behind it. There was something black and fearful where its head should have been... The apparition was coming in my direction.

My nerves were already frazzled as it was. I could hardly restrain myself from screaming aloud.

Suddenly the apparition went off somewhere; it just disappeared like it had never been. Yes, it had been there, floating purposefully above the grass, and then it wasn't there any more, like it had gone underground. My nerves finally gave out and I fled. Please, I don't want a heart attack, at my age I'm due for one...

Walking through the forest to the cemetery hadn't scared me — if you're born to be hanged, you won't drown, as the saying goes. I had absolutely no qualms at all about being in the cemetery in the evening — after all, many of the people there were relatives of mine, or had been close to me, and their ancestors were there as well; I am absolutely certain that none of them would harm me either in life or in death. That gigantic apparition, however, was the last straw. I don't know about the camel, but it certainly felt as though my back was broken. There was no way I could possibly explain what I had seen with my own eyes for the second time! I ran away as fast as I could, constantly looking round in the expectation of seeing the white ghost emerge silently from the ground and come chasing after me. I didn't care that I'm fifty, I didn't care that I'm surrounded by the noise of cars and diesel locomotives, that there were phone wires humming and electromagnetic waves criss-crossing over my head. I did know that I was filled with a fear — a fear that has become rooted in us over the centuries, maybe we're even born with it — a terror of the Evil One, a feeling that I was utterly defenceless; it lifted me off the ground and hounded me out of the cemetery. My heart thumped heavily against my ribcage, I was panting for breath from running and looking behind me. I felt certain that there was *something* coming after me, with a gaping maw dripping blood.

That night I couldn't sleep. My guardians barked from time to time, I could hear the noise of cars on the road, and the frontier signal alarm howled a few times — all the usual nocturnal sounds. It was very dark, I could hardly make out where the windows were. The injury on my back felt like it was on fire and I twisted and turned, trying to find a comfortable position in bed.

If you think about it carefully, what on Earth did I go to the cemetery for, just when night was coming on? I had a terrible fright, and once again I had a sneaky look at somebody else's secrets. And is granny really there, in the grave? If there is anything left of her anywhere, then surely it's going to be here in the house. Here where she lived out her life, day after day, not in the cemetery where they buried her body three days after she died. Good grief, to think I fell weeping on her grave! How sentimental! Granny would never have done anything like that. That wasn't her way at all. No, it's all down to the whisky! Bloody alcohol! I must lay off the booze, life will become a lot easier! Continuing in the same vein: if the Evil One had already led you there and you had become embroiled in somebody else's dark secret, then you should have had a proper look at where Lyonikha had gone, and what kind of devil was bouncing around just over the frontier, and found out where it went. If Lyonikha could clamber in through the window to the vault, then you should have gone in after her. And exactly what would

I have seen there? — this was me quarrelling with myself. My imagination, well trained by a reading of Stephen King's books, immediately conjured up a vision of Satan in a white shroud sucking blood from Lyonikha's neck in the abandoned vault. I turned over in bed for the umpteenth time.

No, I can't go on like this. Now, I think a productive thought flashed through my mind a few moments ago, didn't it? Ah yes, that if granny is to be found anywhere, it's worth looking for her here at home, not in the forest cemetery. Sorrow and insomnia welled up in me together, I threw off the sheet and got up. Without switching the light on, I felt my way through the kitchen to granny's room in "that part of the house". That's how granny walked round the house, no lights. She often used to get up at night. The bare soles of her feet trod on grains of sand, pine needles, dry twigs. The soles of my feet are like hers — broad, with large bones and rough, cracked heels, and there are still pine needles all over the floor. But I will never, ever feel like she, Makrynya, did, an old, strong woman with a difficult character. A woman who brought me up and sent me out into the world. A woman about whom I know very little, and about whom I will now never learn anything new. I will never find out what she was thinking about when she walked around the house at night — the house as it was, old and wooden, and then after it had been completely remodelled inside and virtually rebuilt. Did she ever know what happiness is? I had never even tried to find an answer to this question, and it was now beyond the powers of my imagination and my reason to look for it. There's another question to which I don't know the answer: will I ever know what it is to be happy? Will I even once feel myself happy in the years that are left to me?

In "that part of the house" everything was still as it had been when granny was alive. There was her bed, her table, the embroidered pictures on the walls — a woman with a deer, a couple dancing the Krakowiak, cornflowers in bloom... And the smell was still the same — her body, straw from the mattress, feathers from her pillows, and there was a smell of sand as well. I sat on the bed and closed my eyes. There's no movement in the air, no human touch... Outside in the yard, right by the window, Jeanie barked, shaking her chain. I lifted up a corner of the curtain — it came as no surprise to me to see a dark figure on the other side of the fence. Someone, whoever it was, was watching the house in the middle of the night. The figure moved along the fence, and Jeanie followed, running along the wire to which her chain was attached. Then Jeda started barking and running. I went from room to room, keeping track of whoever it was walking around the house from the outside. Between us the dogs were running in a state of agitation. I completed a circle of the house and returned to "that part". The dark figure stood still for a moment and then retreated into the blackness.

TIME TO CALL A SPADE A SPADE

With a brusque movement of his hand Anton shoved some papers at me.

"Try to understand, I really need this…"

We were seated at the old wooden table in the yard — the one that had gone all black with age. Anton's Mercedes sparkled on the other side of the fence and the blokes who had come with him had gone off for a walk in the forest. My husband — who, according to the documents before me, had become my "former" husband seventeen years ago — looked at me coldly and said: "Let's start calling a spade a spade, shall we? You, or more precisely, certain facts in your biography, are going to be stones around my neck in my election campaign, and they are capable of pulling me down to the bottom."

I wanted to say, "But that was all seventeen years ago," but he went on, as though he had heard me say it:

"And you managed to get yourself involved in lots of different stories, didn't you? Yes, it was all seventeen years ago, yes, OK. A woman made a mistake, she stumbled and fell, there had been a tragedy in her life, but she picked herself up and returned to lead a normal life." He stood up quickly and started pacing up and down in front of the bench. The whole business obviously irritated him. "OK, they closed the case against you, but it's still on record, and they can dig it up at any time, they're bound to! Try to understand, there's only one way out — to do like I'm suggesting: have back-dated documents drawn up to make it look as though we were already divorced back then. It's the only way to draw their fire away from you, and from me too. I've got it all fixed up already. There are people I know who will sign all the necessary papers. It's necessary for both of us..."

Anton was asking me to sign documents, making out that we had been divorced seventeen years ago. I was flabbergasted. I leafed through the papers, struggling to read them but not understanding a single word. That phrase of his had cut me to the quick: "you managed to get yourself involved in lots of different stories."

Once again I was forced to lower my gaze, just as I had had to when my sister levelled the same charges at me. Now, however, there was a difference. The wave of guilt that swept over me, and to which I had become so accustomed over the years — to the point at which it was my constant companion — now crashed headlong into a wave of indignation that Anton himself had set in motion. "But it wasn't you who looked after my affairs back then, it was my sister. For all you cared I could have snuffed it on Roza Luxembourg Street, or they could have put me in prison for life."

"Your sister's another fine one." The circles Anton was walking round in were getting bigger and bigger. "She refused to come and work for me in my campaign. Instead she went and became election agent for Harabets. Wonderful! My wife's a drug addict and her sister's a nationalist! Good start to a presidential campaign..."

My eyes flew wide open at this news. Ulia was election agent for Harabets? That's really something. Harabets was one of the politicians that even I had heard of. In fact you can hardly call him a politician, he doesn't know how to grin the compulsory grin that all politicians have to put on. He had remained in the country for as long as he could; he was forced to leave only after the attempted assassination that he miraculously survived. He continued his political activity abroad, so that once a week the toads on the television had to 'unmask this political bankrupt'. They had to react to him somehow. Even people who never listen to Radio Liberty are up-to-date with what he's doing. Today he was received by the President of Poland, yesterday he addressed the US Senate in Washington, tomorrow he'll be at the United Nations. It was either an oversight or a desire to have as many opposition candidates as possible and so split the vote, but the Electoral Commission did register him as a candidate. True, the toads' tactics had to be changed, and they stopped mentioning him altogether, just as they failed to mention any of the other alternative candidates. And to think that my sister was now this man's election agent!

Anton lowered his voice.

"Have the people from the television already been to see you? Not yet? They will. They've been to see me. They asked about you and your sister. I told them that I don't know anything, we haven't been together for seventeen years and even back then I had lost all contact with you. It was after that visit that I decided to come and ask you to do what I am now asking. Please, don't spoil it, let's get the divorce sorted out! Here are the papers for the flat — I've bought you a two-roomed flat on Red Army Street. I've already had your things taken there. Here are the keys. Sign the papers. If they come to see you, I would ask just one thing: simply say what I said — that you've had no contact with me.

The phrase "lost for words" has a literal meaning as well as a metaphorical one. I wanted to say something, but couldn't get my vocal chords to work. He wants to get the teletoads off his back by getting rid of me. Is he being naïve, or is this just a chance to do what he has wanted to do for a long time?

A change came over his face. His face was still hard and his eyes cold, but his lips seemed to be trembling ever so slightly... Rather than having to see him cry, I quickly took a pen and put my signature on the papers.

With a "thank you" and a well-practised gesture, he shuffled all the papers into a neat pile. He hesitated a bit, then leaned forward to give me a kiss. I turned away abruptly. His bodyguards, or advisers — judging by the look of them they were more likely to be his bodyguards — were casting sidelong glances in our direction and keeping themselves at a distance. Then they all went over to the car, and the Mercedes drove off.

I can still remember very well the feelings from my student days, when we returned from a skiing trip or during a game of basketball, how I could sense the wonder of simply being young bubble up within me, that sense of pure joy at having muscles, of the world being like one long festival. I remember how, after giving birth, I had that quite unexpected feeling of being life itself. I remember the solemn music, my music as it played within me then. And now I have come to realise something quite clearly — just as at one time I had a sense of youth and then of motherhood — something that I have been dimly, in my most secret thoughts, aware of for seventeen years: I am old, old and dried up.

There's something else I realised: throughout the whole time I spent with Anton after he had put his proposal to me, I didn't say a single word.

Old age means keeping your mouth shut.

I FEEL OLD

I took a bottle of whisky from behind the fridge. Jack Daniels. A true, but treacherous friend, a shapeshifter that can burn the roof of your mouth off.

My thoughts had got their tails all tangled up in trying to hang on to each other.

What am I supposed to be thinking about now? Knocking the neck of the bottle against the rim of the glass, I poured myself a drink.

Calm down. Get a grip. I gulped down some of the whisky, went out and sat on the porch. The view that stretched out before me was one I had known since my childhood: the canopy of fir trees, then the meadow with hummocks of willow entangled with blackberry bushes, sand dunes with clumps of juniper, and a winding road in the midst of it all. The Earth's clothing — grey, green and bitter. The snakes leave green tracks, the black paths are trod by humans. There are hawks in the sky, and above them aircraft leaving their trails.

I'm old. An old woman who, setting her tumbler of whisky to one side, weeps on the porch, and the chickens stand around with their heads cocked.

A few moments later the old woman wipes away her tears, goes to fetch some grain for the chickens, strews it on the ground for them to peck at, sits herself down again on the porch and reaches for the whisky.

Now that was another nasty piece of news. Good God, I should have got used to it over the summer. Anton's chucked me away like an old dog-end, just because I'm in the way. I loved the man, believed he was my heaven-sent husband, now it turns out that he stayed me with me because he couldn't think of anything better. How long was it like that? Maybe right from the start? A sense of grievance was growing in me in direct proportion to the amount I had drunk. I suppose now he'll arrange a marriage — also back-dated, I don't doubt — with some iron bloody business-lady, or the complete opposite, a fancy bit of fluff with bright blue eyes. It's a shame I didn't ask what kind of floozy is going to have the honour of considering herself his wife... Consider? That's all I did, consider myself his wife... Maybe he had a second family all those years, a real one. If you think about it, what kind of wife was I to him?

After my daughter's death, after I had come to realise that I would never get pregnant again, I went right off the rails, and, frankly, I didn't give a fuck. There are certain secret places in Mensk, and the feeble shadows who inhabit them do have many genuinely human qualities. Anton tried to get me to stop drinking and took me to see private doctors (at a time when they didn't exactly advertise their services in public). Ulia made the same attempts to get me off the drink — she even hit me — and she too took me to a variety of doctors, but I would always run off and get plastered again. I could feel that my mind was going, and that my liver was beginning to play up, but I didn't care. The only way I could drown out the thoughts about my children who would now never be born, about all those embryos that were walled up within me and would never be aroused to life, was in the company of my shadow comrades on Roza Luxembourg Street. They knew the drug I needed.

Then I met Gosha. He wasn't like one of the shadows. He was a big, calm man with a broad, pleasant face. He simply radiated attractiveness. We became friends. At the time I was incapable of any kind of love — either spiritual or physical — but I certainly saw him as a friend. As it later turned out he used a lot of silly women like me. "Could you do me a favour, please, could you take this package to this address. I simply don't have time now." So it was that, before I knew it, I became a drug runner. Well, no, I guessed that that was probably what I had become, because by that time I was already an addict, but I really didn't care. On one occasion he sent me off on a routine job, gave me a key, told me exactly where to leave the package, then lock up the flat and come back. When I got to the flat, I found a dead teenage boy lying on the bed. Before I had time even to scream, some policemen broke down the door of the flat, grabbed me and twisted my arms behind my back. They opened the package I was holding in my hands — there was heroin inside.

That's how I ended up in prison. Eighteen months on remand in the prison on Valadarskaya Street. It was there in the prison hospital they cured me of my drug addiction. Anyone who has been through that can go through anything else. At least that's what I thought then.

I hadn't spoken to my sister for a year before all this, but she came to see me as soon as I was allowed a visitor. She looked just as worn out, thin and sallow as I did, although she hadn't been in prison. The case was quite clear: the charming Gosha was in charge of a whole drug ring. He was a smooth operator who made use of dopey idiots like me to draw the fire away from himself and other sharks in the drugs business. He made no mistakes: when that sixteen-year old kid died of an overdose — and Gosha may well have been there when it happened — he sent me to the flat where the body was exactly at the time when the police were due to show up. Everyone played their parts, just as if they were acting from a script. The police had the corpse of a drug addict, and they had me with proof of the crime — the heroin. They were especially pleased with that. I was facing a long prison sentence. Gosha moved on and found himself somewhere else to carry on his business, and all my attempts to explain what had happened got nowhere. There was no one living at the addresses I gave, no one hanging out in any of the apartment blocks or alleyways I knew about. The investigating officer — for obvious reasons I'm not going to give his name here — didn't believe me. He didn't believe Ulia either, but met with her on several occasions. In short, taking into account my past history they sentenced me to eighteenth months inside. The court also looked at the time I had already spent on remand and determined that I had already served my sentence. I left the court a free woman.

Ulia took me by the arm and Anton walked alongside me. But it wasn't them I was with.

I felt less crushed by the dirt and pain of prison life than by the knowledge that I had somehow — even if indirectly and involuntarily — contributed to the boy's death. I'm never going to be able to forget the faces of the boy's parents in court.

I learned from experience and no longer sought the company of people, or even of shadows. I simply bought the alcohol I needed and drank on my own.

Why hadn't Anton divorced me back then? It wouldn't have been so painful. At that time I could scarcely feel anything at all.

From time to time I would set off — bottle in bag — on a circular trip: the maternity hospital on Padlesnaya Street, general hospital no. 2, Baraulyany (where the cancer hospital is), the Northern Cemetery. By each fence I would stop and have a swig from the bottle. On one occasion the trip ended up with my going to sleep on that same grating in front of the food store near general hospital no. 2, the one on which I collapsed after finding out that my little girl had cancer, and Vaytsyashonak — with her little dog — once again got me back on my feet, like some vigilante going around the streets of Mensk with the task of picking up repulsive deadbeat drunks out of the dirty snow. A week later she was the one who got me into the psychiatric hospital in Navinki. The methods they used weren't all that different from what I had experienced in prison, but they didn't charge for them, and maybe that was how I managed to clamber out of my own private pit. Relatively speaking. My status was raised from that of "alcoholic" to being merely a "drunk".

However, I'm on their books and they're always keeping an eye on me, especially to make sure that I don't have any alcohol in the house.

But that's enough of that. What do I keep going on these excursions down memory lane for? Why go on tearing my heart to shreds? Everything's covered in ashes.

THE DIESEL TRAIN SOUTH FROM BREST TO VLADAVA

At dawn the light played in the sky, then it became brighter and finally the sun came up in glory. I fed the animals and cleaned them out, and then ran off to catch the train: I wanted to meet Ulia. Right at that moment she must have been somewhere near Baranavichy — she was on the train from Mensk. However, the train I travelled on was different, and better. Or rather, it used to be better.

Ever since Dobratyche had become surrounded with dachas and a halt built for the folk who bought or rented them, I have tried to avoid travelling on the diesel. Even for someone as thick-skinned as me, I find it really difficult to accept what the train has become. You can hear people on the station asking for a ticket "to Dobratichi" at the booking office; there are hordes of them.

The diesel contributed to the grievance that all the villagers felt. Or to time's implacability — what happened was going to happen anyway.

I well remember the train as it used to be. It left Dobratyche when it was already getting light, and then returned. It was a long hike through the forest along the railway lines to get to the station. You could see the sun either rising or setting through the huge windows of the carriages. People used the train to get to work and to return home: cleaners, hospital staff, casual labourers, loaders, gravediggers, dishwashers, railway workers, road workers ("he's got himself a nice job working on the highway", is how they were respectfully referred to) and night-watchmen at the electromechanical equipment factory;

there were also a few representatives of the elite: cashiers, shop assistants and waitresses. The diesel that arrived at half past nine brought our teachers from Berastse, ready to begin classes in the school at ten. Very occasionally the farm labourers would don their best clothes at the weekends and go off on the train to the city. Firemen, plumbers, drivers and low-ranking police officers would use the train to come and visit their abandoned parents in the country. On the train people used to talk about big things, like life and death; they would always address older people as "auntie" or "uncle", they played cards, but there was never any singing, and the young people usually gathered in the third carriage. Later on it became more common to hear people talk about death, and less and less about life. The tradition of the third carriage was lost. Once, when I was on the early morning diesel I recall seeing a woman from one of the dachas wake up an older railway worker who was lying asleep at full stretch on one of the long wooden seats. She tugged at his shoulder, he sat up without a word, held his puttee-wrapped feet off the ground so as not to get them dirty on the floor, pushed them into his workboots, leant hard against the window and fell asleep again. Right at that moment something happened to my eyes. Instead of this middle-aged woman I saw a lime-coated coffin in a brightly-coloured suit, clean, well dowsed in perfume, with lipstick, lacquered fingernails and permed hair. I saw it quite distinctly.

The coffin even managed to say sorry to "uncle": "The train's packed today, isn't it?" it said as it sat down. "There aren't any seats."

I haven't told you yet that I don't like people, have I? I'm warning you about it now. And I don't believe in time's implacability — I don't believe that we have to accept things simply because we are told we have to "keep up with the times." I'm a bit like a mollusc — thick-skinned on the outside, but completely spineless when it comes to dealing with other people, so there was no danger of my creating an explosive situation in the carriage. Best not to take any chances though, so keep your distance. There weren't many of us villagers from Dobratyche, Zakazanka and Stradche. But people descended on us and trampled the places where we lived. And so we became people as well. Even I became a person, in a certain sense anyway. My children, if I had had any, would also have become people. There's nothing I can do about it, but I try to avoid travelling on the diesel, except on those rare occasions when I absolutely have to.

MY SISTER
AND TWO STATIONS

I was a little late to meet the train from Mensk. Ulia was already marching up and down the platform. She turned round when I called out to her and burst out laughing. So did I.

If it hadn't been for my slight limp, the only way people could tell us apart was by the way we dressed and did our hair. I wore my hair long and liked to colour it fairer than it was. Ulia had her hair cut short and dyed it black. I always wore billowing skirts, loose trousers, dresses with quite fantastical lines; the colours I chose were always delicate, pastel shades, somehow amorphous — sandy, greenish (like green russule mushrooms), lilac. My sister's character positively demanded precise, simple outlines and bright colours — her favourites were red, blue and a kind of striking shade of violet that Maria Vaytsyashonak insisted on calling magenta.

On this particular day, however, without any prior arrangement we had reversed our styles and so undergone a kind of polarity change.

Zarnitskaya's red suit sat well on me. It literally oozed scarlet success, the kind of colour you wear when you are very sure of yourself and your purpose. Just for a laugh I decided to launch myself into everything associated with red clothing. I do have to admit that it didn't feel quite right at first, but once I had had my hair dyed "Spanish crow" black (which explains why I arrived late at the station — I got held up at the hairdresser's), I felt myself a completely different person.

"The lock to my flat broke. I couldn't get in", my sister explained, giving me the once-over, "so I had to spend the night at your place and put some of your clothes on in the morning. How come you're dressed up like this? But first things first, how are you feeling? Have you spoken to Aksana yet?"

"No, I haven't," I began to answer her questions in order of importance. "I hardly notice the wound on my back any more. The suit I borrowed from Zarnitskaya. Have you seen Anton?"

Ulia took my by the arm and together we strolled across the empty platform to the bridge.

"No. The flat's a good one, it's quite big," and my sister started telling me about the flat that Anton had bought for me and which I hadn't yet seen. "True, all your stuff is in a heap on the floor of one of the rooms. Anton didn't show up, he's got a lot on his plate at the moment. It looks like he knows what he's doing. Don't worry. We can talk about him later, but right now I want to tell you something that happened to me just now. I had already got out of the train, and was standing on the platform looking out for you when suddenly somebody comes up to me from behind and says 'Are you Ala Babylyova?' I look around, and there's a youngish woman standing there, a real mean-looking type, if you ask me, hair obviously dyed; without waiting for an answer she goes on 'You don't know me but it doesn't matter. I just want to warn you to be careful. You're in danger'. With that she turned round and off she went. I shout after her: 'Hang on. Who are you? What danger? Tell me!' She shouts back, 'It doesn't matter who I am. But remember, keep away from Antanina Dluskaya', or Hluskaya. I didn't catch the name properly. She jumped on a train as it was already moving, and that was the last I saw of her."

"Dluskaya or Hluskaya. Who's that then?"

"How should I know?"

We stood still. The sun shone on the empty, dusty platform, but overhead there were dark clouds gathering.

"Note, this woman mistook me for you, because I'm in a dress of yours. That can only mean that she knows you and you, therefore, know her, or at least you must have seen her sometime."

"Tell me again what she looks like."

"There's nothing special to tell," and my sister shrugged her shoulders. "She's about thirty, a redhead, obviously dyed, normal kind of figure, know what I mean, average height, and a face that isn't what you would call good to look at."

"That description doesn't tell me anything," and it was my turn to shrug my shoulders.

We crossed the footbridge and walked through the old streets of the city towards the bus station. The sun beat down on us through a slight haze, it was getting hot; the heavy air of the city weighed down oppressively on us. In 1596, when Sir Francis Drake was laying seige to Riohacha, the Berastse city fathers were preoccupied with the purchase of a new clock for the town hall tower and with preserving the peace, because the forthcoming Church Council had attracted far too many people to the city, all of them in a state of high agitation about questions of religion and politics. I don't know about Riohacha, or, to be honest, whether Drake was really there in that year or earlier — I may have studied history at university, but I'm not very strong on dates[*] — but I do know there's not a single stone left from the Berastse of those days. There's nothing left of the town hall, or of the clock tower, not even one of the clock hands. Even so, there was some kind of magic in the air on this hot, hazy summer's day: the houses and roofs of the fair *city of Bereste* — the city the Russians erased from the face of the Earth — were still pulsating with life. I could distinctly feel their breath on me.

The new city was living and breathing as well. On the brick wall of what had once — in the Polish days — been the Traugutt Grammar School, and was now the Pushkin Pedagogical University, someone had written in beautifully formed letters a metre high:

---

[*] Ala certainly isn't very strong on dates. The Church Council did indeed meet in Brest in 1596, but Drake laid siege to Riohacha in 1569.

If to Tarasenka you pledge your all,
Bash your stupid head against this wall.

A simple message, clearly expressed. There were a lot of people hanging around, women in light silk dresses, girls — obviously students — in tight jeans with rips in interesting places, shaven-headed body-building types, and all of them smiling, until a police car drove up. A solemn-faced guy with a brush got out and set about painting over the offending inscription.

"Ulia, the train the woman jumped on, where was it going?" I asked.

"Moscow."

"Maybe you saw something odd, something that struck you, on the platform? You know, bags full of knitwear from Pinsk, boxes of cartons of sour cream, trombones in cases, that sort of thing?

"Well, yes," and my sister thought for a moment, "there were bags, cartons of sour cream, and trombones. Well, maybe not trombones, but I do remember seeing some guitars."

There was nowhere to sit at the bus station, so we settled ourselves on the window sill. It was a little cooler here than out on the street. My fellow countrymen amused themselves as best they could while waiting for their bus. Sun-tanned children, sun-tanned women, sun-tanned men and sun-tanned old folk, some of them with such deep-set eyes...

Who was this woman who had stopped my sister on the railway station? What am I supposed to make of it? Is somebody after me? Why? Am I in somebody's way?

Danila Zhukouski once complained that what I write fails to satisfy my readers' feelings of justice, that I disappoint them by not fulfilling their natural desire to see good triumph. Perhaps I've offended somebody or disappointed them so seriously that they want to wreak their vengeance on me?

I suddenly felt Ulia tugging at my sleeve.

"Ala!"

I was instantly aroused from my reverie.

His face could have been handsome, but wasn't. There was nothing aggressive about him, but he could make you feel afraid. The lad was moving in a way that made you think he wasn't quite where he wanted to be. All the same he was clearly heading in our direction. He was looking right through us and swaying slightly in the hot air.

Ulia pulled me over to another corner of the waiting room. "He's a druggie," she whispered.

A moment later he was once again standing near us: sunken cheeks, darks eyes, that same feeling of horror.

Just at that moment came the announcement that our bus was ready for boarding. We hastily made for the exit. He followed us as if trying to move through water, reached the door and then turned back.

Ulia and I looked at each other.

"He's a druggie," she repeated. "And I know who he is. He's Charota's son."

That he was the son of the director of Agrovitalika Plus was news to me, but I had spotted at once that he was a drug addict. There's no one better than me at spotting them. After all, I had already been in rehab — twice, in fact. What did he want from us? I had the feeling that he had been specially sent by someone to remind me of what I was.

AKSANA'S NOT AT HOME

I finally plucked up my courage to go to Stradche to see Aksana and have it out with her. It turned out that I had got myself all worked up for nothing. Her house was locked up. A neighbour told me that Aksana and Syarhey had gone off to Brest for the whole day and tomorrow they would be going to Mensk, and they would be there for some time. They needed to see some doctors. So back home I went, having achieved precisely nothing.

WHAT DID YOU ASK ME THAT FOR?

Ulia and I had a row today.

It all started because I was in dire need of a drink, something that was quite out of the question while my sister was around. Any alcoholic will instantly recognise the irritability that had been growing inside me since early morning. I was complaining, muttering under my breath, moaning, just looking for something to have an argument about. And finally I found it: I confronted her about her getting involved in politics by becoming Harabets' election agent.

"What kind of politician is he? He's a buffoon, nothing more! And you're just the same. Do you think you'll change anything? Look around you, girl! You're trying to do the impossible simply by believing it's possible. They're all like Tarasenka, he's just the one for them."

Ulia had also been in a bad mood all morning — something was obviously troubling her — so she readily snapped at the bait:

"How dare you say that to me? I might have expected other people to say that, but not you. You're asking me why I've got myself involved in politics? What did you ask me that for? You might as well ask me what we live for! What is it you live for? To get drunk? So go ahead and drink.

Throughout the remainder of the day we tried to avoid each other as much as possible. I was busy with the animals, and she was on the phone all the time, down in the root cellar — the only place in the house where you could keep reasonably cool.

In the evening my sister informed me in a cold voice that she had to go off again, and off she went.

My pride wouldn't allow me to ask where she was going or why.

Now I could have a drink.

ANOTHER SOUL,
ANOTHER LANGUAGE

I don't know how to talk to people. There's always a thick wall of transparent cotton wool between us. I don't understand anyone. There are those who pick and choose lemons from the bottom of the box and spend hours wandering around clothes shops. Then there are those who don't give a toss about the first lot. Power-dressing business women in top management. Middle-aged men with paunches. Pedagogues, ha-bloody-ha. My fellow alcoholics. Not forgetting the wretched "yoof", of course. The way they behave is predictable. Explainable. Even if why they do what they do is a big mystery to them. All their jokes fall completely flat.

Anyone who learns a new language acquires another soul. Or so the Czech saying goes — it always used to surprise me, even back in the days when the word *soul* was considered as indecent as the word *shit*. They taught me a new language — it happened to be Russian — and gave me another soul. *This new soul of mine* is something I know nothing about. Or the tricks it gets up to from time to time... What happened to my old soul? To my old language? Where did they go? There are odd occasions when the old soul makes itself felt in an unexpected gesture or unarticulated sound... It's still alive, my old soul. Souls don't die, they just get squeezed into your heel, or your appendix, or some other tiny living space. These days everyone's got a new soul, the language the occupiers gave us: those who consume and those who produce, business women, men, my fellow alcoholics, even my sister... My ideal sister's old soul is sitting all curled up in her pinkie. Her old soul is crying just like mine, precisely because it's old. Our mum never did read the primary grade Russian reader with us, because she couldn't understand it — it wasn't her mother tongue, and it wasn't ours either. OK, I could understand Russian, the language my new soul spoke, right from the start, but what did the souls of the Red Indians feel when faced with the onslaught of English? Or the Bushmen? Or, damn it, all the people who inhabit the vast expanses of Black Africa?

The phone rang. Grabbing the tumbler of whisky I heaved myself up from the porch where I was sitting and made my way into the house, full of loathing for a life that had turned out quite differently to what I had hoped for.

A man's voice was asking for my sister by her full name, *Mrs Ulia Anatoleuna Barysievich.*

Maybe I was still annoyed by the row we had had on the previous day, and hurt by Ulia's refusal to share with me the details of what she was doing, but instead of simply saying that my sister had left and would be back the next day, I took a sip of whisky and blurted into the receiver:

"That's me."

"Ivan Kukal here, my apologies for troubling you," the man was speaking at a fast rate and very energetically. "We need to meet. There are a number of urgent matters we need to discuss, and some of them are of direct concern to both you and your sister. I have some information about her that I want to pass on to you. I would ask you not to say anything to her just yet about our conversation. Could you perhaps come up to Brest tomorrow?"

I didn't know what surprised me more: the fact that Kukal had phoned and spoken Belarusian, or the fact that he wanted to have a meeting with Ulia. Nevertheless I agreed to come next morning to the café that's called simply "At the Market".

I was amazed at myself: it had never in my life before today occurred to me to pass myself off as my sister, and I really could not understand why I did so now. Maybe it was my old soul shifting around and showing what it was still capable of? It's like Squire Burulbash says in the Gogol story*, "Katerina, you don't know one tenth of what your soul knows!"

---

* The Gogol story is *A Terrible Vengeance*.

A CHARMING NEIGHBOUR

The café "At the Market" really is situated right on the Market Square, on the first floor of a new white building, above rows and rows of market stalls with multicoloured canopies. On the inside the walls of the café are faced with a really attractive kind of brick that has been made to look old. The interior walls look a bit like what you would see in an old castle. What makes it look different are the glass tables, the ultra-modern seating and the little pieces of mirror dangling from the ceiling on chains that slowly revolve, casting their fragmented light like sunbeams on to the walls. It is pleasantly cool inside the café, probably the result of air conditioning. Kukal got up at once to greet me, and was the first to hold out his hand.

"I must ask you to forgive me, and beg your permission to speak Russian," he said straightaway, "I know Belarusian, but whenever I speak it I am always thinking about the right word to use, rather than what I actually want to say. This way, please," and he led me to a table hidden behind a column.

After everything I had heard about this man, I took an especially close look at his strong, deeply tanned face with its sharply chiselled features. I could see nothing unpleasant in it.

The waiter — who looked rather more professional than might have been expected in a drinking establishment on the market place — immediately brought a bowl, opened a bottle of French champagne and poured the foaming contents into the round glass vessel where there were already peaches soaking in white wine.

Kukal raised his glass.

"Here's to you! Many thanks for coming. Well, what do you

think?" he asked, tasting the champagne. "It's your favourite, isn't it?"

"Yes, it is."

Kukal leaned back in his chair and ruffled his hair.

"You know, I don't really know how to talk to you," he grinned and suddenly his face changed; it became softer. "At the moment you see me almost as an enemy, I can see on your face that you don't trust me. Before we part today I hope to have persuaded you that you can trust me. As I see it, the only way I can do that, when talking to someone like you, is to be completely open and honest."

I decided yesterday that I would allow myself to be guided by that old student principle: don't say anything, and they'll think you're intelligent. So I said nothing and Kukal went on.

"I'm a businessman. Maybe I'm a little hard, but that's how you have to be if you're going to get things done. I did ask my people to gather some information about you, in order to find something that would make it possible for me to force you — and I'm telling you this quite frankly — to sell your land to me. However, what I learned about you has in fact forced me to change my plans," here he paused for a moment. "I have given up my idea of building in Dobratyche. Instead I want to hand over some money to you for Mr Harabets' election campaign." He lowered his voice quite noticeably when he said that. Then he wrote a figure with four zeroes on a serviette and pushed it over to me. "Here!"

"What do you want to do that for?" I asked.

"I'm a patriot," he said completely seriously, and got out the money. "Do you think that I'm a rootless cosmopolitan, with no feeling for the land where I was born? That my country is nothing more than money? You're wrong. I come from the Lahoysk region, just like Mr Harabets. I can tell you this: when the time came for me to go to school, they had to teach me Russian in a hurry, because there wasn't a Belarusian school in the area. I've always been sympathetic to the ideas of the

Popular Front*, although I haven't always — in the present circumstances, you understand what I mean — been able to display that sympathy openly."

This was a turn of events that I hadn't foreseen. The personal relations between me and Kukal were one thing, but the elections were a different matter altogether. I didn't pretend to understand anything about them. Not a thing. Would Ulia have taken the money for Harabets? There they were, US dollars, thick bundles of them, tied up with rubber bands. They would certainly come in handy. If I don't take them, will I be making a mistake? There's quite a big sum of money there...

Kukal pushed the notes across the table towards me.

"Hide them somewhere. Large sums of money like that ought not to be lying around on tables. Even when you're sitting in a café that belongs to you."

"I can't accept the responsibility just like that," I mumbled. "I need to talk to Mr Harabets first."

"I understand. Go ahead, here's a telephone."

"No, I can't ring him right now (and I don't know his number anyway, I thought to myself). Let's put it off till tomorrow."

"Sorry, but I'm leaving tomorrow, and I'll be away for three months. We must settle it today. That's why I said yesterday that it's urgent."

"You also mentioned yesterday that you had something you wanted to tell me about my sister Ala," I reminded him.

"Yes, I did, but let's get this matter of the money out of the way first. Let's keep the chalk and the cheese well apart," and he smirked, as if we were already best mates. "Please, take the money and give it to Harabets. I very much want him to win, and he can do it, I'm sure of that. It's time for change, and I want to be part of it. It would be short-sighted of me to let it all happen without being involved."

He was so sure of himself when he spoke, so cool and

* *Popular Front:* there is an opposition political party of this name.

collected, that I believed him. I had already lifted my hand to take the money, I could already taste the triumph that I would feel when I handed it over to Ulia, and how it would make up for her previous lack of trust in me, and my lips were already in position to say "Right, OK then," when a stroke of good luck suddenly came to my rescue, as it often does to clumsy types like me.

The café interior, as I have already mentioned, is decorated with pieces of mirror that hang down from the ceiling and slowly rotate around their axis. It was just at that moment — I had already straightened out my fingers to reach across the table — when one of the mirrors was in the right position for me to catch out of the corner of my eye the silhouettes of men concealed round the corner. I saw them. I even saw the weapons they were holding. I saw their masked faces, the word SPETSNAZ* on their black outfits. Then I understood. It was a trap. An ambush. They were lying in wait for me, or rather for my sister, the election agent for Harabets. Perhaps Kukal had prepared bundles of forged banknotes for me, perhaps financing an election campaign with actual cash is not permitted in this country unless you hold an official position, perhaps there's some kind of law that makes it illegal to hold dollars in your hands. What do I know? What I did know, however, was that, if I took the money, those men in hiding round the corner would jump out and arrest me on the spot... My hand circled over the money and took hold of my glass.

"Right, OK then... can I have another bowl?" I asked, trying to smile in as friendly a manner as my host. "I can only thank you most sincerely and inform the candidate whom I represent of your generous offer. He is the one who must make the decision. I do not think that your departure tomorrow will in any way hinder what you intend to do. You can entrust one of your people to meet with me at another time, or you could always

---

* *Spetsnaz*: 'special purpose police'

transfer the money into the account that the Central Electoral Commission has opened for each candidate..."

"Our past has left us with a heavy burden," Kukal shook his head. He obviously realised that his plan had failed, but his face didn't show it. "You don't trust me for some reason. As God is my witness, you're being overcautious. Even so, my offer is still open. Mr Harabets can phone me."

"I'll pass on your message."

"Right, let's leave it at that. And now that matter of your sister," his face clouded over: he was obviously preparing me for some news about my sister that I would find unpleasant, but should most definitely know about. "Your sister is spying on you. She's working for her husband. Are you aware that he came down to see her? It was then that he gave her the job of watching you. She's recording all the conversations you have and passing them on to him. Just listen to this." At this point Kukal took out a tiny tape recorder from his pocket and switched it on. I heard the row that Ulia and I had had yesterday.

My spine refused to support my body. I slumped back in the chair.

"You did the right thing, telling her off like that. Have you ever had reason not to trust her?" he enquired and switched off the tape recorder.

I was in a state of complete shock. I thought I knew what this man was capable of, but this I hadn't expected. It meant our house was bugged. I was so unprepared for what I had just heard that I was even ready to believe that I had installed the bug myself because Anton had instructed me to!

"Where did you get this recording from?"

"Let's not go into details. I have my own ways. For example, one of the men on Babylyov's campaign staff works for me."

Kukal's eyes sparkled in what I thought was a distinctly threatening manner. I began to feel that I understood less and less of the world he inhabited. What the hell does he want from us? Perhaps the drink was poisoned. He took the antidote, but I'm going to keel over at any moment and kick the bucket because of the champagne I've drunk. Money and power — I understand less about them than I do about everything else that goes to make up our lives, yet here I am, mired in them right up to the eyeballs... How would Ulia have behaved in this situation? What would she have done?

"By the way, how did you know that a bowl of peaches with white wine and champagne was my favourite?"

"I told you, I've made enquiries about you."

"What do you need to know such personal details for?"

"I'm interested. Curious, if you like. I wanted to know as much as possible about the charming lady who is to be my future neighbour. Well, if, that is, I eventually do decide to build somewhere near you and if you have still not sold your land to me."

As it turned out, there was no poison in the bowl. On the other hand, the alcohol it contained started to play its usual games with me. I was engulfed by a sense of euphoria as the world began to sway ever so slightly before my eyes. I really couldn't care less any more.

"Kukal!" I exclaimed in an impressive tone, dropping all pretence at politeness. "Do you take me for a complete fool? I trust my sister, she's not the one recording our conversations. And tell the special fuzz you brought here," I pointed to the ceiling and Kukal, in shock, raised his eyes in that direction, "that they should learn to hide themselves better. So, don't bother to see me out, but know this: if you ever get in the way of me and my sister, you'll live to regret it! You can record that on your crap machine and stick it you know where!"

I rose to my feet and, trying to hold myself upright, made for the exit. Kukal suddenly burst into loud guffaws. I could feel the sound of his raucous laughter hitting me in the back until I reached the door.

I raced down the stairs and went out into the heat of the city.

The market place was a hive of activity. Some Uzbek tried to get me to buy his dates. It was still early, but there were already queues of people in front of the health centres, waiting to have blood tests. The engines of "Ikarus" buses were making their usual racket, and minibus taxis were dodging their way through the traffic. Thank God I don't have any children! It's much simpler that way. Water off a duck's back. To drink or not to drink — that is the greatest question I face. Just imagine if I had three sons and them asking me "Mum! What have you done with the world, what kind of inheritance have you left us?" — then what would I have felt?

I wiped my tipsy tears away and headed straight for the Palesie railway station. I had a beer in the station buffet and returned to Dobratyche on the eleven o'clock train.

The euphoria and swaying sensation of earlier had now given way to a deep melancholy (every alcoholic knows what I mean), almost depression. Rage, even.

Ulia was already home (she had returned in her nice new Škoda). There was a load of people fussing around on the hill. They were measuring something, placing striped poles at set intervals and peering through the eyepieces of theodolites. I spotted them as I got closer to the house.

"Where have you been?" my sister asked.

"Who are all these people?" I asked her.

"They must be Kukal's surveyors. Or builders. Good God, where are you off to!? Stop!" and she chased after me.

At the words "Kukal's surveyors" my undefined rage suddenly found a target. We kept an axe standing in a corner inside the front door of the house — granny had used it for chopping wood. I grabbed hold of it and silently — without a single word — charged up the hill. A red veil of anger blinded my eyes. Ulia set off running after me. "Stop! Stop!" I could hear her shouting. The people on the hill turned and looked in our direction. "Get out of here, she'll kill you," Ulia screamed. "Run, she's mad! Save yourselves!"

Just to make sure the message got across, she repeated the same thing in Russian.

It was quite a sight! Up ahead was a woman dressed in red wielding an axe, her face contorted with rage. Behind her ran another, but identical-looking woman, also dressed in red, shouting in a wild voice "Save yourselves!"

The two young women and a young fellow working on the hill stood stock still and watched us. They had no idea of what was going on. They had never seen anything like it before. The lad was the first to realise the danger. He seized the theodolite and raced off down the hill. The women squealed and ran after him. All three of them dived into the Land Rover that was standing at the bottom of the hill, and drove off at top speed. I threw the axe after the vehicle and almost hit it (I wonder — is axe throwing an Olympic sport? I could be entered for championship competitions). Triumph! I immediately set about hacking to pieces the trophy that I had awarded myself — a striped surveyor's pole they had left behind.

Ulia fell to the ground and started laughing out loud.

"God, you really are quite mad! What was all that about? How could you do that? It's not their fault — they were sent here!"

"What was I supposed to do? Put up with it? Not bloody likely! They'll think twice before showing their noses back here."

I also sat down on the grass, drinking handfuls of water from the spring that was bubbling and gurgling close by.

"That bastard son of a bitch Kukal said to me just this morning that he'd had second thoughts about building here, and then he goes and sends his builders in anyway. I couldn't stop myself and I don't regret it. The only thing I am sorry about is that Kukal wasn't here in person. I'd have aimed the axe right at him."

"Kukal? Where did you see him?" My sister was obviously on her guard.

The moment had come for me to drink of the cup of responsibility, and I told her everything.

"I don't know if I did the right thing. If it hadn't been for that blasted alcohol, I might have been able to find out a lot more..."

Ulia looked pensively at me.

"Ala, there's never a dull moment when you're around. That's for sure. I don't think you have any reason to reproach yourself. Everything's clear as it is. If the half of what we know about Kukal is true — and I am convinced it is — then we have a real problem on our hands. He works for the régime and the régime works for him. As for our conversations being recorded, well, who would have thought that we were so important! They're afraid of Harabets, and that means my phone's being tapped. I'll ask our local campaign office to send us some specialists to go on a bug hunt."

In a way I was even grateful to Kukal: thanks to him my sister and I were once again the best of friends.

THE RED JACKET

In addition to drowning in the amount of work she had to do, Ulia was also feeling unwell, so she sent me to Harabets' campaign office in Brest to fetch some documents.

She gave me clear instructions, her face twisted with pain and holding her stomach: "Go to such-and-such an address and find Ales Bakunovich. Tell him you're my sister. He'll give you a green folder. Bring it to me.

I gave her a quick salute, buttoned up the red jacket that Zarnitskaya had lent me and ran for the diesel.

I got off the train at the Palesie station and set off on foot for Harabets' campaign office, totally wrapped up in my own thoughts. I wasn't paying attention to anything in particular, until, when I was already on Kuybyshev Street, just a few metres away from the office, two tough guys in black suddenly jumped on me, grabbed me under the arms and dragged into a bus with darkened windows. I had no time even to squeal before they beat me down to the floor.

The transition from being in bright sunlight one minute to finding myself in the darkness of captivity the next was too much.

"Did you feel that, bitch? You're really going to get it now, you fucking whore, you'll never get up again!"

I lifted my head, and tried to get up.

"Lie still, bitch, don't dare fucking move!"

One of the boys in black, with the word SPETSNAZ above his pocket, swung his boot in business-like fashion and smashed it down on the fingers of my right hand. The pain was unbearable. I screamed "No, don't!", curled up in a ball on my back and drew my legs in, trying to shield my hand.

"What are you twisting around for, you fucking cunt, you piece of shit? Kiss your life goodbye, whore, it's fucking curtains for you." The other took the safety catch off of the automatic weapon he was holding in his hand, laughed and added: "Right now we're going to take you to the firing range, 'no, don't' won't fucking help you there, you fascist bitch cunt!"

The bus moved off.

I was in shock, lying on the floor, trying to make out what was happening. There were two of these yobs from the special forces. They were of an age when they should be in the full bloom of youth, but there was nothing of the kind about this pair. On the contrary, there was an aggressive madness simply oozing out of their bodies. The heavy smell made me shiver, as if I was cold. Both of them were made from the same mould: the same bull necks, the same fat faces and muscle-bound bodies. Both were utterly calm and assured of their own rightness and the rightness of their cause.

My hand was filling up with some kind of liquid and swelling up.

"Right, you fucker. Want another one, do you?"

The blow caught me on the broken hand. Fortunately for me I passed out with the fear and pain.

I came to when they were again holding me under the arms and dragging me off somewhere. I managed to raise my head and saw a board saying "Frunze District Court, City of Brest", and lapsed back into unconsciousness.

Then out of the mist floated a woman in black, someone I'm going to remember for a long time in spite of my poor memory, E.A. Graychik, judge.

"Stand!" she ordered, "The court is now in session to examine the case brought against Borisevich Ulia Anatolevna. The accused is charged with offences classified under Article 156, paragraph 1 as "petty hooliganism". The court has been presented with a police report of administrative offences committed by citizen Borisevich, namely using obscene language in a public place, making a nuisance of herself in public, repeatedly ignoring warnings given to her by police officers Shushko and Pochtivy..."

The judge was wearing a black robe. Sticking out of it, underneath the table at which she was sitting, I could see a pair of desiccated legs. For some odd reason she had a pair of rubber flip-flops on her feet. Her heels were like a face. A thin, black-eyed, blurry face. Her face was like a malevolent, impotent heel with a nervous tic. My hand hurt so much that I was on the verge of crying out loud. The judge was looking at her papers.

Pochtivy tapped my shoulder to get me to stand up. Pain flared up in my broken fingers and I howled in agony. The woman in the black robe cast a brief glance at me and the swollen, blue hand that I was cuddling like a child, and went on:

"The court has witness statements from officers Shushko and Pochtivy. The accused is sentenced to ten days' administrative detention!"

The flip-flops made a damp, squishing sound under the table. That's all. I had no form of ID on me, and I was wearing a red jacket. These slobs had mistaken me for Ulia. I had no interest whatsoever in politics, but I was well aware that in the current election campaign charging someone with an administrative offence and then detaining them was a normal way of promoting the régime's slogan of "Belarus for the people".

I caught the eye of one of the special police thugs.

I could of course state right now that I am not Ulia. Maybe they would even let me go. But then they would start to go after Ulia. No, if that's the case, it's better for her to be at liberty. She really must be a pain in a body part where it hurts them most. I can put up with it, after all, they're not going to kill me, are they?

However, my bravery began to drain out of my body when Shushko dragged me back to the bus. At least they didn't beat me any more.

Spetsnaz, the country's elite policemen, took me — as I found out later — to the Brest remand prison. There they handed me over to the local security staff and departed, leaving a trail of swearwords to dissolve in the cool air.

A chubby, taciturn man of about my age, dressed not in black but in an ordinary grey police uniform (I have no idea what rank he was), took down my details in the logbook. He glanced at my right hand and picked up the receiver of the telephone on the desk.

"Doctor to the duty room."

The doctor also turned out to be a middle-aged man of few words. He gave me an injection which eased the pain, and then two regular policemen took me off to the hospital, where they put my hand in plaster. The doctor in reception there whispered to me as he worked his magic on my hand: "I'm putting some Scotch cast plaster on it. It's much lighter than ordinary plaster, it'll be easier for you." The policemen took me back to the remand prison.

I was in prison for the second time in my life.

I shuffled over to the wooden board that served as a bed, sank down on it, curled up and — to my own surprise — went to sleep.

IT SMELLS OF PEOPLE

I woke up at dawn. The cell was lined with red brick. The window aperture was set deep in the thick exterior wall. The early-morning summer sun cast its red on my breasts.

I recalled everything that had happened.

I tried to stir myself. My body responded with aches in various places. All the same I got up.

Ulia would by now be beside herself with worry that I hadn't returned. Although someone in the campaign office may perhaps have seen me being arrested. After all, the office is close to the scene.

I looked around. Bare walls with no plaster, a bench for a bed, a table and a stool, all of them fixed to the floor. A proper loo that you can sit on. A washbasin. Just like a sanatorium! And — surprisingly — there was a pleasant smell. A smell of old, damp brick mixed with old dust and a little sweat. You could say that it smelt of people, or even of humanity in general.

I went over to the window. Standing on tiptoe I could see part of the yard, a wall made of the same brick as the walls of my cell, beyond it there was a bit of empty street and then the river Mukhavets. A fine mist was rising off the river and I could hear birds singing in the bushes along the bank. Fish were splashing in the water. I could hear the noise of cars driving by.

So, this is the Brest remand prison. In fact the building is the old jail, put up when the city was moved from its old location on the river Buh to where it is now. That makes it one of the oldest buildings of Byarestse.

The door creaked and I looked round. A young police officer

came into the cell. I knew what to do in situations like this, so stood up and stated my name, "Barysevich Ulia!"

He looked a bit taken aback, but managed to nod in response.

In his hands he was holding a plastic mug of tea and some sandwiches wrapped in a piece of squared paper that had obviously been torn out of an exercise book.

"Do you want something to eat?" he asked me. That was obviously not a question you would find in the rule book. I realised that I was indeed very hungry; it was almost twenty four hours since I had last had a bite to eat.

"Yes, I do."

"Here, take this."

"What's this?"

"Don't worry. It's part of the packed lunch my mum gave me to take to work. They won't put you on the list until later today, so you won't get anything to eat until supper this evening. Have a little something now," and he put the mug on the table.

I felt the tears begin to flow, and there was a lump in my throat. I couldn't even thank the lad. He left.

Very little has ever affected me quite so much as that plastic mug of not very hot tea.

There was no question that Zarnitskaya's red jacket had brought me to this place, the old Brest jail, but the warm liquid the policeman had brought me was going to be the cause of my getting out, and of much else that would happen later.

For there was simple human kindness in that tea.

Looking at the tea and wiping away my tears, I realised that I could not retreat.

I had no right to.

I realised that God had not turned His face away from this land of Belarus.

That I would be on the side of God, and not of the devil while I still lived. And after my death as well.

My fear left me. The fear that had crushed me utterly down

yesterday — fear of spetsnaz, fear of life itself — disappeared in an instant. I was no longer afraid of anything.

It was then that granny came to me.

With the mug of tea in my hand I once again went over to the window.

I took a sip.

A light-headed giddiness came over me, and my broken fingers were hurting.

Something strange happened to my sight. I was gradually beginning to notice everything in such detail that I could no longer see entire objects.

The old brick of the walls, pockmarked and scratched. Dust on the glass of the open window. Bars on the window made of thick wire. The asphalt on the surface of the yard suddenly seemed to melt and flow away. The mist coming off the river grew thicker. The noise of the city ceased. The sound of cars seemed to be coming from further and further away, and then it disappeared altogether. It was just as if I had dived into water and emerged in a totally different place.

No, I was still standing by the window, holding the mug of tea in my left, uninjured hand, but out there, beyond the bars, beyond the open window, everything had changed.

The air was different and the mist had dispersed. The street was no longer the same. The asphalt disappeared as though someone had torn it away. In its place were cobblestones. There were no cars. The birds were much noisier. Someone somewhere was chopping wood — the sound carried across the river. There was a smell of smoke. Far off I could hear women's voices, speaking in a language I didn't recognise.

A dog with a reddish coat came running round the corner of the street.

A horse and cart appeared on the scene. A man was walking alongside the cart, barefoot in a cap and jacket, holding the reins in his hand. Next to him was a girl in a headscarf, also barefoot.

I fixed my gaze on this pair.

On the horse.

On the cart.

The red dog was sniffing the dust on the road and then began leaping around by the wall.

The cart came nearer, and I could see that it was full of fish. Huge dark sheatfish were lying on the hay, next to them were several large wicker baskets.

The girl raised her head and looked at the windows of the jail. She asked the man something.

The sounds became much clearer, and I could hear the man's voice.

"No, Paval's not here, they put him in Biaroza."*

"Why did they put him in jail, dad?"

"For politics."

"But what did he do?"

"He said something against Piłsudski."**

"What did he say?"

Without stopping, the man leant down and whispered something in her ear.

I could hear her laughter.

By now they were very close, no more than a stone's throw away. I peered closely at the faces of these people — there was something familiar about them. Dark hair, broad noses, strong, uneven teeth...

The girl bent down to scratch her leg, and I noticed that half of the little finger on her left hand was missing... Wait a minute... That means she's my granny! She told us many times about how she had chopped off part of her finger with a scythe when she was a girl. It's her, it really is, and there are her toes, all bent and crooked! It really is her, with her father.

---

* *Biaroza:* the reference is to the Polish town then called Bereza Kartuska, where a detention camp was established in 1934 to house perceived enemies of the Polish state, frequently without charge or trial. The town is now in Belarus.

** *Piłsudski:* Józef Piłsudski was effectively head of the Polish state between the coup d'état of 1926 and his death in 1935.

A swarthy dishevelled woman came running round the corner; she was holding a child in her arms. Now and again she turned round and shouted something in a guttural language I had never heard before. She was quarrelling with another woman I couldn't see, who was yelling her responses from behind the wall.

"Dad, what are those Jewish women yelling about?"

"They're having an argument. One's accusing the other of..."

Right at that moment the door to my cell creaked open. I turned round instantly when I heard the sound, and then looked back through the window — there was no one there. The girl, her father, the Jewish woman with the child — they had all disappeared. The asphalt had grown back on the roadway, and once again I could hear the noise of cars.

"Barysevich, you're going somewhere!"

It was the chubby taciturn police officer who had signed me in yesterday evening.

I was still holding the plastic mug. The tea was still quite warm. The whole vision had lasted for no more than a few seconds. Had I really had a vision? Yes, I had. Of that I had no doubts at all. I really did see all of it, alive and real. Granny had come to me from places about which we know nothing.

"Barysevich, did you hear what I said? You're going somewhere!"

"Yes, I heard you. Where am I going?"

"To the KBB.*"

"Is that supposed to be a joke?"

"Do you think I would joke about that? We've had orders to deliver you to the KBB, that's serious."

"Can I take my tea and sandwiches with me?"

"Yes, take them."

---

* *KBB* — the Committee for the Security of Belarus. An institution invented by the author. Belarus has retained the name of the Soviet secret police: in Russian KGB, in Belarusian KDB.

During the trip I fortified myself with the tea and bread the young policemen had brought me earlier. The Brest KBB is located in an old building dating back to Polish times on Levaneuski Street. It reeks of peace and olde worlde charm. I was taken to room 156 on the ground floor.

A serious, sedate man was waiting for me in the room. The desk he was sitting at was completely empty. The heavy burden of his honourable mission was imprinted on his forehead. A man of authority, whether you look at him from his dexter or his sinister side. He rose from his chair to greet me, and then offered me a seat. He didn't give his name. His voice was well modulated, and his head well coiffed — every single hair in its allocated place.

His face assumed an expression of official severity, with even a hint of paternal sorrow.

"Ulia Anatolevna, you are an intelligent person. I am certain that you realise the severity — the gravity, even — of the situation in which you have placed yourself. You face criminal charges. I am sure you understand what it is I am talking about."

"I have absolutely no idea."

He was, of course, speaking Russian.

"In that case I will explain in more detail. But before I do, please sign this," and he placed a piece of paper in front of me.

"What's this?"

"It's a document you have to sign, to say that you will not divulge anything to anyone of what we are going to be talking about."

"I won't sign that."

"What do you mean, you won't? You have to."

"I don't have to do anything. You haven't yet brought criminal charges against me, have you? No, you haven't. According to the law, I have the right to refuse not only to sign this piece of paper, but also even to talk to you at all."

This caught him by surprise. He resorted to shouting.

"What do you think you are doing? Do you realise where you

are? Believe me, stronger people than you have signed anything we put before them."

"And do you realise that you are talking to a woman who is old enough to be your mother? How dare you raise your voice to me in that manner!"

He sat up straight. I detected a slight shiver in his otherwise firmly set jaw. His cheeks twitched. He changed his tone.

"It's in your interests to collaborate with us, and not to go all out for confrontation."

"I am perfectly capable of looking out for my own interests."

"Why are you so aggressive? Would it not be better for us to have a peacable and constructive chat?"

"My hand hurts. Your colleagues broke it when they were arresting me yesterday."

"You were arrested by the elite force. They aren't my colleagues. They work for a different ministry. Would you like me to call a doctor to give you something to alleviate your pain?"

"There's no need. I am prepared to hear what you have to say, but I will not sign anything."

"Well, then.. If you don't want to, you don't want to." He thought for a moment and then brought out an opaque folder. "In this file, citizen Borisevich, I have a statement from a citizen of our country to the effect that you sought to persuade him to commit an act of terrorism, namely, to poison the Mensk water supply..."

I couldn't stand it any more. My head sank on to my uninjured hand, and I groaned.

He must have interpreted my gesture in the wrong way, because he was clearly very happy.

"I can tell you frankly that if you agree to collaborate with us, I in my turn am prepared to ensure that this statement goes no further... After all, you are a person who is capable of thinking logically. Think about my offer. You perhaps do not fully understand who it is you have become involved with. Harabets is a dreamer, a political idealist. He does have a certain level of support, I agree, but he's weak, he lacks the force of character to manage people. We would never support such a man, and without our support he doesn't have a chance of winning the elections. Surely a person such as yourself cannot fail to realise that your struggle is senseless. Take, for example, that relative of yours, the husband of your sister the alcoholic", and he looked straight at me, "he realised that he had backed the wrong horse and withdrew his candidature in favour of the current president. Once he had done so he was granted tax concessions for his business and a licence to sell vodka. Believe me, we know how to reward collaboration properly."

"What kind of collaboration are you talking about?"

"You know Mr Harabets very well, don't you? You spend a lot of time with him and with people in his team. There is some information which is of interest to us. No, I'm not asking you to become an informer; I am well aware that you would not do that. But if, let's say, you were to give me the gist of the conversation that Harabets had with the American President — I'm sure he told you about that, didn't he?"

"And here am I thinking that you can listen in on all our conversations, or can't you?"

"You saw for yourself that that man Sanaleyeu from the Harabets campaign team found all our bugs, did you not?"

"Well, yes, I did."

"So, there we are then, I am interested in the conversations that Harabets had with the American President, the German Chancellor and..."

On and on went the secret policeman, listing all the things he expected my sister to do for him. His voice was smooth and self-assured; while he was talking I was looking into his face. So he had succeeded in pushing Anton to the wall... Or maybe Anton had planned the whole scenario beforehand. Perhaps he haggled a bit and won some advantages for himself by withdrawing from the campaign? The régime acts in a variety of ways when campaigning on its own behalf. Some people it packs off to prison, others it gives tax concessions to — the main thing is to get them out of the way. But this business of the statement "from a citizen" about Ulia wanting him to poison the Mensk water supply — that's really creative! Did he think it all up by himself?

"Wait a minute, why would I want to poison the water supply?"

This stopped his flow.

"To cause mass disturbances that could lead to the overthrow of the lawful government of the country."

"Oh, I see, sorry for interrupting you. Please go on. Just tell me, please, what is your name?"

"Stepan Fyodorovich."

"Are you married?"

"That has nothing to do with the topic of our conversation."

"No, indeed it doesn't. Do you know what, Stepan Fyodorovich? I'm not going to collaborate with you. Charge me with a criminal offence."

"You're making a big mistake."

"If I'm making a mistake, it means that I'm still alive."

"You're facing a twelve-year sentence."

"That's just you threatening me with twelve years inside. It doesn't mean that that is what I'll get."

"Oh, yes, you will. You can be certain of that."

"In that case, I'll serve my sentence."

"You might be brave now, but you won't be so brave once you get inside your cell. I can assure you of that."

"Oh, yes, talking of cells. Right now I'm serving ten days' administrative detention, aren't I? So send me back to the remand prison. I have nothing else to say to you today."

Stepan Fyodorovich tried to frighten me with a variety of other punishments, but in the end made arrangements for me to be sent back, after telling me that he would call me in again tomorrow and warning me to think very carefully about what he had said.

As soon as I had been returned to the remand prison and brought to my cell, I asked the guard to let his superiors know that I wanted to make a statement. Almost at once an officer came to my cell, and I said for the record that I was not the person they thought I was. I was Ala Anatoleuna Babylyova, and did not therefore wish to serve a sentence that was intended for someone else, and that I wished to make a formal written statement to that effect, and to be released.

"What do you mean — you aren't the person we thought you were?" the police officer looked completely confused.

"That's it exactly. I am Ala Babylyova."

"Why didn't you say so earlier?"

"I was in a state of shock. It's only now that I feel in full control of what I'm doing. Give me a pen and a piece of paper, I want to make a written statement."

"This is a right turn-up for the books. You'll have to wait, I've got to report this to the prison authorities."

He told me to sit and wait, and left the cell.

And so I started waiting. I realised that they might release me, but equally they might not. If they really need to lock Ulia up, they will probably release me, after all, what use am I to them? If, for example, Ulia is somewhere out there making a noise about my disappearance and draws the attention of the boys from the KBB, they will arrest her and they may well not let me go (after all, I swore loudly and in public at those spetsnaz boys, didn't I?); I was counting on the regular police being under no obligation to do what the KBB wants them to do, unless forced. From a purely formal point of view, if I am not the person they thought I was, then the whole of the arrest warrant is invalid, and that in itself would be grounds for declaring the trial and sentence invalid. That ought to be enough to get me released. At least that was my reasoning.

There was now a group of three policemen entering my cell.

"Who can confirm that you are Ala Babylyova?"

"Here in Brest there's my friend Lena Heorheuna Zarnitskaya, and an acquaintance of mine called Fyodar Kopats, I don't know his patronymic.

"Is Anton Babylyou your former husband?"

"He certainly is."

"Is Ulia Barysevich your sister?"

"Yes."

"Where is she now?"

"She's gone to Moscow for a week on business."

"Wait."

The policemen left; when they returned the group had grown to five. They looked at me with a fascinated curiosity that they didn't trouble to conceal, as if I was some kind of fairground sideshow. Then another officer appeared, this time one with great big stars on his epaulettes. He raised his eyebrows and all the others immediately left the cell.

"Sign this, Ala Anatoleuna."

"What is it?"

"It's a document for your release from temporary detention prison in accordance with the provisions of Article 234, paragraph 3, dealing with the discovery of new evidence that shows a detainee to be the victim of mistaken identity.

"Oho, so there is an article that says that, is there?"

"There is, we dug it up."

I read the document and signed it.

"Thank you very much."

The officer looked at me with a mixture of irony and sympathy on his still youthful, clean-shaven face. He was probably about my age.

"You're a sharp one, you are. These days that's not a good thing," he shook his head, and tried to hide a faint smile. His tone had become really friendly. "Perhaps we could have a bite to eat together this evening, to mark your liberation?"

"I'd love to. But are you allowed to meet up with inmates privately?"

"Once they've been released, no problem."

"Well, in that case not this evening. I'm going home to wash prison off me. A bit later, then."

"That's fine. Go home and wash. By the way, Stepan Fyodorovich won't hear that you've been released until tomorrow morning. He's already gone home by now." The officer left the cell, closing the door behind him.

I was released soon after that. I went out into the street, that same street over which the mist had spread this morning and seeped into the barred windows of the jail, and where the barefoot carter and his daughter had been taking fish to market.

Now the evening sun was warming the huge leaves of the old plane tree by the entrance to the jail, and the carter's great-granddaughter, holding her injured hand to her chest, didn't have the slightest idea what to do next.

FULL CIRCLE

I made my way home by taxi. I had to let six taxis go by before I found a driver brave enough to pick up a dirty dishevelled scarecrow with one hand in plaster.

Ulia burst into tears when she saw me in the doorway; in her mind she had already buried me.

I tried to put things in their proper order as I told her what had happened to me.

"They're going to hunt you down. I don't know why you are so important to them, but they're going to put you in prison. You've got to go underground, if you know how it's done."

"That's something I do know... Let's think what we need to do first. And you... You've simply... I don't have the right words... You're ace, as my Lina would say. For what you've done all your sins will be forgiven. What *scum* they all are."

We hugged each other. A mighty electric bolt of sisterly feelings shot between our intertwined fingers.

"What should we do with you now?" The question Ulia posed as she wiped her eyes was somewhat rhetorical. "Let's go to Mensk together."

"No," I said firmly. "That's something I won't do. Who's going to feed the animals? I'll stay here, I won't leave the house, the dogs will protect me. Now that ex-husband of mine has withdrawn from the election in exchange for some tax concessions, nothing's going to happen to me. But it's different for you... The main thing is for you not to get trapped in their claws. For one thing, how do you intend to get to Mensk? They'll grab you straightaway."

"Maybe not. They aren't all-powerful. Yesterday they mistook you for me, and today they don't know that I never did go to Moscow."

"That was just the ordinary police in the remand prison who didn't know, but by tomorrow the KBB people will know everything."

"That means I must leave today, right away." My sister had obviously made up her mind. She looked at her watch. "There's just enough time for me to make the train from Prague."

She went over to the phone and dialled.

"Tolik, it's me. Our pig's snuffed it. Can you come over at once, so that we can bury it before nightfall? Yes, I have. OK, I'll wait, but please hurry."

I was worried by what I heard.

"What's all this about my pig, then?"

She reassured me in a whisper: "It's nothing to do with the pig, it's a code phrase. Tolik and I got together when you disappeared and we started looking for you."

Ulia was ready and waiting when Tolik burst into the house.

"Ala, what happened to you?" he shouted from the doorway. Where were you? We didn't know what to think."

There was something in his voice... His voice that today sounded so strong and sure of itself... Never mind, let's not think about it now. I must have imagined it. After all, I'm an old woman.

"Tolik, take me to the station. I'll tell you everything on the way, but let's go now, otherwise we'll be late for the train. I'll tell you everything." Ulia pulled him towards the door.

I shut the door behind them and sat down on the bench. For quite some time I simply wasn't able to stand up.

I sat there shivering for about twenty minutes before I could pull myself together and go off for a shower.

I washed the last two days off of me, holding my injured hand up so as not to get the plaster wet.

I got the whisky out of the fridge and drank straight from the bottle.

There was the sound of a car outside in the yard.

It was Tolik.

I went out to meet him and to hold the dogs back.

We didn't go into the house. We didn't go into a house which was probably stuffed with bugs, where someone had poisoned granny and I couldn't do anything to save her, where there were telephones that could ring at any moment with people trying to get hold of us.

Tolik took me firmly by the hand and we walked in silence into the depths of the forest.

Where the silvery light of the moon mingled with the pitch-black emptiness of the shadows.

Where there was silky moss and sand.

Where forty years ago we had dug ourselves great hidey-holes where we could hang out.

Where thirty years ago clumps of moss had stuck to our cool skin.

Now, after thirty years, time had come full circle.

Two alconauts in the moonlight.

Except that now it wasn't quite so easy to count each other's ribs.

MARIA VAYTSYASHONAK GIVES ME A GOOD TELLING OFF

Maria's voice sounded sad and listless on the phone. She was burbling something about the amazing properties of certain medicinal herbs, but I got the impression that she really wanted to talk about something else.

"Did you read my article in *Nasha Niva*?" I asked, fishing for compliments. In the article I described my adventures in court and the remand prison, and quite a few people I know had already phoned me that morning. There was even an American journalist who phoned me — Horst David, if I heard his name correctly. He asked me for permission to translate the article for the newspaper he works for.

"Yes, I did," Maria answered. There was a distinct note of bitterness in her voice now. "Something that you wrote in it cut right through me, I was absolutely horrified by it. How could you write such a thing, after the tragedy you've been through?!"

"What are you talking about?" I was stunned by her reaction.

"I don't know how to talk to you people, how many times do you have to be told? When are you going to learn?"

"I still don't understand what you're talking about."

"How could you bring yourself to write something like this: 'Those who bear false witness in the courts, those who beat us up in buses with darkened windows, those who tell blatant lies on the TV — they will all one day be punished by life itself. Life is always just. They cannot avoid retribution. People will spit at them. Their tongues will be affected by malignant growths. Their children's eyes will be blank. Their spiritual emptiness will bore them to death."

There was a threatening silence.

"So what's the problem? What do you find so upsetting? Do you think that life won't punish them?" I asked.

"How could you write something like that about children? About children's eyes being blank? You of all people, a mother who has lost a child. There have to be certain limits, at least there ought to be. Children are a taboo subject. Take what happened to me. The people in the village where I was brought up could have been hostile towards me. Remember that I am the daughter of one of those Poles who were given land in the eastern marches* before the war and for whom the local people had to work — probably for no more than a handful of rye — until the communists came in 1939 and took everything away from him. But like I said, the people in the village weren't hostile, they regarded me simply as a child. Who do you think you are to write something like that about children? How could you wish that on anybody, that their children's eyes will be blank?"

I felt as if Maria had slapped me hard across the face. My blood boiled, but only for a moment. I often get cross when I'm talking to Maria, but not for long. She likes making blunt statements that brook no opposition, but then I can see her defenceless eyes looking at the world through spectacles with a thin gold frame, and I am immediately mollified.

I had just put the receiver down on the telephone in the kitchen when the old door latch was lifted and Mishyk came in.

"Hi, Ala! Is your telephone working?"

"It was just now."

---

* *Eastern marches:* in Polish 'kresy' — the territorial gains in the East made by Poland after the Russo-Polish War of 1919-1920 and the ensuing Treaty of Riga of 1921. The Polish government pursued a policy of settling Polish peasants in the region as a means of consolidating their authority over the native Belarusian and Ukrainian populations.

"Can I make a call? Our line seems to be dead, and as usual we've got no credit on the mobile."

"Of course, go ahead."

Out of politeness I stepped out of the house so as not to interfere with Mishyk's phone call.

It was evening before I could get Maria's words out of my head. Might I possibly be some kind of moral imbecile not so very far removed from the lying bastards I had written about in *Nasha Niva*?

YOU AREN'T GOING TO WIN THE ELECTIONS

Horst David turned out to be a flaxen-haired young fellow with a firm professional approach to his work. He gave me a choice: either I would go to him to give my approval to his translation, or he would bring the translation to me. He had to have my signature; neither an e-mail nor a fax would do.

I decided to go to Mensk myself. Harabets' campaign staff had put Ulia in charge of the campaign in Brest Province, and so she was now living in Dobratyche. She had two powerfully-built bodyguards — Sasha and Dzima — who accompanied her everywhere in Brest and on the campaign trail at meetings with voters. The two of them relaxed when they were with her in Dobratyche: they changed and enthusiastically pumped water from the well to pour on the allotment, they started training the pig (and by the third day it had already found its first porcino mushroom). With those two around Ulia would be able to cope perfectly well. I'll have a chance to look at my new flat and I might even see my ex-husband. Once away from Dobratyche, I will also be able to think over what has been developing recently between me and Tolik...

I arrived in Mensk in the evening. It was still hot and sticky. People were going home after work, pale and tired, sun-tanned pensioners were returning after a day in their dachas. The city was enveloped in a heat haze that contrasted starkly with the open expanses of Dobratyche. Travelling in a packed underground train was a terrible experience; it was no better when I emerged from the station and joined the crowds on the embankment of the river Svislach to look for the building where my flat was. True, the building wasn't a new one: a pompous Stalinist construction with heavy exterior mouldings, wholly in the spirit of the time when millions were living in poverty and dreaming of being allocated a flat in a palace like this one that in reality was accessible only to the chosen few. A few workers and a couple of cleaners did in fact get flats in such buildings back in those days, but that was only to maintain the illusion. Now the masonry is crumbling and the residents are all busy with major repairs to the interiors of the flats and with the installation of new windows. My flat is on the first floor. I opened the door and stood for a moment in the doorway before taking that first small step that is so important for mankind. Wasn't it Armstrong that said something like that on the Moon? Now I'm going to take a small step... The flat had high ceilings, the wallpaper was in shreds and there were children's scribblings on the doors. Anton, or someone else, had brought our furniture. It was all in a pile in one of the two rooms. My bedlinen was on the shelves of the cupboard. There was mouldy food on the shelves of the fridge.

I looked at the unbelievably beautiful growth of mould on the salami and decided that I wasn't going to meet Anton.

The vodka on the fridge door hadn't gone off, but it was very warm.

The daylight grew gradually dimmer. I spent the lamplit city night on the unmade bed and went to sleep before I had finished the vodka.

So, back to Horst David. He was a tall young man, thoroughly professional in everything connected — however slightly — with his job. As for everything else, he had a ready smile and a wild shock of hair. We somehow managed to hit it off at once, and he asked me to show him Mensk. He turned down the idea of going to Mir and Niasvizh, the Stalin line, Khatyn and the Glory Mound.[*] He even rejected my offer of booking a city tour from a tourist agency.

---

[*] These are the standard tourist sites in Belarus — the first two have UNESCO World Heritage status: Niasvizh (famous for the Radziwiłł Palace and its surrounding parkland, and for the baroque parish church of Corpus Christi) and Mir (restored Gothic castle of the 15th and 16th centuries). The other two sites are connected with the Second World War.

"So where do you want to go and what do you want to see?"

"I just want to see the city, to see and try to understand how people live here."

Off we went.

Whatever it was that Horst was trying to understand, he certainly went about it in the most extraordinary way. We drove round the city in circles, and each time the circles became wider. We began by taking a taxi on what everyone calls the Round Square, but is officially known as Victory Square. First we drove round the Victory Monument, then we made a start on the streets around the city centre. These were followed by the wider boulevards as we circled further and further away from the centre. Horst interrogated me about the buildings we passed. Whenever he saw a building site he would stop, get out and ask the builders about the cost per square metre, we walked around crowded markets and empty shopping malls, dropped into a car showroom and a Registry Office. He chatted with traders, locals, bridegrooms just about to get married, and even went up to traffic policemen holding radar guns to ask how many tickets they had handed out that day. By now the metre in the cab had gone right off the scale; our driver was delirious with joy at having a fare like Horst. Finally we reached the Ring Road, the kingdom of "cottages" — huge detached houses, many of them unfinished. The villages of Tarasava, Zhdanovichy, Kamennaya Horka, Zatsan and Tsnyanka were coming closer and closer to the main road, much like the nobility queueing up to approach the King at a session of the old Commonwealth Parliament: they were dressed in their best clothing, but still had a deep-seated sense of their own unworthiness. In Tsna Horst asked the driver to take a side road and go through the village. I had never been there either, and was flabbergasted by the thousands and thousands of hectares taken up by enormous mansions and the potholed roads laid to reach them. Some of these piles had towers, some didn't, some were built of red brick, others of natural stone. All had wrought iron gates and mighty walls, higher than a man. Many of them had "For Sale" signs, together with a price — 500,000 a.c.u. ("agreed currency unit", in normal parlance US dollars), 600,000 a.c.u. The record was held by a real palace on the lakeside, higher than Everest, going for a million. That's the one we stopped at. The lake was covered in green slime, and it stank. The wind was blowing up the dust on the gravel that we had been driving on, and driving empty plastic bottles across the yellow grass. Horst headed for the house, but I didn't bother getting out of the taxi — nobody would ever take me for a person who had a million dollars to spend on somewhere to live.

When we were driving to the airport, the lad (who was at most no more than twenty five) delivered his verdict on our political situation with the utmost self-assuredness:

"You aren't going to win the elections, you know. Your problem is not that the people vote for the incumbent president. In all probability they won't vote for him. Most people have a sense of justice as well as a sense of responsibility. Your real problem is that you now have in this country a newly-formed class of wealthy people who are a cross between property owners and bureaucrats. This is a numerically strong class of people who have no moral values whatsoever, or are at best totally demoralised. Every minute of the day they receive really big — or, as you say here, crazy — money, and they are never going to risk losing it all by voting a completely new government into power. There's too much at stake, and they haven't yet managed to rid themselves of their sense of insecurity. That will come later, when they start to live off their fat and indulge their every whim. For the moment they are winning. Rabies is a fatal disease and your society is infected with it."

GREETINGS FROM TARAS SLYOZKA

As our cavalcade moved off, Lyonikha continued to stare at us so intensely that I began to be a little nervous: what if one of the wives were to suddenly leap out on Ulia and me tomorrow, armed with a sharpened stake? (Volya is Valik's wife, and Handzya is Tolik's. Handzya milks the Agrovitalika Plus cows, and Volya is a toilet attendant in Brest. Handzya is very house-proud, and in Volya's eyes you can always spot that sadness that is so specific to Dobratyche.) After all, Aksana had attacked me with a hoe, and she had much less reason to do so — I hadn't gone fishing with her Syarhey.

That's exactly what we were doing now — going on a fishing trip. Ulia — who had a seemingly unending pile of work to get through, what with constantly travelling around the Brest region and never getting more than five hours' sleep a night — for some reason suddenly suggested going on a fishing trip. The equally busy Valik and Tolik — who seemed to spend night and day in that Agrovitalika of theirs — readily agreed. I was amazed.

We arrived at the Kopany Rou, a tiny tributary of the Buh, a stream which, in spite of its strange name — "Dug Ditch" — had never been dug out or straightened. There weren't as many fish here as in the lakes of the fishery, but there were far fewer people.

It was a wonderful evening, thanks to anti-mosquito cream.

There was a little inlet surrounded by willows where all of us except Ulia cast our lines. The two men looked as though they were really worked up about something, especially Tolik.

Silence fell.

An otter surfaced noiselessly and just as noiselessly dived down into the water again.

"Well..."

"I want to," Ulia and Tolik both started to speak at the same time and then stopped. "Go ahead, you first," and Tolik nodded towards Ulia.

"Well, right then," and for some reason Ulia heaved a sigh. "Greetings to everyone from Taras Slyozka."

The men looked at her in blank incomprehension. I, on the other hand, had at least heard the name before.

It must have been in 1996 that Taras and his mates from the UNSO* came to Mensk to take part in one of the "Charnobyl Way"** processions. In one of his poems the poet Andrei Khadanovich*** asks "So tell me, sonny, these ways of yours, do they take you where you want to go?"; not long afterwards the Ukrainian Consul in Mensk was to put the same question to Slyozka when he visited him in prison. Who had brought the UNSO boys to join the procession was a mystery at the time, and we still don't know — whether it was our people, or a group that wanted there to be trouble during the demonstration. Was it the Ukrainians who overturned cars or provocateurs from the KBB? Or had any cars really been overturned? Whatever the truth of the matter, on the evening after the procession the Ukrainians were all rounded up and sentenced to eighteen months in prison. When Ulia found out what had happened, she began to take them food parcels. Later, after the authorities had shown who was in charge and had released them, she got to know them; Slyozka was the leader of the group. The interesting

---

* *UNSO:* a Ukrainian political party. Full name: Ukrainian National Assembly-Ukrainian National Self-Defence.

** *Charnobyl Way:* an annual rally and procession organised by the opposition in Belarus on 26 April every year to commemorate the nuclear power station disaster of 1986. These rallies always attract the hostility of the authorities.

*** *Andrey Khadanovich (b. 1973):* one of the best-known Belarusian poets of the younger generation.

thing is that, during the course of these events, he had found himself a bride, and after serving his sentence he took her back home. Maybe he's intending to return to Belarus, this time for the elections.

Ulia told the men briefly about how she had met Slyozka, took a folded piece of paper from her pocket and handed it to me.

"Can you read it? No, not like that, turn it over."

Tolik and Valik came closer; they were obviously curious to know what was on the piece of paper.

No more than a strip of pinkish light was left from the setting sun, but it was enough to make out what was written on the paper.

It was a xerox copy of an old scrap of paper or parchment. Old Slavonic letters were clearly visible on it, faded, grey, almost without gaps between words, and with no punctuation:

"Opposite Kostomloty mill" — I read it slowly, peering closely at the letters — *"on the right bank where there's a hillock in the hole under the oak karpus will show* … What is this?"

"It's Master Tryzna's note!" yelled Tolik.

Ulia heaved another deep sigh and nodded.

After that evening when we held the repast for granny Ulia reckoned that it might be worthwhile writing to her friend and colleague Dr Ponomariv, the head of the Department of Historical Records in the Lviv City Archives to ask him if there were by any chance any records in his collection connected with the Tryzna family of jewellers. Sitting on the grass by the banks of the Dug Ditch, Ulia told the story of how the little scrap of paper had been found: "To be perfectly honest I didn't expect him to find anything. They haven't computerised their catalogues yet. The archives are enormous, packed to overflowing in fact, and it was quite unrealistic to think that he would find anything of use, plus Ponomariv is a very busy man... So it came as a real surprise when he phoned me a week later to ask if he should send what he had found by express post or by giving the package to a train conductor to pass on to me. "So quickly?" I asked in amazement. "How did you manage it?" "I had a pistol pointed at my head," Ponomariv replied, laughing. "The head of security in the archives is Taras Slyozka. Quite by chance he saw your letter on my computer and after that he literally terrorised me with a gun until the two of us went to the stacks and pulled out everything that might be of use to you. He sends his greetings, by the way."

In short they sent me a whole pile of xeroxes — wills, petitions, even a proclamation of Bohdan Khmelnytsky's[*] in which the Tryzna family is mentioned. The family was well known; the King granted them a special licence to trade with the Hanseatic League... In among it all was this little note."

"So what do you keep sighing for?" asked Tolik. His face was shining, even his deep wrinkles had smoothed themselves out.

"I know that now you're going to rush off hunting for the Tryzna treasure, and I won't be able to stop you. I should never have shown you this piece of paper, but my conscience simply would not allow me to keep it hidden."

"Why would you want to stop us?"

"Because there's precious little chance that you'll find the treasure, and I can foresee a whole bundle of trouble ahead."

"What do you mean, little chance? It's all clear, here it is: opposite Kastamaloty, so the mill must have been somewhere nearby... "

"What's karpus then?" I put my penn'orth into the discussion.

"Karpus is a man's name. Karp."

"That means the mill must have been on the right bank."

"Yes."

---

[*] *Bohdan Khmelnytsky (1595-1657):* Hetman (Commander-in-Chief) of the Cossacks of Zaporizhzhya on the river Dniapro (now in Ukraine, but in the seventeenth century part of Poland). He led a rebellion against the Commonwealth of Poland and the Grand Duchy of Lithuania under the pretext of defending Orthodox Christians, but which amounted to little more than random savagery and wanton acts of destruction.

"So what are we going to do then, turn the whole of the right bank over? Plough it up with your tractor? And how do you suggest we get to the bank in the first place? It's over there, on the other side of the frontier, beyond the barbed wire."

"Why should we need to plough it up? We're going to get hold of a metal detector tomorrow. It's what Valik and I have been wanting to tell you."

"What are you going to get hold of?"

"A metal detector."

"What sort of metal detector?"

"One they use in the army."

"Good grief!"

It was Valik's turn to join in the conversation: "Tolik and I have come to the conclusion that finding the treasure is our only hope. Frankly, we need the cash. We've got to do something. That's why we wanted to meet up with you anyway, to discuss our plan of campaign."

"I have to fork out seven hundred dollars every semester for my son's education, and I've got another three kids growing up...

"And to think I'm dealing with grown-ups here," Ulia held her head in desperation. "You need to work, take action, change the government, and all they do is put their hopes in finding treasure. It's just a joke!"

"They said something like that on the radio today about Harabets. He's a joke of a politician, playing kid's games. He doesn't know what life is all about. What people need to do is work and not mess around with silly things that won't get us anywhere."

Valik nodded in agreement: "We're grown up, we know what the score is. This particular foreman has had it up to here with real life. For as long as I can remember, people have been telling me how to live. Just look around you, can't you see what deep shit we're in? Why shouldn't we at least give it a try?"

"Where did you dig up that metal detector of yours?"

"Handzia's brother's getting one for us. He's in the army, at South Base."

"I suppose he's in a unit that calls itself 'Labouring in vain'." This was Ulia being sarcastic.

"On the contrary," me again. "I agree with the lads. Why not try? I'm ready to give it a go, even if only to get across the frontier again. I was ten when I did it last, and still didn't know anything about the world."

"That's very interesting," said Ulia, for some reason putting on a foreign accent, "but how do you intend getting to the frontier? Are you going to attach elk's hooves to a pair of stilts? Or perhaps dig a tunnel?"

"Yes, even dig a...," suddenly a light bulb went off in my head. "We don't need to dig a tunnel! One's already been dug for us, and I think I know where it is."

The men greeted my story about Lyonikha scrambling into the vault with ill-concealed mistrust, but that was soon followed by a level of enthusiasm that they couldn't conceal. Ulia reacted in a cool, collected way.

"I don't know. We got ourselves into that vault God knows how many times when we were kids — do you remember, Tolik? — and we never found any way through."

"That was forty odd years ago. Let's go there now and see."

"Yes, and let's put up a banner on the tractor saying 'Folks, we're off to find the tunnel under the frontier', shall we? What do you want, for the whole gang of us all to go together? No, we've got to do this quietly... Lyonikha was always keeping her eyes peeled even though she was on her own..."

"Let me go down there tonight," Tolik offered. "I'll have a look and see what's what. And as for getting across the frontier, well, Valik and I have an idea..."

TO THE FRONTIER AND BEYOND

Do you know what a real frontier is like? You can always recognise people who live on one.

There is sadness in their eyes.

Their living space is open only eastwards. To the west there is barbed wire. Only hawks can fly freely to and fro.

Take the fellow in the marengo jacket, standing right by the doors of the train. There's a place on the line where the train runs right next to the frontier. For three seconds it's just about possible to see a corner of old Kodan*; he stands on tip-toe, cranes his neck, and looks...

On a summer's day, when the heat shimmers among the reeds growing on the sand dunes, you begin to get the feeling that somewhere over there, beyond the barbed wire, is a land of immeasurable beauty, a beauty that you have never experienced before. That you will never be able to reach.

Over there on the other side of the Buh stands Kodan, with the ruins of the old castle that was once home to the Sapieha family.** Then comes Kastamaloty and its wooden church that was built sixteen years after the Church Union of Brest. We mustn't forget the Orthodox Monastery in Yablachyna*** with its miracle-working icon. They're all behind the frontier that Stalin imposed on us. You will never get there to see them. The

---

* *Kodan:* in Polish Kodeń.

** *Sapieha family:* a wealthy family of nobility back in the times of the Commonwealth of Poland and the Grand Duchy of Lithuania.

*** *Yablachyna:* in Polish Jabłeczna.

diesel train that says it runs from Brest to Vladava* never actually reaches Vladava, because the town is on the Polish side of the frontier. It stops in a little place called Tamashouka on our side of the Buh.**

There are special lists of people who are permitted to proceed across the frontier, over to the other side of the barbed wire and the ploughed strip patrolled by guards, to reach the neutral zone. The attractiveness of this place lies precisely in the fact that it is unreachable for ordinary mortals. In the main, the lucky people on the list work for Agrovitalika Plus. They graze the company's cows and sow rye on the kilometre-wide neutral zone that stretches along the Buh. At one time, when I was still a schoolgirl, they used to send us kids down there to gather the aftergrass for the collective farm. Just once I found myself on the site where our Dobratyche used to be. We ran wild in the old gardens. I can still recall the taste of old apple varieties that people no longer know anything about.

There is nothing left of the old village, but as I grow older, I find that it comes to me in dreams more and more often. The slanting rays of the sun always appear much more sharply defined in dreams. I see the blackened log walls of the houses, the blackened stiles in the fences, the black earth... Every time a powerful urge takes hold of me: I have to go back. To take a closer look. To listen.

Tolik turned up at nine o'clock, just as we had agreed.

For the benefit of anyone who happened to be listening in on our conversation, we swapped a few harmless phrases and then said our goodbyes. Tolik looked me straight in the eyes and with a hand gesture invited me to climb in.

Which is exactly what I did. Glancing cautiously all around I slithered through the open hatch of a cistern used for carrying water.

---

* *Vladava:* in Polish Włodawa.

** *Tamashouka:* just to confuse everyone, the station there is actually called, in transliteration from Russian Cyrillic, 'Vlodava'.

There's a lot of pasture in the neutral zone, but absolutely no water — going right up to the river is strictly forbidden — so Tolik uses his tractor every day to pull the cistern of water for the cows to drink. The idea was to transport the metal detector in the cistern, and to go treasure hunting whenever an opportunity arose. Both Tolik and Valik often have to go over to the zone for their work.

It was back that evening when Tolik and I met in the forest that I asked him to take me over the frontier in the cistern, together with the water. My adventuresome little head can sometimes come up with ideas like that!

The idea seemed realistic, because Tolik agreed almost at once. He assured me that it had been a long time since the frontier guards had last used their long pole to poke around inside the cistern, as they should according to the regulations. At most they occasionally asked him to open the hatch, so that they could cast a bored glance inside. If that did happen and I heard the sound of the hatch being opened, I was to dive down into the water and sit there for as long as I could hold my breath.

Anyway, I'm a free person in all senses, and have the right to do something silly every now and again. After all, I've been without a husband for the past seventeen years! So I persuaded Tolik and he came to pick me up.

Have you ever crossed a frontier inside a water cistern attached to a tractor? No? I can recommend the experience. Once you've done it, diving, rafting and yachting will lose most of their charm. Frantically hanging on to a kind of handle on the hatch cover, spitting water out and dancing a mad tarantella on the slippery round floor of the cistern in order to stay on my feet, I soon lost all fear of discovery by the frontier guards. In fact, being discovered by them would have been a kind of salvation. In the five minutes it took to get from our house to the frontier crossing, I was eight times literally a hair's breadth away from drowning, and had given up all hope of arriving at our destination alive.

The tractor braked sharply. A silence fell beyond the iron walls that enclosed me. Then, several centuries later, the tractor moved off again. There was no rhyme or reason to the way in which the waves splashed wildly against the sides of the cistern and sometimes covered me completely. It was another few centuries before the tractor stopped and Tolik pulled me out into the light of God's world — already on the other side of the frontier. I looked really splendid: a fetching shade of pale green, algae in my hair, no shoes on my feet and cross. A real fish.

"Bloody Hell!" was all I could manage to say. "I nearly croaked in there. You could have driven more carefully! And where did you get that water from? Have you been draining the marshes for it?"

"Quite the opposite. I was trying to drive as carefully as I could." Tolik was trying to justify himself. "I take the water from the pump, just as I'm supposed to. That green stuff must be something growing on the walls," and he plucked a necklace of water weed off me.

"That's what you call careful, is it?" Water was pouring off me, but I had nothing to change into, or even wipe myself down with. My teeth were chattering with the cold. However, the heat of the sun soon began to dry me out and warm me up. I wasn't so cross any more.

I looked around. Here I am at last, after so many years of following the hawks in this direction with my eyes. It really isn't quite the same here as on our side of the wire. Are there really no plastic bottles and bits of paper scattered all over the place? Is there really no noise? What about the air — is it less dry than the air we breathe in the village? And where's the scent of the fir trees? The old road makes a huge loop to avoid the marsh... We don't have such winding roads on our side any more.

"This is the first and last time! The main thing is we got here. Sit here for a bit under this pear tree." Tolik took a pole with a hook at one end and fished my shoes off the bottom of the cistern. "I'm just going over to where the cows are, and then we can start on the treasure hunt. And I've got something to tell you that will cheer you up."

Puffing and chugging, the tractor disappeared from view.

The sunlight sparkled on the shiny leaves of the wild pear tree as they fluttered in the light breeze.

Plants spread like a carpet over the water meadows.

Once again I looked carefully all around me. Not a soul to be seen anywhere. The noise of the tractor was growing fainter and fainter. The road was completely empty in both directions. There was a slight dip, and beyond that was a wall of willows and sycamores. And beyond the trees, I knew, was the Buh.

The river that bursts its banks at flood time.

The river that people used to cross in dugout boats.

The river down which a mill once floated, and on the mill was a cockerel.[*]

I felt the urge to run down to the river, the Buh that had been a god[**] for so many generations of my ancestors.

But since Tolik had given me strict instructions to wait for him here, I lay down on the ground, closed my eyes and listened.

Suddenly... Suddenly it all happened again. I could suddenly see everything in such detail that I stopped being able to see the whole picture. There was a blade of grass next to my eye, then another one. The beetroot-red stem of a sticky catchfly. The wind. The leaves of the wild pear tree were shining in the sun. The ground beneath me began to tremble. Horses were being ridden somewhere close by. And the air! It smelled completely different.

The ground was shaking now, the riders were coming closer. Then I heard the sound of feet — two people running, a man and a boy. What a curious hat the man was wearing, a large round fur hat, broader than his shoulders.

The tractor was rattling towards me.

---

[*] Reference to a real event that once occurred during the annual spring flood.

[**] The wordplay depends on two Polish words, both of which are pronounced alike: the name of the river 'Bug' and the word for God 'Bóg'.

The air now smelled like it always did.

The vision faded before it had even properly begun. The tractor came to a halt by the pear tree.

"OK, up you get," Tolik jumped out of the cabin, pulled me up and began to tug me off somewhere. "There's been a slight change of plan. I went to the cemetery yesterday. There really is a secret door hidden behind a stone slab in the vault, but I couldn't open it. It's got a special kind of padlock on it and we'll have to find a key that fits. Let's go to the river now and have a look to see if we can spot a mill somewhere on the other bank. We can do a bit of reconnoitring to see where things are. It might also be a good idea to go down to the cemetery and try to find where that underground passage comes out. We've to get a move on. The pass they gave me is only valid till four o'clock."

I really wanted to take a long look at the river of my dreams, but Tolik didn't give me a chance. He dragged me at a trot along the overgrown riverbank. He darted about and sniffed the air like a hunting dog. From time to time he would nimbly climb up a tree to have a better look around. He lifted the drooping branches of fir trees, wriggled his way into overgrown clumps of bushes and along moss-covered ditches, sticking his nose into the thick grass that grew everywhere. He was clearly trying to prepare himself as well as he could for a methodical treasure hunt. All the while he was telling me about what he had found in the vault.

"If there's an entrance, there has to be an exit somewhere, don't you think? The door's new, looks as though it was made quite recently. Most likely it's a way of getting over the frontier, what do you think? Just imagine how much easier our lives will become if we can make use of it. We'll be able to come and go as many times as we want. And at any time."

I remembered the trip in the cistern and agreed with him wholeheartedly.

We ran across little dips in the ground, plunged into thickets and fought our way through brushwood.

"The interesting thing is, what does Lyonikha use the tunnel for?" Tolik was thinking aloud.

"Dobratyche used to be somewhere around here, didn't it?"

Tolik raised his head and gazed around.

"Yes, it must have been. Let's find out where we are exactly. Over there is the railway crossing," he said, pointing to the Belarusian side, then you've got that big sycamore there, and over there..."

Suddenly he grabbed me by the shoulders and pushed me hard to the ground. His eyes were wide in alarm, and the finger pressed tightly to his lips begged me to be quiet.

"Frontier guards," he mouthed silently. I tried to hug the grass even tighter.

The guards were patrolling the strip. We could hear their voices. Their dog was barking frantically, and trying to come charging over towards us. Then we heard one of the lads say, in Russian and with a note of regret in his voice:

"He's caught the scent of a hare. Pity we can't let him off the lead."

The return journey in the empty cistern was a little more pleasant — I even managed to find a position in which I could stand without having to dance — and Tolik dropped me off at my house.

Half-an-hour later, Tolik, Valik and I were in the pit that was all that remained of the hidey-hole we had dug for ourselves forty years earlier in the forest, discussing 'the situation as it has unfolded', as the news agencies love to put it.

Tolik had brought along the metal detector that looked like a vacuum cleaner. You had to switch it on and hold it in front of you; a red light came on and it made a sort of whistling noise. When Tolik shoved a rusty old tin can right under its snout, the red light went green and the whistling became a howl.

"It reacts to every kind of metal, not only ferrous. It has a radius of two metres, and that includes down in the ground as well." While telling us how the apparatus worked he made a sweep of the clearing where we were sitting. "They've let me have it for a week. Right, what have we got? First off, we've got the note that tells us where we should look for the treasure — on the right bank, opposite Kastamaloty, opposite the mill. Ala and I took a look along the bank earlier today, and we didn't see any sign of a mill. We'll have to go to Kastamaloty to get a closer look at the spot. That'll take at least a day."

"We don't have to go to Kastamaloty," I said. "Zarnitskaya's over there at the moment. We can give her a call and she can tell us if there's a mill somewhere nearby. What's more, she can come right down to the river on that side."

"That's great. All that's left then is to sort out the lock on the door in the vault."

Tolik told Valik about the door and the problem with the padlock.

"Maybe we should just go to Lyonikha and ask her straight out," I suggested.

"What do you think will happen then? We don't know what she's doing in the tunnel. Will she want to talk to you about it at all? And anyway, she's deaf. You'll have to yell so loudly that they'll hear you right over in Pryluki... No, that's not the right way to go about it."

"We'll just have to follow her," said Valik. "She went there once, she'll go again, sooner or later."

"What are you looking at me for?" I said with all the indignation I could muster, although I knew full well why they were looking at me.

"Ulia's busy, Valik and I are at work... You're the only one who can keep an eye on what she's doing."

"Only you," sang Valik with a smile on his face. He gave a passable imitation of Elvis.

I shook my head. What was I supposed to do? Act the good little girl guide and lie in wait for Lyonikha for days on end?

"So let's just break the door open, and that'll be the end of it," that was my suggestion.

"Oh yes, that will really put Lyonikha or whoever on their guard, it will be their turn to keep watch and try to find out what's going on, and then before we know it they'll be on to us. No, that won't work. We don't need publicity."

"What if she doesn't go to the vault for a whole month? Or doesn't go at all?"

"Just keep an eye on her for the time being. Valik and I are going to make a start on the hunt tomorrow. We'll take the metal detector over in the cistern and hide it somewhere secure. We won't have much time though — the passes they issue for the neutral zone are only ever for a short period. It'll have to do for the moment. Can you give Zarnitskaya a call right now?"

Zarnitskaya was unfazed by my question about whether there was an old mill somewhere in Kastamaloty. Her answer, however, was not what we wanted to hear. She told me very firmly that the nearest mill was ten kilometres away and it was in the open-air museum in Siemiatycze, not on the Buh.

Tolik's reaction to the news was that we would have to search right along the river bank from one end of Kastamaloty to the other, and that we would have to ask Zarnitskaya to somehow mark those two points tomorrow. I was just reaching out to pick up the phone when Zarnitskaya herself rang.

"She says," I was addressing the honourable assembly of treasure hunters, "she has just asked an old lady she met on the street, who told her that she had never seen a mill in Kastamaloty in her lifetime, but there are some piles in the ground, which people say are all that's left of a mill." I spoke into the receiver again, " Listen, Lena, could you try to find out today where those piles are, and tomorrow at …" I looked at the men inquiringly.

"At twelve."

"At twelve, that's eleven o'clock Polish time, can you come down to the bank close to where those piles are and sit there for about half-an-hour? No, I can't at the moment. I'll tell you later.

You can just sit there, or you can fish, float flower garlands down the river, whatever. Or you could go there with the children. The main thing is to be right by where the piles are, and so that you can be seen from the other side. That will be a really great help to us. OK, fine, all the best, I'll call you again later."

NOT EVERY BOOMERANG CHOOSES FREEDOM

Thanks be to God, and to Sasha and Dzima as well — they returned home today a bit earlier than usual and took upon themselves the job of watering the allotment. I had some time in the evening to think calmly about what was happening to me. Ulia was down in the root cellar where it's cool, drafting the text of some new leaflets. Sasha and Dzima were working and I had been put in charge of getting the supper ready: potatoes with some chanterelle mushrooms that our trained pig had helped me gather.

The water flowed in a wondrous transparent stream from bucket to saucepan, and from bucket to kettle.

The most interesting thing was that I had been able to bear all that had happened over this insane summer with relative tranquillity. At the age of fifty I could look back and see that life had treated me in all sorts of different ways, so much so in fact that nothing would ever break me. I had fallen into a kind of moral numbness which helped me bear everything so calmly: granny's death, Kukal's dark deeds and my arrest... Perhaps this trance-like state is in fact spiritual strength, I just don't know. Perhaps it's nothing more than my stupidity, my underdeveloped intellect, so to speak. Just imagine what people might be thinking: all these crazy events happening to her day after day, and there she sits, the silly woman, in that Dobratyche of hers, looking after her pig... But then again, firstly, if I don't look after the pig, who will, and, secondly, even if I do leave here, what does it change? Kukal will still be able to get me in Mensk, won't he? Here in the country I can go for a walk in the forest, I can listen to the eternal rustling sound of the fir trees, I can even go for a swing on their copper-coloured branches, and I can be at peace, just for a little while.

Ulia had always been able to think logically, she could always find causes and effects, but even she, or so it seemed to me, did not fully appreciate the situation. At least she knows what has to be done at any specific moment. Yesterday I helped shift the whole print run of 100,000 copies of a special edition of *Tavarysh* ('Comrade') from one van to another in order to cover their tracks — the driver of the first van had managed to lose his KBB tail, and we only had twenty minutes to load everything into another van, and get it out of Dobratyche. The six of us — Ulia, me, Sasha, Dzima and the two drivers — had to work so hard that by the time we had finished and the vans had driven off in different directions my healthy arm was visibly shaking. When I tried to pour myself some water it just splashed out of the glass. Ulia first helped me drink, then she took a long drink herself, wiped the sweat from her forehead, sat heavily on the bench and began to sing my praises.

"Ala, Ala, you're a real hero. A one-armed hero, there's no other word to describe you. We would never have managed without you. I would never have thought that one day I would have to get behind a steering wheel, let alone have to escape KBB tails. And yet here I am, doing all that and writing leaflets and printing them on a risograph in the root cellar... And, forgive me, Lord, I never thought I would ever smile at bosses of ideology departments when trying to book a room for a meeting or waste time chatting to editors of local newspapers that haven't changed their names since the communist times. Although I do have to admit that they are quite interesting characters in their own right..." Ulia's face became more serious: "I don't believe that granny died because of me, because I'm helping Harabets. I simply don't want to believe it, although that's exactly what Yurka reckons. I don't want to believe it. God simply wouldn't allow such a thing to happen. But if I had to decide all over again what I was going to do, I'd do exactly the same. Do you remember the saying: Do what you have to, whatever will be, will be? I have to do what I'm doing. Even if you suffer because of it as well. There's so much going on every day, everyone's so busy, that there simply isn't time to sit and make sense of what has happened. We can only pray that we will be able to find a way of averting future misfortunes.

I had grown accustomed to agreeing with my sister, and so I agreed with her on this occasion too.

Whatever will be, will be.

But there was a desire burning within me, burning so strongly that it was physically painful: I needed to understand how it was that I could go back in time, and how it might be possible for me to do it whenever I wanted. I tried to figure it out, this way and that, but could not find any logic in it. The two incidents that I had already experienced had nothing in common, as far as I could see. My train of thought was interrupted by a smell of something burning, but fortunately I was in time to salvage the supper.

Right at that moment Sasha and Dzima returned from the allotment and started to wash their hands in the old washbasin in the yard. Ulia and I set about laying the table outside. I was bringing the saucepan of potatoes and Ulia had the plates and forks in her hands, when all of a sudden Sasha, looking in our direction, raised his soapy arms, made a giant leap and fell on us from the air, knocking everyone to the ground. I landed on my side, and an agonising pain shot up my arm — my injured hand had taken the full weight of Sasha's body as he fell. Something whizzed right past my nose — a boomerang! A genuine boomerang, a big one, one edge honed really sharp, was spinning in the air and flying with tremendous force and speed. It turned, and, following the laws of all boomerangs, returned back to where it had presumably been thrown — somewhere up the hill. The dogs were barking and straining at their leashes. Sasha and Dzima freed Jida and raced off to where the boomerang had disappeared in a green tangle of bushes. Ulia and I somehow managed to get to our feet.

"Ulia, look! I didn't spill the potatoes. That's the second time I've come to the supper's rescued this evening," I simply blurted out the first thing that came to my mind as I stood up, holding out the saucepan in my hand.

"You should be pleased that we weren't hurt. Did you hear how that thing whistled?!"

"And how!"

"I don't think that boomerangs have figured very large in the KBB's armoury before... Just imagine what a thing like that could do to you if it struck you in the back of your neck. Even so, I'm quickly getting used to the idea that every day they're going to try to either arrest me or kill me!"

"Anyway, a boomerang is not exactly a nuclear bomb," me burbling again. "It's not even a nuclear pistol. And the only way they're going to get us is if they nuke us."

We were struck by a fit of laughter. Nervous laughter, I have to admit.

Sasha and Dzima returned out of breath. They ordered us into the house and eat our supper there. They totally rejected our suggestion that the boomerang had something to do with the KBB.

"No, it doesn't. Categorically no!"

"So who then?"

Dzima answered: "That we don't know. There was no one up on the hill, and no sign of the boomerang either. You know, not every boomerang chooses freedom. Some do choose to return to whoever threw them. But you can believe me when I say that it wasn't the KBB. They don't have any instructions to use boomerangs, and without proper instructions they won't do anything. I used to work in the KBB, and so did Sasha. So you really can believe what we say."

And so we sat down to have our supper. We believed Dzima, but didn't feel a bit easier.

ON STAKEOUT

Tolik had more or less appointed himself leader in all matters related to the treasure hunt. He took control of everything, and dished out orders right, left and centre. The only problem was that you need to have a good head on your shoulders if you're going to be a leader. And I was beginning to wonder if Tolik's head was fully in order.

No, don't get me wrong. At first I was quite comfortable when I was on stakeout duty. I chose a spot in our yard where I had a good view of Lyonikha's place. I brought out a rocking chair to sit on — fortunately it was in the shade — and began the job of keeping a close watch on my neighbour's comings and goings. After some time, however, her constant moving about, doing this and that, going here and there, aroused rebellious thoughts in me about the purpose of all this time-wasting and about the state of Tolik's mental health. After all, it was his idea. Put yourself in my position. How long would you last if you had a day like this one? I had only just sat down, when Lyonikha ran off in the direction of the oval lake; I suspected that she was going to see to her cow, but what if she were to run off to the cemetery once she'd tied the cow up again? So I hurried after her, hiding behind the bushes. When she returned, she spent a bit of time in the house, but I had hardly had time to get my breath back when she set off again, this time on her bike. So — what else was I supposed to do? — I had to follow her again, this time to the dachas. I didn't have a bike, so it was just as well that she rode slowly... Then off we went again to the cow, and after that to the allotment (fortunately for me, our allotments are next to each other, so I was able to use the chance to do some weeding

in the rows of carrots). When Yarashykha called on Lyonikha
to let her know that they were earthing up the potatoes with
a tractor down by the river (thanks to Lyonikha's deafness I
could hear perfectly well what was going on), and they went
off, I was unable to limp after them. I consoled myself with
the thought that they would come back together; someone like
Lyonikha would not head for the cemetery while Yarashykha
was around. I was correct in my assumption, but then I had
to tag after the object of my surveillance once more when she
went to the station, and hang around while she tried to sell
her apples there. Don't forget that in the midst of all this I still
had to feed the animals, including the pig, and rake over the
mountains of earth that the wretched animal had dug up, and
you'll have some idea of why by the time the evening gloom was
beginning to descend on the fir trees of the Dobratyche forest
I was incapable of dragging one foot after the other... Imagine,
then, my feelings when — after I had seen Lyonikha milk her
cow — the indefatigable woman got her bike out, hung a bag
on the handlebars and rode off.

On this occasion she rode along the path that runs right
by the railway. There was nothing for it but for me to follow
immediately behind her. If Lyonikha had turned round, she
would certainly have seen me, but I was banking on her not
looking round. It's not so easy for a seventy-year-old woman
to twist herself around when sitting on the saddle of a bike. It
was beginning to look as if my persistence would pay off at last.
She was obviously going to the cemetery; once there, I planned
to run down the slope and somehow make my way along the
bottom. Lyonikha's deafness gave me a big advantage — there
was no chance of her hearing me. I had seen her goodness knows
how many times happily riding her bike at her usual solemn
pace along the narrow Dobratyche road, followed by a Ford or
a Mazda from the dachas, honking away, desperately trying —
and failing — to get past.

When we were close to the cemetery, Lyonikha began to

brake — using her foot, like all the women do round here. This was a sign for me to get off the path and plunge into the bushes. She got off the bike, looked around and then went down the path that led to the cemetery. My heart was thumping with excitement and the effort of trying to get my breath back. She made her way stealthily over the fence, and still looking cautiously round, once again climbed in through the window of the abandoned vault, taking her bag with her. I watched her through the window. She drew the stone slab to one side, undid the padlock and opened the door. She bent down and disappeared into the blackness beyond. Then it was my turn to wriggle through the window and creep towards the door, trying not to make any noise. I took the piece of plasticine that I had prepared beforehand out of my pocket and removed the key; it was a good thing that Lyonikha had left it in the padlock. It was then an easy task to take an impression of the key and put it back. Job done!

Nothing disturbed the utter stillness of the evening.

I didn't have a watch with me; it seemed like an eternity before Lyonikha appeared in the window again. We returned to Dobratyche by the same route that we had come. Once back in the house, I phoned Tolik and, in the course of our general chat about nothing in particular, threw in our previously arranged code phrase: "No, there aren't any good mushrooms at all, but I did find an orange oak bolete." That evening Tolik dropped by to pick up the impression of the key. He solemnly thanked me for successfully executing my allotted task. Well, didn't I say that he was starting to behave like a leader?

Before going to sleep I lay in bed with my legs up the wall. Granny had taught me long ago that this was the best way to relieve pain and fatigue in the legs.

SASHA AND DZIMA
DO THEIR JOB

"Hold it here, Ala Anatoleuna." Dzima passed me a piece of wood through the hole. "Good, now shift it this way a bit."

Dzima and I were repairing the roof. There was a big hole in the shingle that we simply hadn't noticed because it hadn't rained for such a long time; last night an owl had got into the attic through it and given us all a scare. It had made a tremendous racket, flapping frantically round the roof space and causing destruction with its wings. It was just as well that the lads were by now sleeping in the house, otherwise Ulia and I would have lain awake all night, trembling in fear and then not daring to go up to the attic to see what had happened. Blinded by the light from our torches, the owl landed heavily on the old loom and Sasha managed to throw a large piece of cloth over it and carry it outside. The owl's claws looked really threatening; there are no words to describe the expression on its face with that sharp, crooked beak, but perhaps the bird was thinking to itself "What should I do? Bite the bastards or crap myself in fear?"

In short, early in the morning Dzima and I had climbed up to repair the roof. While working together we got talking.

"I was in the security services for ten years. They came recruiting while I was still a student at the polytechnic, they offered me a job and I agreed. Here, hold this piece of wood right here, that's it. I agreed. I graduated from the special KBB school and joined their Mensk office. Everything was going fine. I was in the narcotics unit and not doing at all badly. I was proud of the fact that we managed to reduce the drug turnover in Mensk by 28 percent. Then, all of a sudden, about ten years ago, I began to get the feeling that things weren't going right. No, I don't mean that piece of wood, just continue to hold it there. I mean not going right in the sense of what our department was doing. Of course I already knew, back when I started working there, that the KBB had a very specific job to do, but at least the people who worked there were professionals and, by and large, perfectly normal. Then gradually everything started to change. The people I had respected simply left. They disappeared into thin air. Some went quietly, others slammed the door loudly behind them. There were even some who went abroad and sought political asylum. The types who came in their stead were more like..."

"Wild pigs?" I asked, remembering Stepan Fyodorovich.

"Wild pigs?" There was surprise in Dzima's voice. "No, more like wild dogs. A real witch-hunt began. I was stunned by the way in which they tried to turn us into zombies. Even worse was the number of my colleagues who allowed themselves to be zombified and would begin to foam at the mouth as soon as they heard the command to attack. Then individuals that I can best describe as fixers started to take over. One of them took charge of the department I was working in. Quite by chance I discovered that the drug hauls we seized were finding their way back on to the market, but through entirely different channels. It was then that I handed in my notice."

"You didn't try to stay on and fight?"

"You can't fight the KBB from inside. You either play by the rules or you don't play at all. I decided to get out before I became involved in anything risky. I drifted around for a bit and then I met Sasha. He was already working for Harabets. So I joined him."

"What did Sasha do before that?"

"He was in military intelligence. We don't know each other all that well. Oh, look, there's your neighbour over there."

I was lying flat on the roof; from there I had a good view of Dobratyche from an unusual angle. Mishyk the Poet was walking slowly somewhere along the bottom of the hill, holding his head down. He didn't spot us.

There were really lovely clouds floating over the Dobratyche forest. I was afraid of crashing down to the ground, so I crawled across the roof tiles like a fly, feverishly hanging on to the ladder all the while. I was just edging myself into the right position to climb down when I turned my head, quite by chance. I froze. Beneath the hill, at the spot where one of the springs in our area bubbles to the surface, a living circle of people was whirling round and round. There were boys, some sporting pudding-basin haircuts, others with a topknot of long hair at the back, and well-built country girls with broad smiles and happy eyes, dancing in pairs, holding each other by the hands and singing along. I realised that they were dancing the Krakowiak. The sounds came to me through the trees, I could hear the Polish words, the ground beneath the dancers' bare feet was damp, and the grass all around them was lush and green — I could see the raindrops still on it. I had once again fallen through a hole in time; these must of course be people from the years between the two world wars. Who were they? I couldn't tear my eyes away from the circle of dancers, afraid that it would disappear, just as all my previous visions had vanished. How beautifully they all moved, their bare feet softly beating the rhythm on the ground, their voices weaving the melody in perfect harmony! I noticed one girl who was not dancing, but laughing at something. Were they fellow countrymen of mine from Dobratyche or did they come from somewhere else? Granny must be here somewhere, otherwise why am I seeing this vision? But where is she? Yes, there she is, I can see her now, that good-looking girl in a white headscarf tied under her chin and a pinafore. Her eyes are sparkling and her smooth face seems to be shining with happiness. The lad she's dancing with holds her hand up high, and has his other hand round her waist. Perhaps that's Stsyapan? Or maybe my grandfather. No, it can't be my grandfather, they say he had black hair and was round-shouldered, whereas this lad has fair hair and stands upright. And is that Lyalka? Dark, round eyes, nicely-shaped calves — tucked into her belt was a sprig of dogroses. The dancers turned all at the same time and the circle went in the opposite direction. Good God, how wonderful this all is! Can I really be the only one seeing and hearing it? I looked cautiously at Dzima and made a fatal error. Dzima was concentrating on tightening a screw and had obviously not heard anything. When I looked back, there was nothing to see or hear. I nearly groaned out loud in disappointment. Why, oh why did I take eyes off the scene? Next time — if there ever is a next time — I won't budge, I won't move a muscle. The spring was still bubbling just like in the vision, but nothing else remained. A deep sigh escaped my lips of its own accord.

"Is it too heavy for you to hold? Here's Sasha, he can take over."

Sasha really had just emerged from the forest, carrying a hefty stick on his shoulder.

A minute later he was already up on the roof with us, and I got ready to go down the ladder.

"Wait a sec, Ala Anatoleuna. Tell me, how do you get on with that neighbour of yours, Mikhas Yarash?" Sasha asked.

"We're neighbours, I get on with him well enough," I shrugged my shoulders. "When he was little and I was a girl, I looked after him a few times whenever his mother was busy at work and couldn't get away. But he never dedicated any of his poems to me."

"He's spying either on you or on Ulia Anatoleuna."

"What?"

"Spying on you, keeping an eye on you, grassing on you, if you like."

"What makes you think that?"

"In the forest I overheard him talking to somebody on his mobile, he mentioned that he had seen how you were nearly hit by a boomerang yesterday. Almost word for word this is what he said: 'While I was keeping the target under observation, an assault on Babylyova and Barysevich was attempted with the aid of a boomerang.'"

"Mishyk spying? I don't believe it," I blurted out.

"No, there's no doubt that he is spying on you. All we have to do now is to find out who he's reporting to."

"I'll just go straight up to him and ask him. I'm sure it's all a misunderstanding."

"I wouldn't do that," Sasha shook his head. "He won't tell you the truth. You will simply put him on his guard; he'll realise that he's been unmasked. Whoever or whatever is behind this, we have to tread very carefully. Quietly. We'll keep tabs on him ourselves. I reckon we'll soon find out what it's all about."

FROM AMERICA
WITH SORROW

Never mind this terrible drought that seems like it's never going to end — every morning in Dobratyche comes as a gift from Heaven. On the horizon the sky grows lighter. The pearl-tinted clouds part at the point where the sun is about to rise. The air is cool and fresh. In the village houses the women light the stoves — blue flames for gas, yellow for wood — and the dough sizzles in the frying pans, ready to turn into pancakes. It's high summer, but there are still some birds singing in the bushes nearby.

A man was coming up the path that leads to our house. At first I thought it must be one of the townies from the dachas, but when he came closer I shrieked with joy and ran out to meet him. It was Valeryk the Uruguayan — although it would be more accurate to call him Valeryk the American. He was the only one of the natives of Dobratyche not to have been incorporated by Russia. The United States took him instead. Like his great-grandfather before him, he went out into the world to seek his fortune, but — unlike his great-grandfather — he didn't come back. Great-grandfather Ivan chopped down sequoias in the jungles of the Amazon, and he often used to get beaten up by the local macho types because of his excessively pale-skinned and blonde-haired wife. Valeryk, by contrast, was some kind of manager and had married a local woman — I don't know anything about the colour of her hair or skin. I last saw Valeryk eight years ago, and the time before that we were both at the school-leavers' ball. And now here he was, walking towards our house along the needle-strewn path, and smiling. With his knobbly forehead and broad, flat nose you could tell he was from Dobratyche, only his skin had been tanned by winds that were gentler than the ones we get round here. In fact, everything about him screamed that he was "not from round here" — the shorts he was wearing, the expression on his face, the slip-on shoes on his foreign-looking feet and legs. I took it all in at a single glance before putting my arms round his neck and hugging him tightly.

"Why don't we have women like you in America? God, how I miss eyes like yours."

"What about you? Are you bringing ice down from the mountains?" I could still remember the conversation we had had more than thirty years ago, when he told me that he was off to the Americas to look for the ice the Indians used to bring down to the valley from the tops of the Andes, because they regarded it as one of the greatest miracles there was. "What kind of eyes is it you miss so much? Tiny, sleep-deprived and with fat all around them?"

"I don't even know if such mountains exist. And as for the eyes... Over there in the States the eyes really are surrounded by cholesterol deposits. Everyone has them, except actors in Hollywood and on Broadway. What do you expect; loads of money, loads of cheap food, and the result? Waists broader than shoulders."

We sat ourselves down on the bench under the pear tree.

"Do you want some whisky?" I asked. "I've even got some ice."

"Absolutely not," replied Valeryk with a dismissive wave of the hand. "That's a drink for my father. In America we treat ourselves to the occasional beer and coke, but even then only in the evenings. Just let me have some water from the well. All I do here is drink the water, it's the taste of my childhood."

Valeryk really did drink the water like a connoisseur drinking the finest cognac, one sip at a time, not letting the cup out of his hand. We sat talking softly.

"So how are things in America that, oh, I shall never see?!" I joked, quoting a line from the song "Gudbai Amerika" that the group Nautilus Pompilius used to sing at the end of the eighties. "How's democracy doing? Still flourishing?"

"There are black clouds hanging over America, just as there are here," Valeryk answered in all seriousness. He had obviously not understood my joke.

"Can you see any black clouds hanging over us?"

"Do you mean you can't?"

"I don't know," and I took a swift look at the sky. "Maybe I can."

"My parents have aged terribly. Dad drinks, mum cries all the time. My sister's too busy with her family, and I can't take them back to America with me," said Valeryk, holding his head down.

I was struck by this involuntary, boyish gesture.

"Why not? Won't they get visas?"

"I simply can't take them. It would be just like killing them. They wouldn't be able to live there. My wife and children don't speak any Ukrainian or Belarusian."

"I get the point about your wife and children, but they wouldn't be speaking Ukrainian or Belarusian if they lived here either. I understand what you mean, though."

"Do you? I'm afraid you don't. Living overseas, among people who are completely different, you just feel so homesick."

"Believe me, Valeryk, you get the same kind of feeling even if you live here. I think the reason your sister Halya hasn't taken your parents to live with her in Brest is not that she doesn't want them or love them. It's simply that she's also aware that it would kill them. It's unfortunate, but there's nothing you can do about it, wherever you live. They're looking Death in the face. They live, just waiting to die, and that's terrifying. That's why your dad drinks and your mum cries."

Valeryk went on. "I even feel that my own children aren't

really mine. They look like me on the outside, but that's all. I don't even love them. All I have to do is leave the house and I forget all about them — out of sight, out of mind. I don't even have the feeling that I'm somehow weighed down by my kids."

"Why should you think that's a bad feeling to have? No one should ever weigh you down, especially your own children. But it's not a topic I'm qualified to talk about. I don't have any children and, come to think of it, I never really had any parents either."

"I'm sorry."

"It's OK, don't worry."

"So you don't think I'm to blame, do you?"

"For going to America? Of course not. But you know, all of us — you included — we all have a load of guilt to bear. Quite what we're guilty of, I'm not sure, but I am certain that we're guilty. You yourself talk about black clouds. They don't hang in the sky over the innocent..."

Valeryk was silent for a moment, and then said, in quite a different tone, "I've brought a present for you." He dug around in his pocket. "Here, look at this. It's a German map of this area from the World War I. Just look at the detail, and here — someone's written on it."

I bent over the map. It was well preserved, despite its age, probably because it was printed on oilcloth rather than ordinary paper. The placenames were in Latin script with German-type spellings that reproduced the pronunciation exactly: Dobratytschy, Jablotschyn, Granne. In the villages even individual houses and barns were marked. Farmsteads that I knew nothing about were placed on the banks of rivers that had long since dried up. The handwritten notes had been made by some German officer; Valeryk translated them for me: 'Village-owned field here, make detour one kilometre to the south', 'Russian line of defence', and the like. It was interesting to examine the map, of course, but I couldn't imagine that this product of German geodesy would be of any more use to us than it had been to the Kaiser's troops back in 1914.

Valeryk sat with me for a long time, until the senior Uruguayan came to fetch him. He was already in a merry mood and singing. The old man sang me a few jolly refrains and then took his son home.

IT'S BETTER TO BOW DOWN AND WORSHIP YOUR OWN ARSE

The conversation with Valeryk touched me deeply. Valeryk was one of us, he was from Dobratyche and we don't talk much. We're not like Dostoevsky's heroes who ramble on and on in monologues that last for three chapters. The fact that Valeryk had started talking like that at all must mean that there was something hurting deep inside. That's not surprising, though, is it? Doesn't everyone feel some kind of guilt about their parents or, in my case, my granny?

Granny was afraid of dying. Every one of us must presumably, at a certain time or age, feel themselves alone with their fear of death, even if they have been longing for death to come. She often used to start on about how much she wanted to die, how difficult it was for her to go on living, and then she would look at me as if she was hoping, in the very depths of her soul, that I would comfort her by saying "What are you talking about, granny, you're going to live for ever." How can you possibly comfort this final fear? In spite of everything granny never agreed to come and live with me or with Ulia, and she loved Ulia more than she did me. She was a strong, hard woman, and here she stayed, alone and lonely, but ever faithful to her favourite saying "It's better to bow down and worship your own arse, rather than someone else's head", always chopping wood and lighting the fire. Perhaps she never would have died, perhaps she would have gone on holding the world on her shoulders, but somebody poisoned her.

I lived my whole life with her, but I didn't really know her at all. She never shared her thoughts with me, and never took any interest in what I was doing. She never consented to come and stay with me for the winter, or simply to come on a short visit, and it's only now that I have come to realise why: she didn't think of me as her *real* granddaughter. She didn't regard Ulia as her real granddaughter either — and she never went to see her — but granny was always a little more gentle with her. Perhaps Ulia reminded her somehow of what she had been in her younger years. Nevertheless, it was a fact that she didn't see us as in any way connected to her, and placed none of her hopes in us. Tangled up in the threads spun by time, bound with the cords that emanate from the land, inextricably tied with ropes to the rains and frosts, she knew that she, Makrynya, was the last of the line, and that the burden of our entire family was now resting on her. She knew that no one would help her or come to her rescue and that the threads, cords and ropes would snap under the weight at any moment.

She knew that we were *different*.

I DON'T EVEN
HAVE A CATAPULT

Kukal rang again. I can already recognise his voice.

"Well then, Ala Anatoleuna, how are you feeling? How did you like the bowl with peaches? Hallo, why don't you say something? Ala Anatoleuna!!"

So Kukal knows that it was me who went to see him in the café that day, and not Ulia!

"Yes, I'm here, but I don't understand what you are talking about."

"Oh yes, you do, you understand perfectly well what I'm talking about. I think we need to meet again. Not at your place, and you can guess why, and not at that café where we were last time. As it turned out, that can also be a dangerous place. Let's meet in the 'Goliath' this time — I've got my own people there..."

"Weren't you supposed to be going out of town for three months? Or have you come back already? To put it bluntly, I don't want to meet you."

"Believe me, I was set up. That's one of the reasons why I would very much like to meet you. And I also have some news about a certain person..."

"About my sister?"

"I can understand your irony. I can also explain that particular episode, but it would be better if we were to meet. No, I have some news about your grandmother, or more precisely, about her death. I was mistaken about you, when I was under the impression that I was talking to your sister, but I don't think I'm making a mistake now..."

Early next morning Khvedzka drove me right up to the doors

of the 'Goliath', the poshest restaurant in Brest. Zarnitskaya had insisted on this.

"Khvedzka will take you in the pick-up. He may be useful, you never know," she said firmly when I phoned to tell her about Kukal.

We got to the 'Goliath' very early, somewhere around half past nine, so I decided to stay inside the vehicle until it was time to meet Kukal.

"Look, while you're waiting here, I could just run quickly over to the bazaar where they sell car parts, I've been wanting to get hold of a new pair of windscreen wipers for ages, but couldn't get round to it, what do you think?" asked Khvedzka.

"Go on," I agreed. "I'm not going to go in there for another thirty minutes."

"OK, I'll be back here in half an hour," and Khvedzka ran off.

His back had literally only just disappeared round the corner when Kukal's black Merc rolled smoothly up to the pavement and parked next to the pick-up. The King of Brest stepped out. One of his young thugs emerged from the restaurant to greet him.

I had no desire for Kukal to see that I had arrived early and was waiting for him, so I bent down as low as I could in my seat in order not to be seen from the outside.

I heard Kukal's stern voice: "You're going to drive down to Dobratyche right away, pick up that daft old biddy and her loony daughter and take them you-know-where. Watch it! No foul-ups, no loose ends!"

"Of course, Ivan Dmitrevich. Don't worry. It'll be a nice, clean job. Consider it done."

"Then come back straight to me."

I sat up straight.

Kukal strode off into the restaurant and the thug he'd been talking to was just getting into his jeep.

They were talking about the two Lyalkas! They're going to kill them. What the hell do I do? Phone someone? Who?

Ulia's not around, and I don't even know the Uruguayan's phone number. He doesn't sit around in the house anyway! Should I run and look for Khvedzka? But he could be anywhere in the car bazaar, and it covers a huge area. Should I wait for him? But it'll be half an hour before he gets back, and by that time Kukal's hired killer will have finished off the two Lyalkas. Should I go straight to Kukal and try to scare him by saying that I heard what he said and I'm going to the police? He'd just laugh in my face. There's no alternative: I've got to drive down there myself. My only experience of driving a car was a month's practice twenty years ago. Thirty days after I received my licence I drove into a wall when I was a bit under the influence. Anton solemnly tore up my licence on the spot and never let me get behind a steering wheel again.

I stared wildly at the key that Khvedzka had left in the ignition. The keyring was still shaking slightly. My heart was thumping. Would I be able to drive that far? There was no time to have any doubts: I couldn't allow these bandits to murder my neighbours. Que serà, serà, but I've absolutely got to do this.

I scrawled "I've gone back to Dobratyche. A." on a scrap of paper, placed it on the pavement and weighed it down with a handful of earth I took from a nearby flowerbed. I got into the driver's seat, telling myself to get a grip and try to remember what I've got to do now. Ah, that's it, turn the key. The pick-up lurched sharply forwards and died. No, that's not right, you have to put it in neutral first, then push the clutch down, at the same time pressing gently on the accelerator, and don't forget to turn the wheel, otherwise you'll drive straight into the back of the Merc. The engine roared, but the vehicle stayed put. Oh, sod it, I need to put it in gear first. Sweet Jesus, I'm going to crash right into Kukal's Merc. The engine began to growl quietly to itself. Oh, bugger, what do I do next? I took my foot off the clutch too quickly and the pick-up stalled, with its snout right in the middle of the roadway. On the fifth attempt I managed to get it going.

And so, by fits and starts, I drove off. I was being assailed by several problems all at once: how to get to Dobratyche before Kukal's thug, how to avoid hitting anybody, how not to fall into the clutches of the police — how would I explain to them why I'm driving without papers for the vehicle and with no licence. Will Khvedzka find the scrap of paper, or will he raise a hue and cry because the truck's been stolen? And how, for God's sake, do I change gear?

I completely forgot about minor details, like signalling before making a turn.

Oh, you my readers, who take your gleaming new Beemer just to drive down to the nearest convenience store to buy a loaf of bread, you will never be able to understand me! Feverishly gripping the steering wheel, pressing hard on the accelerator and not daring to shift up from third, I drove as fast as I could out of the city. A thick cloud of black exhaust fumes spread across the road behind me. Passers-by looked up when they heard the roar the pick-up was making; even when I stopped at a red light I kept my foot hard down on the accelerator so as not to let the engine stall on me.

That I managed to escape the city at all was little short of a divine miracle in itself.

It was only when I was on the country road that I dared shift into fourth. I succeeded! I pressed the pedal down to the floor and sped away.

I might just be in time. I reckoned with the likelihood that Kukal's thug would take the asphalted highway that goes in an arc towards the border with Ukraine. There was another, older road; it was much shorter but in a poor state of repair. Not many people knew about it, so it wasn't used very much. This was the road along which I was now racing. The road runs between empty fields. There were no pedestrians and no on-coming traffic. Now at least I could wipe the sweat from my forehead. And then a thought suddenly struck me: how was I going to defend the two Lyalkas? Have a fight with this thug? What with? I remembered that Anton always used to keep a small axe under the driver's seat, in case it came in handy when driving. Perhaps Khvedzka has something like that? Without taking my right foot off the accelerator, I tried to feel around under the seat with my left foot, but all I managed to do was lose my backless clog. Anyway, what use would an axe be against the pistol this bandit's got? If I get there before Kukal's men, I will at least be able to hide my neighbours somewhere, but what if the thugs get there first?

I had no time to think. I was already racing into Dobratyche, and a moment later I could see Lyalka's house.

The silver jeep was already standing there in the yard.

The young slob who had been talking to Kukal was dragging Lyalka senior along the ground towards it. Her legs were trailing behind her over the dry sand, like swollen blue logs. There was another slob pushing Lyalka junior into the jeep.

It was at that moment that I realised I couldn't stop. I had completely forgotten how to brake! The answer came in a flash. I was driving really fast. It was this that saved the two women's lives, plus the eagerness of Kukal's helpers to protect their lovely car.

I stuck my head out of the window — just as well it was already open, I would never have been able to open it by myself — and yelled as loudly as I could:

"I'm going to smash into your car! Run! The brakes have failed. I'll smash the car! Get out of the way!"

All heads were turned when they heard me yell. The bandits' reaction was instantaneous; they leapt into the jeep and sped forwards.

I missed hitting them right in the backside by no more than about thirty centimetres. The jeep hurtled away quite literally from under the nose of my elderly Russian-built pick-up. The jeep's engine was obviously much more powerful than mine, but even so I was able to keep up with them. If we had been on the asphalted road, then they would easily have been able to get away much faster. As it was, I was chasing after them along the old Dobratyche road, little more than a sand track with pebbles and deep ruts. I was being thrown around in the cabin, but I kept my foot down on the pedal. I couldn't even think of leaving the road — the waves of dry sand that were being churned up on both sides of the road as we hurtled out of the village were replaced by ditches and mounds that had been specially dug as military fortifications back when the communists were still in power. At the speed we were driving any attempt to veer off the road would have meant ending up on the roof in a ditch. Even I could understand that. So how was the chase going to end? I couldn't go on chasing them indefinitely, could I? I had just started to think about this when a hand holding a pistol appeared out of the jeep window and fired a shot at me!

It must have been the fright, but I suddenly remembered how to brake. More precisely, my feet remembered; they instinctively pressed the right pedals and the pick-up stopped with a jerk. I hit my head against the windscreen with such force that later a bump came up on my forehead.

The jeep disappeared into the distance. Through the open window I could feel the dry heat and hear the chirping of the crickets and the trembling rustle of the aspen leaves above the ditches.

After four attempts at a three-point turn on the narrow road, I succeeded in getting the pick-up to face the opposite direction. A bit more practice and I'll be ready for figure driving championships!

When I got back to Lyalka's place, Lyalka junior was trying to pick her mother up off the ground. I braked quite smoothly and got out.

"Auntie, I'll take you to our place now. Those crooks might be back. Come on, Lyalka, let's try to lift her together."

Lyalka senior could only groan; she seemed to have lost the power of speech altogether. Somehow, with Lyalka junior's help, I managed to get her into the pick-up. She was really heavy, just like all sick people. I instructed Lyalka junior to run over to

our place. Once back home I left old Lyalka in the pick-up —
without her daughter's help I would never have been able to
lift her on my own — and raced for the phone. I quickly found
Kukal's number in the list of received calls and pushed the right
buttons. Kukal himself answered.

"You bastard," I shouted, "I'm going to phone Ulia and a
friend who works on *Narodnaya Volya* (People's Will)*, and if
anything happens to me or my neighbours, they'll raise such a
stink! You're not going to get out of this one. I have proof. I've
got it all on video: that conversation you had with your thug,
how they were dragging old Lyalka into the jeep and how they
shot at me. Ulia and my friend will go to the police, to the public
prosecutor, to the United Nations if they have to. Just try and
touch anyone from Dobratyche again and you'll regret it!" and I
slammed the phone down without waiting for a reply.

Of course, it was probably not very sensible to talk to so
widely respected a man as *Ivan Dmitrevich* in that manner, but
what was I to do in the circumstances? David had a sling in his
fight with Goliath, but I didn't even have a catapult against the
owner of the 'Goliath' restaurant. The only weapons I possessed
were the burning inner rage that I had inherited from my
ancestors and the despair that had accumulated in me over the
past fifty years. Plus the fact that I wasn't clinging to life.

* *Narodnaya Volya*: an opposition weekly newspaper.

DEATH HANGS OVER DOBRATYCHE

Lyalka senior took a serious turn for the worse and we had to call for a doctor from one of the private clinics in Brest. Lyalka was unable to move and couldn't speak.

"Stroke," was the doctor's diagnosis after he had examined her. He began to write out a whole pile of prescriptions.

When we had left the house the doctor looked round to make sure that Lyalka couldn't hear him, and added in response to my question:

"God knows, it's often difficult to pinpoint the exact cause of a stroke. Maybe it's just her age, perhaps she's been through some kind of stress or she's become overanxious about something. But you should know that she has absolutely no chance of recovery. Be prepared for the worst. Only a miracle..."

But no miracle ever came. Lyalka died the next day.

This was the second funeral we had had in Dobratyche that summer. And it was much worse than the first.

Lyalka junior watched calmly as the women washed her mother, dressed her, put her in the coffin and then put a candle in her hands. She stood calmly in the church and at the cemetery — until the moment when the gravediggers started filling in the grave. Then she became really disturbed, hurled herself at the gravediggers, grabbed the spades out of their hands and threw them to one side. She jumped into the grave and began to throw out handfuls of the sand that had landed on the lid of the coffin. She then tried to prise open the lid itself. She wanted her mother to rise from the dead. We all stood, rooted to the spot in shock. Ulia, who was standing next to me, suddenly burst into loud sobs. Valeryk the Uruguayan and the other men at the funeral came to their senses first, rushed at Lyalka and pulled her out of the grave. She fought and struggled to get away, but finally they managed to bundle her into a car, so that the young priest — who was standing there observing the scene with a sheep-like expression on his face — could complete the burial service.

The intention was that after the funeral Lyalka's relatives were going to take her to a nursing home — there was no way she could look after herself, and none of them were able to take her in. However, it didn't work out as planned. She refused to be put into another car. When the relatives started discussing what to do next and took their eyes off her for a second, she simply ran away. They couldn't find her anywhere and towards evening they went their separate ways home.

Early next morning we found Lyalka junior sitting on the ground in our yard; next to her was the body of her mother. She had dug her up overnight. The dead woman's arms, which yesterday had been folded neatly across her chest, were now twisted behind her back, her legs were spread over the grass with the soles of her feet turned outwards... Rigor mortis had given way to the next phase of decomposition...

While Ulia was phoning Brest, I fed Lyalka. She wouldn't leave her mother, so sat eating next to the corpse. How had she been able to carry the body so far? Either Lyalka senior had become lighter after death, or insanity had given Lyalka junior inhuman strength... Watching Lyalka greedily gulping beetroot soup alongside her dead mother, I felt as though I was going out of my mind. The relatives returned, their numbers strengthened by a brigade of orderlies from the psychiatric hospital. Lyalka took off into the forest as soon as she saw them, and once again it proved impossible to find her. The relatives took the body away for reburial.

When we were at last left on our own, Ulia had a gloomy prediction to make: "Now we're going to have her dump her mother's body in our yard on a daily basis. It won't stop her even if they put a large block of granite on the grave."

Ignoring her words, I went out on to the veranda and took the whisky from behind the fridge. My sister said nothing, and I swallowed the burning liquid straight from the bottle until I felt I had had enough. Then I groped my way along the wall to my room, reached out for the bed, collapsed on it and switched off.

EVERYONE CAN HAVE
THEIR SAY

We were having breakfast: me, Ulia, our two bodyguards, Sasha and Dzima, and Khvedzka. Khvedzka, who was standing in for the still absent Zarnitskaya, had spent the night with the Agravitalika cows. The negligent guard who was supposed to have been watching them (already a 'former' guard, as Khvedzka put it) had allowed the cows to graze on a field of dewy clover. Once the danger had passed Director Charota was so pleased that he presented Khvedzka with some money in an envelope. The amount of money in the envelope put Khvedzka in such a good mood that he called on us very early in the morning to invite us for breakfast. Just so that we didn't throw him out for waking us up so early, he had been to the all-night shop on the frontier crossing and bought a load of tasty things to eat: caviar, salted herrings, smoked chicken wings, pickled cucumbers, shiitake mushrooms and sushi. Obviously it was impossible to resist the sushi and his high spirits.

"Don't bother to get dressed," he shouted, putting out the food hastily on to plates. "What could be better: having caviare and fresh coffee for breakfast in your pyjamas! This will be something for you to remember! Breakfasting Japanese-style. Or maybe European-style. Or American. Whatever. Come and eat!"

"Great! Shamelessly breaking all the rules! Nobody has breakfast like this anywhere." This was Ulia, She looked around to make sure that Lyalka was nowhere to be seen, then stood stretching on the porch. We were all soon infected by Khvedzka's good humour. Let's forget all our problems, at least for a short time.

"Right! This is an original Dobratyche breakfast. I'm getting it patented. Come and get it, I'm hungry," and Khvedzka called us to the table as soon as he had finished setting out the food.

And so we ate our breakfast: in our pyjamas, with fresh coffee, caviare and other delicacies. Khvedzka was unstoppable; he came out with one joke after another. The cool of the early morning reached us through the open doors, and the dogs were busy running round the yard. They had been let off their chains in honour of Khvedzka's arrival.

"Death to anyone who doesn't love us," he declared. "Long live the stork, our very own Belarusian bird!" and again he raised his mug, and the aroma of fresh coffee wafted into the Dobratyche forest. "Let's switch on some music."

"Or the TV," Dzima pressed some buttons on the remote. "Only there won't be any music on at the moment, but at least we'll be able to watch Ala Anatoleuna as a star of the TV screen."

Khvedzka, who didn't know anything about this story, looked at me with surprise.

On one of the two days that I spent in Mensk when I went to see Horst, the telephone suddenly rang in my new flat. I thought that it must be for the people who used to live here — I didn't even know the number — so I automatically lifted the receiver, ready to say "Wrong number". But no, as it turned out, it was for me. There was a woman on the phone wanting to speak to me. She said she was from Belarusian TV and had what I thought was an extremely pleasant voice for someone who worked in that particular establishment. She told me she was the editor of some analytical — her word — programme called *Talking on contemporary issues*. They would like to get my opinions on a few matters.

"My opinions?" I could not conceal my surprise. "Why? What sort of opinions?"

"Well, you are the sister of a well-known public figure, and you're a writer... I'm sure it would be very interesting for our viewers to hear your thoughts on what is going on in the country today."

"My thoughts are unlikely to appeal to you. I consider that what is going on in the country today shows a complete disregard for the law."

"Well, there you are, then. You can talk about that."

"But you will never show a programme where I say what I want to say."

"Why ever not? You obviously don't watch our channel very often (that's certainly true, I thought to myself). Everyone can have their say on our channel."

"Can you give me your word, I mean, can you promise that you will cut nothing out of what I say, and that you won't distort my meaning? What kind of questions do you intend putting to me?"

"Of course we can. The question is simply this: what do you reckon the chances are of the incumbent president winning the forthcoming election?"

I phoned Ulia. She advised me to agree to the interview: she reckoned that we should use every opportunity to state our case, but to think very carefully about what we say. We know only too well how the people on Belarusian TV are capable of twisting everything, and of showing that white is not only black, but also a greyish-brownish-raspberry colour as well.

I met with the team that was to conduct the interview beside the river Svislach. The team consisted of a gloomy cameraman, the programme editor — the one who had phoned me — and the programme presenter, an inveterate smoker by the look of her, eyes like saucers, fingertips offering fine examples of nail art. Passers-by gave us a wide berth.

I once again tried to extract from them a solemn promise that my words would not be distorted.

"Don't be so worried. Everything will be fine," and the editor gave me a sweet smile. She had the inevitable blonde hair, striking pink lips and heavy black and brown eye make-up. Her teeth seemed to have been subjected to the attention of a dentist who doubled as an enemy of the state.

"No, no, I want you to give me a clear, firm promise."

"Fine. I promise clearly and firmly."

The specimen with the nail art spat out her chewing gum and shoved a microphone under my nose.

"Tell us, by what kind of margin do you think the current president of our country will win the election?"

"I don't think he will win. They're telling us now on the radio and the TV that he will win with 86% of the vote, but that's complete nonsense. Along with the beatings, arrests, hounding of anyone actively involved in the other candidates' campaigns, it simply shows that the results will be falsified, and the falsification will be crude, blatant and with utter disregard for the people's right to exercise their freedom of choice. I think that in actual fact a large part of the electorate will support the other candidates. Harabets has a real chance of winning the election. I urge everyone to vote for him. In contrast to the current president he has never lied, has never been mixed up in murky scandals and is genuinely concerned for the people of this country."

"That's excellent," said the editor, "OK, it's a wrap. Let's go."

Off they went.

It's today that this "conversation" is due to be broadcast — I checked the programme schedule in the paper. This morning, and then later, at prime time in the evening.

And broadcast it was, much to our "enjoyment".

The topics were all the usual ones. You got the impression that the programme had been cobbled together by idiots for the benefit of mental retards. First there was a parade of women school teachers — all with the same blonde hair colour and with the same hair style, military types in peaked caps, students against a background of drawing boards, construction workers in brand new safety helmets, well-fed looking OAPs and mustaschioed Italian parliamentarians, all of them rabbiting on about how the current president will win, the current president cannot fail to win, the current president is the best, and how we pray to God for the current president to win, blah, blah, blah...

Khvedzka said that he was just going to pop out to the car to get something to stop him being sick, because he could feel the vomit rising in his throat. But he had no time to do it. The programme presenter contorted his face in an effort to wipe off the saccharine smile, put on his serious mien and uttered:

"Our president is a man of such grand stature that even our so-called opposition have no doubt that he will win. As we well know, many members of this opposition are drug addicts and alcoholics, who are prepared to sell their honour and their country for a bottle of vodka or a dirty dollar bill. And there are even women among them, long-standing drug addicts and alcoholics, the sisters Ala Babylyova and Ulia Barysevich. One of them is the election agent of the emissary of the American intelligence agencies, who is striving to fight his way through to the presidential chair. He harbours nefarious plans to become president in order to repay his masters by handing our country's wealth over to them. However, even the election agents of this so-called candidate for election as president are convinced that he has no chance whatsoever of being elected."

Then I appeared on the screen. Do I really look like that? Dark circles under the eyes, twisted, swollen mug. And the mug, hiccuping slightly, mumbled:

"I think the president will win with 86% of the vote. I urge everyone to vote for the president. He has never lied, has never been involved in murky scandals and is genuinely concerned for the people of this country."

Then I disappeared from the screen.

The presenter was back again. "As we can see, even the déclassé elements of our pseudo-intellectual Bohemian subculture realise that it is our president who is the undoubted leader in the present election campaign, and that therefore there can be no doubt of his victory. And now for news from abroad. By contrast to our own dear Belarus, foreign countries continue to be struck by natural disasters. A terrible hurricane has hit the seaboard of the United States..."

Everyone sat thunderstruck. No one looked at me. Khvedzka put his coffee on the table. I could feel my ears turning red.

"I didn't say that."

"In that case I must have said it," and there was a distinctively sarcastic note in Ulia's voice. Her hands were trembling slightly.

"I swear I never said anything like that. I can repeat word for word everything I said, because I've been mulling it over and over again in my mind ever since," and then I told them exactly what I had really said.

"That's it," said Dzima when he had heard my response. "They simply threw out everything they didn't need, and then stuck all the remaining bits together. It's not difficult, and it's easy to touch up anything they took on video to make Ala Anatoleuna look like a goblin. You've got to admire the way in which they used the fact that you're twins. You get the impression that it's Ulia Anatoleuna who's doing the talking."

"I'll take them to court," I said, completely at a loss to know what to do.

"Ha, ha! They'll destroy the tape as soon as it's been broadcast. It'll be impossible to prove anything."

"I'll record it all on tape this evening."

"Recordings like that aren't accepted by the courts as evidence."

"Then I'll simply tear that editor's eyes out."

"That's enough! Stop being silly!" Ulia struck the table with her hand. You've already shown what you're capable of. Enough!"

I jumped to my feet.

"What are you shouting at me for? By the way, I phoned you beforehand, to ask your advice about agreeing to the interview."

"Yes, what a fool I was to advise you to do it. I completely forgot that you bring nothing but trouble, whatever you do.

You simply destroy everything. You're a real destroyer, do you know that? Whether you want to or not, you destroy everything. You've destroyed your own life, and now you're destroying mine. What did God tie us so closely together for? When is he going to rid me of you?"

Ulia grabbed my bottle of whisky from behind the fridge, smashed it against the wall and ran out into the yard.

Everyone sat looking down at the floor.

I realised that my sister was very tired and that her nerves were on edge. I understood just how difficult things were for her at the moment. But that didn't make it any easier for me.

So ended my career as a political commentator.

All the same, I did phone that editor woman, just to give vent to my wrath. She parried my chaotic, hysterical thrusts in a totally calm, unhurried manner:

"I'm afraid that we had some problems with the recording, so for purely technical reasons we had to omit some parts of what you said. However, we didn't add a single word. You really did say everything that was on the broadcast."

These people are not made of marble or of iron.* They're made of rubber.

---

* The reference is to two films by the Polish director Andrzej Wajda: *Man of Marble* (1976) and *Man of Iron* (1981).

A BLOOD-SOAKED RAG COMES TO MY RESCUE AGAIN

A sense of anxiety was being to grow inside me. I wasn't sure about why I was feeling so anxious, but I was, and it was weighing me down. My head was beginning to ache. I crawled quietly down from the roof (this time the lads and I had gone up there to attach a satellite aerial). Sasha and Dzima watched me as I climbed down the ladder.

"Are you feeling OK?"

"Yes, I'm all right, but I think I'll get down. My head's playing up a bit."

Dzima started banging with his hammer again.

I stepped on to the ground. My legs buckled beneath me. I sat on the bench and wiped the sweat from my forehead. My stomach was churning uncontrollably. I felt the blood pouring out of me. The pain eased off a little. The blood flowed in waves, sometimes there was a lot of it, at other times less.

I hadn't had anything like this for about the last ten years.

At that time I hadn't realised what it meant.

In the evening a girl I didn't know delivered a summons for me to appear at the public prosecutor's office. *"Alla Anatolevna Bobylyova is hereby summoned for the purpose of making a statement in connection with charges that have been made against her. You are to appear at the Office of the Public Prosecutor in Brest..."* The girl asked me to sign a piece of paper to confirm that I had received the summons and then departed in the car that had brought her here.

"What's this?" I asked myself, holding the yellowish document in my hand. The question, of course, was rhetorical. "What am I charged with? Is this another piece of their nonsense?"

The following morning found me walking along the recently and expensively refurbished office of the public prosecutor, looking for the right door. Like all the rest of them, the right door was massive, and covered in leather.

"Can I come in? I've been summoned."

From behind the desk there looked up at me a man with dark hair combed back, swarthy skin and a potato nose. He was dressed in an black suit that obviously cost a great deal, but which didn't seem to fit him very well — one size too big, perhaps? Then there was the tie sitting like a red blob on his frontage. His eyes were like bottomless wells. A thought flashed through my mind — "Old Nick in person, coal and fire."

"Citizen Bobylyova? Enter."

I made a few tentative steps into the room and stopped. There were several comfy-looking leather armchairs next to the prosecutor's huge desk, and three well-worn stools against the wall, but I made no move to sit down. I stood and waited for the ashen-faced prosecutor to finish off what he was so intently writing. A few moments later he finished.

"Sit," and he pointed to the ancient stools by the door. I approached the desk and sat in one of the leather chairs.

"Thank you."

The prosecutor raised his head, and the fire on his face took on a different hue; a wave of hatred hit me so powerfully that I involuntarily shrank back in my seat. I had often encountered hate-filled faces like this one over the past few weeks. At the election campaign meetings organised by my sister there would invariably be men in tracksuits and heavily made-up women trying to provoke fights, whistling, spitting and booing whenever Harabets was speaking. The expression on their faces was the same, but then the hatred was not directed at me. I was able to sit back and watch young men from the audience remove the tracksuited troublemakers from the hall, or a young slip of a girl from the campaign team deliver a stinging slap to the face of some painted bitch from the local council, or a frail old lady — you would think one puff of wind would be enough to blow her away — seize the leader of a gang of rowdies from the régime's youth organisation by the ear and drag him out, saying loud enough for all to hear:

"Just you wait, you silly little boy, I'm going to tell your mummy..."

However, the hatred was now aimed directly at me. For a second I thought the prosecutor — *"A.T. Kuleshov, Prosecutor, Brest"*, read the badge pinned to his black suit — would at any moment draw a pistol from its holster and say some thing like "Well, bitch, your final hour has come, pray, if you believe in God!", but he didn't do anything so dramatic. Instead he just stared straight into my eyes, presumably in the hope that I would turn my gaze away from him. I don't fall for that kind of thing.

"Tell me, why have you summoned me here, and in what capacity?" I asked.

"You are accused of the wilful murder of Makrynya Lukashauna Hadun," he replied curtly.

I would have been less astonished if he had in fact drawn a pistol. I had been expecting that he would accuse me of something connected with my helping Ulia in this ridiculous election campaign — like passing myself off as her, or swearing in a public place, or beating a squad of spetsnaz boys to a pulp — it's become a common occurrence for people to be charged with offences like these in recent months. Anything but this bolt from the blue!

"What proof do you have?" my voice must have sounded strangled. I was trying to suppress a lump in my throat.

"I'm the one who asks the questions here."

"What do you mean, then? That I'm not allowed to know what you base your charges on? What happened to the presumption of innocence?"

"Don't be insolent! How dare you talk of innocence!"

"What then?" There was indignation and astonishment in my voice. "Is it not the done thing to talk about such things here?"

The prosecutor narrowed his eyes. The expression on his face became tenser.

"How do you explain the presence of the drug Cardiostom Forte in the coffee the victim drank?"

"How do you know it was present?"

"An search was made, and then a forensic analysis…"

"You made a search in my absence? Without the knowledge of the people who live in the house? That's against the law! And what's more, you need a warrant from the prosecutor to conduct a search!"

"I am a prosecutor, and I issued the necessary warrant! The search was conducted in the presence of properly sworn witnesses, in strict accordance with the provisions of the Procedural Code. The exhumation of the victim…"

"What?! You exhumed my granny?! How could you do such a thing!"

"How could we?" The prosecutor stood and leaned right over me. "Do you take us for fools? Do you think we're complete idiots? You simply wanted to speed up the process of getting your hands on the inheritance, didn't you? But it didn't work out like that, did it? You've been unmasked, and there's no way you are going to be able to wriggle out of it. There's more than enough evidence against you to convince the court of your guilt. I could with complete justification detain you in prison for the duration of the investigation, but there is one highly respected person in Brest who has requested me not to do so, so I will therefore restrict myself to granting you bail on condition that you do not leave the area. Write!" and he shoved a piece of paper into my face. "You, and you alone, carried out this criminal act that you and your sister had concocted together." He was now talking down to me in an unpleasantly familiar way. "The two of you were the only ones to knew that the victim had a weak heart, and only you had the opportunity to put the drug in the coffee. Both of you had a motive for wanting the victim dead, so you could get your inheritance as soon as possible and free yourself of the burden of looking after the old lady. You set it all up so cleverly, didn't you? What was it you were going to say when asked about the death? Something like 'It wasn't me, I wasn't even home when the old girl kicked the bucket'? Unlucky for you that we've got a witness who overheard the conversation you had with your sister. What was it you said? 'The old girl's going on for too long. Time to help her fall off her perch'. I'm certain that in the course of the investigation we'll turn up more incontrovertible evidence. We haven't done a fingerprint analysis yet. That's what will send you to prison, which is just where you deserve to be!"

I was shaking all over when I left the prosecutor's office. Not only as a result of the questions he had asked me — and from them it emerged that I was the murderer — but also because of the photographs that the police photographer had taken after they had exhumed granny and which Old Nick had just shown me. I fell against the wall in a state of complete shock. I looked unsteadily around — and who should I see standing at the far end of the corridor, leaning on the plastic sill of one of the ultramodern windows that had been installed everywhere in this establishment? None other than Milord Kukal himself, gazing at me with curiosity. The realisation came to me — he's the one behind all this! He killed granny and he set up the summons to the prosecutor. And therefore he must be the 'highly respected person' who urged that I should not be detained but released on bail. After all, it isn't possible to conclude a contract of purchase and sale of real estate with someone in jail, but if that someone is out on bail, there's no problem... My eyes were able to see properly again, and the expression on my face literally radiated determination. I still had the picture in my mind of Lyalka senior's body, dug up by her daughter and lying in our yard. I still had the picture in my mind of my granny's body, dug out of her grave and lying on the pathologist's table... And the inner fury of the Haduns, so well-known throughout the area round Dobratyche, let loose a red haze that coloured my vision.

I began to advance on Kukal, walking faster and faster. Without slowing down I bent over in what might be considered an indecent manner, tugged out from under me a blood-soaked rag — Kukal twisted his face in disgust — and without saying a word ran right up to him and hit him across the head with it, just as I had done to the Devil. Unlike the Devil, however, Kukal didn't just crumble and disappear. He fought back. At first he tried to push me away and protect himself from the rag, but when I took aim for his nose with my plaster-covered hand, he gave me a mighty punch to the face which sent me flying backwards some three metres. I slid down the wall to the floor.

Kukal swore loudly, gave me one final kick, spat and quickly ran downstairs.

Covered in the blood that was pouring from my nose and cut lip, tears streaming down my face — as hard as I tried not to cry — and my head still ringing from the blow that Kukal gave me, I lay against the wall of the prosecutor's office, quite unable to stand up. Meanwhile the folk who worked here were bustling to and fro about their business: secretaries tottering along on high heels, men in uniform marching, women of a certain age filing past with their large behinds and extravagant hair-dos. Not one of them came to my aid, not one offered me a hand to help me up, no one even called the policeman who was on guard duty downstairs. Somehow, I don't know how, I managed to get up and literally crawl out on to the street. The tooth that Kukal had nearly knocked out was wobbling loose in my mouth. Passers-by scurried to the edge of the pavement in an attempt to avoid coming anywhere near me. I could hardly make out what was going on around me. I couldn't see very much and shuffled along without knowing where I was going. There was only one thing that kept me moving forwards: the awareness that the very unrespected Mr Kukal was as much blood-spattered as I was, even if the blood was mine rather than his. Come to think of it, though, I had caught him right on the nose — perhaps it's bleeding now... As I stumbled through the streets I came across a pump — one of those pumps that had survived in Brest since the Polish times. I tried to use it to wash the blood off, but to no avail. The water came out only when I pressed the handle down. As soon as I let it go to collect some water in my hands, the flow stopped. I tried this way and that to stretch so as to keep my hand on the handle all the time, but I managed to catch no more than a few drops. I was beginning to feel that these few drops would be my last, in the metaphorical as well as the literal sense, and that I would howl out my desperation for the whole street to hear, when suddenly I heard a familiar voice behind me:

"Here, let me help you."

I looked round. There by the pump stood Aksana. She even looked pleased to see me. She pressed the handle down, there was a gurgling sound and a plentiful stream of water gushed out. With a feeling of relief and joy I put my head under it. I put myself more or less in order. Wiping the blood stains off the plaster took the most time.

"What are you doing here?" I asked.

"I'll tell you in a minute. Let's go and sit over there in that little square, and let's buy an ice-cream. It'll be good for your lip to have something cold put on it, and I can't remember the last time I ate ice cream. For some reason I want to remember what it was like being young."

We bought a choc ice each (and some hygienic things in a nearby kiosk). The passers-by no longer tried to avoid us, but instead cast strange looks at two middle-aged women sitting in the shade on a bench: one with plaster on her hand, a cut lip and a wet head, the other in a dress of the kind OAPs wear, and both of them licking ice cream...

We sat in silence for a bit.

At last Aksana sighed and took my hand: "I need to ask you to forgive me."

"What for? For slashing me with a hoe?" I mumbled. The ice cream eased my swollen lip a little, but all the same I still could not pronounce words clearly. Try to imagine what this would come out like if you had a potato in your mouth. "Don'th wowy. I'fe almosht thothally forgothen abouth ith alreathy, and the cuth hath almosht healdth. Buth thinth then I'fe hadt fingerth broken, a tooth knockedth outh, and my headth almosht shmashed open by a boomerang. Tho you thon't needth to apologithe."

"No, it's not only about the hoe. The fact of the matter is that it's my fault you were called to the prosecutor's office today. Yes, my fault," she confirmed, in response to my raised eyebrows.

CANCER

I now had aches and pains over virtually the whole of my body. The hand beneath the plaster cast throbbed and itched, my lips and nose were still stinging from Kukal's blows, my jaw ached, and in it my loose tooth was dangling like a child's swing. To add to it all, I had severe cramp in the lower belly. Now that the fit of fury had passed, the snake of uncertainty and bitterness was gnawing at my heart. I'm not the terminator. The old dear is fifty years of age. Hidden behind an alcoholic haze she didn't want to see the world, she lacked the strength to carry on and put up with things, she was neither steadfast in faith nor brave in the face of trials... Aksana held my hand and looked at me. It was a long time since we had last seen each other: what did I know about her? Only that for many years we had sat at the same desk in school, that she was the headteacher of our local school, that she had three children and two grandchildren, that she was wearing an old dress that I had seen her mother wear — little roses on a green background (artificial silk, was it?), that on her feet she had a pair of slip-ons with rubber soles. I knew too that her body was still thin, but it had lost some of its suppleness.

"It's cancer," said Aksana, and smiled a wan, unhappy smile. Then she got ahold of herself. "Cancer, you know, it's crazy, you live like you're going to live forever, you worry, you struggle, children, money, and then all of a sudden it hits you: cancer."

"Do you have... a tumour?" I couldn't bring myself to mention the dreaded Big C.

"No, Syarhey. He was diagnosed recently. Although he had already been suffering from frequent headaches for some time. That's why he never drank. Like he said, if he has a drink, his head feels like it's about to burst. Like a fool I even made a joke about it: better to have a headache than lie dead-drunk by some fence somewhere. But the headaches were a sign of his illness. Then — like a tiny snowball rolling down a mountain, the tumour began to grow and grow, blocking his nose, making it difficult for him to breathe, the pressure of it was so great that one of his eyes began to bulge out horribly. Finally he got down from his tractor and went to see the doctor. But it was already too late."

"Oh, God! Why did you let it get that far? Why didn't you both go to see the doctor earlier?"

"That's the question I keep asking myself. But we let it go. I was in the school all the time, I couldn't think about anything else. I come home — the allotment needs watering, there are the cows and geese to feed, the children need your help... There's no time to wipe your nose, have something to eat, or just sit down and talk. And Syarhey and I haven't slept together for ages. Syarhey spent all his time with his vehicles. You know how he is, likes everything to be just right. A perfectionist. There was always something going on, like that drunken idiot Yuzik getting his hand caught in the combine harvester, or somebody stealing the petrol at night, or something else. That's how we lived. A visit to the doctor would mean going to Brest or Rechytsa and losing at least one whole day, if not more. And then — oh yes, I remember, we had an inspection at school, I was absolutely delighted that the school was praised. I flew home just as if I had wings, and there was Syarhey sitting on the porch. I made a joke: has the sun set then? He lifted his head and looked at me. My heart trembled and then seemed to stop. My God, what's wrong with him? He was all skinny and yellow, the expression on his face showed that he was in pain...

It took a month to get his condition diagnosed. The cancer specialist in the provincial clinic — he himself looked like he had cancer and was already knocking on death's door — told me that Syarhey had at most six months to live. 'In situations like this', he said, 'there's not much that drug can do.' I don't know how we drove back home. Our son said at once: 'You should go to the cancer hospital at Barauliany, and see a private specialist there.' Of course we went, and it wasn't entirely in vain. They made some analyses, a scan, ultra-sound, and some other things. The doctor there — one of the senior doctors, in fact, called Henadz Yafimavich — told us: 'Well, I don't have any good news for you. The cancer is already at an advanced stage, I agree with the diagnosis of my colleague in Brest. I can say one thing with complete certainty: that the only treatment we can offer within the limitations of established procedures will be palliative, aimed at relieving as far as possible the sufferings of the patient. But,' and at this point he put his glasses to one side, 'science doesn't stand still. There's a new drug on the market in Europe — Xaratex — which is showing results that give cause for hope, even in conditions such as that of your husband. We are unable to use it in the clinic because it is extremely expensive; a one-month course of treatment costs around three thousand dollars, and the treatment has to last at least a year. However, after twelve to eighteen months the tumours shrink to a size at which it becomes possible to treat them with normal methods, radiation or chemotherapy. Therefore,' he said, 'if your financial circumstances permit, I recommend trying a course of Xaratex. I realise, of course, that when I tell patients about this drug, I make the situation of their families even harder to bear. Nevertheless, I consider it my duty to pass on this information, so that you can then decide... I can only add that, if you do decide to commence a course of treatment with Xaratex, I will personally look after your husband free of charge.'

Ala, love, you may have had to bury your daughter, but at least you never had to face anything like this, knowing that salvation is possible, but just out of reach. I started to do the maths: even if we sell everything — the house, the car, the farm — we might get about thirty thousand. That's not even enough for a year. Then where would we live? What about the children and the grandchildren? There'll be nothing left to leave them. Nothing, not a penny. And we've still got to pay for our daughter's education... No, it's impossible. But then what? Do I just let my husband die, the man I love so much?

Then I start thinking about what he's going to suffer. With me and the children in the house, and not being able to do anything to help him. I remember how our grandma used to scream for days on end while she was dying. So what do I do, get a noose ready? Do I hang myself, or does he hang himself? The night we came back from Barauliany the two of us cried; for the first time in months, probably in a year, the two of us sat together and wept... It was a dark, stuffy night, and there was loud music playing in the neighbours' place. Our house was silent; it could sense that Death was approaching.

Early the next morning I was called urgently to the local education authority. They phoned me at home, because I hadn't gone in to work. I was on autopilot by this time, so I just went to find out what they wanted without thinking. There were two men waiting for me in the director's office, the director — a man of surprisingly few words on this occasion — and someone else. The director said that the other man wanted a word with me and left.

The someone else remained behind. He was fair-haired, with stony features — the kind of face you can never quite recall, however hard you try. He flashed his ID from some special secret organisation. The first thought that came to my mind was that one of the kids in my school must have been caught with leaflets again, and that I was going to get it in the neck. But he started talking about something completely different. He said that I had been under observation for some time. His organisation had noted that I was a conscientious worker with a well-developed sense of responsibility, and that I realised how essential it was for us all to stand together in these difficult times. He also told me that they were aware of my husband's illness... Then he offered me the post of Chair of our local electoral commission. If I accepted, his organisation would find the necessary means to fund my husband's course of treatment with Xaratex. I accepted the offer the moment he finished speaking."

"These types know exactly what they're doing, they're real smooth operators. What organisation was he from? What was his name?"

"That's something I won't tell you. To continue then, he said that he has no doubts whatsoever about me, that he's happy a good-looking woman like me will be meeting up with him regularly, and so on and so forth. I said that I would do everything they ask of me provided they pass me the money for the drug, or the drug itself, as soon as possible. He promised that we would receive the first package on the next day, and the rest every month after that. And he's keeping his promise." Aksana gave a long sigh — not a deep one, but the kind you emit when you're checking to see if your heart hurts. "Henadz Yafimavich has confirmed that there's been a significant improvement in Syarhey's condition. Soon, as you well know, it's going to be pay-back time..."

"What then? What happens once the elections are over? Are they going to give Syarhey a chance to finish his treatment?"

"We agreed initially that they would. But I was called in again recently — this time to the prosecutor's office, where I had a conversation with Kuleshov. He wasn't so pleasant. He has this way of keeping his eyes down and looking at you only when he wants to bore right into you with that scornful stare he puts on. He got straight down to business with me, telling me that he had called me in on the advice of that fair-haired secret service type I was telling you about. Then he told me that he — the prosecutor — was dealing with a dangerous group of flagrant enemies of our country which has recently become active, and that the members of this group were planning all kinds of provocative actions, including bombings and the poisoning of wells and water supplies in towns, all of course aimed at destabilising the current stable situation in the country, and that I know personally two of these dangerous individuals — you and Ulia. Your criminal activities had to be stopped before you trapped a whole lot of young people in your web of intrigue, and before you actually killed anybody."

"And you believed all that drivel and attacked me with the hoe?"

"No, I didn't, I didn't believe a single word of it. Just listen, there's more. It turned out the prosecutor had summoned me because he needed my assistance. Apparently it was in my power to stop your evil doings. All I had to do was to write a statement to the effect that I had overhead you and your sister talking about how it was time for granny to depart this life because she had gone on living for far too long. This would help him neutralise you. He, the prosecutor, is aware that what he is proposing is, strictly speaking, not entirely legal, but when it's a matter of preserving the peace and saving lives, then surely a noble aim justifies any means... He was certain that I understood what he meant. Especially when the completion of my husband's course of treatment depended on my doing what he wanted of me. Etc., etc."

"So that means that the witness for the prosecution whose name cannot be divulged in the interests of security is actually you?"

"It is me. There's no getting away from it. I gave them an inch, and they took a whole yard. I blew up. I refused to write a statement like that, I shouted at the prosecutor and he shouted back. I left the room and slammed the door behind me. But when I was walking along the corridor of the prosecution service building, I realised that there was no escape, I would have to write the statement that the prosecutor wanted, because I could see Syarhey's bulging eye floating in the air before me... And so I went home. I was furious with myself and with all those bastards, the blood was boiling in me. On the next morning I had to go to see the Anisichuk family about their son Sasha, you know — the ones that live on that isolated farmstead outside the village. He had skipped the practical work sessions on the collective farm, because, as he said, he didn't want to waste time on pointless activities. I was walking there through Dobratyche and thinking about what I ought to do now, although the answer was obvious. The fury inside me needed to find a target, and then you suddenly appeared from behind a bush. You know what it's like when you're furious with yourself but you take your anger out on someone else. It's at moments like that that something disgusting, something quite inhuman wells up from deep inside you. It's then that you become capable of hitting a child or smashing a kitten against a brick wall. And that was precisely the moment you turned up. When we came face to face by the allotments, it was you, you alone, who was guilty of all my misfortunes. You sit there in that Mensk of yours, you've got too much of everything, theatres, cafés, trips abroad, but what do we have here? We go for years without knowing what real joy is, then we feel death coming, and there's no alternative, you have to sell your soul cheap to the devil. I'm also a Hadun, I know exactly what kind of fury burns in us... So that's how I came to slash your back with the hoe... I suffered afterwards, I really did. Then I decided what I would do. I would write their bloody statement, but I would let you know what I had done. Before signing the statement I got them to agree to provide Syarhey with the drug for the next nine months. I wanted it for a whole year but we compromised on nine months."

"Well, that's good at least."

"There's nothing good about it, but we have to be satisfied with what we've got. When I heard that you had been summoned to the prosecution service — it took Lyonikha no more than an hour to spread the news around the neighbourhood — I decided to try to warn you. I was a bit late and you had already left for Brest, so I set off after you. I was afraid that they would arrest you, imagine how pleased I was that they let you out. So who did you have a fight with? Surely not with the prosecutor himself?"

"With Kukal."

"With Kukal! So he's involved in this, is he? Scumbags really do flock together, don't they?"

She fell silent, obviously thinking deeply about something.

What did I really know about Aksana, apart from what she had just told me? Just that we had grown up together in Dobratyche. I leant over, put my arm around her, and kissed her with my swollen lips.

"Don't concern yourself any more. We'll get through this. The main thing is to get Syarhey cured. You did the right thing. I would even go so far as to say you did the only thing possible in the circumstances."

"Forgive me."

"There's not going to be any talk of forgiveness. That's exactly what these pieces of shit wanted — to split us up and make us quarrel. We won't surrender."

"Does your shoulder still hurt."

"It's nearly healed. But by God, you've got some strength in you."

Aksana nodded her head in agreement.

"I hope that when Syarhey gets better I will have a chance to show these — as you so elegantly put it — pieces of shit just how strong I am."

Pieces of shit. Sacks of shit. Guts topped off with, in some cases, white hair, in other cases, black hair. Stomachs where their food rots. Bladders full of piss. Pricks living in their swanky new apartments, all freshly tiled with the very latest in kitchen equipment, sweating in their saunas or sitting in their deep leather armchairs. But I'm not going to lose hope. I still have Aksana, Dobratyche and, yes, even Sasha Anisichuk who skips practical work sessions on the collective farm.

I reckoned at the time that all that was enough to make life worthwhile.

We spent a lot of time sitting together on the bench. I told Aksana about the poison in the coffee, the boomerang, Kukal's plans to build in Dobratyche and old Lyalka's death... I was itching to tell her about the treasure — if we found it, there would no longer be the problem of finding money for Syarhey's drugs — but I held back. What if we don't find it? I would have got her hopes up, only to dash them to the ground...

"There's a law of life that's set in stone, truth never dies, as is well-known," murmured Aksana to herself when we were saying our goodbyes.

"What was that?" I had no idea what she was talking about.

"It's a quote from Dubouka*," she explained. "After all, I am a teacher of Belarusian language and literature, it's a couple of lines that just came to me..."

---

* *Uladzimir Dubouka (1900-1976):* Belarusian poet.

TRAP FOR A MIDDLE-AGED WOMAN WHO KICKS HORNETS' NESTS

Getting someone to come to the door of the Brest remand prison is no easy task. This is where I was headed after I had said goodbye to Aksana. After much banging on the little window of the thick iron doors of this institution of the penitentiary system of the Republic of Belarus — the metallic racket must have instilled the fear of God into the neighbourhood and driven away all the fish in the Mukhavets — a police officer on door duty at last peered out at me. He made no attempt to conceal his doubts regarding the request of a suspicious-looking woman to inform the prison governor that a Mrs A. A. Babylyova wished to see him, but he did order me to wait.

About fifteen minutes later the governor himself opened the door. He still looked just as jolly as the last time we met, although I thought he seemed worried about something.

"Anatoleuna! What's brought you here again? Come on in." He admitted me to the 'clink'.

"So, what did bring you here?" he asked me again as he sat me down at the desk in his office. "It's quite rare for someone to come to this place of their own volition. Did you like it here with us?"

"Yes, in fact I did. Could you please put me back in the cell where I was before, and don't let anybody come near until I call to be let out."

He pushed his chair back from the table.

"Wow, you're a strange one, Anatoleuna. You've kicked your

way right into the hornets' nest. What do you want to do that for? Do you actually want to be caught in a trap, and get yourself stung to death?"

So I told this police officer everything. This man in uniform, with his clean-shaven chubby cheeks, neatly trimmed hair and a smile playing round his lips, heard things I had been too ashamed even to tell my sister or Tolik. I told him about the vision I had had in the cell. The sober might regard it as the product of a feverish, alcohol-addled brain, but I was convinced that it was in fact a hole in time, one that didn't open up just by chance. I told him I desperately wanted to find my way back into the hole again. And I had thought long and hard about how to do it, and I had decided that the best way would be to return to the place where the vision had first occurred. (I was afraid to climb up to the roof. In my present condition, when I felt permanently giddy, I would more than likely fall off, but in prison I didn't need to climb anywhere.) I described to him what I had seen and heard on the previous occasion: horses' hooves clopping along in the mist, huge grey sheatfish on the cart, their whiskers drooping in resignation at their fate, the sounds of Yiddish being carried through the fresh, clear air of the riverside...

"So you're certain that it isn't all a figment of your imagination?" he asked after a long pause.

"Absolutely, and even if it is, I still want to see it again. I want to see granny as a young girl. At least I want to try, and for that I have to be in the same place."

He said nothing for a bit, and then:

"Well, all right then, I'll get someone to take you to that cell. Have a try!"

"Thank you! Thank you so much!"

"You can thank me afterwards!" He was trying to cool my enthusiasm. "Perhaps it's best for the person who broke Kukal's nose to spend a bit of time in a prison cell. At least he can't get you here. He shouted to someone in the corridor: "Kaspyarovich, take the lady to cell 23!"

How quickly news spreads in their system!

Once again the door of the cell shut behind me. There they all are — the wooden boards that serve as a bed, the washbasin and the toilet — a real rest cure.

I sat on the grey boards. Maybe I'm being foolish? Here I am. What next? Do I really believe that I'm going to be able to go back to the past, especially since I've set it all up in such an artificial way? All I've done is amuse the prison governor.

With no hope at all of seeing anything I went over to the window.

And it happened. At once. Immediately.

Once more I began to see everything in great detail, without being able to form an impression of the whole scene. Wall of unplastered brick. Dust. Bars made of thick wire. I shifted my gaze to beyond the bars.

The prison yard was gone. The cobblestones that I had hoped to see were no longer there either. My lungs almost stopped functioning for a second; they needed time to grow accustomed to the totally different air that was now reaching them. Everything I could see was so beautiful, more beautiful than anything I had ever experienced before.

There's a stream, bubbling and gurgling as it winds its way across the scene. The water is transparent; in the depths I can see a murky brown colour. There are shoals in the stream where the water tumbles and splashes around rocks. Through the rich green grass next to the stream there run two scarcely noticeable ruts, the signs of a roadway. There are thousands of water lilies dotted along the stream, with their white petals and yellow centres, their leaves like green plates floating on the water. What flowers there are on both sides of the stream! I've never seen anything like them before and have no idea what they're called. There are pink ones, and white ones that look like stars, there are wonderful flowers that remind me of lilac, and lilies with black spots on their petals. Oh yes, over there I can see some flowers I do recognise, they're gladioli. And what are these, are they chrysanthemums? There's something quite miraculous about the light that seems to flow from the sky. Rain has just been falling, the sun is hidden behind light grey clouds. In the light reflected back from the water the flowers take on a fantastic, dream-like quality. Where am I?

A dark red figure has appeared on the roadway, looking for all the world like an unusually large flower. It's a woman. A thin woman of medium height in a dark red dress that appears to hug her waist. I don't recognise the kind of cloth it's made from, and the cut is like nothing I've ever seen before. It's obvious that I've gone further back in time. Her face is framed by a tall, white coif with folds on the sides. There's not a single hair to be seen. Her face is tanned, her eyes are wide open and gleaming. Her forehead is knobbly and her lips are narrow. I could have had a face like that if I had been strong-willed and if I had organised my life properly. Granny could have had a face like that if it hadn't been for radio and the collective farm. My daughter would have had a face like that if she had lived, and if the world had not been sown with sin like tares. I am certain that this woman is a Hadun.

The woman reached a crooked willow and stopped. I could hear the sound of a horse approaching at a gallop from the direction in which she had come. The rider was short and slim; he called out "Whoa" to his small horse, and jumped down from the saddle.

"Ah, Mistress Makrynya, I am so pleased that you have come." The man kissed her hands and pressed them to his chest. I could see the black, uneven edges of their fingernails, even the hairs and pores on their skin.

"Master Staryma, are we doing the right thing by meeting here like this?" she whispered. "What if they find out?"

"Why are you whispering, dear heart? There is no one here."

"True," Makrynya started speaking aloud, and a smile lit up her face. "I have grown so accustomed to the need for stealth."

They were speaking in a language that I could understand

perfectly. That is exactly how the people of Dobratyche spoke, how granny spoke, indeed how I myself used to speak. Just occasionally some words slipped out that I had never heard before. The old tongue that people used to speak in these parts was an addition to our polyphony.

"But why should we be stealthy?" said Staryma gently. "Surely we are doing nothing of which we should be ashamed. We have nothing to hide from God or other people. Mistress Makrynya, let us speak of what matters most. I have called you here for a purpose, away from the town, so that no one will hinder us. Are you prepared to give me an answer? Will you consent to be my wife?"

"I told them at home that I was going to Mlyny."

"Mistress Makrynya, my dearest, will you consent to be my wife?"

"Ah, there is nothing that I wish for more than that." She uttered the words with conviction. "But is it really possible that we should be married?"

"Why should it not be?"

"We are of different faiths. You are a Uniate, I am a Calvinist."

"What of that? In our times every other marriage brings together two people of different faiths. A neighbour of mine recently took a Calvinist girl as his wife, and last spring Prince Sanhushka married a Protestant... I have nothing against your faith, you have nothing against mine, so why should faith be an impediment?"

"Maybe faith need not be an impediment. But what about the mayor and his wife? They say the mayor's wife swore an oath that she would rather die than permit me to marry."

"So let her die!"

Makrynya clung to her Staryma in a loving embrace.

"I now swear that if that scrawny chicken attempts to hinder what I intend to do, I," she lowered her voice," will help her fulfil her oath. I will, I'll marry you and help her die. Ever since my husband died, the mayor and his wife have been looking askance at me and making things as difficult as possible. I can see why, it's so much easier to wrong a widow than it is to hurt a woman who has a husband to stand up for her. Last spring I dug over a piece of land out beyond Nalozki that didn't belong to anyone, but the mayor's wife swore blind that it had once belonged to her family. That was the time when I tore the coif from her head, she-devil that she is. That night she ordered her man Martynak to slip out to the field and sow rye. The woman has absolutely no fear of Judgement Day! Obviously the magistrates and councillors aren't going to do anything to thwart the mayor, so she thought I would just knuckle down and give in. That's just where she was wrong — if I'm not going to get something, I'll make sure that nobody else gets it either. When the rye was ripe, I sent my boy Nachko out to cut it. And who was it who tore my fishing nets? She did, the mayor's wife, with her own hands — she wasn't even squeamish about going right into the mud where I'd stood them."

I formed the impression that Makrynya was, as we say nowadays, having a rant. That's the way people talk when there's something burning deep inside, when they don't care if anyone is actually listening or interested in what they have to say. But Staryma was listening to every word.

"They want to use the courts to get their hands on what my husband left me, because he was some kind of distant relative of theirs. After all, the mayor's wife is a Kukal and they're supposed to be related to the Haduns. Honestly, do I look like somebody who would allow her children to starve, while some fat toad lorded it over them?"

"No, you don't," Staryma was trying to calm her down. "Your children are fortunate to have such a mother, an eagle protecting her fledglings. I wish that my children had just such a mother. You've seen my children, haven't you? My Khrystof is the only one who could look after himself if anything happens. The others are too young to be of any help to each other. Please become a loving mother to them! God took your husband, just as He took my wife. I do believe that God wishes us to marry."

"You won't treat any of my children badly, will you, Staryma?"

"Never, I swear it. I have been meaning to tell you that God has blessed my labours. You have no cause for concern. I have property and goods aplenty. Even His Majesty the King buys the jewellery I make. I export my wares to the Germans, and, thank God, they sell very well in my shops in Lviv, Lutsk, Lublin and Berastse. I have just purchased gold wire and stones in the Netherlands and Turkey, and with them I have produced many different..."

I suddenly heard someone say "Anatoleuna, come on down from your Nirvana!" right into my ear, and I missed the end of Staryma's phrase.

"I did ask you not to disturb me!"

"I'm sorry, but I have some urgent news for you. Information has just been released that a certain Ala Anatoleuna Babylyova — let's not go into the year of birth — is on the most wanted list. Do you understand what that means?"

"What?"

"It means that once a description of you has been circulated, every member of the law enforcement agencies — from a humble traffic policeman to a KBB officer — has the duty to arrest you as soon as he sees you. And then you'll be back here — officially, but not for long. Something tells me that they will very quickly pack you off to prison, after convicting you of course. And, as you know, our courts are just and swift. In talking to you now I am in fact in breach of police regulations. So, not to worry, I'm going to go even further and take you to a safe place somewhere; they won't stop my car. Don't go home; the chances are they're already waiting for you there, and by that I don't mean the regular police, but something much worse. Let's go."

A part of me was desperate to stay on the damp bank of the

fast-flowing stream, so I was still not thinking very clearly. I'm a wanted person? Where am I? What was the jeweller talking about? The governor shook me by the shoulder.

"Oy, come one, what's up with you? Come on out of that hole in time. Did you understand what I said?"

I sighed and reluctantly returned to the present. "Yes, I understood. Since you're not afraid of being charged with breaching regulations, you can take me to Zarnitskaya's veterinary clinic."

"Zarnitskaya? I know her. But she's not there!"

"She may not be there in person, but her cause lives on."*

On the way, while the prison governor's little Kia twisted and turned through the narrow streets of tsarist Brest-Litovsk, we finally got to know each other a little better. I discovered that he had the same first name as my father — Anatol.

"Tell me, Anatol, why are you helping me? What about police regulations?"

He snorted.

"I like people who kick hornets' nests and I like what you write as well. Don't look so surprised. Yes, I do read *Nasha Niva*. But now get out of the car. It's best for us not to be seen together for the time being. I'll call you."

Zarnitskaya's clinic is located in a quiet cul-de-sac in the old corner of the city. There was no real need for the prison governor to have been so concerned, because there was no one around to see us. The clinic itself consisted of several small rooms that proudly bore the title of 'surgeries'. There were neat little doorplates right along the corridor: 'Cats, dogs and other animals', 'Birds', 'Reptiles and amphibians', 'Administration'. That was the room I needed. I went in.

I was met with a barrage of expletives.

I had never heard Khvedzka use such language before. In

---

* Sardonic adaptation of an old Soviet slogan 'Lenin's cause lives on and will be victorious'.

fact I had never heard anything like that before — even from the spetsnaz.

"Are you talking to me?"

"What, is it really you? Yes, I'm sorry," Khvedzka blushed a deep shade of red. "It's just that they've really worn me down. Here, look, they've sent me another *instruction*," and he handed me a piece of paper. "The bastards. I'm totally pissed off with it all. Sit down."

The document came with the letterhead of the Committee for Sanitation, Hygiene and Veterinary Services.

It was addressed to the Veterinary Clinic registered name 'Doberman Pinscher', Owner E.G. Zarnitskaya, registered address *such-and-such*, Bank a/c no. *such-and-such*, Licence no. *such-and-such*, Date of issue *such-as-such*.

Instruction.

In order to ensure stability and the maintenance of public order, as well as to avert provocative acts on the part of antisocial elements, you are hereby instructed to ensure that at least 86% of the staff employed in your establishment, together with members of their families who have the vote, turn out to register their vote in the period of early voting before election day. In addition, you are also required to ensure that no discussions on the election campaign are held on the premises occupied by your establishment, especially where the names of the candidates for election are mentioned (with the exception of the current President). We hereby give notice that, in the event of your non-compliance with these instructions, your licence to provide veterinary services will be revoked in accordance with the provisions of Article 36a of the Law on Veterinary Services (non-compliance with the legitimate demands of higher authority). In order to check that these instructions are being carried out in your establishment spot checks will be made by our investigators, incognito.

Signed: Chairman of the Committee for Sanitation, Hygiene and Veterinary Services.

"That's completely absurd," I said, and handed the paper back to him.

"Absurd and stupid. Yesterday I received an identical document from the City Council (we rent this place from them). The only difference is what they're threatening us with: if we don't ensure a high-enough turnout for early voting and permit the names of alternative candidates to be mentioned on the premises, they'll tear up the rental agreement 'in connection with the conduct of activities not foreseen in the contract.'"

"What are you going to do, observe their instructions to the letter?"

Another barrage of expletives.

"But then they'll take your licence away and put you out on the street!"

"The boss said she's not afraid of them, that, if it comes to the crunch, we'll simply move over the border to Ukraine. Now tell me, what are you here for? What's happened? And why, in God's name, do you look as though someone's beaten you up again?!"

I told him briefly about what had happended that day, omitting the bit about going to the remand prison of my own accord. Instead I said that I had met Anatol the prison governor in the prosecution service building.

"And he advised me to hide out somewhere for a time."

Khvedzka thought for a moment and then announced: "I know exactly where we can hide you away. In the beaver lodges!"

"In where?"

"Where the beavers are. In the fortress. There's a fellow called Vital Kanapatski who stands guard over them, he doesn't let anyone near them, not even the police. That's where you can sit it out.

I knew what he was talking about. I knew the whole story. There's a quiet spot in the fortress where not many people go, the place where the Mukhavets joins the Buh, and this year beavers had suddenly arrived there. They must have come from Poland, because there's hardly any animal life left in Belarus for miles around. The beavers chewed down several trees and, as they always do, made a dam. Then they built themselves a few lodges and settled in. The director of the fortress museum wanted to have them shot. He reckoned that the beavers spoiled the view by felling the willows along the river, and, whenever they emerged from the river they would distract the tourist groups being led around the museum. And they would have been shot if it hadn't been for Vital Kanapatski, a biology teacher at the Pedagogical University. He managed to persuade the city authorities to set up a nature reserve 'of local significance'. He went to the museum, thrust the freshly signed document right under the nose of the director and announced that, now he had been appointed to safeguard the reserve, tour groups had to stay at least five hundred metres away from it. A real battle broke out between him and the director, but an official document cannot be ignored, and there it was on the table. Besides, Vital was known to be a seasoned fighter. He had already successfully defended the flood-lands of the Mukhavets, an area of impenetrable undergrowth in which many species of bird have their favourite nesting places. The plan had been to build yet another 'ice palace' on it. Then there was the time when he came to the rescue of an area of woodland where black herons nest — someone wanted to build dachas on the land. There were other instances as well; landowners and developers had become wary of having any dealings with him. According to what Khvedzka told me, he had built two little huts near the beavers' lodges; one was nearer the fortress, which he used to make sure that no one came any closer, the other was right by the lodges themselves. It was from this one that in quiet moments he could observe the beavers' comings and goings.

"That's the one where you'll be. Don't worry, we won't make you live underwater right next to the beavers."

---

* The current president of Belarus has an obsession with ice hockey, and building 'ice palaces' where the sport can be played.

"Why not? I suppose in principle I could go down there. Didn't Jules Verne's heroes spend some time in a termite mound? Pity I don't remember how things turned out for them. But all the same, Khvedzka, listen a minute, are we perhaps being a bit overcautious? Perhaps I should just go home to Dobratyche. Could you perhaps just pop down there to see if things are OK…

The phone rang and Khvedzka picked up the receiver.

"Hallo. Yes, it's me. Got it. I'll pass it on."

He replaced the receiver and looked at me.

"There's the answer to your question about being overcautious. That was Lilka from *Narodnaya Volya*. Ulia was arrested today. She said there was a wave of arrests today, and asked me to pass on the message that you shouldn't worry. She'll do everything she can for Ulia. So off we go to the beavers. You won't be able to help Ulia if you yourself land up in prison. You can still be useful if you're at liberty.

On the way there I slid down the seat of the pickup, trying to avoid being seen by any passing police officers, and thought about the reasons for Ulia's arrest. Using obscene language in a public place again or something worse?

Khvedzka was obviously still thinking about the instructions he had received.

"It looks like they're going to declare that he won the election with 86% of the vote. They've got this figure of 86% on the brain and they keep trumpeting it all over the place. They might at least try to hide their intentions, even if only for decency's sake. As it is, they don't regard the rest of us as people with any modicum of intelligence. It's all so bloody stupid."

The country was being smothered by a blanket of stupidity and absurdity, just like this unprecedented heatwave. And it seemed as though the blanket would never be lifted. Everywhere, from all the billboards along all the roads, we were greeted by the same teeth bared in the same mocking laugh on the same repulsive face.

DOWN AMONG THE FISHES

Above my head a thousand birds joined in chorus were puffing out their chests and straining their vocal chords. The lady beavers — Vital had taught me how to recognise the difference between the males and females by the expression of the muzzle — emerged from the lodges, and, with their paws resting on their bellies like housewives with their hands on their aprons, listened pensively to the concert. Later they were aroused from their land of dreams by the squealing of one of the kits, or by the discontented grumbling of one of their menfolk; they shook themselves and dived back into the water, down to their homes where duty was calling. A worried-looking male took the place of his mate and, paying not the slightest attention to the frivolous singing of the birds, dragged his flat tail to an alder tree and attacked the bark with his teeth... Observing the life of these large-toothed rodents had a more calming effect on me than any tranquilliser. It was like a balm for the soul to watch the beaver couples show their affection for each other, and see the young ones fool around. If it hadn't been for the mosquitoes... Vital had forbidden me to use any sprays or creams to keep them off, so as not to disturb the beavers with chemical smells. It was just about tolerable during the day, but I was dreading the moment when the sun set.

The hut I was in would have been too small for a large dog. The only thing you could do was sit in it. But, as Vital said, it was better to sit in a beaver lodge than to walk up and down in a prison cell. There was no flooring, so I simply settled down on the ground. At least it was warm.

I stretched out my legs. I really felt like sleeping. I knew

Vital was sitting in the hut closer to the fortress, on guard. I leant with my back to the wicker wall.

It was then I felt a sudden jolt.

I shuddered and opened my eyes. There was the woven willow of the wicker wall, and an old board covering the entrance. Further off I could see the castle wall, the road, carts with sacks, carts with hay, carts with bales, I could hear the commotion. It had happened again. Once more I had fallen into a hole.

There was a tremendous noise and bustle all around the road leading into the town; shouts, bits of conversation, people gesticulating. I drank in the sight with my eyes. There was a bridge. Large puddles in the mud. People in unfamiliar, fascinating clothes...

I turned my head a little and everything disappeared.

Trembling with excitement, I shut my eyes again and waited for the jolt. You mustn't move. Don't move, don't let your attention wander.

Then another jolt came.

The bridge; puddles beneath the wheels; wooden shafts and leather harness; light red dogs.

Two boys sitting with their backs to me, right by my hut. Coarse grey coats. One of them has fair hair, the other is dark — the hair has been cut in an unusual way, unevenly, as if with a knife. They're both wearing caps, or, to be more precise, pieces of grey cloth that have been wound round and round their heads to look like cones.

"Look, look," I heard one of them say in Ukrainian, "There's mama galloping."

I followed the direction in which the boy was pointing. Makrynya really was coming at a gallop, spurring her stocky black horse on with her bare heels. She disappeared through the gate without stopping or taking any notice of the boys.

"Shall we go home?" asked the older of the two boys. Perhaps she'll give us something to eat."

"No, she won't." The other boy was tying something that

looked like an iron hook to a thick grey strip of leather. "She doesn't have any time. Raina's not at home, neither is Nachko. We'd be better off going to the mayor's wife, she'll feed us."

"Mum'll thrash us when she finds out. She told us not to go there."

"How's she going to find out if we don't tell her?"

"Come on, better go down to the river and catch a sheatfish. Mum'll be pleased."

"The last couple of times we went down there we didn't catch anything."

The boys stood up. I could see their bare dirty heels. The calves of their thin legs were blue with cold.

"Look, it's like there's another town down there in the river." The younger boy pointed to the water. "Down among the fishes."

The calm waters of the river were level with the bank; I could see the reflection of the castle walls, the shutters on the windows, bridges, field elms. Shapes and colours were exactly like those above the water, even sharper and clearer. It really did look as though there was another town down there where the fishes lived, a submerged, mystic town where the roofs of the houses look down instead of up. It's like there are two inseparable towns that have suddenly sprung out of the ground from one single root, and flourish together amid green foliage, like a shoot ready to burst into life, like the flower of a mallow with its translucent, silky petals — bridges, walls, trees above the water and beneath it. As if there were people living in both towns.

The boys ran off; they were all skin and bone, their faces — both the fair-haired lad and the dark one — slightly more delicate versions of Makrynya's stern features. Beyond the bridge the boys slithered down to the Buh.

Trying my utmost not to move a muscle, I let my eyes feast on the scene; as I did so, I wept and the tears burned my mosquito-bitten cheeks. I was afraid to wipe them away, in case I fell out of the hole.

Small horses with long, flowing manes were pulling carts; some men were carrying axes and spades on their shoulders.

I relished the sounds of the language they were speaking. Each word was stamped in my mind, just as a gold coin takes shape when cast in a mould.

A pregnant woman was walking slowly across the bridge in the direction of the town; she seemed to be concentrating solely on what was happening inside her body. Makrynya came galloping out of the gate on horseback towards her. The woman looked up and smiled; Makrynya saw her right at the last minute and, rather unwillingly, tugged on the reins. There was a huge contrast between the two women; one was energetic and purposeful, the other soft and somehow not fully formed; her dress was riding up up over her belly and badly crumpled around the hem. Her round face was swollen, making it look even rounder. Her time was obviously close.

The pregnant woman walked over to Makrynya, and, clearly in an attempt to prevent her riding away, leant against her leg.

"Praised be Jesus Christ!"

"Now and for ever!"

"You're always in a hurry to get somewhere, Makrynya! Where are you off to now?"

"Nachko's at Zahorane, ploughing our land there. The harrow broke and he sent me to fetch some wire. I've got to get it fixed before the ground dries out."

Makrynya jerked the reins.

"Oh, you'll manage it alright. Stay with me for a minute, I must catch my breath. We may never see each other again."

Makrynya's stern face softened a little, but she didn't dismount.

"What do you mean, won't see each other? Nonsense!"

"I'm really afraid, Makrynya. I know I'm going to die. I keep having these bad dreams."

"When you sleep, you have dreams, that's all. It's always frightening when you give birth. I've had five children, and I was scared each time. But whether you're scared or not, it's going to happen. Just look around at how many people there are in Berastse — they all had mothers who gave birth to them."

"Our Volka was in agony for six days, and even then the baby didn't appear. Zhoska Kuleshykha, and Maryna from Valynka both died in childbirth, so did Tanka Hnalyova... I've already said a prayer to St Paraskeva, and I sent Anna off to the Carmelites to light a candle to Marketa*, which is what they expect you to do. All the same, I still feel nervous."

Makrynya bent down and stroked the pregnant woman's pale arm.

"It'll be all right, you'll see. You asked God for a child and he's given you one at last. The Blessed Virgin will surely come to your aid, won't she? If you want, I'll come when it's your time. Anyway, that mother-in-law of yours has had enough experience. How many children has she had? Eleven?"

"Yes, Makrynya, please come, I'll feel easier. I'm not telling anyone about the baby, I don't want them putting the evil eye on me, you're the only one I wanted to tell. It's been such a long time since we last saw each other and had a chat. You've always got so much to do. Do you remember the fun we used to have when we got together in the evenings? How we went to Master Kopets' place for Maryna's wedding?"

"Sure I remember. I will come, I'll come to you when you send for me. But right now Nachko's waiting." Makrynya had already got her horse to move on, and these last words were shouted from the bridge.

The poor pregnant woman dragged her feet slowly through the gate.

Vital brought me some soup in a thermos.

---

* St Margaret of Antioch

YET ANOTHER DECREE

I spent three days in the hut. The mosquitoes had bitten me so much that my face had come to resemble the full moon. "Your cheeks have filled out a bit," my sister would have said. She was in prison, but — I do have to admit — I wasn't particularly concerned about it, just as I wasn't particularly concerned about the mosquitoes; every day, when all was quiet except for their buzzing and the beavers were busy beavering in their lodges, I found myself back in old Berastse, right down there with the fishes, on the road that led from the district where the townsfolk lived to the castle, right past where my hut stood. I should make it clear that I always returned to the same period of time: it was summer, a cold, wet summer somewhere in the middle of the seventeenth century. It took me a long time to work this out, and even then I was not absolutely certain. To be quite honest, I didn't have enough to go on in order to reach a definite conclusion. Yes, the clothes people were wearing bore some resemblance to what you can see on the canvasses of some seventeenth-century painter, and yes, I heard a word a few times that I took to mean the Swedes*, and there were those two townsmen who stopped on the bridge and began to talk about someone they called Khmel, by which I understood Bohdan Khmelnytskyi, but they may have been referring to somebody else. Never mind, whether it was the seventeenth century or not, it absorbed me totally. I forgot about everything else. A starving man cannot tear himself away from food, a love-struck girl

---

* There was war between Sweden and the Polish-Lithuanian Commonwealth in the years 1655-1660.

cannot bear to be parted from her beloved, and I could not get my fill of this place with its mirror image in the water, my town, with all its people and horses, full of life and disappointments, full of fresh air. From time to time the wind brought me all manner of scents: the aroma of fresh bread and other good food, the stench of rotting vegetation, the smell of hay, coal, smoke and sheep. I heard the trumpet call in the town that marked the passing hours. I heard laughter, shouting, the clatter of hooves on the cobblestones and singing — long drawn-out, loud songs. Now and again Makrynya would hurry past me — either on her stocky, black horse, or in a cart. I also saw her two daughters, but I never did see her fifth child, nor heard anything about it. Had it died? I eagerly drank in everything I saw before me. I was like that old woman, the fisherman's wife from the fairy story, who was no longer satisfied with what she had; I no longer wanted just to sit perfectly still and find myself right by the gates to the town. I was already dreaming about finding my way through the massive log walls into the very heart of the town. I never for one moment thought about what I had done to deserve an opportunity like this, who was offering it to me and for what purpose.

It was then, in the time I spent in the hut next to the beaver lodges, that I succeeded in formulating with absolute clarity a thought that had often occurred to me before, but only in the vaguest of ways. God had made a slight miscalculation with his raw materials. Back then, in the seventeenth century, there was a soul for every body. In our twenty-first century there were far more bodies than souls.

Where had this thought come from? I don't even know how to explain it. I had seen these people — all of them short and dressed in rags — for at most a few hours. Well, how long does it take to cross the bridge and disappear through the gate into the town? Or emerge from the gate, and go off round the bend in the road beyond the bridge? Even so, there was a spark of something in each of these filthy ragamuffins, vagabonds, building workers, townsfolk and peasants that I had not seen in my contemporaries...

Hiding here was easy: in all the time I was here no one had appeared on the broad pathway that leads in an arc from the casemates of the fortress to the river. It wasn't a place for the youth of the town to hang out — it was much too far away; the tramps 'of no fixed abode' didn't bother either — there was nothing here for them, and Vital barred the way to the occasional group of tourists. Once a day he brought me food. While pouring me soup or tea from his thermos, he would briefly tell me the latest news: altogether some two hundred people, including my sister, had been arrested and charged with organising a terrorist gang under the guise of holding a staff meeting at the election campaign headquarters. A news item had been shown on TV which purported to show the things that had been found in the room where the meeting had taken place: automatic weapons, money, drugs and — for no obvious reason — pornographic films. The situation was not exactly a very pleasant one, but, as I have said before, I wasn't very worried.

On the fourth day Vital and Khvedzka turned up together.

"Lilka phoned today. She said that Ulia's been let out, along with all the others."

"I smell a rat. All of them? Without a trial?"

"Absolutely. Your friend said that the spetsnaz had picked up two international observers along with the rest without bothering to check, so the authorities had to beat a hasty retreat."

"How can that happen? Since when has our régime had any sense of shame when dealing with observers?"

"These things can happen," Vital joined in the conversation. "Our marvellous régime has really landed in the shit with this one. Radio Liberty reported that there were two women from the OSCE at that meeting. Evidently they aren't the type who are easily frightened. When the spetsnaz broke in, these observers didn't say who they were. In fact they left it until they were already in prison to show their credentials. Someone had managed to smuggle in a mobile phone, so they phoned and stirred up a real noise. But the best of it is that one of the women is the niece of the president of a very powerful European country. Apparently he himself phoned our man and gave him an earful. They simply had to let everyone go — they had no other choice. Lilka says that there'll be a thaw for a time. So what do you want to do — stay here for a bit longer or risk coming out of hiding?"

I was in two minds. On the one hand I really did want to stay here, to be close to where the fishes are. On the other hand I realised that I was causing problems for Khvedzka by not being in Dobratyche, because he had to look after my animals, and for Vital, who risked getting into serious trouble because of me. If the authorities found me here they would close down his reserve and kill off all these beavers... If Lilka thinks that there's going to be a thaw (and she has a nose for that sort of thing), then it's probably worthwhile to take a risk.

"I'll go home. I think it must be safe there now."

On the way from the fortress I gave Ulia a call. The conversation wasn't entirely vacuous, but there was no warmth in it. My sister was totally engrossed with the tasks of the day — her time was noisy, it whistled and shouted slogans; she didn't even have anything special to say about being arrested — "we're over that now, we have to look to the future." I, on the other hand, was still down where the fishes are. My time gurgled and flowed with the brown-tinged water of the Buh, where people catch sheatfish with hook and line in the shallows. Only one piece of my sister's news was of any concern to me:

"By the way, do you know that the other day a decree was issued that makes it illegal for private individuals to go treasure hunting? From now on only the state has the right to engage in such activities. If any person or organisation wishes to hunt for treasure, they have to have a licence. Treasure hunting without a licence is now a criminal offence, and you can get up to two years inside for it."

"Do you think that's aimed at us?"

"I don't doubt it. Just bear it in mind when you're talking on the phone. There's something else: I think we were quite right to make a start on this."

"Make a start on what?"

"Make a start on everything. Only, I beg you, don't get worked up, don't make a mess of things, and don't do anything stupid, like you've shown yourself so capable of doing in the past."

That's how my sister talks to me, and she's no older than I am. Oh well, let her if she wants to.

Khvedzka reported that everything in Dobratyche had been quiet during my absence. He had fed my livestock, keeping them on the same rations as the animals in their clinic; every day he went over to the provincial hospital to fetch a few buckets of leftovers from the canteen. Khvedzka dropped me off at the Central Department Store. After the isolation of the beaver lodges in the fortress it felt a little strange to be walking along the busy streets of Brest. I was also a little disturbed by the unusually loud honking of car horns. What on earth was all the racket about? I thought it was supposed to be forbidden. It was only when I had taken a few more steps down Masherau Avenue that I realised what it was all about. There were some young people standing about ten metres apart on both sides of the road all the way along the carriageway. Each one of them was wearing a T-shirt with a letter of the alphabet painted on it. Altogether the letters spelled out the words "Harabets means freedom". Car drivers and their passengers sounded their horns in approval and waved in greeting to the girls and boys. I spotted Iryna Lauraneuskaya among them; she was also wearing a T-shirt with one of the letters. I knew this woman; she was about my age, and the only person in Brest to have made a serious study of the original town, the one that had been completely destroyed to make way for the fortress. At a time when you could be instantly dismissed from your job simply for mentioning aloud the name of any of the candidates for election (except, of course, One Name in particular), when the radio and TV were packed with rubber people, and the few remaining independent newspapers weren't printed at all the week before, this was a brave and creative action to undertake. I looked around in an attempt to gauge the reaction of people on the street. Most of them were smiling in appreciation of what the young people were doing, but then I saw something that wiped the smile off my face: there was a large military lorry taking up position in the street by the river, just beyond School no. 13. It stopped, and out jumped a herd of spetsnaz in black. I know the type only too well; I had already opened my mouth to yell "Police!" but fortunately didn't have time to make a sound of any sort. An old chap sitting on a bench with a newspaper quietly muttered "Achtung!" into his mobile. At that moment the chain broke up — the youngsters hastily removed their T-shirts and without fuss simply dissolved in the crowds on the pavement. It took the spetsnaz no more than thirty seconds to reach the scene, but all that was left for them to seize were the T-shirts. Mrs Lauraneuskaya, who had also taken off her T-shirt by this time, walked straight into the very thick of the policemen. The look of fierce determination on her face, the dark glasses, the long cigarette in a cigarette holder and the high heels all combined to make her the spitting image of Sophia Loren. She simply carved her way through the crowd of men in black, and they parted for her. It didn't occur to them that this *grande dame* had been in charge of the young people on that risky demo.

I sat down next to the old fellow on the bench.

"What do you think our president's next decree will be about?" I asked him, pointing to the newspaper and unable to suppress a smile.

He looked me over very carefully.

"Well, if I was in his position — God forbid — I would make it a legal requirement for everyone to speak with the same accent as he does. He should have done it a long time ago. Now please allow me to wish you good day," and the old boy gallantly raised his hat, stood up and set off after Lauraneuskaya.

Once they had picked up the T-shirts, the lads in black surged back to their lorry.

A car suddenly braked sharply right next to me. It was a miracle of technology; everything about it — the wheels, the ancient, rusty wings, the doors — all seemed to be hanging on with wire, and about to fall off completely. Inside there were only two well-worn seats. The driver — a swarthy, jolly-looking type with gleaming white teeth and a shock of thick brown curls — nodded in the direction of where the youngsters had just been standing in their T-shirts.

"Wicked! Good for them, they didn't fuck up. Sometimes you look at kids who come out on demos and they're already shaking like sheep before anything happens. That's not the way to do it. Can I take you somewhere, milady?"

"I don't have any money for a taxi," I informed him.

"And I'm not a taxi driver," he replied. "I'm a racing driver. I need to train for the next race. Would you care to join me? That is, of course, if you're not afraid.

I looked at this crazy individual in surprise. I've had a lot of luck recently in meeting odd-ball types. His white teeth were shining against the dark background of his face.

"I need to get to Dobratyche. If you can give me a lift, let's go."

"OK, let's go," he readily agreed. "I can do my training anywhere."

His way of driving the car — nosing his way into the slightest gap in the traffic, ceaselessly manoeuvring this way and that, speeding up and then stepping hard on the brakes — was so enjoyable that we got to know each other on the way. He told me that his name was Lyavi — with the stress on the second syllable, Lyavi, not Leu — that he was a Gypsy, and that he's been racing for ten years.

"Well, it's not exactly Formula 1 stuff. We hold competitions for normal people who simply love driving fast. I've been in Germany, in Poland and in Catalonia. Just where haven't I been! I can drive fast in any car," he said, "it's just that I smash them up quite a lot. That's why I buy really old ones. This one is my favourite, she's a veteran, her name is Anita."

I showed Lyavi the road which I had taken to Dobratyche, and told him all about that incident. Lyavi was impressed.

"Wicked!" was how he praised me. "Do you want to learn how to drive like a racing driver?"

I did.

Lyavi was eager to teach me.

In spite of her — how shall I put it? — "Bohemian" appearance, Anita was a powerful, well-disciplined car, ready to obey the slightest movement of the steering wheel. We simply flew round sharp bends, the engine roared across the emptiness of what had once been marshlands, the air whipped past us. On a couple of occasions I nearly hurtled into the ditch, but managed to straighten up in time. Liavi laughed and smacked the palms of his hands on his jeans-encased knees.

"Wicked!" he shouted, when I dropped the speed as we drove into Dobratyche. "Do you know, there are some races where there have to be two people in the car, would you like to come with me? I'll be happy to take you. Come on, say you will."

The events of the day — the news that all those arrested had been let out, the shit that the authorities had got themselves into, the demo that I had witnessed, meeting Lyavi, the hairy drive — had boosted my spirits incredibly. That evening I felt as though I was twenty again, and that my whole life still lay ahead.

However, that night I had a bad dream, and waking up from it was even worse.

MAD MEG ON THE MARCH

Mad Meg the vacant-eyed still roams the world, sword in hand. The bee-keepers, with cocoons for faces, still tramp and tramp around... Pieter Brueghel — the older one — couldn't paint. I realised that when I tried in my younger years to copy "Mad Meg" and "The Bee-keepers". He may not have been able to paint, but he could certainly see. He married the boss's daughter and designed etchings to sell... Today Brueghel's heroes came to me in a dream. Dreaming in colour is the first sign of schizophrenia.

Barking, shots and groaning all got mixed up in my dream; the dream burst like a soap bubble. What's going on out there? I jumped out of bed. The dogs — for some reason I could hear only three of them — were barking furiously; there was hatred in the sound. Then the barking gave way to howling and yelping, high-pitched, pathetic and helpless.

I looked out of the window and nearly jumped out of my skin. It was Kukal!

Kukal with his bodyguards — or whatever I am supposed to call them. All of them, except Kukal, held automatic weapons.

I sat weakly back down on the bed. At that moment I knew I had lost. A person loses when he concedes defeat. Now it was my turn to concede defeat. I was frightened, although nothing had yet happened, and that wasn't the way to do it, as Lyavi had so rightly said. Now the end was inevitable. Should I run out to them with the axe that granny always used to keep under her bed? That's just a joke, and a bitter one at that. Should I phone the police? Pointless — Kukal's got them in his pocket. You can't reason with brute force. There was no ring tone in the telephone in the kitchen — it had been cut off. I picked up my mobile —

should I phone Ulia, or Zarnitskaya or Anatol? But what for? What could they do to help?

So I went out into the yard to surrender and throw myself on the mercy of the enemy. I knew I was deceiving myself; in my heart of hearts I was well aware that this particular enemy did not know what mercy was.

I had gone to bed without getting undressed. My bent fingers — I had torn off the plaster yesterday — wouldn't obey me, so I didn't even try to tidy up my hair. Dishevelled, in my crumpled clothes and mechanically putting one foot in front of the other, I went out on to the porch, to the accompaniment of merry shouts of "Come on out! Come on out!"

I was greeted with applause. The guards with their automatics lined up in a corridor, and along this corridor I walked towards Kukal, who sat lounging on a chair at our table under the pear tree. Jean, with a wound in her belly, was lying with her paws stretched out in a pool of blood. She was obviously dying. The other dogs were yelping.

"What do you want from me?" I asked when I reached the table. "How could you kill the dog?"

"It wouldn't let us pass, so we shot it," he answered in his usual manner, calmly, without emotion. He was dressed tastefully but ever so slightly casually, in the way that sensible and successful artists or photographers normally do. "If you don't want to end up the same way, you will stop being a nuisance. I mean that quite literally. So," he clicked the lock of his leather briefcase, "here you have the deed of inheritance, so the title to the property has now been transferred to you and your sister, this is a document granting you permission to sell the house and land within six months of the decease of the testator, and this is a contract of sale and purchase. That is the one you will sign now, and which you will bring back to me tomorrow with the signature of your sister."

Without saying a word I shook my head to show that I would do no such thing, and turned to go back into the house.

One of his thugs turned me around again; I could feel the cold barrel of an automatic pressing against my ribs.

The dogs were still howling disconsolately; above me was an empty washed-out sky; there was no one to help me.

Calmly and unhurriedly Kukal reached into his pocket for a mobile and pressed a few buttons.

"Hi. How are things with you? Excellent. Wait a second," and now to me: "Your sister's kids are bathing in the Buh right now. Will you sign or do you want me to tell my man over there to shoot them?"

"I-I'll sign."

"On your knees."

I got down on my knees. He pushed the document and a pen into my face. I signed the contract and one of the guards took it from me.

"Now kiss my feet," said Kukal, still holding the telephone next to his ear.

I crawled towards him and kissed his feet, first one, and then the other — his fat feet in their leather sandals.

"Good, you can come back now, the problem's been solved," Kukal said into the telephone.

I was still kneeling before him.

He stood up, and swiftly, professionally, without taking a swing, kicked me in the solar plexus. I fell forwards.

"We're off," said Kukal. "You'll bring the document to me in the 'Goliath' tomorrow with your sister's signature. No, I'm busy tomorrow, make it the day after. You know what will happen if you don't. Finish off the dogs." He barked his last order just as he was leaving.

Then the shooting began. I lay on the sand, pressing my hands hard against my ears, but still the sounds got through — through my skin, my bones, my muscles and my sinews. Each groan from the dogs was like a whiplash... The guards needed a lot more than three bullets to kill them.

They left at last.

For a time I lay where I had fallen, but then gathered my strength, stood up and went off to fetch a spade and bury the dogs. I also had to go and find an axe to chop through the thick tree roots that run everywhere through the ground beneath Dobratyche.

When I had finished digging a huge pit under the bird cherry tree, I spread a thick layer of walnut tree leaves on the bottom and then brought the dogs, carrying each one of them on my arms. At first I tried not to get their blood on me, but they were heavy and it was awkward to carry them. I didn't want to drag them along the ground. Very soon my arms and dressing gown were all red with blood. There were even some crimson drops on my lips and face.

I managed to place all four dogs in the pit, lying next to each other. I put more walnut leaves on top of them, to stop sand getting into their wounds. On top of all that I placed several bright pink dahlias, the ones with the transparent petals that are called round here — rather inappropriately, given the circumstances — 'jolly lads'.

It was then that Lyalka junior appeared from behind the bird cherry tree with her back to me. She was dragging her mother's body along the ground.

"Put her in there," she said, pointing to the pit. These were the first meaningful words that I had ever heard her utter in all my life.

The corpse had now been several days without the merciful covering of the earth and was terrible to look at. How I could possibly bury auntie Lyalka together with the dogs?

"Lyalka, love, let's take your mother to the cemetery. I'll dig another pit for her there, just like this one, and I'll spread the same kind of leaves in it, and put the same kind of flowers on top. The cemetery is next to the church, and the ground is hallowed. Your mother will lie there just as if she was in church."

"No. We were in church last Sunday and the Sunday before that. Put her here."

"Fine. Let's do it. Let's put her here."

I didn't know what else I could do, and I really didn't care either.

We had to carry auntie to the pit and somehow lower her into it.

Everything was quiet all around. Dobratyche was silent. No one had come running to see what the shooting and noise was all about, no one was interested in what had happened, or if anyone was still alive.

But no, I was wrong, someone had come to the gate and was now walking towards us.

"Good day, what...," our poet Mikhas Yarash, smiling as always, had reached the two of us; he took in the whole picture at a glance and the smile vanished, — "what's going on? I've just come from the train, and granny told me that there's something happening here..." He couldn't say any more. He just stood there, transfixed by the terrible sight that old Lyalka's corpse had become by now.

"Oh, it's you. Good that you've come. You can help me put auntie into the pit. I can't manage it by myself, and I don't want to step on the dogs. Come here and help me."

Mishyk retreated.

"Where are you going? Come back here," I insisted. "And by the way, who were you spying on us for? Was it Kukal? Or the KBB? Answer me, say something!"

When I started speaking Misha was still walking backwards, but then he turned and fled.

"Oy, poet, did they pay you well?"

The last words were shouted to his back.

Somehow Lyalka and I managed to lower her mother into the grave without dropping her. The sharp smell of the walnut leaves overcame the fetid stench of the corpse; we covered the pit with pink dahlia heads and then filled it in with sand. We had made an impressive mound. Lyalka smoothed it down with her hands and then — while I was putting the spade back in its place — disappeared silently into the forest.

I was alone again.

The contract that Kukal had left for me was lying on the verandah. I read it, staining the paper with the blood on my fingers.

Kukal had bought our land and house for a ridiculous sum of money. There was my pathetic signature, the space for Ulia's signature, and Kukal's cocky, insolent signature — in facsimile.

So I had messed up. I had given way. I had let my sister down yet again.

How am I going to tell Ulia about all this?

Why did I ever come out of hiding? Why can't I ever do anything right? Why does nothing turn out as it should? Nothing ever does. Why do I need a life like this at all? I seized hold of this last thought. Why should I go on living? What for? What's the point? I'm of no use to anyone. There's absolutely no one who wants me to go on living. My sister? She's already tired of me. My husband? My *former* husband, I don't have any children. There are no children. I've outlived my daughter. I don't have granny any more, and there's no one left in the village that I grew up with. I don't have Tolik either: will he really be sorry if I'm not around any more? No. As far as he's concerned, I'm just an adventure, a memory of his youth, proof that he's still alive and strong. No, I don't have Tolik either. What I do have is Kukal, Shushko and Pochtivy, Graychik and Kuleshov. They are spreading over the body of the earth like a disease, a malignant tumour.

And soon the tumour will burst here in Dobratyche, and pus will flow everywhere.

Kukal will reign here. Pus will rule over all.

WHAT KIND OF MEDICINAL HERBS DO WE HAVE IN DOBRATYCHE?

I felt no better during the night. I was unable to get to sleep. Thoughts cawed in my head like ravens. Thoughts weighed me down like stones. Thoughts kept going round and round in my head like rats in a wheel, or running up the rope that led to the Cardiostim on the shelf.

All the mean and nasty things that I had experienced or of which I was guilty kept coming back to me that night. I remembered how granny beat me when the cow died because of me. My first wedding night (I've never told anyone about that, and never will). The face of my little daughter lying in her coffin. Gosha. Prison. Anton's treachery. My fear and hesitancy. My weak will. And the most perfect example of them all: Kukal's puffy, damp foot that I am about to kiss.

All I have to do is swallow a few tablets and I'll never see any of this again. I'll forget about it all, and everyone will forget about me. Life isn't for people like me.

It was growing lighter, then the sun came up. In order to get enough water for the animals, I had to drop the bucket down into the well four times. That's what drought means. There was a bitter taste in my mouth, bitterness inside me, bitterness in my soul. My black thoughts blotted out the light of the mercilessly burning sun. I covered my eyes with my hand and felt my tears flow between my fingers. I want to die. That will be simpler than trying to prove my innocence to my sister, to the prosecutor or to myself. It will certainly be easier than seeing those people with their theodolites again up here on the hill. I'm already fifty, I've lived for as long as I could.

When granny was seventy eight she had wanted to drown herself. Eventually she went off the idea after she had had a dream in which she was in Heaven, and someone there refused to give her a communion wafer because she had committed suicide, and then turned his back on her. She took this as a sign: she, after all, believed in the Kingdom of Heaven, but I don't.

A pain, far worse than any pain suffered as a result the beatings I had received, welled up in me. I drowned in it, and the words seemed to come of their own accord:

"Oh, mother, why did you bring me into this world?"

The Cardiostim Forte was waiting for me on the shelf, and the rope that I was crawling along led directly to it.

I was completely calm and totally aware of what I was doing as I poured a large handful of the little white tablets from the bottle into the palm of my hand. Then I heard your deep, bass voice:

"Hi! What are you doing?"

There was never anything more between us other than what there was. You never even once said to me that you loved me — not then, when we were young and lying on the green silky-damp moss, nor even more now, in the forest at night, when the shadows are like emptiness. But in the end it was you who saved me from death and from something even worse. I hadn't heard you drive up — in my state I was incapable of hearing any sounds from the outside world — but I couldn't fail to notice you when you appeared on the verandah.

Tolik, your figure, when you were standing there in the doorway with the light behind you, was darker than usual. I could scarcely make out your face. You took a few steps towards me, took my hand and turned it over, and you caught the tablets in your other hand and then went to the kitchen. I dragged myself after you. You poured the tablets into the stove, where they fell straight into the ash that I had not got around to cleaning out for so long.

"What's happened?" you asked quietly.

Sitting at the kitchen table, covered with old, well-worn oilcloth, I told you everything. How granny beat me because it was my fault the cow died. How the little face of my daughter looked accusingly at me when she was lying in her coffin. How Gosha had used me as a drug runner. How they had tortured me in prison. How Anton had betrayed me. How my sister had finally grown tired of my being so timid, hesitant and weak-willed. And how you had never said to me that you loved me. And how, after crawling on my knees to kiss Kukal's puffy, damp foot, I didn't want anything more than just to able to forget everything. That I simply cannot watch Kukal turn Dobratyche into one huge brothel.

You hung your head and said nothing. There was nothing you could say, and I understood that.

But then you did find some words. You had called on me quite by chance, you never did say "I love you", you asked me to go with you into the forest only out of pity and a feeling of tenderness. I understood that, but it was enough.

"Let's go," you said to me on that day, the seventh of July. "It's Kupala* today, we need to gather lime leaves and wild rosemary. Let's do it together. There's some wine in the cabin of the tractor, " you added after a short pause.

That settled it for me.

Ever since Ulia hurled the words "You destroy everything!" into my face, ever since she smashed the bottle of whisky against the wall, I haven't had so much as a sniff of alcohol.

Tolik quickly unhitched the cistern and climbed up to me in the cabin. He produced the bottle from under the driver's seat, pulled out the cork with his teeth and passed me the wine. Then he started the engine, and the tractor — now without its burden — drove away at a lively pace along the dusty road.

---

* The Feast of the Nativity of St John the Baptist, celebrated by the Orthodox in Belarus and Russia on 7 July.

I drank straight from the bottle and then put it down by my feet.

It's quite a long way to Hory. First you have to drive along a track through the forest, then along the main road (there was a notice fixed to a post by the roadside: "Incidents of rabies have been observed in the area. Keep away from wild animals"), then along an unpaved road across a flat dried-out field, with yellow grass on both sides of us. The short shadow of the tractor ran alongside. There were no wild animals to be seen.

We didn't say a word.

Both of us saw the Mercedes at the same time. There's a sizeable bay beyond the sluice gates; right on a sharp bend and parked just to one side of the road, stood the black car that I knew only too well. Next to it stood another car, silver-coloured. Tolik switched off the engine at once. My heart began to thump so loudly that it drowned out the roar of the water in the sluice.

"Turn round. I don't want to meet him. For the love of God turn round!"

"Just keep calm. I'll go and have a look to see what's going on."

Without shutting the cabin door, Tolik climbed down from the tractor. Keeping to the shadows cast by the bushes and stooping slightly, he moved swiftly forwards. He stopped suddenly, stood quite still for a second, then turned and waved, signalling me to come as quickly as I could. Cautiously I got down from the tractor, and the sun's heat immediately struck me on the back of my head.

Tolik warned me to be quiet by putting a finger to his lips.

We could see everything perfectly from behind the bush where we were standing.

Kukal was standing about ten metres away with his back to us, wearing only his swimming trunks. You could see how powerfully built he was, but you could also tell from his back that he was a little drunk. A bit further away, beyond the bushes, some people were splashing around in the bay. Kukal's people,

NATALKA BABINA

presumably. Now and again the roar of the water in the sluice was drowned by the squeals of the women in the group. A blue tablecloth with food and drink was spread on the grass.

I had no time to notice anything else, or to think or to look around before Tolik suddenly bent low, spurted forward, raced across the few metres that separated us from Kukal and jumped on him from behind like a lynx. Kukal was not expecting an attack from that quarter, and both of them tumbled into the water together.

I stood rooted to the spot, mouth agape, and watched as Tolik struggled to keep Kukal's head under water. Tolik is wiry and tenacious, but Kukal's body is big and well-fed. An overwhelming urge drove me forward to join them. I jumped into the water and grabbed hold of Kukal's legs with the full weight of my body, trying with all the strength I could muster to stop him from getting his head above water. I knew that if he had the chance to break free, he would shout out and his mates would come running from the bay. He was big, but there were two of us, and he was probably drunk. You only need three minutes to drown a man. And three minutes was the time that Tolik and I managed to hold out.

When he stopped struggling and stayed perfectly still, it sunk into me what we had done.

I got up from my knees and began to shake all over. A high-voltage bolt of electricity crackled right through my head, heart and arms.

The drowned man rocked gently in the shallow water, face down.

Kukal was drunk and fell from the shore into the water and drowned. The water is shallow by the shore, barely reaches the knees, but, then, how much water does a drunk need? Or even someone who isn't drunk? Man's life hangs by a thread. That's what everyone will say if we manage to get away from here.

We're murderers.

It all went blank, then I find myself in the cabin of the

tractor and Tolik is starting the engine. The tractor turns round. There is a puddle under me. Tolik's wet outline and his squinting dark eye.

What's happening back there now, by the bushes on the bay? What if Kukal's people have suddenly returned, perhaps they've found him already. What if they saw us, and even now are chasing after us or phoning the police? We're done for.

Tolik drove the tractor hard, I was thrown around the cabin.

"We should go to Hory through where the dachas are. We have to be seen there. It's not exactly an alibi, but it's better than nothing. We might be spotted if we went through Dobratyche, and if anything happens, we can more easily insist that, yes, we really had been to Hory, but we didn't go on that road, but by the road that goes past the dachas. The people in the dachas rarely wear watches on their wrists when they're working on their allotments. They tend to guess the time by the sun, and that could come in handy for us. Don't worry, it's more than likely that no one will trouble us. "Sod it," he muttered through his teeth as we emerged on to the main road.

"What is it?"

"It's Charota. He must have seen the tractor. That's his car over there.

A white 'Niva'* was turning on to the main road from the Dobratyche road about a kilometre away from us. It turned in the opposite direction but certainly could have seen us just as we were coming out from the road that leads to the sluice.

"What are we going to do now?"

"Whatever. Whatever will be, will be.

Tolik deliberately drove the tractor past the dachas in such a way as to make it produce a lot of noise, but I didn't actually see anyone. Maybe the dacha people were all hiding away from the baking heat in their hovels, watching the clock for the moment when they could run to catch the train. Then they

---

* Four-wheel drive vehicle like a Land Rover.

would certainly notice the exact time when we chugged past. Perhaps we're making a mistake that will cost us dear. I can just imagine the dialogue: "forensic analysis has ascertained that death occurred at 12.30. According to the statements of witnesses you emerged on to the main road from this road at 12.40, and at 12.50 you drove through the territory of the "Veteran" gardening club. This is all indirect proof that you could have committed the murder." Come off it, what are we talking about indirect proof for?! No, the dialogue will go like this: "Tracks from your tractor were found at the scene of the crime, as were your tracks on the shore. Taken together with the statements of witnesses who saw the tractor, this is almost certain proof of your guilt." And it will be a monologue, not a dialogue, because what answer can you give the investigator? Prosecutor Kuleshov with the sunburnt skin and the fire in his eyes?

Tolik turned the tractor into a cluster of oak trees and switched off the engine.

"Quick as you can." He shoved a basket into my hands and pushed me out of the cabin.

"Pick some savory." He gave me another push in the back. "Come on, we don't have time to hang around. There'll be time for gawping later on."

I gripped the basket feverishly and slowly looked at my surroundings.

A strong wind blew up. The old conifers in the Hory forest produced their own echoes — there was a constant rattling, cracking and crashing among the tree stumps and the sun's rays. A row of fragrant lime trees marked the spot where the farmhouse had once stood, on a slight rise in the ground. It was here that Tolik stood, rapidly breaking off small branches of fragrant lime flowers. There were some plum trees growing nearby that had long since gone wild. He tore the fruit from them too. Small clumps of savory and stonecrop luxuriated in the sun. Lower down, where there was once a stream, the valley was filled with misty waves of ragged robin. That's where the damp, marshy smell was coming from.

"Get ahold of yourself," yelled Tolik at me, in a rather nasty way I thought, and snatched the basket out of my hands. "You look like you've been turned into a pillar of salt, Everything's all right. It was a clean job. So what's wrong?"

"Tolik, I feel sick. I'm afraid!"

"Stop it!" Tolik fell to his knees and began to load up the basket with savory, all mixed up with fir needles, moss and sand. "OK, then, tell me, when I came to you this morning, you wanted to poison yourself, didn't you? Well, you did, didn't you? Yes, you did. That means you're not afraid of dying, doesn't it? Yes, it does. Then what the hell are you afraid of?" he thundered. "What do you have to be afraid of if you aren't even afraid of death?"

He slung both baskets on one arm, picked me up with the other arm and dragged me to the tractor.

"Now all you've got to do is to sit indoors and not go anywhere. I'll take the water, then I'll go and fetch Valik. If someone suddenly starts asking questions — but no one will ask any questions — you know nothing, we weren't anywhere near the sluice, we saw nothing." Tolik instructed me in what to say as we drove back at the maximum possible speed — past the dachas, along the main road and through the Dobratyche forest. "Lock yourself in and don't open the door. When's Ulia coming?"

"I don't know. Sometime late in the afternoon, I think. She has to be in a lot of places today."

"We'll be back before she arrives. Please God, everything's going to be OK. No more hysterics."

With these final words of command Tolik left me, and the tractor disappeared behind the fir trees. He had left me the bottle with what was left of the wine.

I opened the gate with an unsteady hand, and in so doing accidentally knocked my hip on the gatepost. I wasn't prepared for how painful it was. I lifted up my skirt, which still hadn't dried out. My thighs were covered in bruises.

These were the marks of where Kukal had lashed out at me. I could feel the vomit rising in my gullet. He had kicked out with his legs when he was trying to stand up, and now the marks of our struggle by the sluice are adorning my thighs. The whole picture suddenly rose before my eyes, every single detail: the noise of the water, Tolik, Kukal's legs kicking me hard in the belly, the hairs on his legs. I can't even say that I killed him with my bare hands. No, I killed him with the whole of my body, the fat body of a foolish fifty-year-old woman.

So, there you are then. You're a murderer. You're assuming the functions of the Lord God Himself.

I locked myself in the verandah, closed the curtains and, just as I was — still in my damp clothes — I stretched out on the floor. I only had to close my eyes, and once again I could hear the sound of water, I could see the straining muscles in Tolik's wiry arms, and feel Kukal's feet kicking me in the belly. I removed the cork from the bottle of wine, but then the realisation suddenly came over me that I couldn't. I couldn't swallow. Simply couldn't. My throat was constricted. The body of a murderer can't take alcohol. Drinking is a celebration. And my days of celebrating are over.

Somewhere inside me it felt like the tension in a coiled spring was suddenly released. It immediately straightened itself out and the two ends of it hit me so hard that I groaned with the pain. That's the kind of pain you get from an ulcer or a heart attack. It's the kind of pain you get when you're giving birth. Perhaps it's like that when you're being born. Or when you're dying.

But I didn't die.

THE DOG IT WAS THAT DIED

Ulia and Valik didn't react to Tolik's story in the way I had expected. Neither did they react in the way I had expected to the fact that they were sitting on the same bed cover as two murderers. We had spread the cover in the garden and were sitting on it so that we could talk without the risk of eavesdroppers listening in on our conversation.

Ulia arrived in a state of nervous tension, hiding her eyes. At one point in Tolik's story she raised her head and never took her eyes off me until the tale was told.

We phoned Zarnitskaya to tell her not to let Lina and Kazik out of the house, but to keep them in their room until Yurka came to collect them.

"So, Kukal's no longer with us. Well, he was a mad dog, so I'm not going to be writing an elegy for him. Now the question of selling your house is off the agenda. But there is one question still remaining: what happens next?" said Tolik, rounding off his story.

"Oh yes, it completely slipped my mind with all these other things." Ulia waved her hand and turned to her case. "I've brought you a proof copy of your book," and she held out a green volume for me to take.

"Good that there's a strong wind today — sand has probably already covered the tracks of the tractor on the road," Valik said, obviously concerned that suspicion should not fall on us.

Looking straight at me, he added in a perfectly calm voice:

"You don't need to tremble. It was the only way out. You can be proud of yourselves. I'll tell my grandchildren about you if I live that long."

In short, I found myself in the company of individuals who were even more amoral than I was; for them Kukal's death was almost a cause for rejoicing rather than an occasion for examining one's conscience and repentance.

I had a good look at them all, and then opened the book that Ulia had brought.

DESPAIR IS THE DAMP
OF HELL...

I was in a sort of disturbed mood for the next few days; I couldn't calm down and I couldn't concentrate on anything.

I was left virtually alone with my frayed nerves. Ulia hugged me when she left for another of her trips with her campaign team, on this occasion around the villages of the Stolin district. Charota had yoked Tolik and Valik so firmly together in the fight for the harvest that the metal detector lay idle for several days where it had been stashed away in the lumber-room — true, Tolik had arranged for us to be able to keep it for a bit longer. Yurka dropped by with the children to see me — just for an hour. He went to granny's grave, and then they all rushed off to Mensk.

So here I was all huddled up by myself in the yard.

To be quite honest, my conscience was no longer troubling me, and Kukal's ghost didn't come visiting me at night. I thought over everything very coldly and rationally and came to the conclusion that there was no reason for me to be upset: I had broken the commandment "Thou shalt not kill", and killed a man, but — as Azazello* said — "he absolutely had to be killed." I was greatly heartened by what Valik had said — and he's a man who always chooses his words carefully: that he would tell his grandchildren about us. OK, when I die I'll go to Hell, but Kukal was turning our lives into a living hell here, and I feel no regret at having stopped him.

---

* *Azazello:* One of Satan's companions on his visit to Moscow in Bulgakov's novel *The Master and Margarita.*

However, as much as I may not have regretted committing the crime, I certainly did regret the likely punishment.

I was in a state of panic about ending up in prison again. It's one thing to be in prison when you're young, although even then it's not exactly a bed of roses, but to find yourself inside again at the age of fifty, especially because of a piece of shit like Kukal... It wasn't difficult to imagine what that programme editor on Belarus TV would make of it. It would mean letting Ulia down again, yet again everything would be my fault. No, I won't be able to go through all that again. It really would be better for me to... I looked once more at the Cardiostim on the shelf.

There were moments — what am I talking about? There weren't just moments, there were whole long hours — when I fell into a state of utter despair. Every now and again I would look out on to the road, expecting to see the police arrive at any moment from behind the big hazelnut bush: (a) bearing greetings from the dark-haired prosecutor, to arrest me for the murder of granny, (b) bearing greetings from some other higher authority, to arrest me for the murder of Kukal or (c) not the police, but a gang of spetsnaz bearing no greetings whatsoever, but calling on me for the sole purpose of smashing my face in — after all, the election campaign hadn't yet come to an end!

It would probably have been easier for me if I had been able to get drunk. But I couldn't. My throat was too tight, my body wouldn't accept alcohol, so, holding the glass in my trembling hand, I tipped the wine out on to the floor.

… AS JOY IS THE SERENITY OF HEAVEN

Finally I did see someone appear from behind the bush: it was our local police officer. The pig's dinner landed up on the ground instead of in the trough. I would have said a prayer if I had only known how. Retribution, after keeping me waiting for a week and reducing me to a nervous wreck, had finally arrived in the shape of a smart young man with an honest, open face — a great rarity these days. He shut the gate behind him and walked over to me.

"Good day."

"Good day to you."

"Could you spare me some time? We need to have a talk."

"Of course, just go and sit over there, on the bench by the table. I'll be over in a minute, I've just got to give the pig its food."

"Keep calm, just keep calm," I kept repeating to my thoughts as I levelled the mounds of earth that the pig had dug up, and spread out some straw. This served only to make me even more nervous.

From under the pear tree the officer watched intently as I washed my hands.

"Just a sec," I said to him, contorting my face into a smile, and stepped up on to the verandah.

I took a bottle out of the fridge. No, I realised at once that I would not be able to take so much as a small sip, but all the same I grabbed hold of the whisky and took a glass and some ice.

"Would you like a drop?" and I offered the bottle to the officer.

He turned his head a little in order to read the label and, quite unexpectedly, accepted.

"Yes, go on, pour me out a little. Plenty of ice, please."

It was a blisteringly hot morning. Although the yard outside was well shaded by trees, it was no cooler.

The officer took the glass, shook it a bit, tried the whisky and said:

"Good stuff. Tasty. But let's get down to why I'm here. If you remember, we first met because the body of a man had been found not far from here. The body of a man brings me here again, although it's not the same one."

A cold shiver ran down my spine. Should I say something? Or keep my mouth shut?

The policeman looked sharply at me and continued:

"Exactly a week ago the body of a man was found near here. He was lying in the water next to the sluice. He had drowned. He was a wealthy, influential businessman, well-known round here. You knew him, didn't you?

"Mmm" and a demented look on my face was the only answer I could offer.

"Ivan Kukal," explained the police officer. "I know that there was some sort of major disagreement between the two of you."

I was being to shake all over. Another second and I would faint. I could feel a fit of hysteria coming on. But then I looked up: behind the policeman's back I could see the knoll, the oak woods, the oval shape of the lake and a piece of the blue horizon. Whatever happens to me, no one is going to level the knoll, or fill in the lake, or chop down the oaks... At least, not for now. For the time being there'll be no whores or gangland scum trampling the Dobratyche paths. Unexpectedly, I calmed down. I no longer gave a damn. Que serà, serà.

The bowl of ice that I had taken from the fridge had now melted in the heat. I poured the water into my glass and tipped it all over my head.

"It's very hot," I said to the police officer. "I need to freshen up. Don't take any notice. What was it you were saying? Something about Kukal drowning? That's something I didn't know. Yes, there were indeed major disagreements between us, so I'm not going to weep for him. Good riddance."

The policeman seemed to cheer up when I poured the water on my head. He took another sip from his glass, and his face showed how satisfied he felt.

"The provincial prosecution service has taken charge of the investigation, but because the death occurred in the district for which I am responsible, I'm also involved. However, and I will be quite open with you, I am not here in an official capacity, but simply as a private individual," he pointed to his glass of whisky as proof that this was a private visit. "The investigation is almost complete. I thought you might be interested to know what conclusions we have reached."

"Well, if that's what you thought..."

"Briefly then. The death occurred when Kukal was at a picnic with colleagues and friends. As is usual on such occasions, there was a lot to drink, and soon the whole company was unable to put two coherent words together, so that when they were questioned it was difficult to make any sense of what they said. The soberest among them was Kukal's driver. He showed us where they found Kukal's body in the water. They fished him out at once and tried to resuscitate him as best they could, but without success. Then they took him to the hospital... On the next day a criminal investigation into the death was begun, and a forensic team was called in to examine the scene... They were working on two basic theories of what had happened. The first was that the victim, in a drunken state, fell into the water and drowned. This version was rejected. I won't go into the finer points, but I can say that there are ways of determining whether a person drowned, or, so to speak, was helped to drown. Forensic analysis showed with absolute certainty that he had been helped. Then the question becomes: who? This then became two separate questions: was it someone who had come with Kukal, or someone outside the group who had come on foot — or, let's say, arrived by tractor?

An examination of the scene produced little by way of hard

evidence — the strong wind had literally blown away any traces that there may have been — so we had to rely primarily on witness statements.

There was something that put the investigators on their guard at once: there were two cars at the picnic — something that one of the good ladies of the company let slip. There was only one car when they brought the body to the hospital — the other car didn't show up. What's more, when the investigators started questioning Kukal's companions about this, they at first denied that there were two cars. It was only when the investigators had pushed them into a corner, that they confirmed that, yes, there were two cars, that... then the bluster and blather began again, but when they were pressed really hard, they admitted that Kulya and his men were in the other car. Kulya is a recognised authority in the criminal world who's been on the wanted list for ages. What's more, it's no secret that Kulya and Kukal were at daggers drawn; we've known about it for a long time. Witnesses said that the picnic had been organised with the aim of bringing about a reconciliation between the "two Ks". According to their account Kulya was also bathing, but with the others some way off. They all came back together. When they found Kukal's body, Kulya left immediately; he knew full well that the police would have to be dragged in, and he had absolutely no desire to be around when the police arrived. We may assume, then, either that a quarrel was somehow sparked off between the two old enemies, or that Kulya had intended right from the very start to remove his rival, and was using the pretext of a reconciliation as cover. Choosing a convenient moment, either Kulya or one of his gang drowned Kukal. The witnesses said nothing that backs up this version, but it's highly likely they didn't see anything. It's even more likely that, if they had indeed seen anything, they're keeping quiet because they're afraid of Kulya.

During the investigation of the other version of events — that someone not involved with the meeting of Kukal and Kulya was responsible for the murder — some people fishing near the scene and some of the people in the dachas were questioned. It was one of these who said that at about the time of the murder he had seen the tractor belonging to citizen Anatol Hadun drive past, with "one of the twin sisters from Dobratyche with him in the cabin". Tractor tracks were indeed found near the scene of the incident, but unfortunately it was impossible to identify them with any certainty; too much sand had been blown on top of them. Nevertheless, this was sufficient for the investigators to begin to look more closely at this line of inquiry. However, it soon became clear that this was a dead end; two witnesses that the investigators held in high regard had seen you, and it was plain from their statements that you could not possibly have been at the scene of the crime. This means that the tracks left at the scene must have been from a different tractor. The first of these witnesses is Director Charota of Agrovitalika Plus — you probably don't know him. He stated that at 12.40 precisely he turned on to the main road from Dobratyche and saw Hadun's tractor driving from Stradche towards the road to Hory. The tractor turned on to the road that leads to "the dachas on the furthest edge of the settlement", in the witness's own words. The tractor must therefore have been coming in the opposite direction to where the sluice is. The witness went on to say that he recognises the sounds made by all the vehicles in his firm, and besides, this particular tractor has a distinguishing mark — one of its wings is red. Charota later spoke with Hadun. Hadun explained that he had been going into the forest on a personal matter — he wanted to gather some medicinal herbs — and Charota had become very angry because Hadun had been driving around looking for herbs instead of going where he was told. The second witness recalled seeing a blue tractor with a red wing ten minutes earlier, at 12.30, in Stradche itself. So there you have your alibi.

"Who is the other witness?" I asked, trying hard to conceal my amazement.

"I am," the young man answered calmly. "I was in Stradche

on a case, and saw your tractor near the shop. I remembered the time because I was completing a report right at that moment which needed to be timed exactly."

We looked straight into each other's eyes, and I felt the tears well up...

Charota, whose son had become a drug addict thanks to Kukal, had seen us *driving out* of the road from the sluice, but said that we were *driving towards* the road that leads to Hory from the other direction and turned towards "the dachas on the furthest edge of the settlement"... And this young police officer hated Kukal no less than I did, and also saw our tractor in a place where it wasn't...

"So, you see, sometimes it's not so bad having a blue tractor with a red wing, even if the traffic police might cause you trouble because of it. And sometimes it's good to have a snifter in the morning like this. What is it the Russians say: *Have a stiff drink in the morning and you're free for the rest of the day?* Right then, *all the best*," — these last words he said in the local dialect. "I'll go for a walk through the forest. I hear that there's a good crop of mushrooms."

Against all the rules of etiquette, he proffered me his hand first and held my cold, weak claw in a powerful grip.

I said goodbye, hoped that he would enjoy his break and invited him to drop by any morning whenever he felt in need of freedom. I watched him for a long time, until his back disappeared behind the bushes.

I DIDN'T GET HIS AUTOGRAPH

The morning had come to such a triumphant conclusion that I spent the rest of the day in a state of blissful euphoria. I felt unusually light-headed, and didn't try to conceal it. It was exactly like the feeling I had as a child when the long plait that I had nurtured for all my short life was ceremonially cut off. Domestic tasks that used to weigh heavily on my shoulders suddenly did themselves. I made a pool for the geese out of an old trough and scratched the pig's back — it lay down on the ground at once and waggled its trotters in the air for sheer joy. And I had a natter by the mobile shop with Yarashykha, Lyonikha and the Uruguayan about how long the street lights in Dobratyche that they switched on yesterday would stay on once the election was over and done with. Judging by how everyone turned towards me as I approached, by how friendly people were to me and by the jokes that flew around, I gathered that they all knew about the business with Kukal, and that the whole of Dobratyche approved. This raised my spirits even higher. I even dismantled the dogs' kennels without feeling as upset as I thought I would. I had a bite to eat, then decided to go up on the roof. I was coming back to life, and once again I was feeling the urge to return to the hole in time. While looking at the roof from below in the yard, I tried to puzzle out what this ability of mine to travel to the past depended on. What was most important? Was it a particular place or time of the day? And, for Heaven's sake, did I really travel back in time, or was it all in my imagination? Everything that I had seen in my trips into the holes was so clear, so life-like and varied, and the trips themselves occurred so unexpectedly, that it all seemed — as Feuerbach might have said — like objective reality. However, common sense and my own materialist experience of life suggested that it was nothing but a series of subjective hallucinations. I turned to go and fetch the ladder, and jumped in surprise. Mikhas Yarash was standing right behind me. He must have come through the gate without making a sound and was just standing there silently.

"I want to talk to you," he said, without a word of greeting. "I want to say I'm sorry," he added after a pause.

"OK, let's go and sit down."

We sat at the table under the pear tree, where I had already been sitting that morning with the police officer.

"I'm the one who's guilty of granny Makrynya's death," he obviously found it difficult to get the words out. "But I didn't want her to die."

I jumped again.

"You? Why? How? It wasn't Kukal? I don't understand..."

"You have some xerox copies of old documents lying around in the house..."

"Yes."

"It's all because of them. Do you remember I came round to ask you to show me how to switch on the Ukrainian spell check in Word? Ulia phoned and you left the room, I had nothing else to do, so I started to flick through the pile on the table. Almost at once I came across a very interesting document..."

"Khrystof Tryzna's complaint against the squire of Kastamaloty?"

"So you've seen it?

I nodded.

"I know how much the pieces his father made are worth nowadays. For about fifteen years I've had a passion for numismatics and antiques. That explains it all really. What was I supposed to do? Show you the document? But that would have meant letting the treasure slip out of my hands. I had no way of knowing how you would react, you're so unpredictable! I needed to look right through all the piles of documents calmly and without haste; who know what other documents I might find? But how could I do it unnoticed? Should I steal them? There's always somebody in the house. I didn't worry too much about granny Makrynya — she was already a bit deaf and her eyesight was poor; I had no doubt that I would be able to creep into the house quietly, even if she was inside. But it was different with you around... I knew that you were a light sleeper, and you never go far from the house, so I decided to find a way of getting you into a deep sleep. It had to be a way that was safe for both me and you. I did a search on the internet and found something that would do the trick on one of the forums: Cardiostim Forte mixed with coffee. According to the bloke who posted the information the mixture guarantees a long, sound sleep. I knew that they had Cardiostim in our local chemist's, and that granny takes it anyway. I also knew that you could buy it without prescription, unlike sleeping tablets. I did some more searching on the net, but I soon realised that I wouldn't find anything simpler and more effective. I ground the tablets into a fine powder; it filled about half a little bottle. The next question I had to deal with was how to mix it with ground coffee beans and, even more important, how to get it to you. Should I buy some exotic brand of coffee, mix in the Cardiostim and give it to you as a present? Too risky, you might probably suspect that something was up. Should I try to add the Cardiostim to coffee you already had in the house? I set off for your place that night more with the aim of 'casing the joint' than hoping for anything else, but — miraculously — the door was unlocked. What, don't you lock your door at night?"

"Yes, we do!"

And then it struck me that Mishyk had got into our verandah on the night that I went off to earth up the potatoes! It was like being hit on the head with a big stick. That means it was my fault after all! If I hadn't felt compelled to go to the allotment that night, Mishyk would never have been able to get into the house, and granny would not have been poisoned. God! I remembered how angry she had been with me for going gallivanting around at night. At the time I had laughed it off, but she had been absolutely right, fatally so in fact!

My young neighbour continued his story: "I went quietly into your house, I knew where you kept the coffee — you've made me coffee enough times whenever I've called... On the next day I felt really uneasy, early in the morning I decided to go to your house and wait close by for you to drink some coffee and fall asleep."

And I would indeed have had some coffee if I hadn't decided to break the ban on alcohol after the fright I had had that night! The whisky saved me, but it killed granny!

"Then I could have hidden myself somewhere and read all the documents in peace. But there was something troubling me, so I went back on to the forum where I found the recipe. I was horrified when I saw that there was a new comment, this time from a doctor who wrote that the mixture offered as a sleeping potion was in fact dangerous for a healthy person, and for anyone with a weak heart it could be fatal! I rushed over to your place without closing the computer, but... Your granny was sitting at the table and there was a mug of coffee in front of her. I could see just by looking at her that it was too late. I was in shock. Granny Makrynya had died because of me... I didn't know what to do. This I hadn't expected. You can't imagine what it's like to know that you've murdered someone. (A thought flashed through my mind: 'I can now. Yarashikha evidently hasn't shared her suspicions about me and Kukal with her grandson'). If I had been able to think calmly and rationally, I would have walked right into the house and do what I had planned to do, but no such thought entered my head. I rushed home as fast as I could. I sat staring blankly at the computer screen. I was in a right panic, I can tell you. Finally I decided to return, take the packet of coffee that I had laced with Cardiostim and pour away what was left of the coffee in the mug. For a time I was unable to move, but finally I got up and went over to your house. I could see Zarnitskaya's car by the fence, then I heard you crying, and I knew I had come too late again.

I was in a state of shock. I cursed myself that things had turned out that way. I simply wanted to find a way to get rich and as a result ended up killing someone! More than that, I was afraid that you were in danger! You might make yourself some coffee from the same packet! I made up my mind to take the packet at the first opportunity, but that evening when my grandma and I came to sit by the coffin, I noticed that it wasn't where I expected to find it. What happened to it?"

"Zarnitskaya took it. She smelled the Cardiostim."

"Did she?" Mishyk looked surprised. "I didn't know that. Even so, I came several times to try to see where the pack of coffee was, and to take it away if I could... So that's how it all happened. Forgive me if you can. It was when I saw you with old Lyalka's body that I knew that I had to ask your forgiveness."

I didn't say anything. There's been something about me that I've had for as long as I can remember — apart from my lame leg, that is. I've never been able to distinguish between truth and falsehood. I was always ready to believe anything I read, or anything that people told me... Even when what they said was quite patently false, I could never say to the liar's face: "You're a liar!" I just couldn't say it. The most I could do was to say sorry, turn my back and walk away However, probably as a result of what I had been through over the previous few days, I was now no longer the same person. There was something about what Mishyk was saying — I could still remember when he was a boy and his grandmother had saved my life a few weeks before — that made me feel uneasy inside. Were his words unnatural? Or theatrical? Yes, he was telling the truth, but was he being completely open with me?

"You know, Mishyk, I don't think you've come here just to say you're sorry. I think you've got something else in mind. I don't believe a word you're saying."

Mishyk's head drooped.

"OK, that's your privilege," he said after a few seconds, and the tone of his voice had changed. "Why should I try to deceive you? Why should I put the blame for your granny's death on myself? I didn't have to admit to it, after all. Especially now that you're finished. You may be strong and brave, but they will sweep you away, chew you up and spit you out. It's not long now till the elections, and once they're over I don't envy what's going to happen to you. I have to go on living here, and God will go on sending me poetry. You do believe that my poetry is sent to me by God, don't you?" I felt compelled to nod my agreement. "Well, there you are then. In fifty years' time people will have forgotten about these elections and about you, but they will remember me. And they will remember Dobratyche, the village I write about. Remember that what is written lasts for ever."

"So write down everything that you've just told me. And sign it. Leave me your autograph. I've been accused of granny's death, but you know that, don't you? Your account of events will be the proof that I'm innocent."

"No, that's something I'm not going to get involved in. My confession won't help you in any way, and you know it. If they've made up their minds to put you in prison, they'll do it regardless. All the prosecutor will do is tear up my statement in front of you, and there won't be anything you can do about it. The only way out for you and Ulia is to flee and hide somewhere abroad."

"Ah! So that's what this is all about! We should run abroad, should we? You really are so concerned for our welfare, are you? No, these aren't your own words! They've sent you here to be all nice and friendly, and persuade us to leave and hide out somewhere. I'm right, aren't I? They're trying a different tack now, are they? They've realised that beating us up and bringing criminal charges against us won't work, so they want to persuade us to leave, do they? So they send the best poet of Belarus round to ask us — strong, brave people (your words) — to save our own skins by running way abroad? It isn't to their advantage to kill us, much better if we give up of our own accord."

"You can't say that I'm not right, can you? It's like banging your head against a brick wall, you'll never get anywhere. All you'll do is ruin your own lives and the lives of Ulia's children. The conditions aren't yet right for régime change in this country, because people really do support what we've got now. You don't know the people here at all. I can re-educate them with my poetry much sooner than you can with your meetings and calls to action."

Suddenly it struck me what all this was about. All the pieces fell into place.

"Now I understand what happened! They were keeping an eye on you, you're a potentially dangerous type. After all, you write in Belarusian, you publish your poetry in *Nasha Niva* and *ARCHE*.* Obviously they're going to watch you at a time like this. And then all of a sudden they find out that you poisoned my granny. What a gift that was! So they came to you and offered you a choice: either work for them or go to prison. And you made your choice. Am I right?"

"What else was I supposed to do?"

"Obviously, nothing else. They, of course, pulled the wool over your eyes like they always do, made it seem that they knew a great deal more than they were letting on. You must have thought that they had also got hold of the pack of coffee, didn't you? It's all quite clear. But why do you go on deceiving yourself?"

"What do you mean, deceiving myself? How am I doing that?"

"What about believing that you can educate people with your poetry? You won't be able to write real poetry any more, don't you understand that? Who's going to let you? From now on, matey,

---

* *ARCHE (Beginning):* Belarusian-language monthly journal, publishing lite-
rary works as well as articles on history, literature and philosophy. In opposition to the present regime in Belarus.

all you'll do is compose propaganda verses about happy children in our country. You're concerned about people remembering you in fifty years' time? You poor man! You've signed your own death warrant, not as a man, but as a poet. It's over, there's no Mikhas Yarash any more, only Mishyk Yarashyshyn: *Mikey, Yarash's missus's grandson!*"

Now he was really angry.

"All I wanted was to ask your forgiveness, and lift this burden from my soul. And I really did want to warn you of the terrible danger you're in. But you're incapable of reacting in a normal way, aren't you?"

"The one thing I hate more than anything is demagoguery. Take that to your present employers. Now go home, Mishyk, and never come here again."

I felt very tired. Perhaps not so much tired as completely drained; it was as if people had been throwing stones at me until I was almost dead, and then at the last minute they had left me alive.

Mishyk stood up and, without a word, went out through the gate.

So that was it, then — first euphoria, then shock. And all in one day!

But I will say this: who would have thought that there could be so many murderers in Dobratyche? The end of the world is nigh.

I got up as well, intending to go back into the house. The route was exactly the same as the one I had taken when I crawled on my knees towards Kukal's feet. All of a sudden — right after I had stood up and taken a few steps — the world dissolved before my very eyes. The scene changed completely. Our house vanished, as if it had never been. There was no more pear tree. The walnut tree had also gone. The air became colder. The trees had shifted their position. There were no people around. Where was I? Previously, whenever I had fallen into a hole in time, I had always seen people. Now everything was quiet and cold. And totally empty. Why was I being shown this bleak scene?

It reminded me of my thoughts about the world ending soon, and I felt very afraid. I needed to escape this desolate vision and overcome my fear, so I shouted out loud, and the scene disappeared. I sank down on the bench. What was that? I still don't know. Maybe, the future. Perhaps it was a moment in the past. I haven't the faintest idea.

However, that was the day, the very moment even, when I finally realised where I needed to look for doors to the holes in time: anywhere where dramatic events had taken place, or where someone had experienced powerful emotions. Just think of all the times I had walked up to that bench and back, and nothing ever happened, but now this was the spot where I had known humiliation and fear, and a door in time opened up before me. That explains what happened in the prison. It's not difficult to guess the horrors that the prisoners had experienced there in the years of its existence. Exactly the same applies to the fortress; how many people had died in torment there, or had lived in fear of death every waking moment? But what about our roof? Unable to conceal my excitement at what I had discovered, I hurried off to see the Uruguayan.

He was just in the process of smoking his bees, and was very unwilling to break off. Nevertheless I asked him:

"Uncle Henik, it was you who built our house, wasn't it?"

"Yes."

"Then tell me, did something unusual happen while you were raising the roof?"

The Uruguayan looked at me suspiciously.

"Why are you asking me that?"

"I just need to know, that's all.

He took off his beekeeper's hat and veil.

"Something did happen. Even now it still strikes fear into my heart when I think about it. We were putting up the rafters. Your granddad, me and Yovik. Makrynya was helping. My little Valeryk — he was about three at the time — was down on the ground playing. Just as we were pulling up one of the beams,

I lost my balance and the beam fell. One more second and it would have killed Valeryk. But your granddad, God rest him, leapt down, put both arms under the beam and held it. It broke both his arms, but Valeryk lived. That's how it was."

I thanked the Uruguayan.

So I had guessed right!

Holes in time occur in those places where people — God's creatures or descendants of the apes — have experienced something terrifying.

MAKRYNYA'S FIFTH CHILD

Good Lord, what on earth is going on!

The townsfolk were in a state of open rebellion. Discontent had been swelling for some time; in Berastse — and, I suspect, everywhere else — the people had become loud and angry at life in general. I often heard furious shouting: in the market when the price of salt had gone up, on the bridge when a toll was introduced for local carts. Both Polish and Ruthenian* voices were raised in anger in the town hall, when the councillors were in session. There was tumult in the churches whenever delegates to the national and provincial parliaments met together... A wife had somehow displeased her husband, and immediately there would be yelling so loud that the whole street could hear it. An apprentice has cut the leg of a boot crooked — cause for wailing and lamentation. A tailor steals a client from his neighbour — a scuffle breaks out at once. When the tax-collector comes round for the taxes owing, there's howling like someone's been murdered. I already knew a lot about the town and the people living there.

Now that I understood the mechanics — if that is the right word — of where I could pass through a portal to the holes in time, I began to make as much use of it as I could. I had the feeling that there wasn't much time left. On the very next day I set off for the fortress. Thanks to Lauraneuskaya, I knew more

---

* *Ruthenian:* adjective applied to people of the Commonwealth who spoke a Slavonic language other than Polish, i.e. the ancestors of modern Belarusians and Ukrainians. By religion they would in the seventeenth century have been mainly Uniate or Orthodox.

or less exactly where the old town had been. I wandered around
the completely empty open-air museum of the "Brest hero-
fortress", along the grey and red asphalt paths, among the forts,
casemates and concrete monuments that had been painted to
make them look as though they were made of bronze. This was
the ground once trampled with much pomp and circumstance by
the feet of the great of this world: Trotsky, Pilsudski, Hitler and
his Mussolini, Brezhnev and Masherau*, Lukashenka, and now
Tarasenka, and many others besides. This was the ground where
I now walked quietly, listening intently to myself and arousing
the suspicions of two security guards who were obviously bored
out of their minds with having nothing to do. My task was to
unwind the clockwork of time to a point much further back; to
go past the clear air of wars and periods of construction, fires
and starvation where everything can be clearly understood, and
through the murk of history seek an answer to a question that
no one has thought of asking. I continued to trail around the
fortress; I was apparently the only visitor. The guards — a couple
of tough-looking young lads — followed me. I could understand
them, but they prevented me from concentrating on finding an
entrance to the hole. I was saved by a chance occurrence. Sitting
on the grass I desperately tried — and failed — again to reach
the state where I could see the world in sharp relief, down to
the tiniest detail. At first the guards just hung around but then
finally made up their minds to come over to me.

"It's forbidden to sit on the lawns," one of them informed
me. "The grass wasn't sown just so you could have a sit down."

Instead of replying, I just pointed with my finger. The two
guards turned round at the same time, one of them gasped and
they both set off at a run. Behind their backs, in the car park of the

---

* *Masherau (1918-1980):* in Russian Piotr Masherov. There is still something of
a Masherau cult in Belarus. He was appointed First Secretary of the Central
Committee of the Communist Party of Belarus in 1965. It was widely believed
that he defended Belarusian national interests against Brezhnev. His death in
a car accident has never been fully explained.

restaurant called "Defence" — it was situated in the casemates near the entrance; specialities of the house included vodka labelled "Citadel" and beef cutlets of unimaginable toughness rejoicing in the name "Batallion Commander Zubachov"* — so, as I was saying, near this restaurant there were two yobbos avidly attacking a flashy car with metal rods. You could see a heavy rain of glass fragments falling to the ground, but — because of the distance — you couldn't hear anything. The guards ran up to the car and started a fight with the two lads, who had no intention of giving up easily. Diners in the restaurant were also anxious to join in the fray. It was then that a police 'Opel' drove up at speed and screeched to a halt. As soon as I was left alone, I immediately fell into a hole. I had worked it out correctly!

After that day the guards never troubled me again. The owner of the flashy car was clearly well-versed in such matters, and sued the museum management for an enormous sum of money because of their failure to ensure adequate security on the territory under their control. Consequently the museum director ordered the security personnel to be stationed permanently by the restaurant. He reckoned, justifiably, that another such incident would bankrupt the whole establishment.

By now I was familiar with the old town, and could even recognise some of its noisier inhabitants. My wanderings led me to quite different places. Naturally I was most interested in Makrynya. I already knew where her house stood — in the northern part of the fortress, on the bank of the Buh, where there is now a wasteland strewn with broken bricks and over-grown with hogweed — and have been inside it. I've found Master Tryzna's shop in the market. Makrynya and Tryzna did get married, and the mayor's wife didn't die. I have seen this imperious woman many times in the market.

---

* *Ivan Zubachov:* commanded the defence of the Brest Fortress from the moment of the German attack on 22 June 1941 until his capture a few days later.

The Calvinists (including Makrynya and her children) went to their services in the large old church of St Nicholas. It had a leaky roof, with the result that the floors and plastered walls were almost always disfigured by damp stains. Master Tryzna and his sons went every Sunday to their recently built little wooden church of St Paraskeva by the river. It had jolly little tin-covered cupolas. On one occasion I even found my way into a school. The schoolmaster — I heard them use the word *'dydyktar'* — was conducting a class of quite grown-up youths who were seated around him. They were learning how to draw the graph of the function $y=x^2$ in order to calculate the trajectory of shot fired from a harquebus; my eyes widened in amazement. I spent half a day there and was absolutely astounded at what was being studied. Judging by the topknots worn by the students, this must have been the Brest fraternity school.*

I liked the inn very much. It was kept by a swarthy Jewish woman called Esterka. She never took off her little round cap that was stitched all over with glass beads and always wore a clean coarse-cloth apron. I really wanted to taste the *palyukhi* [dumplings made of buckwheat flour, eggs and milk and boiled in bouillon] and the *hrechanaya babka* [savoury cake of buckwheat flour filled with fried pork fat and onions] that were served up to anyone with a couple of pennies, and the sausages that were brought out on a board to those who had a groat, and a piece of smoked sheatfish. But the most frequent item brought out for the guests was drink; it made everyone merry, irrespective of how much money they had — pennies, groats or even the large silver coins they called *tynfy*. Looking cautiously to left and right, Esterka would now and again run over to her neighbour's house — Makrynya's — and return holding a bottle or jug that she had covered with a cloth, and again she would

---

* *Fraternity Schools:* such schools were set up by the Orthodox laity in the seventeenth century in an attempt to counter the Catholic Church's active promotion of education.

keep her eyes peeled. By running to and fro I was able to work out that Esterka the innkeeper was doing business with Nachko, Makrynya's servant boy. In his turn, he was distilling moonshine and brewing beer in a root cellar behind where Makrynya lived.

The life of the town fascinated me.

There were gangs of skinny-legged youths who crept along the castle walls in the evening twilight with daggers in their hands.

There were the women on the Buh, with their weaving paddles and baskets. Their voices carried, and every single one of them was pregnant.

There was the market with its talk of the exchange rates of numerous European currencies, and endless complaints about taxes: there seemed to be taxes on everything. Of course there was a poll tax, but then there were taxes on the manufacture and sale of alcohol, on salt and on herrings, as well as a tax for the maintenance of roads and bridges.

There was the trumpet call every morning.

And in the new district of the city called Nalozki there were ceaseless quarrels among the builders. The city was growing, there was a real building boom. Grand stone houses were springing up all over the place. Agents showed them to potential buyers; they would turn up their noses, the prices fell, and Milord the Mayor, a truly insatiable type, was dissatisfied.

The street called Rotten was where the Jews lived; a Jewish apothecary has on offer a remedy for fever — a decoction of willow bark and something else (exactly what that 'something else' is the apothecary won't say), but he guarantees it will relieve the symptoms. It costs three *tynfy*. This isn't real money for the Lady Mayoress, but her coins — as it turns out — are from Moscow, and the apothecary refuses to take them. They settle on payment of one goat.

Goats are a whole subject to themselves. A young leaseholder from Kastamaloty, coming out of Esterka's inn in a merry state, chased away Milady Bahushova's herd of forty goats with his sword, and four got lost somewhere. Shouts and yells in the magistrates' court on this account (I am lying pressed against the fortress museum's giant piece of statuary entitled *"Thirst"* so as not to miss a single word). Milady Bahushova's got her teeth into this one. Let the young man do what he likes on the land he leases, but there's no law against goats walking in the streets of the city!

I'm hearing the name Khmel more and more: Khmel will cut taxes, Khmel will strip the Jews of the right to levy customs dues, Khmel is giving land to the Cossacks, Khmel is giving land to the peasants, Khmel is fighting for the faith, Khmel will cut taxes. The Virgin Mary appeared to some boys in Kastamaloty when they were grazing the cattle, and told the to wait for Khmel... Khmel — the very name had an intoxicating effect on people.*

It's all so fascinating, it simply takes my breath away.

Early this morning the market place was buzzing with rumour, and finally it exploded. The plague's here, in Berastse! The King ordered the transfer of sessions of the city court to Kobryn. The first to give vent to their discontent at this were the salters from Kodan, who had come to the city for a hearing of their dispute with the elders of the Berastse Jewish community. Now they will have to waste another day in getting to Kobryn, and meanwhile everything is just standing idle in Kodan. The expenses are mounting up! The salters were ganging up together in a hostile group by the town hall, shouting and yelling threats. (I recalled one of granny's sayings: "When from Kodan blows the wind, it's the surest sign that God is kind", but I had no idea that they produced salt there at one time.)

Meanwhile Herman of Valynka, the gravedigger, had arrived in the shop of Master Yarash, the butcher — who also dealt in animal skins — and announced that in the previous week he had

---

* *Khmel:* a shortened form of the name Khmelnytsky, but also a word in its own right, meaning 'hops' or, more generally, 'tipsiness'.

earned a tidy sum, but from now on he was only going to bury the dead in communal graves, and only if the magistrates paid him for it, otherwise...Then the Lady Mayoress came into the fly-covered butcher's shop, the crowd inside parted to make way for her, she began to poke and sniff the pork legs from all sides and examine the ribs — only the best for the Lady Mayoress. The tension showed on Master Yarash's face.

Then Titus, the clown from Volhynia, a tall, strong man who could lift a millstone, tottered across the market square in a zig-zag pattern and fell where the cobblestones ended and the weeds began.

A priest in the butcher's shop crossed himself and said:

"God is angry with the people of Berastse."

The salters began to shout even louder.

Up spoke the Lady Mayoress, wiping her fingers on her skirt:

"Because the heathens have multiplied, they that do deals with the enemy of the human race, they cast spells and poison good Christian souls."

I could hear Titus vomiting (a thought suddenly occurred to me: can I catch the plague? That's all I need).

"We should go in solemn procession round the city." This suggestion came from Milady Bahushova. I had noticed that she almost invariably appeared on the scene whenever the Lady Mayoress was around.

"How will that help, now that we have all manner of wizardry and heresy running wild in the city?"

"What was that about wizardry?" The priest obviously felt that the Lady Mayoress was encroaching on his professional interests.

"What, you don't know?" The Lady Mayoress certainly knew how to put pregnant pauses to good use. "Makrynya's youngest boy has six toes on each foot! And you know what that means, don't you, Father?"

"But he's been baptised!"

"And we know where he was baptised, don't we? Over there in Mlyny, where the priest's never sober and he's a bigamist, and the other year they made that deacon of his do penance. That man would even permit the Antichrist to take communion! It's God's honest truth I'm telling you, Makrynya's had carnal knowledge of the Unclean One, and there's the result — this six-toed monstrosity! I noticed a long time ago how he walks around with shoes on his feet even in summer. Who does he think he is, the son of a king? There we are, then. That clinches it."

This line of argument affected the whole company — they were all bare-footed, including the Lady Mayoress and the Reverend Father.

"Lyauko has six toes on each foot? How do you know that, milady?" The priest expressed his doubts very delicately. "Milady Makrynya performs many good deeds that are pleasing to God. Last year she gave money to build a church in Stradche, and the year before that in Kastamaloty…"

"Father, you shouldn't let the money cloud your eyes. She's very generous with her donations to the Church precisely because she's committed so many sins. She's the reason why God has sent plague and starvation down upon us in Berastse!"

"Let's kill the Devil's spawn!" shouted someone in the mob that had begun to gather round the butcher's shop after the Lady Mayoress had appeared there.

"Kill! Kill!" The words ran across the market square and turned round the corners of the houses into the surrounding streets and alleyways.

"We know why Makrynya always has such good fortune. She's built herself a fine town house, and the King has issued her with a special charter, granting her relief from payment of taxes. Which of us can boast of something like that, eh? The Devil comes to her aid!"

A cart came on to the market square, piled high with corpses. The carter himself was a really weird-looking type, probably drunk. This was what the plague looked like.

At the sight Milady Bahushova began to wail:

"We're going to die, we're going to die like dogs, God has turned His face from us because we have forgotten to fear Him!"

"Let's kill the monster, we can strangle him, use our knives on him!" The mob surrounding the butcher's shop was growing larger by the minute. "Let them pay, it's all their fault!"

"On to Makrynya's house! Let's make her hand over the monster! We'll kill him for the glory of God!"

The salters from Kodan were already waving their knives.

Across the market square, where the stone shops stand, where the wind flaps the awnings, where deep black muddy puddles glisten, the mob moved on to Makrynya's house. I raced after them, trembling with excitement — past museum exhibits of World War II heavy guns, past the restored Russian church. I was afraid that some unforeseen event might stop me from finding out what happened in the end. I needn't have worried. I reached the hole before the mob got anywhere near Makrynya's house. I emerged right at the moment when Esterka realised what was going on and hurriedly put up the shutters on the windows of the inn. The hubbub was getting closer. The Lady Mayoress was at the head of the mob, followed closely — as if they were pinned together — by Milady Bahushova. The mob had doubled in size. There was not a sound from Makrynya's house.

"Makrynya! Come out and face us! Bring out your Devil's spawn!" This was Ivan Kukal shouting, a nephew of the Lady Mayoress; I knew this strapping youth, I had already seen him a couple of times in the city. And now here he was, at the head of the mob, standing side by side with his aunt.

A stone was thrown at one of the windows; it pierced the oiled paper stretched across the frame.

As white as her coif, Makrynya was now standing on her stone doorstep; she held a sword in her hand.

The rumpus the mob was making quietened down a little.

"Bring Lyauko out and make him show us his feet!" Milady

Bahushova yelled. "Bring him out. Why do you fear to show him to us, if he is not the Devil's spawn?"

"I'll take you to court for those words. Why have you come here, you feeble-minded wastrels. So you've heard that Master Tryzna is away on his travels, have you? The mayor's wife brought you, I know. She's always causing trouble for me, because I'm not prepared to kiss the ground she walks on! Off with the lot of you. You've no right to stand around here, stopping law-abiding folk from going about their business, and stopping me from working. Be off before Nachko goes to fetch the guard."

"Just listen to her threatening us!" Kukal was indignant. "Bring Lyauko out here, witch! It's because of you the people of Berastse are dying! Death to the witch and her devil child!"

Suddenly from somewhere deep inside the house little Lyauko came running out to the doorway; he had obviously been left unattended. He had his little shoes on. This chubby child could not have been more than two years old, and he really did have six toes on each foot — I knew it for a fact because of my unseen presence in Makrynya's house. Master Tryzna, Makrynya and the other children in the family worshipped the lad and did everything they could to keep his deformity hidden. This year Master Tryzna had been planning to take the boy to Cieplice, where a well-known surgeon had guaranteed that he could perform the necessary operation. They didn't manage it in time.

"Grab him," shouted Kukal, and made a dive for the boy.

Raina the servant girl, as pale as her mistress, slipped out through the doorway, picked up the little boy and, with a swing of her skirt, disappeared with him into the darkness of the house, slamming the door shut behind her. I could hear her turn the key in the lock. Makrynya stood on the doorstep alone.

"Break down the doors, let's get the whole brood of them and burn them."

"It's an unlucky child as is conceived on a Friday," wailed Mistress Bahushova.

There were shouts from the crowd: "Seize them! We'll all of us take the sin on ourselves", and Kukal ran towards the door. He drew his sword, but came face to face with Makrynya's weapon. She kicked him in the groin and slashed him from shoulder to neck. Kukal fell, blood spurting out on to the ground. The mob gasped and surged forwards. Things could have gone badly for Makrynya, but right at that moment Nachko was heard shouting at the end of the street, followed by the sound of horses' hooves; a company of the city guard rode up. The mob parted to make way for the well-nourished horses. Nachko even managed to lash one or two in the crowd with his whip.

The lady mayoress made her way to the front of the mob:

"Arrest that murderous woman!" and she pointed an accusatory finger, "Arrest the murderer of my nephew. She's a witch and the mother of a warlock."

Master Uladyslau, the thin, moustachioed captain of the guard, knew how to calm situations like this, even without drawing his weapon.

"Disperse, good people, in the name of His Majesty the King. The court and the lords in council will examine the matter and deliver their just ruling. Disperse!"

The guards acted swiftly.

Some of them dismounted, ran to Makrynya and surrounded her. She was still standing on the porch with her bloodied sword in her hand. The others used their horses to push back the crowd. Only the mayoress refused to move away from the body of her nephew.

"Master Uladislau, I am a relative of this murdered man and demand that you arrest that murderer."

"I was only defending myself and my children from the mob that she herself had incited. And Kukal attacked me with his sword first!"

Master Uladislau bowed to the mayoress, then turned to Makrynya:

"By the power vested in me by His Majesty the King, I arrest you prior to the questioning of witnesses and the trial. The clerk to the court will conduct the investigation, and in the meantime, you, Mistress Makrynya, in accordance with the relevant article of the Statute and the orders of the King, will be held in the castle.

Makrynya's sword was taken away from her. Raina came running out to the doorway and Makrynya was allowed to take the packet of food. Master Uladislau did not bother to check it, even though the mayoress insisted that he should. The children — both Makrynya's and Staryma's — all came out of the house. Lyauko realised that his mother was going away, burst into tears and ran towards her. Raina picked him up; the poor little lad, still no more than a baby really, screamed and struggled to escape from her grasp. Makrynya was taken off to the castle.

I sat by the house until evening. From time to time I could hear screams and shouts coming from the city, something was going on there, but I decided not to move from the spot. Master Tryzna returned when it was beginning to get dark. Nachko took the reins of his horse and both disappeared through the gate.

I shifted my position a little along the river bank, so as to be right inside the house. At first I was in the kitchen, and the voices were coming from the main room. I moved a little further and found myself exactly where I wanted to be.

Raina was speaking:

"I've got everything ready that you'll need, Master Staryma. Don't wait. Take the children away from here, even if only as far as Dobratyche, but better still — take them to Lviv. Who knows how things are going to turn out here..."

"That evil woman is bound to say in court that we've taken Lyauko away because Makrynya really is guilty."

"You can say that we took him and the other children out of the city because you were afraid of the plague. In any case we can't show the boy to the court."

"That's true. Maybe we can have the operation done in Lviv, then we won't have to go to Cieplice."

"That'll be good."

"We'll move off when it gets dark. We'll go the roundabout way, so that we don't have to cross the bridge. It's better that no one sees us for the time being."

"Yes, that's right."

Khrystof spoke up from the corner of the room: "We'll take swords with us, it'll be safer as we've got the children. Nachko can get the guns ready."

"Agreed."

"The lock needs to be repaired on that Turkish gun." Nachko stood up. "Come on, young master, you can help me."

Nachko and Khrystof left the room, leaving Raina and Staryma alone. The last of the washed-out yellowish light of day struggled through the paper that was stretched across the window frames.

"I never expected to come back to something like this. So, Raina, I'll take the children to Lviv and try to arrange things with the doctor, then I'll come straight back. Or perhaps it would be better if you and Nachko take them, and I stay here to be close to Makrynya?"

Raina shook her head.

"It's a long way, and it's dangerous. It's better for you to go. Makrynya will feel easier knowing that the children are with you. And I can cope well on my own. Tomorrow I'll go and see the court's clerk."

Staryma drew out a small leather bag from beneath his red waistcoat and handed it to Raina.

"Spare no expense."

There was a piercing squeal nearby, and I couldn't make out at first whether I was still in the old city or back in the new one. No, I was in the new city, by the restaurant again. I had come back to my own time.

To the time when Ala and Ulia of the Haduns had fought off Ivan of the Kukals.

Where Master Tryzna's treasure was waiting for someone to find it.

Where a repulsive face bared its teeth at everyone on the roads.

Where new children are born and grow up.

Where — and I was beginning to realise this more and more — the fate of these children and the content of those roadside hoardings depended in a way that I as yet did not understand on whoever found that treasure.

WIVES ON THE CATWALK ABOARD THE "ROYAL BARGE"

It was already completely dark. For some reason, nothing came of any of my attempts to go back through the hole. After about an hour of trying I decided to go home. Well, not home exactly, but to Zarnitskaya's — she had arranged for her housekeeper to let me have the keys so that I could spend the night there whenever I needed to. This is actually what I had done on several occasions after spending too long in the fortress.

I slowed down a little when I finally emerged from the dark fortress on to a well-lit street. I phoned Khvedzka on my mobile and arranged for him to feed the animals, and then realised that I could do with something to eat as well.

I was walking along the river, moving from bright pools of sodium lighting to dark areas shrouded by huge trees. I could hear the quiet whirring of the cranes in the port. The white of the remand prison's freshly plastered walls stood out in the gloom. A little further on there were some golden-coloured lights flashing: this was a new restaurant, a place where people who like that kind of thing can relax. It stands right on the water's edge, with what can only be called an open-air terrace on a barge moored alongside. It's this feature that presumably gives the restaurant its name: "The Royal Barge". There was a fragrant, tasty smell of coffee, bigos*, and mulled wine. I decided to stop for a meal. The barge was packed and I wanted some peace and quiet, so I entered the indoor part of the restaurant. The room was in semi-darkness and there was hardly anyone there. I could

---

* *Bigos:* a Polish dish of stewed cabbage and meat.

just about make out the sounds of a small oompah band playing on the barge. It sounded like they were playing *The Charm of Polesie*, a tango from the old Polish times.

I ordered my food and sat thinking.

This six-toed little lad, Lyauko Tryzna, aroused feelings of deep affection in me every time I saw the fair hair on his head and his coarse cotton shirt. I am sure that I would look at my own son in that way, if I had one. We, the Haduns, were all descended from him — of that I had little doubt. The fact that our surname came down to us from his mother, and not from his father, can also be easily explained. The people of the time often had double-barrelled surnames, apart from which they frequently made use of nicknames which then became official: So *Lyauko Tryznin Hadunou* (Lyauko son of Tryzna Hadunou) or *Lyauko Makrynchyn z Hadunou* (Lyauko son of Makrynya of the Haduns) could easily become Lyauko Hadun. And there was a reason why Raina mentioned Dobratyche. The family had either bought the estate there, or founded it on previously unowned land. I felt my heart begin to beat faster: beyond the oval lake in Dobratyche there are two valleys — Lyaukova, as if named after Lyauko, and Sirotsina (Orphan Valley)...Does that mean that Makrynya was burned as a witch and little Lyauko left as an orphan?

"There's a note for you."

The sound of the voice tore me away from my thoughts. I raised my head. The waitress was standing right over me. There was a piece of paper folded double on the little tray which she was holding out to me.

"For me?"

"Yes. I was asked to give it to you."

I opened the paper and began to read by the light of the small lamp on the table:

"I know that your sister has been asking around about me, don't think that she's done it without my knowing about it. I know that certain people who wish me ill have been filling her head with all sorts of lies about me. But even if she had come straight to me, I would have said it to her face: Yes, I despise you, Ala. What kind of person are you? You're nothing but a blank space, an old woman. You're not a wife to him any more, so why did Anton buy you that flat, why has he left you part of his estate in his will? Do you remember that day when you were nearly hit by the boomerang. That was a little greeting from me. I've got lots more ideas like that, and lots of friends. I'm warning you, leave Anton alone. I'm his wife now, he's mine."

And the signature: A. Tluskaya.

For some considerable I sat and stared at this piece of paper. I was utterly stupefied.

What on earth is this? Who is this A. Tluskaya? Then I suddenly remembered my sister telling me about a meeting with a woman on Brest station, and what that woman had warned her about: "Remind Ala to keep away from Antanina Dluskaya". At the time my sister wasn't sure if she had heard the surname correctly. Could it be that this Antanina Dluskaya and A. Tluskaya are one and the same person?

The waitress brought the crudités and juice I had ordered.

"Tell me, who gave you this note for me?" I asked.

"Antanina Tluskaya," she answered calmly.

"Who's that then?"

"The singer, have you never heard of her?"

The singer! So that's what all this is about! Yes, now I remember that Ukrainian lad telling me about a singer that Anton was promoting. It's all clear now! It's her, Anton's new wife!

"Where is she now?"

"She was sitting at the bar here, then she saw you, wrote the note, asked me to give to you and left. But we've got a cassette. I can put it on if you want to hear her."

"Yes, please put it on."

The huge screen above the bar lit up and I saw her.

Inevitably, I suppose, she sang the songs of Edith Piaf. Girls of a certain type always choose her songs in the hope that they will make the grade with a great repertoire, but they never do. She was so well groomed that she quite literally shone, but this was grooming for the screen, and not for real life. In life she was just an ordinary and rather unpleasant woman. When she was singing her mouth gaped open, and she smiled the whole time, a meaningless, sickly-sweet smile that had nothing to do with the words she was singing. You know, it says a lot about a person who can sing "Je ne regrette rien" like that. No, this isn't jealousy talking (who am I to play the role of Hecuba?), but this woman had no talent and no real beauty. Anton, Anton, where were your eyes? Or where were my eyes when I failed to notice the cardinal changes in your tastes...

I signalled the barman to switch the recording off, something that he seemed very ready to do.

The oompah band on the barge continued to play the tunes of yesteryear; they seemed to have found a new popularity in these parts.

The waitress came up to my table again: "Excuse me, but the chef is wondering why you aren't eating. If you don't like it, we can suggest something else..."

"No, thank you, everything's fine..."

The waitress apologised for troubling me and left. I took hold of the fork. I was now alone in the room; there were still quite a lot of people on the barge. A noisy group that had driven up in a huge jeep and had not been able to find anywhere to sit on the barge now trooped into the room where I was; they ordered vodka. My fork clattered on the plate. I recognised one of the men in the group: the spetsnaz officer Pochtivy. He was in civvies today. But there was the same shaved head, and the rolls of fat around the neck. It was him, no doubt. Next to him was a dark-haired, vivacious female. Every now and then Pochtivy would bend down to give her a hug. With a look of utter indifference on his face he cast a glance in my direction. He hadn't recognised me.

They filled the restaurant with their loud conversation. The first toast they drank was for the young couple, and Pochtivy kissed the dark-haired girl. So, they're husband and wife then! I looked more closely and saw a shiny wedding ring on his hand. A constant torrent of swearwords flowed from their table. There was I thinking that this was their way of communicating only with inveterate enemies of their president, but no, apparently they talk like that with the ones they love as well. The women at the table also began each phrase with "Fucking hell, bitch", as in *"Fucking hell, bitch, you've got to try this salad! Fucking hell, bitch, let's go and dance!"*. When Pochtivy and his wife got up to go and dance on the barge, the two ladies who stayed behind immediately started gossiping about them. I learnt that the girl was called Elka and she was four months pregnant, that when Sashka — Pochtivy's first name — was on duty she would go off to Gazman, and that Sashka was a fool for allowing her to twist him around her little finger. I shifted my gaze to the barge where the young couple was dancing. Drinking like that and four months pregnant? No, Maria Vaytsyashonak can say what she likes, but these people will be punished in the end when they see the vacant eyes of their children.

Shushko and Pochtivy, Stepan Fyodorovich, Graychik and Kuleshov are all on my special shortlist. I couldn't yet say whether or not I would drop all my plans for them after this evening, but I did feel calmer inside; what I had seen this evening only convinced me even more of just how right I was to think that people like them get what they deserve in life. And they will get what they deserve without my having to do anything about it.

In the restaurant on the bank of the river Mukhavets that evening one of the spectacles that anyone curious enough to be watching could have seen was a parade of wives on the catwalk:

1. The abandoned wife (me).

2. The pugnacious wife with a stellar career (Tluskaya).

3. The wife who has a few surprises in store for her husband (Madame Pochtivaya).

Before leaving the restaurant I picked up Tluskaya's note, intending to send it to Anton. Another surprise was waiting for me. The letters in the note began to fade and disappear before my very eyes! They had been written with special ink; you can buy pens for writing with this ink everywhere. Either I underestimated Antanina's sense of humour, or she too has some surprises in store for Anton. Anton and Antanina — even their names are alike! They go together like a pair of socks.

BY THE LIGHT OF THE MOON

We were standing on the steep banks of the oval lake, surrounded by clouds of mosquitoes. The frogs and the birds had already fallen silent, leaving only the dry sound of the bats flapping their wings above us. The reflection of the moon on the surface of the water looked like an up-turned 'no entry' sign, and Tolik's treasure-hunting apparatus lay where we had dropped it in our irritation. No one said a word. We had reached a dead end. We had just returned fron the Buh via the vault. Our hopes had been raised sky-high by Tolik's ardent certainty, but now there was no hope left.

For two solid weeks Tolik, Valik and I had been working like demented moles. We had been digging holes, not in time, but in the dry, rock-hard earth. Ulia hadn't been working with us — she was too busy, the electoral campaign was entering its final stage. So the three of us really had to put our backs into it. There wasn't much time left — only two weeks.

Only two weeks. One evening over supper we heard on the news that in two week's time — in connection with the upcoming election and the need to ensure stability and public order — the army and the police were to be placed on emergency standby. This would include the troops guarding the frontier. People always used to say that not even a fly could get across our borders without being noticed; now it wouldn't be possible for a microbe or even an amoeba... And, of course, our moustachioed man of the pot belly with his general's epaulettes went on to add that after the elections this state of emergency would be in place permanently. There would be some serious side-effects on the frontier. All frontier guard units would be on continuous patrol, they would all be armed and under orders to use their weapons without warning against anyone attempting to cross illegally.

Sasha had also got us steamed up about the need to finish the treasure hunt quickly. At one of the campaign rallies he had met a former colleague of his who also used to work in the KBB. He too had left his job there, but still had many contacts in the organisation. Apparently the cloak and dagger boys in Brest had been given a strange kind of order. A special unit was to be put together, consisting of responsible, physically strong officers entrusted with the task of digging for treasure in the region over a period of two weeks.

When we heard this we looked at each other and realised at once that we would have to find the treasure within these two weeks or we would never find it.

Tolik and Valik risked being sacked by their boss Charota but all the same took two weeks' leave, and we got down to work. I shall never forget those two weeks. We slaved away every day like beasts of burden. My back never stopped aching. The spade was virtually stuck to the palms of my hands. The calluses were filled with blood; they never went away — they just burst, to be replaced by abscesses that throbbed intolerably. All the same I gritted my teeth and went on helping the lads. I bandaged both hands in an attempt to ease the pain a little; all I had to do was press lightly on the handle of the spade for the bandage to be instantly stained brown with a mixture of blood and pus. Tolik shouted at me when he first saw this and tried to get me to go home. I shouted back at him and threw to the ground a great lump of sandstone that I had just that moment dug up; I told him in no uncertain terms where he could go, including home if he wanted, adding two or three choice phrases of my own. Valik had trouble keeping us apart. Tolik and I calmed down only when our normally easy-going, sensible friend lost his temper and in his turn sent us both to you know where, saying that he refuses to work with such idiots, that he's had enough of the pair of us, and that if he'd known earlier, he would never have got himself involved.

In other words, our nerves were on edge. We had nothing to show for all our hard work. Nothing, except bits of scythes, pitchforks and sickles, chains, nails, coins of both the Russian and Soviet empires, rusty helmets from the First and Second World Wars, cartridge cases, bits of shrapnel from bombs and shells — Valik had been in the artillery and could tell what kind of gun they had been fired from — a lock, tin cans and shapeless pieces of metal — the metal detector was always squealing, but unfortunately, it was never what we wanted to find.

I was tormented by doubts and pangs of conscience. Doubts that we would ever find anything. That we wouldn't manage in time, that we'll miss it altogether. My conscience was troubled at the prospect of the treasure going to enrich the toad ladies of Belarus TV. I felt some measure of responsibility for it. Nothing is ever that straightforward in life. I had this vague feeling that things don't happen just by chance: the old document in that fat folder, Taras Slyozka and the Lviv Archives, my holes in time... There was no obvious connection between all these things, but surely all these coincidences must have some purpose behind them. Some kind of intention, a plan, or a mystery. Perhaps this is the reason why we plod our weary way along the dark paths of life, as Tolik once said to me. And now look what's happened: the only thing we've been able to do is betray the secret, and before we know where we are, a large group of responsible, physically strong KBB types will snatch the treasure out of our hands. If the treasure is really valuable — and the fact that they've taken KBB officers off election duties to search for it can be taken as proof that they think it is — then actually finding it will be put forward as further evidence that their Leader really is God's anointed.

The wounds inside me hurt me no less than the ones on my hands.

We worked night and day, and slept for just a few hours.

We lost weight and grew more and more exhausted. Tolik and Valik began to have problems with their wives; neither of them had yet admitted what they were doing or where they were going off to every single day. We had to creep along cautiously, keeping our eyes open for frontier guards. Nevertheless, every day and every night we squeezed ourselves through the narrow passageway in the vault and crawled out to the surface. Quietly and methodically we dug over the whole area, going to the left and right and gradually getting closer to the spot where we could see the remains of the thick black piles that had once supported the mill on the Polish side. The more ground we investigated, the more my hopes began to fade. Apart from that one outburst Valik worked steadily and silently (he brought me some gloves on the next day, and I have to admit that it was much easier to work in them). Quite the reverse seemed to be happening to Tolik. His certainty that we would find the treasure grew with every night. When I told him of my growing doubts that we would ever find it, he countered with:

"On the contrary, the smaller the area we still have to search, the greater the chances that we'll find it, maybe even today!"

But this today was invariably followed by another, and we still hadn't found anything.

Ulia arrived with her husband Yurka. On the last night, when all that was left for us to dig over was a small area of land immediately opposite where the old mill had stood, all five of us set off for the river together.

"We'll find it today for sure," Tolik announced as he climbed out of the vault on to the parched grass.

A button from a Polish soldier's uniform, a handful of bits of shrapnel, a piece of chain — that's all we found. Nothing else. Tolik and Yurka fell into the cold water and got themselves all wet and muddy.

Just before dawn we returned to our post-Soviet motherland, weary and depressed, and sat down on the bank of the oval lake.

Valik, completely dry and the least tired of all of us, summed up the situation:

"Well, there we are then, that's exactly what we should have expected. We didn't find the treasure and that's all there is to it. We've been right over the whole area. Not to put too fine a point on it, it would have been a miracle if we had found it."

"Yes, you're right. But you've got nothing to complain about." Yurka was trying to comfort us a little. "In the process you rid the world of a monster, which was a great thing in itself, and you opened up a window into Europe — I mean the tunnel through the vault, and then you got hold of that map. That's a real rarity; Ala can write an article about it."

"What article are you talking about?" and I waved my hand dismissively.

"Anyway, it's no great rarity," added Ulia.

Yurka turned over on to his front, switched on his torch and from his rucksack produced the map that Valeryk had brought from New York.

"I don't know, maybe it isn't a rarity, but it's certainly interesting." Yurka shone his torch on it and examined the map that we had already studied from every possible angle. "Very interesting."

Tolik, who until now had been lying like a stone on the spot where he had flopped to the ground, suddenly showed signs of life. He stirred and cleared his throat.

"Maybe there's a mistake in that old document. Perhaps we should have been looking on the Kastamaloty side, on the left instead of on the right bank."

The full moon cast its pale ghostly light on us. Very soon now it will drop from the sky into the bottomless abyss beyond the Buh, and all at once, from the opposite direction — from Moscow — the red sun will swell and burst forth, the mists will swirl, snake-like, across the drained marshlands and the drops of dew that cool the air will dry up in the merciless, burning wind of time...

Waves of moonlight flooded the scene. No one said a word. All around everything was still: over the marshes where the peat lies hidden, over the tiny calcium shells of molluscs that lived aeons ago, over the skeletons of carp and loach crushed beneath layers of silt, over snake skins and the white bones of hares...

And here it is again: the world breaks up into such fine detail that I cannot see the whole picture. I begin to panic when I realise that something strange is happening to me: there is a sudden firmness to my podgy body, I'm shorter than I was, my bones feel harder, and there's a different wind blowing in my face. I eagerly gulp down the air; it has an unusual taste, it makes me feel giddy. I was seized by a fear that I could not explain. I could still see my sister and her husband, and there were Tolik and Valik, but I was no longer with them. I had shifted to another place, or, more precisely, another time. If only I had had the strength of will to pull myself together, I would probably have been able to throw off this nightmare. But — as you already know — willpower is not exactly one of my strong points. A moment later, and I was no longer myself. I was someone else, running through the moonlit darkness. I was a man, but at the same time I was still me, Ala, one of the Haduns. I had not only fallen into a hole, I had come out on the other side of it! The muscular arms I saw weren't mine, the heavy chest I was carrying pressed hard on my breasts, and I was fighting for breath as I ran along the river bank at night. I finally had to stop and said to the boy who was running alongside me:

"Wait, I have to get my breath back, I can't run any more..."

I could feel the ground tremble beneath my feet, from behind I could hear the sound of horses' hooves fast approaching, the horses were neighing, the riders were shouting, the noises made my flesh crawl.

The man that I had become looked around at the wilderness surrounding him. Bushes, the river sparkling, then more bushes, a bit of a mill wheel just visible above the tops of some trees. Then there was a knoll. On the knoll was an oak, obviously a young one, but already strong. I fixed my gaze on that oak. There was a gaping hole beneath one of its roots.

"I'll write a note," I panted. "Here, take it and run. Give it to young master Khrystof..."

The frightened fair-haired boy grabbed the yellow scrap of paper and raced off into the darkness. The bushes rustled gently behind him.

I ran as fast as I could to the oak tree, used my knife to make the hole wider, pushed the chest into it and covered it up with grass and blackened dry leaves. Now to lead these devils away from here... I've got my knife, they won't be able to take me so easily... Slithering down the wet grass of the river bank in my leather boots, and losing my broad fur cap in the process, I hurled myself into the water. The cold surface of the water broke into ripples beneath the weight of my body... The sudden shock of it brought me back to the present.

I was back on the bank of the oval lake. The moon was still in the same place where I had last seen it... My heart was beating furiously. I patted myself all over like a woman possessed, and then crossed myself — for the third time in my life. No one was paying any attention to me. Everyone was looking at Yurka and listening to what he was saying.

"... flowed along a different channel to the one it takes now. Can you see that bluff there?" Four heads bent intently over the map. "Opposite the church in Pryluki? It's not there any more. After all, we've been there and you've seen for yourselves. Do you remember how Ala got so worked up about the name of the village, how she kept on asking where the bends in the river *(luki)* were that the village was supposed to be next to *(pry)*. Otherwise where did the name come from? The bends aren't there now, and on this map from a hundred years ago there's only a little hook shape left, but — who knows? — maybe around four hundred years ago the Buh really meandered at this point. It's a known fact that rivers change their courses. At one time we studied all this in geology, things like how the whole process could be calculated, but I don't remember much about it. Putting it in very general terms, rivers are deflected from their course in a direction opposite to that of the Earth's rotation about its own axis. So," Yurka stood up, "the Buh flows in that direction," he waved his arm northwards. "The river bank on that side is steep, that means the river is being deflected towards Poland. Which in turn could well mean that at one time it must have flowed somewhere nearer to us. Maybe this oval lake is all that is left of the river's old course."

"That's it!" Valik was so excited he even managed to sit up. "Rivers do change their courses. How could we have forgotten that? So now what do we do?"

"Well, I suppose we could try to find a specialist in these matters; there are such people. He would have to study the terrain, the structure of the soil and the special features of the river, like the speed it flows at and the volume of water — and he would then be able to tell us with a reasonable degree of certainty where the river bed was four hundred and fifty years ago. Of course, there's no guarantee that his calculations will be correct."

"There's no need to find a specialist," I said in a subdued voice, and cleared my throat. "Tolik, pick up the metal detector, let's go."

"Go where?" Tolik was puzzled.

"Over there," and I pointed to the cluster of oak trees on the knoll. "Let's go, I'll explain later."

Tolik looked at me somewhat doubtfully, but stood up and followed without saying a word.

"Come on, then, all of you, let's go."

Iurka, Ulia and Valik hurried after us.

"Start looking."

"Here?"

"Yes, right here."

I must have had a really determined look on my face, because Tolik immediately threw the strap of the metal detector over his shoulder and got down to work. The red light flickered on, the machine began its low squealing. We watched in complete silence as Tolik swept the area methodically, moving from one tree to the next. In the middle of the cluster was a huge spreading oak that must have been some five hundred years old. Its children and grandchildren were growing all around it.

The squealing suddenly changed to a jolly yelping sound. The red light went out, and a green light came on its place. Ulia and I clasped each other's hands. The detector now sounded more like a loud siren.

"There's something here," announced Tolik; his voice was muted. "Can it be...?"

Valik was already bringing up the spades.

"Careful, careful!" The soil was dry and came pouring down in little torrents, making the hole bigger,

"Take a look at this!" and there was the sound of a spade clanging on something metallic. We could see part of a dark object in the ground.

Tolik used his hands to scrape away the sand. Was it the chest? Valik and Yurka got their spades underneath whatever it was to lever it up out of the ground. They took hold of it, and on the grass they placed a large black box.

"It's locked. How are we going to open it? Perhaps we should break it open with the spades?" Tolik was feeling the chest on all sides, impatiently looking for a way to prise it open.

"No, don't use a spade. Ulia, shine the torch on it."

I pressed my torch into Ulia's hand and knelt in front of the chest. I could feel the old tree breathing beneath my fingers; the forged metal fittings on the corners exuded the living cold of the earth. I found something sticking out just under the right foot of the chest and pressed it. Something clicked inside and the lid lifted slightly. The chest was unlocked.

I looked round at Ulia and the three men.

"Go on, open it," whispered Ulia.

My hand trembled as I gingerly reached out for the lid.

"No, I can't. I'm afraid to," I whispered back.

Tolik, apparently, was not afraid. He fell to his knees and jerked the lid open.

The moon lingered in the sky to see what was inside. Over on the horizon the Sun was impatiently rising, eager to catch a glimpse as well.

How wonderfully the gems glowed in the gentle pre-dawn light; the rings were all neatly arranged on wire that had been tied in loops. This jeweller from Lviv was clearly a specialised ring maker. The chest — roughly the size of a ladies' shoe box — was packed full of them: their shining yellow gold set with red, green and transparent stones.

Three oaks there were in a field so wide... Tolik suddenly burst into song in his deep bass voice.

Three oaks in that great field so wide, Valik picked up the song a quarter of a tone higher.

They crowded together side by side,
They crowded together side by side!

The oaks we were singing about rustled gently in the early morning breeze.

We sang. I sang for the first time in my life, if you don't count the singing lessons at school. We stunned our surroundings into silence, the sun was coming up, and I caught the sound of a sixth voice — a powerful voice, one that felt very close to me, one that I had already heard, but then it had been breathless and hoarse. It was the voice in which I had once spoken.

SOTHEBY'S ACQUIRES
A NEW CLIENT

Ulia protested: "He couldn't possibly have specialised just in making rings. There were no specialisations at all in the seventeenth century!!"

I told them everything about how I had found out where to look for the chest. I formed the impression that Ulia and the others would have preferred not to believe me, had the proof that I was telling the truth not been scattered right across the oilcloth on top of the kitchen table. For a long time all four of them looked at me in silence; it's been a long time since I last managed to astonish people to that extent. They were totally gobsmacked by my theory about the holes in time; that was something they had never expected from Ala the Alkie.

The rings with their precious gems lay sprinkled over the kitchen table, and the kitchen itself was sprinkled with our laughter.

We had no hesitation about bringing the treasure into the house, because our trusted friend Sanaleyeu had paid us a visit beforehand and neutralised all the listening devices. He's a man of few words, balding slightly, very pleasant to have dealings with and really clever with his hands. He immediately located two tiny spy devices — one on the door of the ground floor, the other upstairs underneath a clothes rack. He worked his magic on some wires, then placed two of his own devices on top of the ones left by the KBB, opened his notebook, closed it again, and explained to us what he had done:

"That's done. We modelled your voices. Lilka made up some dialogues — that's what the KBB comrades are going to be listening to from now on. I can guarantee you a quiet life for a whole week."

"What do you mean, you've put on a recording instead of our real voices?" I was trying to get my head around this fancy technological stuff.

"Well, yes. Lilka's managed to cook up all sorts of things. She said that after the elections she's going to put in for a job as a script writer for soap operas. Anyway, touch wood, the system's working well in other campaign offices.

So that's why we weren't afraid to come home.

Tolik told us at once what kind of sum we could expect the treasure to fetch. As it eventually turned out, his estimate was a little lower that the final figure.

With the window heavily curtained and the house firmly locked we examined the treasure. We had no words to express our wonder at our discovery and at Tolik himself. Indeed, I found myself amazed by him even more than by the jewellery — and my amazement at the jewellery was little short of boundless.

Picking up each ring in turn and holding it up to the red light of the rising sun as it fell on the oilcloth-covered table, Tolik — remember that he was a tractor driver for the agricultural company "Agrovitalika Plus" — would state with absolute conviction:

"West European style. Gold and emeralds. The work is — well, let's say, just to be on the safe side — satisfactory. How much is it worth? Well, let's start with five thousand." He put the ring to one side and picked up the next one. "Yes, hm, this is in the so-called urban style. Work of outstanding quality. Gold and... I think, sapphires and a diamond. Now this piece is going to be extremely valuable, there aren't many around, maybe no more than a few dozen. It ought to fetch, oh, I don't know, somewhere around ninety nine thousand."

"How much?"

"Ninety nine thousand."

"Where do you get these figures from?"

"From catalogues."

"What catalogues? Where have you got catalogues from?"

"I've been in touch with collectors. They've sent me catalogues," said Tolik in a matter-of-fact voice, as though it was something he did every day. "Even back at the repast after granny Makrynya's funeral, when Ulia read the document for the first time and I made up my mind that it would be worth our while to hunt for the treasure, I realised that actually finding it was not the main problem. The main thing would be to make sure that we got money for it... But how? How to find the right people? Well, the answer was obvious — use the internet. So I bought a computer... The wife was cross about it, but what else was I to do? I'm in correspondence with auction agents, even Sotheby's has written to me.

As I listened to Tolik, I increasingly felt the urge to hit my head against the wall. What a fool I was to turn down his invitation to go to the dance with him back then. What an utterly stupid fool! How could I have failed to see what kind of man *my* Tolik was? How could I have turned down the chance to call him *mine*? There's nothing I can do about it now. There's no going back to the damp moss of those days when we could easily count each other's ribs, or to the magic nights we spent together in the forest. Even the time when he kissed my bloody calluses after one of our digging sessions won't change anything. It's too late. Fatally late. The horse has already bolted. There's no point in trying to shut the stable door now.

I didn't shut the stable door back then when I should have. I ruined my life, and I ruined his too. If only I had had the sense — something that I don't have, I know it! — at the time, if only I had seen what sort of man he was, everything would have turned out differently. Did I really need to go off and study history at university? That's exactly what he should have done. Our teacher always used to say that Tolik Hadun was the only one in the school whose eyes would light up whenever he heard the word "archaeology"; it was our teacher who urged him to go on with his studies. Tolik and I both tried for university at the same time, except I passed the entrance exam and he didn't. Then he was called up, and after that he had to find work, so that his old parents had something to eat. Then came the tractor — he was always either sitting on it or fiddling with it — and I refused to go to the dance with him. That's when Handzia turned up, and he married her. And that's how life passes by — there's always glass to be fitted on the hothouses, there are acres of apple trees to be planted, and the pigs need to be looked after...

And his eyes no longer light up until he's had a drink or two. But true talent will out, even if you try to keep it hidden under the proverbial bushel. And it will burst out into the open when there's a lot at stake. Whenever there's still a glow beneath the ashes, it isn't difficult to get the fire going again.

Our new-fledged antiques expert looked round at us and continued:

"Putting it briefly, then, everything's all set up. What we have to do now is decide how we're going to share out what we've found. Do we divide it into four parts, for each of us to do whatever they want with their share, or do you trust me to sell everything abroad, and you receive the money afterwards? Whatever we do, we must first draw up a list and roughly estimate what each piece is worth. Ala, get some paper and a pen, and get ready to write it all down."

"Hang on," Ulia interrupted him. "Is it right to take the treasure out of the country and sell it? By law treasure trove belongs to the state."

"By law?" There was irony in Tolik's smile. "You talk about law? OK, perhaps you can explain to me exactly what law means in this country?"

"And who the state is," added Yurka in support of what Tolik had said.

"All the same, we ought to hand over the treasure to a museum." Ulia continued to press her point home.

"Right. You'll receive bugger all for your pains, and this selfsame 'state' will immediately grab Master Tryzna's estate from the museum for itself — which means that everyone else will receive bugger all as well."

"Even so, I am categorically against selling the treasure abroad. However pompous it may sound, a hoard like this belongs to the whole nation, and that includes future generations." Ulia insisted.

"In that case, why the hell did we go looking for the treasure in the first place?" Valik was now getting angry.

"That's enough!" Tolik's voice had acquired a firmness that we seldom heard. "I knew right from the start that there would be some kind of argument like this, so I got to thinking and came up with this idea. We've been very lucky all along with this treasure hunting business. Now just listen to this. Over the internet I got to know someone called Maysey Patapchuk. He's the director of Business City Bank, the largest bank in Canada. He also happens to be from the glorious city of Brest, and was born in the same year as granny Makrynya. In fact he even knew her when he was a young man. And what's more, this Mr Patapchuk is the owner of what is probably the largest collection of — sod it, I can never remember the word, oh yes — artefacts that are in one way or another connected with this region. He let it be known ages ago that he would leave his whole collection to the city of Brest on condition that it was freely accessible to everyone and that its security could be guaranteed. In the meantime the collection is to be kept in Canada, in the vaults of his bank. So this Mr Patapchuk is prepared to buy all the items we found. As for making sure that he pays the right price — well, that's something I'm willing to do."

"We mustn't forget that we have to give a share to the Uruguayan, Lyonikha and Yarashykha. They're from Dobratyche too, and we did find the treasure in land by the village." Ulia was making another condition for the sale of the rings abroad.

"Nobody's going to object to that," responded Tolik. "They'll get a share too, but first let's take a closer look at what we have here. Ala, start writing!"

Estimating the value of each item in the hoard, together with breaks to feed the animals and birds, to drink tea and make pancakes, took almost four hours. The total sum was impressive. In fact it was so big that I'm not going to tell you how much it was. All I can tell you is that the euphoria we felt that morning was equivalent to the value of the treasure expressed in US dollars.

The rings were now laid out separately on the worn oilcloth that covered the kitchen table. Never before, and never since, have I seen such a beautiful sight. We stood rooted to the spot, just admiring them and passing them to each other. Finally I simply had to say:

"I would like to leave one for myself as a keepsake. I can take its value out of my share of the money."

"Take one," said Tolik and swept his hand over the whole collection. "I think it's quite right that Ala should keep one of the rings for herself. After all, it was through her that Master Tryzna showed us where the hoard was. I reckon that he would want her to have one."

I lent over the table and moved my hand slowly across the rings. Which one should I choose? Perhaps this one with the tiny seed pearls in a matt gold setting? Or this one, with the ruby so vibrant red that it's like looking into a deep pool of pulsing blood? Or perhaps this one that Tolik described to us as a ring with a rare kind of aquamarine called 'celeste'? All of a sudden I felt something. Some kind of sound in the ears, a warmth on the palm of my hand, a cry from far off... There was a flash of light from a gemstone beneath my hand. Listening intently to myself, I gently picked up the ring. Is this the one I should take? Yes, take it.

Tolik told us that this was a ring on which the master jeweller had not finished working. Tiny unpolished dark agate gemstones were deep-set in a silver band that had also been left unpolished. I tried it on the ring finger of my left hand. It fitted perfectly. It took up almost the whole of the middle phalanx. Once again I felt... was it a sound or did someone touch me? It was a greeting, and I knew who it was from. I could guess why the greeting was especially for me, and I was certain that we would meet again, either in this life, or at least after it. That's when I'll be able to find out about it all in more detail, if, of course, it will be right and proper to talk about such things.

Tolik packed the other rings carefully back into the chest.

"Well, now's the right time to have a drink," suggested Ulia happily. "Ala, love, go and fetch whatever it is you've got hidden away somewhere!"

I brought the wine and five glasses. I spooned out a fruit drink from a jug for myself, and explained:

"I've not been able to drink ever since we bumped Kukal off."

Tolik also held his glass out to the jug so that I could pour some for him:

"I haven't wanted to drink ever since we found the treasure."

"OK, that's two alcoholics less in the world," said Yurka with a broad smile on his face. "Right, let's drink to the successful conclusion of our treasure hunt. Our dreams have come true!"

We clinked glasses and drank.

A WORLD CREATED ANEW. I LEARN WHO THE APPARITION IN THE WHITE SHROUD REALLY IS

Tolik wasted no time. That same day all three of the men — Tolik, Valik and Yurka — submitted their applications to the Polish Consulate in Brest for visas to be issued as a matter of urgency. Then Tolik phoned Zarnitskaya and told her to stay awake that night. Fortunately the border guards can't listen in to all mobile phone conversations.

That evening Tolik and Valik successfully got through the tunnel that leads from the vault and crossed the Buh. Zarnitskaya nearly had a heart attack when they knocked on her window. They handed over the chest with the treasure and told her briefly about their plan.

The men returned the same way, and, still on the same day — now accompanied by Yurka — they crossed the frontier again, only this time quite legally. They swapped jokes with the customs officers, and then went on to Kastamaloty on foot — it took them about an hour to walk there. They relieved Zarnitskaya of the treasure and took the regular bus to the town of Biała Podlaska. From there an architect friend of Yurka's delivered them safely by car to Prague; by the time they arrived there the city was very busy. Once in Prague they set about waiting — in a hotel overlooking the Charles Bridge — for the arrival of that one-time citizen of Brest Maysey Patapchuk.

Meanwhile, back in Dobratyche, we were hit by a terrific storm. The men returned to a world created anew.

Everyone probably remembers that storm. It left its mark right across the country; in Dobratyche its consequences were just the same as everywhere else.

There had never before been a drought like the one we had that summer. Right from the time when the snow thawed the ground lay thirsting for rain, but none came. It didn't rain on Easter Day, or on Ascension. There was no rain at Pentecost, or on Trinity Sunday, or on St John's Day. There was no thunder, not even a drop of rain on the feast day of the prophet Elijah.* In fact it had rained in Dobratyche only once during the summer — on the day I had to go and earth up the potatoes, if you remember.

On the third day after the lads had left I heard a storm warning broadcast on the radio: a gale-force wind was expected over the whole country, together with thunder and torrential rain. The announcer's voice sounded concerned. At first I was even delighted at the prospect. Rain at last! Ulia wasn't around — she had gone off to Mensk yet again. I looked out at the yellow, burned-out grass of the yard, the stretches of dry sand, the withered lilac bushes, and then I raised my eyes to the heavens — no sign of a storm cloud yet.

Even so, I instinctively felt that there was something wrong. The wind had dropped completely — not a leaf stirred. There were no orioles screeching, no sparrows chirping. The copper grey pine trees seemed to be holding themselves tense, as if conserving their strength. The sun was blazing down from the vast emptiness of the sky. The heat weighed heavily on my head. I went over to the barometer, and my eyebrows shot up in stunned amazement — the pressure had dropped to such an extent that the needle was pointing way below the visible scale. I felt a vague kind of unease stir within me. The radio broadcast the storm warning again. The untrained announcer's voice — there were obviously none of the old-school announcers left — was filled

---

* *Elijah:* his feast day is celebrated by the Orthodox on 20 July. He is traditionally associated with thunder.

with ill-concealed panic. Not knowing what else to do I went out on to the porch.

No doubt about it, this was God's wrath.

From way, way over on the other side of the Buh came the sound of distant thunder; first a quiet mumbling, then, a moment later, a louder rumble. Someone was rolling empty barrels across the white sky.

A huge threatening black thundercloud appeared from beyond the Buh. By now up in the cloud the lightning flashes and thunderclaps were unceasing. Then came little grey clouds spotted with white — the harbingers of the storm — flying over the willows, and once again everything calmed down. This was the moment of mystery that comes before every storm, when everything is still, when even the leaves on the ever nervous aspen trees stop trembling. There was the first, delicate, gentle puff of breeze, followed by another — a little stronger this time, then suddenly the wind was blowing at full force, driving the sand before it and stinging the eyes... A split second later the thunderstorm burst upon us in all its rage.

Yes, of course this was God's wrath.

The violent, gale-force wind bent even the tallest and thickest fir trees to the ground. The solid wall of air was enough to knock you off your feet. The rain fell in one never-ending torrent. With loud cracks thick branches broke away from the trees, deafening claps of thunder came one after the other, and flashes of lightning tore the sky apart... The old pine tree in the yard came crashing to the ground. Lightning struck the top of a birch tree up on the hill... I suddenly became aware of a new sound, one that was louder than all the others — roaring, bellowing and moaning all rolled into one. In my imagination that was the kind of terrifying noise that a monster would make, or a fearful dragon, or a devil of some sort, dragging behind it a chunk of the cliff to which it had been chained... This monster was closing in on Dobratyche from the south. A cold shiver sent goosebumps all over my body and I ran upstairs to get a better view of what was happening. I looked out of the window. My hair quite literally stood on end. The monster that roared so scarily was water. A huge wave — a wall of water, in fact, some ten metres high or so it seemed to me — was surging towards Dobratyche. Something in the middle of it was boiling and gurgling frantically; objects would appear for a moment on the surface and then disappear again in the depths — wooden boards, tree stumps, metal pipes. There was a glimpse of the twisted remains of a red car... My hair did not have time to return to its normal position before the monstrous wave struck the walls of our house, and I was being pummelled by a massive weight of cold water. The house began to crack, the floor gave way beneath my feet and I lost consciousness. Not for long, however. Lying on the wet floor, I opened my eyes: the wave had swept on towards the north, and the roaring sound was receding. Trembling, I stood up and looked around. The force of the water seemed to have shifted the house a little. Part of the roof collapsed as I looked up at it, and virtually the whole of the first floor lay in ruins. I started going downstairs with the rain pouring straight on to me. The kitchen was deep under water. I sat on the stairs, halfway between the kitchen and the wrecked upper storey, and felt that I was going to die. All I could see through the kitchen window, in whichever direction I looked, were the grey waves of an angry sea; here and there broken tree trunks were sticking up into the sky. The view had changed completely; there was nothing left to remind me of what I had become accustomed to seeing ever since I was a child.

The pig, working its shoulders in a surprisingly agile manner, was swimming around its sty (I had not had time to shut the door before the storm struck). In spite of the rain I could see its snout concentrating on keeping above the water. I found the whole spectacle — watching the pig make little waves as it swam to and fro from one wall to the other — for some reason so funny that I burst into roars of laughter. So there I was, hysterical, with tears streaming down my face, roaring with laughter to the accompaniment of peals of thunder, sitting in the wreckage of our house, and the storm went on and on and on.

After this storm life never did return to what it had once been.

As we were to learn later, the flooding in our area occurred because the dams in two large reservoirs had failed almost simultaneously: the Shatski in Ukraine and the Miklaszewicki in Poland. The waters from both reservoirs merged at a certain point to form the massive terrifying wave that I had seen. But it wasn't only our area that had suffered. Palesie (the area along the Prypyats river), the Lake District in the north of the country, and the Mensk region had all been inundated. Everywhere people were faced with the same horrors — corpses that had been washed out of their graves floating down the streets, small towns totally destroyed; landscapes had been altered irrevocably, maddened animals attacked people and each other. Scenes that will never fade from the memory.

But let's get back to Dobratyche on that fateful late afternoon.

At last the rain stopped, but the wind was still strong and cold. I decided to go out into the yard to have a look round. Everywhere there were trees lying on the ground. They had been torn out of the ground by the roots. The pig was no longer in its pen, the chickens had disappeared, and the rabbits' cages were under water. I could just make out their little bodies bobbing up and down in the murky soup that had swamped the whole yard... Wading through the water I began a trek round the village; perhaps my help might be needed somewhere to pull somebody out of the ruins of their home...

The only thing to have been smashed in Yarashykha's yard was the bath-house. She wept as she drove her pig up the stairs to the barn loft. Unlike me she's very conscientious about looking after her place; she had made sure to shut the pig up in the barn when the storm hit. I helped her and then we set off to see how the Uruguayan was doing. We soon saw him wading towards us, driving his cow forward. He turned us in the direction of

Lyonikha's house on higher ground. I didn't recognise him at first: his face was distorted, and he spoke like he had potatoes in his mouth; yes, that's it, like he had potatoes in his mouth, and he was crying — something serious must have happened and he was frustrated that we couldn't understand what he was saying. Finally we understood: his wife Katsya had been killed by a tree when it crashed on to their house, and the shock of seeing it had contorted his face... *Get away from here, get to higher ground* — and he continued to drive us up to where Lyonikha lived.

"I have to go back to Katsya, but you should get up to the hill, to Lyonikha's place..."

That night everyone that was still alive in Dobratyche — and I mean everyone, humans and animals — spent the night in Lyonikha's house. It was well above the level of the floodwater.

For several days there was no electricity, the phones didn't work, there were no trains, and they never did rebuild the main road where it had been before it was completely washed away. Nobody had a proper radio. The 'kitchen radios' — the ones that could receive only certain preset stations — stayed silent, and so did my mobile. We were cut off. The only sign of the outside world were the military helicopters that occasionally circled over the flooded fields and the devastated forests. They didn't drop any food for us, not even leaflets urging us to *hang on, because help was coming.* This was the time when political changes were taking place in the country; we only found out about them much later, and now nobody talks about anything else.

The women cried every day: the water hung around for three days, which meant that all the crops would be ruined, the potatoes, the hay, everything. And that in turn meant *hunger.* The women of Dobratyche knew very well what that was...

We buried auntie Katsya on the hill. The Uruguayan was distraught: there was no priest to officiate.

On the fourth day the water began to recede. Little islands of sand began to emerge. The flood left behind a filthy, frothy brown mess, yellow bundles of waterweeds and rotting vegetation. The grass was dead and brown. The tree trunks were beginning to sprout yellow and crimson fungus and mould. Dead snakes lay all over the place in various stages of decomposition. They were of a species I didn't recognise: repulsive brownish, yellowish creatures with white undersides and flat heads... Where had they come from? Had the water washed them out of their holes deep underground, or had it brought them from somewhere else?

Lyonikha complained to me: "Ala, love, I simply can't walk on the ground while these revolting things are there. Where have they come from? It makes me sick to look at them..."

Nevertheless it wasn't long before Lyonikha was back to her old self. On the day after the storm she opened up an outhouse and took out an old boat that had been hollowed out of a tree trunk. Deftly working the single oar, she rowed off somewhere across the frontier that was no longer there. She returned in an hour and, to my horror, I saw that she was accompanied by a *black apparition* in a white shroud.

The "apparition" was called Ngwaasi, he spoke English quite well. Seated at Lyonikha's table and eating her thick beetroot soup, he told me his story:

"We're refugees. There's me, my wife, the families of my two brothers, and my neighbours. We're fleeing. We're from the Congo. There's no life there for us, the only thing you can do is die. There's a lot of sun, but it burns your skin. So we decided to leave the country. I had nine children, now only one is left. They died in my arms." Ngwaasi put down his spoon and held out his arms, so that I could see the pink palms of his hands. "At first we walked to the sea, where we found a captain willing to take us to Turkey. We walked across Turkey, then we managed to get across another sea to Ukraine, and after that we landed up in Belarus. From here we want to get across Poland to Germany."

"Merciful Heavens! How on Earth did you manage to get so far! How long have you been walking for?"

"It's been three years since we set off. Children have been born while we've been on the road, old people have died. Here in Belarus I was arrested by the police, they told me I would be deported. I didn't tell them where I was from and while they were thinking about they were supposed to do with me, I escaped through the toilet window."

"But how did you survive? What did you eat on the way? Where did you get the money from?"

Ngwaasi put his hand into his white robe and fetched out a little bag. From the bag he poured what looked to me like cloudy, whitish pieces of glass into his hand.

"This is our treasure. Back home I used to work in a diamond mine. We had to hand in all the stones we had found during our shift, otherwise we'd be killed. But we decided to take the risk, because we wanted to have a real life. When we had collected a few stones, we moved off. A friend of mine had been a student in Germany and she told me that was the place to make for. I know that now there are some ships' captains who take people across to Spain, but back then there weren't any, and so we had to go through Turkey."

My God. Walking for three years, bringing children into the world and burying the dead. I could just picture these people endlessly trudging along on stony, cold, hostile roads...

Lyonikha appeared in the doorway.

"Right, Vaska," this was what she called Ngwaasi, "eat up, you can leave now. The boat's there for you. I've got everything ready." And she disappeared again.

Ngwaasi spooned up the soup faster and drank the last drops straight from the bowl. He finished his story:

"I met auntie Manya quite by chance. We reached Brest and started wandering up and down the frontier, not knowing what to do. We'd never seen a frontier like that before, with barbed wire. We used to spend the night in the forest. Auntie Manya was out picking those mushroom thingies — you know, the ones with the big caps. She was kind to us, Manya was. She told us to come and stay at her place. It was there in the shed where Manya stores the wood for the stove that my wife gave birth to my son. Then Manya showed me the vault in the cemetery. I dug a passage through to the other side. That's how we could get across the frontier. My family's already in Germany now, we've finally got thereI But there were other people following us, they were refugees too, so I came back to help them get across. I had a hiding place on the other side, and whenever these other people reached the frontier at night, auntie Manya would bring them to me. Auntie Manya didn't want to take any money from us, she used to say we're *God's creatures too*," those last words Ngwaasi spoke in our local dialect. "She never told anyone about us, and brought us food through the vault. I love auntie Manya."

Well, I thought to myself, I love auntie Manya as well! To think of her doing all that to help these poor unfortunates cross the frontier and set them on their way to the country they were so desperate to reach! Good for you, auntie Manya!

The storm caught the last group of Ngwaasi's refugees on the banks of the Buh. They had to seek safety from the flood high up in the trees. They had gone hungry for several days but now, fortified by the hot beetroot soup that Ngwaasi was going to bring them, they would be able to move on.

Ngwaasi placed one of his uncut stones — a good-sized one — on the top shelf of the cabinet, next to the alarm clock and the Bible.

"There, please show it to auntie Manya. It's something for her to remember us people from the Congo by."

Ngwaasi told me that he had seen us digging up the grass on the river bank, and realised that we must be looking for something, but of course neither he nor the people he had with him wanted to show themselves to us.

Ngwaasi steered the dugout into deep water, then turned and waved to us. Auntie Manya waved back energetically, and the narrow boat disappeared from view behind the bushes.

On the fifth day Lyonikha ventured out to the dachas and reported back. There was very little left: most of the shacks had been destroyed, and the others were now standing in a lake so deep that the windows were below the surface of the water...

That same day I helped Lyonikha move the wood for her stove from the covered area where the logs were stacked to the woodshed, and after several hours of hard work clearing away piles of tree debris I managed to dig out a bicycle with bent handlebars and both wheels twisted in a figure of eight.

"What's this, auntie Manya?"

My question obviously embarrassed her somewhat.

"Yes, well, you know, it belonged to that man from the dachas that we used to call Grey Toper. Can you believe it, he actually fancied me! 'Marry me, Manya,' he used to say. I would always answer 'You've already got a wife.' 'I'll leave that snake. She's ruined my whole life, she's sucked all the blood out of me. Marry me, come on, we'll make a great couple.' He was always asking me. Not long before he died he started up again, talking about us living together. He says 'I'll come and live with you. We'll be well off! I'm going to come into some money soon, real money. We'll have enough for the rest of our lives, and there'll still be some over.' Where would he get so much from, eh? Do you know where he worked? At the shithole..."

"The where?!"

Auntie Manya looked even more embarrassed.

"You know, the place where they collect the shit from all over Brest..."

"Ah, yes, the sewage treatment plant!"

"That's it, that's what he called it himself. He used to work there as a security man. One day he saw some people drop a large package of some kind into one of those special pond things they have there: perhaps it was a man's body or something else they wanted to hide. So Toper goes up to these people and says something like 'you can't go throwing stuff into the pond, it's not allowed.' Then that Kukal fellow goes up to him and says: 'Listen, old man, keep your mouth shut and we'll pay you well.' He, like the fool he was, agreed, but they — instead of giving him any money — killed him. That's all there is to it."

"So they were the ones who knocked Toper off his bike..."

"It was them alright. I was in the forest at the time and could see everything clearly. This great silver car came hurtling down the road, knocked him off his bike, turned round and ran over him again, just to make sure... I called the police, but didn't let on that I'd seen it happen. I said that he was already dead when I found him. I was afraid they would kill me as well. People like that — it's nothing for them to bump off anyone they want. But I did take the bicycle for myself. After all, he was going to move in with me, wasn't he? And my bike is old. I'll ask the Uruguayan if he can repair it... "

I could only scratch my head. So the unfortunate drunk and would-be blackmailer that we called Toper had also died at Kukal's hands... What a tight web he had woven round us all...

On the sixth day Tolik and Yurka returned; Ulia was with them. They had had to make their way from Brest on foot, here and there crossing newly-formed lakes on a rubber boat. They found me in the yard, spade in hand, digging holes to bury the dead snakes, chickens and rabbits, and looking from to time at what was left of the house.

The pig came back six months later. And what's more, she wasn't alone — she brought young ones with her. God only knows where she had acquired them, or who the father was. I wasn't in Dobratyche at the time, so Lyonikha took them in. This pig founded a new breed which has since become popular throughout Belarus — the black-snouted. A new age pig, so to speak. The offspring of our pig inherited the mushroom hunting skills that those former KBB officers, Sasha and Dzima, had so patiently taught her, something that came in very handy when a start was made in this country with the cultivation of black Piedmont truffles on an industrial scale. The French were also very happy to buy these pigs — for exactly the same purpose.

E DAY

Ulia has now finished reading through everything that I have written so far. She had just one observation to make. She says that that the book is written in a lively style, with some sharp observations, but I need to go into more detail about how the elections went off. She thinks the readers will want to know my views on the subject. She's probably right. So — although I was cut off from the world in my flooded Dobratyche on E Day — here is my account of the events of that day, put together from what various people have told me.

The elections took place on the day after that terrible storm. Absolutely nobody turned up at the polling stations, and in many places the polling stations themselves — schools, hospitals, rural council offices — lay in ruins. People were looking for relatives and friends who had been swept away, they were burying their dead, they were looking after the injured, they were replacing smashed roofs, repairing whatever they could, clearing out the piles of debris and taking their children to places of safety... Putting it bluntly, the country had no time for elections.

On the other hand, they were of great importance to the authorities. The powers-that-be were clearly nervous and flustered; in fact they were so eager to bring the voting process to a successful conclusion that they lost all sight of reality. The inertia within the system was too powerful; instead of tackling the consequences of the hurricane at once, they decided to finish the election process first, largely because so much time, effort and money had already been spent on it. And so — remember there was no TV or radio — we had military helicopters flying over flooded towns and amphibious vehicles sailing down streets announcing from loudhailers to anyone who cared to listen, that, according to the latest information, as of 12 o'clock midday the elections were proceeding smoothly, that in the polling stations in closed establishments such as prisons, hospitals and military bases the current president was winning with a vote of 99.9%, and that, according to the results of an exit poll organised by activists of the "Rus of the Red and the Green" Party*, the current president was ahead overall with a vote of 86%.

People simply didn't give a damn.

The authorities first realised that something was not quite right when no journalists turned up for the press conference staged by the Central Electoral Commission, at which the results were to be officially announced! The Commission Chairlady's voice trembled as she declared the result to the vast, empty hall — the incumbent president had won an elegant victory. The only response she received was an echo of her own words. The authorities were left alone with their victory.

The billboards along the roads had all been toppled.

There was no longer any respect, or any fear. Anyone who has survived a flood like that is not going to be afraid of anyone except God.

Aksana lost her husband and her son in the flood. As soon as the storm started Syarhey raced out to save his beloved tractors and all the other vehicles. The boy ran out after his father. Their bodies were found that evening, surrounded by twisted and crumpled wreckage...

Aksana fell on the bodies and lay there all night, hugging them, trying to warm them, hoping for a miracle...

The next morning, as soon as it got light, Aksana stood up and, just as she was, left the house. She was the only person in Stradche who actually voted that day. She reached the polling

---

* Red and green are the colours of the Lukashenka flag, introduced in 1995 to replace the Belarusian national white-red-white flag. The political party is an invention of the author's.

station, sat rigidly at her Presiding Officer's table the whole day and signed the real record of activity for the day after tearing up the one that had been prepared in advance. Some functionary turned up on a jeep — the only thing that could be said about his unremarkable face was that he was obviously at his wit's end — and tried to stuff voting slips in the ballot box as he had already done with the boxes used for early voting. Aksana gave him such a look that he immediately beat a hasty retreat without saying a word...

Aksana did everything that was required of her as Presiding Officer, wrote up the official report, sealed the ballot boxes and went back home to her dead husband and son, and her living daughter and grandchildren...

1465 WORDS

You may as well know that I have adopted an American habit when I write. It's one that involves writing a certain number of words every day. It happened quite recently, when I met that Horst David. Apart from working as a journalist, he earns a bit on the side as a screenwriter for Hollywood. When he found out that I was also a writer, his first question was: how many words a day do I write?

I thought: God only knows! So now I have to think about the actual number of words I write rather than about how good those words actually are, do I? So here I am writing this last chapter, and I'm going to count up how many words it takes to tell you how the story ends.

OK then, I'll begin. I'll be sparing.

The first problem we encountered when the money was transferred to Belarus and we were able to withdraw it was this: what pretext could we use when we gave Yarashykha, the Uruguayan and Lyonikha their share? Obviously we couldn't tell them about the treasure: the decree that banned treasure hunting had not been rescinded; at that time I had my doubts as to whether it ever would be. Finally we settled on telling them that it was aid sent by Valeryk in America to the people of Dobratyche who had suffered in the flood. We phoned Valeryk to let him know; he was amazed when he heard what our problem was, and then utterly astounded when he found out just how much he was supposed to have given his fellow villagers, but he didn't make any objections.

"But why can't you tell them the money's from you?"

"Tax problems, we can't tell the authorities," was Ulia's reply.

That was something a citizen of the United States was bound to understand.

"Well, if you must, go ahead... especially since my dad's going to get some of the money."

His dad did indeed get some of the money, and he did go to live with his son in America.

Yarashykha gave the whole of her "aid" to her grandson Mishyk the poet and she too went to live with him. And so my granny's murderer eventually received some of the money for which he committed the murder in the first place — even if he hadn't intended to kill her... Funny, but I don't feel any need for revenge, and I don't hate him. If that's the way fate wants it, let it be. After all, like that singer from Ukraine said, the spirit of our land lives in his verses. I'm not going to judge him: the magic of money has lured greater men than he is away from the straight and narrow... Especially as, given the present situation, he may well go on to write many more fine verses — if God wills it.

Lyonikha donated all her share, as well as the diamond that Ngwaasi had given her, to her Baptist congregation. Thanks to her generosity those energetic Protestants were able to build — with amazing speed — a new chapel for themselves. White and tall, with a cross on the roof pointing to the sky, it stands on a peninsula in the lake that was formed where the dachas had been. It draws the gaze of all those travelling on the railway... The congregation moved Lyonikha away from the now abandoned village of Dobratyche and settled her in a good, solid house in Stradche.

There was nobody in Dobratyche any more. On a map recently published by the Belarusian Geodetical Survey, the name of the village is followed by a word in brackets: *uninhab*. Dobratyche lives no more, but we're still alive, at least for the time being. The flood was something else we survived. It was only when I saw that map that I realised why the treasure had been given to us: we're the last. When we go, the story of our tribe ends; our children — even if they bear our surnames — will be a different tribe, theirs will be a different story. We are the last ones to have seen, heard and played a direct part in everything that went to make up the life the people from this area had led for several centuries. Now there's a new life beginning.

Valik and his Volya still live in Stradche, just like they've always done. Volya no longer works in a public toilet, but the sadness in her eyes has never left her. Valik also gave up his job in "Agrovitalika Plus". He likes to lie down; he reads a lot, and his loneliness is slowly receding into the distance.

Ulia put her share of the money towards setting up an independent satellite TV channel. *Belspad* it's called, on the *Sirius* satellite. I'm sure many of my readers in Belarus watch it. She works there herself and once again she's terribly busy. I rarely see my sister. I talk to her children Lina and Kazik more often. I've become accustomed to speaking to them in our own Dobratyche dialect, something I never did before. They often drop in to see me in my Mensk flat on Red Army Street or at the refuge. I opened a refuge for homeless people and animals; it's where Maria Vaytsyashonak brings all the murderers, drug addicts and alcoholics that she picks up out of the snow. Lyalka junior lives here too. We're always patching people up here, or washing and feeding them. I've got some wonderful people working here, they're not afraid of hard work. Of course they don't know — and they will never find out — that the most homeless person in the whole establishment is me, their director; nothing will ever satisfy my hunger and no doctor will ever be able to help me...

Tolik has successfully managed to multiply his share of the money several times over. He started a tourist company even before the barbed wire was officially removed from the frontier. By the time Stalin's frontiers had ceased to exist he had already acquired an airship with transparent sides in Germany, and opened up an exclusive tourist route which he called "The Sky over the Buh". It's become very popular in Europe. If you should

---

* *Belspad:* from 'spadarozhnik', Belarusian for the Russian 'sputnik'. There is a real TV channel called 'Belsat' broadcasting from Poland.

ever fancy a trip yourself, just phone Tolik's office in Berastse, and a pleasant female voice will offer you a choice of dates — let's say the twentieth of next month. You sign up. You arrive in Berastse on the twentieth, you make your way to the Brest Fortress and board the great airship. It slowly ascends into the sky and floats along at a restful pace above the wide river. You can see it reflected in the endless lakes, beneath your feet you can see the heavy treetops of the forest swaying in the breeze, and there too are all the places that I've been telling you about in this book. All the way from Berastse to Lviv, with stops on both sides of the river — you will see it all for yourselves; the forests, the lakes, the river, the strips where the old roads are. Tolik has made sure that his tour guides are efficient and the places where you will spend the night are comfortable — you're sure to like them. From time to time Tolik himself is the guide. Then you will have the opportunity to question him; I'm sure he'll be willing to tell you his version of the story. Soon the airship will start to descend for its first stop. As you float gently over a slight rise in the land and a little, almost circular lake, Tolik will point out where we once sang in a group of five, where the moon and the sun jumped up and down in the sky in their eagerness to see what was inside the old chest. It's here that the collector — now a centenarian — built his museum. Now people come from all over the world to admire his collection. Without a doubt the *pièces de résistance* of the entire museum are Master Tryzna's rings. The ones we found on this selfsame knoll under the old oak tree.

And, by the way, it turned out that Kukal had an heir. A son. People say he lives somewhere in Russia, in Surgut. They say he's soon going to come and take his considerable inheritance. So what, let him come. If he wants to follow in his father's footsteps, let him do so. Why not? We know the antidote, it's been tried and tested. So let him try.

The holes in time are all interconnected. You can get out of one straight into another one, without coming out to the surface. I found out about it recently, but that's another story.

Glagoslav Publications Catalogue

- *The Time of Women* by Elena Chizhova
- *Sin* by Zakhar Prilepin
- *Hardly Ever Otherwise* by Maria Matios
- *The Lost Button* by Irene Rozdobudko
- *Khatyn* by Ales Adamovich
- *Christened with Crosses* by Eduard Kochergin
- *The Vital Needs of the Dead* by Igor Sakhnovsky
- *METRO 2033* (Dutch Edition) by Dmitry Glukhovsky
- *A Poet and Bin Laden* by Hamid Ismailov
- *Asystole* by Oleg Pavlov
- *Kobzar* by Taras Shevchenko
- *White Shanghai* by Elvira Baryakina
- *The Stone Bridge* by Alexander Terekhov
- *King Stakh's Wild Hunt* by Uladzimir Karatkevich
- *Depeche Mode* by Serhii Zhadan
- *Saraband Sarah's Band* by Larysa Denysenko
- *Herstories*, An Anthology of New Ukrainian Women Prose Writers
- *Watching The Russians* (Dutch Edition) by Maria Konyukova
- *The Hawks of Peace* by Dmitry Rogozin
- *The Grand Slam and Other Stories* (Dutch Edition) by Leonid Andreev

More coming soon…